Joseph and His Friend

A Story of Pennsylvania

by

Bayard Taylor

Joseph and His Friend
A Story of Pennsylvania
by Bayard Taylor

ISBN: 978-93-62764-59-1

Published by

DOUBLE 9 BOOKS
2/13-B, Ansari Road
Daryaganj, New Delhi – 110002
info@double9books.com
www.double9books.com
Tel. 011-40042856

ABOUT THE AUTHOR

Bayard Taylor was an American poet, literary critic, translator, travel author, and diplomat. As a poet, he was extremely popular, with an audience of almost 4,000 attending a poetry reading once, setting a record that remained for 85 years. His travelogues were well-received in both the United States and Britain. He held diplomatic appointments in both Russia and Prussia. Taylor was born January 11, 1825, in Kennett Square, Chester County, Pennsylvania. He was the fourth son of Quaker couple Joseph and Rebecca Taylor, and the first to reach maturity. His mother was of half Swiss descent. His father was an affluent farmer. Charles Frederick Taylor, Bayard's younger brother, was a Union Army colonel killed in action during the Battle of Gettysburg in 1863. Bayard obtained his early education at an academy in West Chester, Pennsylvania, and later in nearby Unionville. At seventeen, he was apprenticed to a printer in West Chester. Rufus Wilmot Griswold, a renowned critic and editor, pushed him to produce poems. The resulting anthology, Ximena, or the Battle of the Sierra Morena and Other Poems, was published in 1844 and dedicated to Griswold.

CONTENTS

The better angel is a man right fair;
The worser spirit a woman colour'd ill.

Shakspeare: Sonnets.

CHAPTER I
JOSEPH

Rachel Miller was not a little surprised when her nephew Joseph came to the supper-table, not from the direction of the barn and through the kitchen, as usual, but from the back room up stairs, where he slept. His work-day dress had disappeared; he wore his best Sunday suit, put on with unusual care, and there were faint pomatum odors in the air when he sat down to the table.

Her face said—and she knew it—as plain as any words, "What in the world does this mean?" Joseph, she saw, endeavored to look as though coming down to supper in that costume were his usual habit; so she poured out the tea in silence. Her silence, however, was eloquent; a hundred interrogation-marks would not have expressed its import; and Dennis, the hired man, who sat on the other side of the table, experienced very much the same apprehension of something forthcoming, as when he had killed her favorite speckled hen by mistake.

Before the meal was over, the tension between Joseph and his aunt had so increased by reason of their mutual silence, that it was very awkward and oppressive to both; yet neither knew how to break it easily. There is always a great deal of unnecessary reticence in the intercourse of country people, and in the case of these two it had been specially strengthened by the want of every relationship except that of blood. They were quite ignorant of the fence, the easy thrust and parry of society, where talk becomes an art; silence or the bluntest utterance were their alternatives, and now the one had neutralized the other. Both felt this, and Dennis, in his dull way, felt it too. Although not a party concerned, he was uncomfortable, yet also internally conscious of a desire to laugh.

The resolution of the crisis, however, came by his aid. When the meal was finished and Joseph betook himself to the window, awkwardly drumming upon the pane, while his aunt gathered the plates and cups together, delaying to remove them as was her wont, Dennis said, with his hand on the door-knob: "Shall I saddle the horse right off?"

"I guess so," Joseph answered, after a moment's hesitation.

Rachel paused, with the two silver spoons in her hand. Joseph was still drumming upon the window, but with very irregular taps. The door closed upon Dennis.

"Well," said she, with singular calmness, "a body is not bound to dress particularly fine for watching, though I would as soon show him that much respect, if need be, as anybody else. Don't forget to ask Maria if there's anything I can do for her."

Joseph turned around with a start, a most innocent surprise on his face.

"Why, aunt, what are you talking about?"

"You are not going to Warne's to watch? They have nearer neighbors, to be sure, but when a man dies, everybody is free to offer their services. He was always strong in the faith."

Joseph knew that he was caught, without suspecting her manœuvre. A brighter color ran over his face, up to the roots of his hair. "Why, no!" he exclaimed; "I am going to Warriner's to spend the evening. There's to be a little company there,—a neighborly gathering. I believe it's been talked of this long while, but I was only invited to-day. I saw Bob, in the road-field."

Rachel endeavored to conceal from her nephew's eye the immediate impression of his words. A constrained smile passed over her face, and was instantly followed by a cheerful relief in his.

"Isn't it rather a strange time of year for evening parties?" she then asked, with a touch of severity in her voice.

"They meant to have it in cherry-time, Bob said, when Anna's visitor had come from town."

"That, indeed! I see!" Rachel exclaimed. "It's to be a sort of celebration for—what's-her-name? Blessing, I know,—but the other? Anna Warriner was there last Christmas, and I don't suppose the high notions are out of her head yet. Well, I hope it'll be some time before they take root here! Peace and quiet, peace and quiet, that's been the token of the neighborhood; but town ways are the reverse."

"All the young people are going," Joseph mildly suggested, "and so—"

"O, I don't say you shouldn't go, *this* time," Rachel interrupted him; "for you ought to be able to judge for yourself what's fit and proper, and what is not. I should be sorry, to be sure, to see you doing anything and going anywhere that would make your mother uneasy if she were living now. It's so hard to be conscientious, and to mind a body's bounden duty, without seeming to interfere."

She heaved a deep sigh, and just touched the corner of her apron to her eyes. The mention of his mother always softened Joseph, and in his earnest desire to live so that his life might be such as to give her joy if she could share it, a film of doubt spread itself over the smooth, pure surface of his mind. A vague consciousness of his inability to express himself clearly upon the question without seeming to slight her memory affected his thoughts.

"But, remember, Aunt Rachel," he said, at last, "I was not old enough, then, to go into society. She surely meant that I should have some independence, when the time came. I am doing no more than all the young men of the neighborhood."

"Ah, yes, I know," she replied, in a melancholy tone; "but they've got used to it by degrees, and mostly in their own homes, and with sisters to caution them; whereas you're younger according to your years, and innocent of the ways and wiles of men, and—and girls."

Joseph painfully felt that this last assertion was true. Suppressing the impulse to exclaim, "Why am I younger 'according to my years?' why am I so much more 'innocent'—which is, ignorant—than others?" he blundered out, with a little display of temper, "Well, how am I ever to learn?"

"By patience, and taking care of yourself. There's always safety in waiting. I don't mean you shouldn't go this evening, since you've promised it, and made yourself smart. But, mark my words, this is only the beginning. The season makes no difference; townspeople never seem to know that there's such things as hay-harvest and corn to be worked. They come out for merry-makings in the busy time, and want us country folks to give up everything for their pleasure. The tired plough-horses must be geared up for 'em, and the cows wait an hour or two longer to be milked while they're driving around; and the chickens killed half-grown, and the washing and baking put off when it comes in their way. They're mighty nice and friendly while it lasts; but go back to 'em in town, six months afterwards, and see whether they'll so much as ask you to take a meal's victuals!"

Joseph began to laugh. "It is not likely," he said, "that I shall ever go to the Blessings for a meal, or that this Miss Julia—as they call her—will ever interfere with our harvesting or milking."

"The airs they put on!" Rachel continued. "She'll very likely think that she's doing you a favor by so much as speaking to you. When the Bishops had boarders, two years ago, one of 'em said,—Maria told me with her own mouth,—'Why don't all the farmers follow your example? It would be so refining for them!' They may be very well in their place, but, for my part, I should like them to stay there."

"There comes the horse," said Joseph. "I must be on the way. I expect to meet Elwood Withers at the lane-end. But—about waiting, Aunt—you hardly need—"

"O, yes, I'll wait for you, of course. Ten o'clock is not so very late for me."

"It might be a little after," he suggested.

"Not much, I hope; but if it should be daybreak, wait I will! Your mother couldn't expect less of me."

When Joseph whirled into the saddle, the thought of his aunt, grimly waiting for his return, was already perched like an imp on the crupper, and clung to his sides with claws of steel. She, looking through the window, also felt that it was so; and, much relieved, went back to her household duties.

He rode very slowly down the lane, with his eyes fixed on the ground. There was a rich orange flush of sunset on the hills across the valley; masses of burning cumuli hung, self-suspended, above the farthest woods, and such depths of purple-gray opened beyond them as are wont to rouse the slumbering fancies and hopes of a young man's heart; but the beauty and fascination, and suggestiveness of the hour could not lift his downcast, absorbed glance. At last his horse, stopping suddenly at the gate, gave a whinny of recognition, which was answered.

Elwood Withers laughed. "Can you tell me where Joseph Asten lives?" he cried,—"an old man, very much bowed and bent."

Joseph also laughed, with a blush, as he met the other's strong, friendly face. "There is plenty of time," he said, leaning over his horse's neck and lifting the latch of the gate.

"All right; but you must now wake up. You're spruce enough to make a figure to-night."

"O, no doubt!" Joseph gravely answered; "but what kind of a figure?"

"Some people, I've heard say," said Elwood, "may look into their looking-glass every day, and never know how they look. If you appeared to yourself as you appear to me, you wouldn't ask such a question as that."

"If I could only not think of myself at all, Elwood,—if I could be as unconcerned as you are—"

"But I'm not, Joseph, my boy!" Elwood interrupted, riding nearer and laying a hand on his friend's shoulder. "I tell you, it weakens my very marrow to walk into a room full o' girls, even though I know every one of 'em. They know it, too, and, shy and quiet as they seem, they're un-merciful. There they sit, all looking so different, somehow,—even a fellow's own sisters and cousins,—filling up all sides of the room, rustling a little and whispering a little, but you feel that every one of 'em has her eyes on you, and would be so glad to see you flustered. There's no help for it, though; we've got to grow case-hardened to that much, or how ever could a man get married?"

"Elwood!" Joseph asked, after a moment's silence, "were you ever in love?"

"Well,"—and Elwood pulled up his horse in surprise,—"well, you *do* come out plump. You take the breath out of my body. Have I been in love? Have I committed murder? One's about as deadly a secret as the other!"

The two looked each other in the face. Elwood's eyes answered the question, but Joseph's,—large, shy, and utterly innocent,—could not read the answer.

"It's easy to see *you've* never been," said the former, dropping his voice to a grave gentleness. "If I should say Yes, what then?"

"Then, how do you know it,—I mean, how did you first begin to find it out? What is the difference between that and the feeling you have towards any pleasant girl whom you like to be with?"

"All the difference in the world!" Elwood exclaimed with energy; then paused, and knitted his brows with a perplexed air; "but I'll be shot if I know exactly what else to say; I never thought of it before. How do I know that I am Elwood Withers? It seems just as plain as that,—and yet—well, for one thing, she's always in your mind, and you think and dream of just nothing but her; and you'd rather have the hem of her dress touch you than kiss anybody else; and you want to be near her, and to have her all to yourself, yet it's hard work to speak a sensible word to her when you come together,—but, what's the use? A fellow must feel it himself, as they say of experiencing religion; he must get converted, or he'll never know. Now, I don't suppose you've understood a word of what I've said!"

"Yes!" Joseph answered; "indeed, I think so. It's only an increase of what we all feel towards some persons. I have been hoping, latterly, that it might come to me, but—but—"

"But your time will come, like every man's," said Elwood; "and, maybe, sooner than you think. When it does, you won't need to ask anybody; though I think you're bound to tell me of it, after pumping my own secret out of me."

Joseph looked grave.

"Never mind; I wasn't obliged to let you have it. I know you're close-mouthed and honest-hearted, Joseph; but I'll never ask your confidence unless you can give it as freely as I give mine to you."

"You shall have it, Elwood, if my time ever comes. And I can't help wishing for the time, although it may not be right. You know how lonely it is on the farm, and yet it's not always easy for me to get away into company. Aunt Rachel stands in mother's place to me, and maybe it's only natural that she should be over-concerned; any way, seeing what she has done for my sake, I am hindered from opposing her wishes too stubbornly. Now, to-night, my going didn't seem right to her, and I shall not get it out of my mind that she is waiting up, and perhaps fretting, on my account."

"A young fellow of your age mustn't be so tender," Elwood said. "If you had your own father and mother, they'd allow you more of a range. Look at me, with mine! Why, I never as much as say 'by your leave.' Quite the contrary; so long as the work isn't slighted, they're rather glad than not to have me go out; and the house is twice as lively since I bring so much fresh gossip into it. But then, I've had a rougher bringing up."

"I wish I had had!" cried Joseph. "Yet, no, when I think of mother, it is wrong to say just that. What I mean is, I wish I could take things as easily as you,—make my way boldly in the world, without being held back by trifles, or getting so confused with all sorts of doubts. The more anxious I am to do right, the more embarrassed I am to know what is the right thing. I don't believe you have any such troubles."

"Well, for my part, I do about as other fellows; no worse, I guess, and likely no better. You must consider, also, that I'm a bit rougher made, besides the bringing up, and that makes a deal of difference. I don't try to make the scales balance to a grain; if there's a handful under or over, I think it's near enough. However, you'll be all right in a while. When you find the right girl and marry her, it'll put a new face on to you. There's nothing like a sharp, wide-awake wife, so they say, to set a man straight. Don't make a mountain of anxiety out of a little molehill of inexperience. I'd take all your doubts and more, I'm sure, if I could get such a two-hundred-acre farm with them."

"Do you know," cried Joseph eagerly, his blue eyes flashing through the gathering dusk, "I have often thought very nearly the same thing! If I were to love,—if I were to marry—"

"Hush!" interrupted Elwood; "I know you don't mean others to hear you. Here come two down the branch road."

The horsemen, neighboring farmers' sons, joined them. They rode together up the knoll towards the Warriner mansion, the lights of which glimmered at intervals through the trees. The gate was open, and a dozen vehicles could be seen in the enclosure between the house and barn. Bright, gliding forms were visible on the portico.

"Just see," whispered Elwood to Joseph; "what a lot of posy-colors! You may be sure they're every one watching us. No flinching, mind; straight to the charge! We'll walk up together, and it won't be half as hard for you."

CHAPTER II
MISS BLESSING

To consider the evening party at Warriner's a scene of "dissipation" — as some of the good old people of the neighborhood undoubtedly did — was about as absurd as to call butter-milk an intoxicating beverage. Anything more simple and innocent could not well be imagined. The very awkwardness which everybody felt, and which no one exactly knew how to overcome, testified of virtuous ignorance. The occasion was no more than sufficed for the barest need of human nature. Young men and women must come together for acquaintance and the possibilities of love, and, fortunately, neither labor nor the severer discipline of their elders can prevent them.

Where social recreation thus only exists under discouraging conditions, ease and grace and self-possession cannot be expected. Had there been more form, in fact, there would have been more ease. A conventional disposition of the guests would have reduced the loose elements of the company to some sort of order; the shy country nature would have taken refuge in fixed laws, and found a sense of freedom therein. But there were no generally understood rules; the young people were brought together, delighted yet uncomfortable, craving yet shrinking from speech and jest and song, and painfully working their several isolations into a warmer common atmosphere.

On this occasion, the presence of a stranger, and that stranger a lady, and that lady a visitor from the city, was an additional restraint. The dread of a critical eye is most keenly felt by those who secretly acknowledge their own lack of social accomplishment. Anna Warriner, to be sure, had been loud in her praises of "dear Julia," and the guests were prepared to find all possible beauty and sweetness; but they expected, none the less, to be scrutinized and judged.

Bob Warriner met his friends at the gate and conducted them to the parlor, whither the young ladies, who had been watching the arrival, had retreated. They were disposed along the walls, silent and cool, except Miss Blessing, who occupied a rocking-chair in front of the mantel-piece, where her figure was in half-shadow, the lamplight only touching some roses in her hair. As the gentlemen were presented, she lifted her face and smiled upon each, graciously offering a slender hand. In manner and attitude, as in dress, she seemed a different being from the plump, ruddy, self-conscious girls on the sofas. Her dark hair fell about her neck in long, shining ringlets; the fairness of her face heightened the brilliancy of her eyes, the lids of which were slightly drooped as if kindly veiling their beams; and her lips, although thin, were very sweetly and delicately curved. Her dress, of some white, foamy texture, hung about her like a trailing cloud, and the cluster of rosebuds on her bosom lay as if tossed there.

The young men, spruce as they had imagined themselves to be, suddenly felt that their clothes were coarse and ill-fitting, and that the girls of the neighborhood, in their neat gingham and muslin dresses, were not quite so airy and charming as on former occasions. Miss Blessing, descending to them out of an unknown higher sphere, made their deficiencies unwelcomely evident; she attracted and fascinated them, yet was none the less a disturbing influence. They made haste to find seats, after which a constrained silence followed.

There could be no doubt of Miss Blessing's amiable nature. She looked about with a pleasant expression, half smiled—but deprecatingly, as if to say, "Pray, don't be offended!"—at the awkward silence, and then said, in a clear, carefully modulated voice: "It is beautiful to arrive at twilight, but how charming it must be to ride home in the moonlight; so different from our lamps!"

The guests looked at each other, but as she had seemed to address no one in particular, so each hesitated, and there was no immediate reply.

"But is it not awful, tell me, Elizabeth, when you get into the shadows of the forests? we are so apt to associate all sorts of unknown dangers with forests, you know," she continued.

The young lady thus singled out made haste to answer: "O, no! I rather like it, when I have company."

Elwood Withers laughed. "To be sure!" he exclaimed; "the shade is full of opportunities."

Then there were little shrieks, and some giggling and blushing. Miss Blessing shook her fan warningly at the speaker.

"*How* wicked in you! I hope you will have to ride home alone to-night, after that speech. But you are all courageous, compared with *us*. We are really so restricted in the city, that it's a wonder we have any independence at all. In many ways, we are like children."

"O Julia, dear!" protested Anna Warriner, "and *such* advantages as you have! I shall never forget the day Mrs. Rockaway called—her husband's cashier of the Commercial Bank" (this was said in a parenthesis to the other guests)—"and brought you all the news direct from head-quarters, as she said."

"Yes," Miss Blessing answered, slowly, casting down her eyes, "there must be two sides to everything, of course; but how much we miss until we know the country! Really, I quite envy you."

Joseph had found himself, almost before he knew it, in a corner, beside Lucy Henderson. He felt soothed and happy, for of all the girls present he liked Lucy best. In the few meetings of the young people which he had attended, he had been drawn towards her by an instinct founded, perhaps, on his shyness and the consciousness of it; for she alone had the power, by a few kindly, simple words, to set him at ease with himself. The straightforward glance of her large brown eyes seemed to reach the self below the troubled surface. However much his ears might have tingled afterwards, as he recalled how frankly and freely he had talked with her, he could only remember the expression of an interest equally frank, upon her face. She never dropped one of those amused side-glances, or uttered one of those pert, satirical remarks, the recollection of which in other girls stung him to the quick.

Their conversation was interrupted, for when Miss Blessing spoke, the others became silent. What Elwood Withers had said of the phenomena of love, however, lingered in Joseph's mind, and he began, involuntarily, to examine the nature of his feeling for Lucy Henderson. Was she not often in his thoughts? He had never before asked himself the question, but now he suddenly became conscious that the hope of meeting her, rather than any curiosity concerning Miss Blessing, had drawn him to Warriner's. Would he rather touch the edge of her dress than kiss anybody else? That question drew his eyes to her lips, and with a soft shock of the heart, he became aware of their freshness and sweetness as never before. To touch the edge of her dress! Elwood had said nothing of the lovelier and bolder desire which brought the blood swiftly to his cheeks. He could not help it that their glances met,—a moment only, but an unmeasured time of delight and fear to him,—and then Lucy quickly turned away her head. He fancied there was a heightened color on her face, but when she spoke to him a few minutes afterwards it was gone, and she was as calm and composed as before.

In the mean time there had been other arrivals; and Joseph was presently called upon to give up his place to some ladies from the neighboring town. Many invitations had been issued, and the capacity of the parlor was soon exhausted. Then the sounds of merry chat on the portico invaded the stately constraint of the room; and Miss Blessing, rising gracefully and not too rapidly, laid her hands together and entreated Anna Warriner, —

"O, *do* let us go outside! I think we are well enough acquainted now to sit on the steps together."

She made a gesture, slight but irresistibly inviting, and all arose. While they were cheerfully pressing out through the hall, she seized Anna's arm and drew her back into the dusky nook under the staircase.

"Quick, Anna!" she whispered; "who is the roguish one they call Elwood? *What* is he?"

"A farmer; works his father's place on shares."

"Ah!" exclaimed Miss Blessing, in a peculiar tone; "and the blue-eyed, handsome one, who came in with him? He looks almost like a boy."

"Joseph Asten? Why, he's twenty-two or three. He has one of the finest properties in the neighborhood, and money besides, they say; lives alone, with an old dragon of an aunt as housekeeper. Now, Julia dear, there's a chance for you!"

"Pshaw, you silly Anna!" whispered Miss Blessing, playfully pinching her ear; "you know I prefer intellect to wealth."

"As for that" — Anna began, but her friend was already dancing down the hall towards the front door, her gossamer skirts puffing and floating out until they brushed the walls on either side. She hummed to herself, "O Night! O lovely Night!" from the *Désert*, skimmed over the doorstep, and sank, subsiding into an ethereal heap, against one of the pillars of the portico. Her eyelids were now fully opened, and the pupils, the color of which could not be distinguished in the moonlight, seemed wonderfully clear and brilliant.

"Now, Mr. Elwood — O, excuse me, I mean Mr. Withers," she began, "you must repeat your joke for my benefit. I missed it, and I feel so foolish when I can't laugh with the rest."

Anna Warriner, standing in the door, opened her eyes very wide at what seemed to her to be the commencement of a flirtation; but before Elwood Withers could repeat his rather stupid fun, she was summoned to the kitchen by her mother, to superintend the preparation of the refreshments.

Miss Blessing made her hay while the moon shone. She so entered into the growing spirit of the scene and accommodated herself to the speech and ways of the guests, that in half an hour it seemed as if they had always known her. She laughed with their merriment, and flattered their sentiment with a tender ballad or two, given in a veiled but not unpleasant voice, and constantly appealed to their good-nature by the phrase: "Pray, don't mind me at all; I'm like a child let out of school!" She tapped Elizabeth Fogg on the shoulder, stealthily tickled Jane McNaughton's neck with a grass-blade, and took the roses from her hair to stick into the buttonholes of the young men.

"Just see Julia!" whispered Anna Warriner to her half-dozen intimates; "didn't I tell you she was the life of society?"

Joseph had quite lost his uncomfortable sense of being watched and criticized; he enjoyed the unrestraint of the hour as much as the rest. He was rather relieved to notice that Elwood Withers seemed uneasy, and almost willing to escape from the lively circle around Miss Blessing. By and by the company broke into smaller groups, and Joseph again found himself near the pale pink dress which he knew. What was it that separated him from her? What had slipped between them during the evening? Nothing, apparently; for Lucy Henderson, perceiving him, quietly moved nearer. He advanced a step, and they were side by side.

"Do you enjoy these meetings, Joseph?" she asked.

"I think I should enjoy everything," he answered, "if I were a little older, or—or—"

"Or more accustomed to society? Is not that what you meant? It is only another kind of schooling, which we must all have. You and I are in the lowest class, as we once were, do you remember?"

"I don't know why," said he, "—but I must be a poor scholar. See Elwood, for instance!"

"Elwood!" Lucy slowly repeated; "he is another kind of nature, altogether."

There was a moment's silence. Joseph was about to speak, when something wonderfully soft touched his cheek, and a delicate, violet-like odor swept upon his senses. A low, musical laugh sounded at his very ear.

"There! Did I frighten you?" said Miss Blessing. She had stolen behind him, and, standing on tiptoe, reached a light arm over his shoulder, to fasten her last rosebud in the upper buttonhole of his coat.

"I quite overlooked you, Mr. Asten," she continued. "Please turn a little towards me. Now!—has it not a charming effect? I do like to see some kind of ornament about the gentlemen, Lucy. And since they can't wear anything in their hair,—but, tell me, wouldn't a wreath of flowers look well on Mr. Asten's head?"

"I can't very well imagine such a thing," said Lucy.

"No? Well, perhaps I am foolish: but when one has escaped from the tiresome conventionalities of city life, and comes back to nature, and delightful natural society, one feels so free to talk and think! Ah, you don't know what a luxury it is, just to be one's true self!"

Joseph's eyes lighted up, and he turned towards Miss Blessing, as if eager that she should continue to speak.

"Lucy," said Elwood Withers, approaching; "you came with the McNaughtons, didn't you?"

"Yes: are they going?"

"They are talking of it now; but the hour is early, and if you don't mind riding on a pillion, you know my horse is gentle and strong—"

"That's right, Mr. Withers!" interrupted Miss Blessing. "I depend upon you to keep Lucy with us. The night is at its loveliest, and we are all just fairly enjoying each other's society. As I was saying, Mr. Asten, you cannot conceive what a new world this is to *me*: oh, I begin to breathe at last!"

Therewith she drew a long, soft inspiration, and gently exhaled it again, ending with a little flutter of the breath, which made it seem like a sigh. A light laugh followed.

"I know, without looking at your face, that you are smiling at me," said she. "But you have never experienced what it is to be shy and uneasy in company; to feel that you are expected to talk, and not know what to say, and when you do say something, to be startled at the sound of your voice; to stand, or walk, or sit, and imagine that everybody is watching you; to be introduced to strangers, and be as awkward as if both spoke different languages, and were unable to exchange a single thought. Here, in the country, you experience nothing of all this."

"Indeed, Miss Blessing," Joseph replied, "it is just the same to us—to me—as city society is to you."

"How glad I am!" she exclaimed, clasping her hands. "It is very selfish in me to say it, but I can't help being sincere towards the Sincere. I shall now feel ever so much more freedom in talking with you, Mr. Asten, since we have one experience in common. Don't you think, if we all knew each other's natures truly, we should be a great deal more at ease,—and consequently happier?"

She spoke the last sentence in a low, sweet, penetrating tone, lifted her face to meet his gaze a moment, the eyes large, clear, and appealing in their expression, the lips parted like those of a child, and then, without waiting for his answer, suddenly darted away, crying, "Yes, Anna dear!"

"What is it, Julia?" Anna Warriner asked.

"O, didn't you call me? Somebody surely called some Julia, and I'm the only one, am I not? I've just arranged Mr. Asten's rosebud so prettily, and now all the gentlemen are decorated. I'm afraid they think I take great liberties for a stranger, but then, you all make me forget that I am strange. Why is it that everybody is so good to me?"

She turned her face upon the others with a radiant expression. Then, there were earnest protestations from the young men, and a few impulsive hugs from the girls, which latter Miss Blessing returned with kisses.

Elwood Withers sat beside Lucy Henderson, on the steps of the portico. "Why, we owe it to you that we're here to-night, Miss Blessing!" he exclaimed. "We don't come together half often enough as it is; and what better could we do than meet again, somewhere else, while you are in the country?"

"O, how delightful! how kind!" she cried. "And while the lovely moonlight lasts! Shall I really have another evening like this?"

The proposition was heartily seconded, and the only difficulty was, how to choose between the three or four invitations which were at once proffered. There was nothing better to do than to accept all, in turn, and the young people pledged themselves to attend. The new element which they had dreaded in advance, as a restraint, had shown itself to be the reverse. They had never been so free, so cheerfully excited. Miss Blessing's unconscious ease of manner, her grace and sweetness, her quick, bright sympathy with country ways, had so warmed and fused them, that they lost the remembrance of their stubborn selves and yielded to the magnetism of the hour. Their manners, moreover, were greatly improved, simply by their forgetting that they were expected to have any.

Joseph was one of the happiest sharers in this change. He eagerly gave his word to be present at the entertainments to come: his heart beat with delight at the prospect of other such evenings. The suspicion of a tenderer feeling towards Lucy Henderson, the charm of Miss Blessing's winning frankness, took equal possession of his thoughts; and not until he had said good night did he think of his companion on the homeward road. But Elwood Withers had already left, carrying Lucy Henderson on a pillion behind him.

"Is it ten o'clock, do you think?" Joseph asked of one of the young men, as they rode out of the gate.

The other answered with a chuckle: "Ten? It's nigher morning than evening!"

The imp on the crupper struck his claws deep into Joseph's sides. He urged his horse into a gallop, crossed the long rise in the road and dashed along the valley-level, with the cool, dewy night air whistling in his locks. After entering the lane leading upward to his home, he dropped the reins and allowed the panting horse to choose his own gait. A light, sparkling through the locust-trees, pierced him with the sting of an unwelcome external conscience, in which he had no part, yet which he could not escape.

Rachel Miller looked wearily up from her knitting as he entered the room. She made a feeble attempt to smile, but the expression of her face suggested imminent tears.

"Aunt, why did you wait?" said he, speaking rapidly. "I forgot to look at my watch, and I really thought it was no more than ten—"

He paused, seeing that her eyes were fixed. She was looking at the tall old-fashioned clock. The hand pointed to half-past twelve, and every cluck of the ponderous pendulum said, distinctly, "Late! late! late!"

He lighted a candle in silence, said, "Good night, Aunt!" and went up to his room.

"Good night, Joseph!" she solemnly responded, and a deep, hollow sigh reached his ear before the door was closed.

CHAPTER III
THE PLACE AND PEOPLE

Joseph Asten's nature was shy and sensitive, but not merely from a habit of introversion. He saw no deeper into himself, in fact, than his moods and sensations, and thus quite failed to recognize what it was that kept him apart from the society in which he should have freely moved. He felt the difference of others, and constantly probed the pain and embarrassment it gave him, but the sources wherefrom it grew were the last which he would have guessed.

A boy's life may be weakened for growth, in all its fibres, by the watchfulness of a too anxious love, and the guidance of a too exquisitely nurtured conscience. He may be so trained in the habits of goodness, and purity, and duty, that every contact with the world is like an abrasion upon the delicate surface of his soul. Every wind visits him too roughly, and he shrinks from the encounters which brace true manliness, and strengthen it for the exercise of good.

The rigid piety of Joseph's mother was warmed and softened by her tenderness towards him, and he never felt it as a yoke. His nature instinctively took the imprint of hers, and she was happy in seeing so clear a reflection of herself in his innocent young heart. She prolonged his childhood, perhaps without intending it, into the years when the unrest of approaching manhood should have led him to severer studies and lustier sports. Her death transferred his guardianship to other hands, but did not change its character. Her sister Rachel was equally good and conscientious, possibly with an equal capacity for tenderness, but her barren life had restrained the habit of its expression. Joseph could not but confess that she was guided by the strictest sense of duty, but she seemed to him cold, severe, unsympathetic. There were times when the alternative presented itself to his mind, of either allowing her absolute control of all his actions, or wounding her to the heart by asserting a moderate amount of independence.

He was called fortunate, but it was impossible for him consciously to feel his fortune. The two hundred acres of the farm, stretching back over the softly swelling hills which enclosed the valley on the east, were as excellent soil as the neighborhood knew; the stock was plentiful; the house, barn, and all the appointments of the place were in the best order, and he was the sole owner of all. The work of his own hands was not needed, but it was a mechanical exhaustion of time,—an enforced occupation of body and mind, which he followed in the vague hope that some richer development of life might come afterwards. But there were times when the fields looked very dreary,—when the trees, rooted in their places, and growing under conditions which they were powerless to choose or change, were but tiresome types of himself,—when even the beckoning heights far down the valley failed to touch his fancy with the hint of a broader world. Duty said to him, "You must be perfectly contented in your place!" but there was the miserable, ungrateful, inexplicable fact of discontent.

Furthermore, he had by this time discovered that certain tastes which he possessed were so many weaknesses—if not, indeed, matters of reproach—in the eyes of his neighbors. The delight and the torture of finer nerves—an inability to use coarse and strong phrases, and a shrinking from all display of rude manners—were peculiarities which he could not overcome, and must endeavor to conceal. There were men of sturdy intelligence in the community; but none of refined culture, through whom he might have measured and understood himself; and the very qualities, therefore, which should have been his pride, gave him only a sense of shame.

Two memories haunted him, after the evening at Warriner's; and, though so different, they were not to be disconnected. No two girls could be more unlike than Lucy Henderson and Miss Julia Blessing; he had known one for years, and the other was the partial acquaintance of an evening; yet the image of either one was swiftly followed by that of the other. When he thought of Lucy's eyes, Miss Julia's hand stole over his shoulder; when he recalled the glossy ringlets of the latter, he saw, beside them, the faintly flushed cheek and the pure, sweet mouth which had awakened in him his first daring desire.

Phantoms as they were, they seemed to have taken equal possession of the house, the garden, and the fields. While Lucy sat quietly by the window, Miss Julia skipped lightly along the adjoining hall. One lifted a fallen rose-branch on the lawn, the other snatched the reddest blossom from it. One leaned against the trunk of the old hemlock-tree, the other fluttered in and out among the clumps of shrubbery; but the lonely green was wonderfully brightened by these visions of pink and white, and Joseph enjoyed the fancy without troubling himself to think what it meant.

The house was seated upon a gentle knoll, near the head of a side-valley sunk like a dimple among the hills which enclosed the river-meadows, scarcely a quarter of a mile away. It was nearly a hundred years old, and its massive walls were faced with checkered bricks, alternately red and black, to which the ivy clung with tenacious feet wherever it was allowed to run. The gables terminated in broad double chimneys, between which a railed walk, intended for a look-out, but rarely used for that or any other purpose, rested on the peak of the roof. A low portico paved with stone extended along the front, which was further shaded by two enormous sycamore-trees as old as the house itself. The evergreens and ornamental shrubs which occupied the remainder of the little lawn denoted the taste of a later generation. To the east, an open turfy space, in the centre of which stood a superb weeping-willow, divided the house from the great stone barn with its flanking cribs and "over-shoots;" on the opposite side lay the sunny garden, with gnarled grape-vines clambering along its walls, and a double row of tall old box-bushes, each grown into a single solid mass, stretching down the centre.

The fields belonging to the property, softly rising and following the undulations of the hills, limited the landscape on three sides; but on the south there was a fair view of the valley of the larger stream, with its herd-speckled meadows, glimpses of water between the fringing trees, and farm-houses sheltered among the knees of the farther hills. It was a region of peace and repose and quiet, drowsy beauty, and there were few farms which were not the ancestral homes of the families who held them. The people were satisfied, for they lived upon a bountiful soil; and if but few were notably rich, still fewer were absolutely poor. They had a sluggish sense of content, a half-conscious feeling that their lines were cast in pleasant places; they were orderly, moral, and generally honest, and their own types were so constantly reproduced and fixed, both by intermarriage and intercourse, that any variation therein was a thing to be suppressed if possible. Any sign of an unusual taste, or a different view of life, excited their suspicion, and the most of them were incapable of discriminating between independent thought on moral and social questions, and "free-thinking" in the religious significance which they attached to the word. Political excitements, it is true, sometimes swept over the neighborhood, but in a mitigated form; and the discussions which then took place between neighbors of opposite faith were generally repetitions of the arguments furnished by their respective county papers.

To one whose twofold nature conformed to the common mould,—into whom, before his birth, no mysterious element had been infused, to be the basis of new sensations, desires, and powers,—the region was a paradise of peaceful days. Even as a boy the probable map of his life was drawn: he could behold himself as young man, as husband, father, and comfortable old man, by simply looking upon these various stages in others.

If, however, his senses were not sluggish, but keen; if his nature reached beyond the ordinary necessities, and hungered for the taste of higher things; if he longed to share in that life of the world, the least part of which was known to his native community; if, not content to accept the mechanical faith of passive minds, he dared to repeat the long struggle of the human race in his own spiritual and mental growth; then,—why, then, the region was not a paradise of peaceful days.

Rachel Miller, now that the dangerous evening was over, was shrewd enough to resume her habitual manner towards her nephew. Her curiosity to know what had been done, and how Joseph had been affected by the merry-making, rendered her careful not to frighten him from the subject by warnings or reproaches. He was frank and communicative, and Rachel found, to her surprise, that the evening at Warriner's was much, and not wholly unpleasantly, in her thoughts during her knitting-hours. The farm-work was briskly forwarded; Joseph was active in the field, and decidedly brighter in the house; and when he announced the new engagement, with an air which hinted that his attendance was a matter of course, she was only able to say:—

"I'm very much mistaken if *that's* the end. Get agoing once, and there's no telling where you'll fetch up. I suppose that town's girl won't stay much longer,—the farm-work of the neighborhood couldn't stand it,—and so she means to have all she can while her visit lasts."

"Indeed, Aunt," Joseph protested, "Elwood Withers first proposed it, and the others all agreed."

"And ready enough they were, I'll be bound."

"Yes, they were," Joseph replied, with a little more firmness than usual. "All of them. And there was no respectable family in the neighborhood that wasn't represented."

Rachel made an effort and kept silence. The innovation might be temporary, and in that case it were prudent to take no further notice; or it might be the beginning of a change in the ways of the young people, and if so, she needed further knowledge in order to work successfully against it in Joseph's case.

She little suspected how swiftly and closely the question would be brought to her own door.

A week afterwards the second of the evening parties was held, and was even more successful than the first. Everybody was there, bringing a cheerful memory of the former occasion, and Miss Julia Blessing, no longer dreaded as an unknown scrutinizing element, was again the life and soul of the company. It was astonishing how correctly she retained the names and characteristics of all those whom she had already met, and how intelligently she seemed to enjoy the gossip of the neighborhood. It was remarked that her dress was studiously simple, as if to conform to country ways, yet the airy, graceful freedom of her manner gave it a character of elegance which sufficiently distinguished her from the other girls.

Joseph felt that she looked to him, as by an innocent natural instinct, for a more delicate and intimate recognition than she expected to find elsewhere. Fragments of sentences, parenthetical expressions, dropped in her lively talk, were always followed by a quick glance which said to him: "We have one feeling in common; I know that *you* understand me." He was fascinated, but the experience was so new that it was rather bewildering. He was drawn to catch her seemingly random looks,—to wait for them, and then shrink timidly when they came, feeling all the while the desire to be in the quiet corner, outside the merry circle of talkers, where sat Lucy Henderson.

When, at last, a change in the diversions of the evening brought him to Lucy's side, she seemed to him grave and preoccupied. Her words lacked the pleasant directness and self-possession which had made her society so comfortable to him. She no longer turned her full face towards him while speaking, and he noticed that her eyes were wandering over the company with a peculiar expression, as if she were trying to listen with them. It seemed to him, also, that Elwood Withers, who was restlessly moving about the room, was watching some one, or waiting for something.

"I have it!" suddenly cried Miss Blessing, floating towards Joseph and Lucy; "it shall be *you*, Mr. Asten!"

"Yes," echoed Anna Warriner, following; "if it could be, how delightful!"

"Hush, Anna dear! Let us keep the matter secret!" whispered Miss Blessing, assuming a mysterious air; "we will slip away and consult; and, of course, Lucy must come with us."

"Now," she resumed, when the four found themselves alone in the old-fashioned dining-room, "we must, first of all, explain everything to Mr. Asten. The question is, where we shall meet, next week. McNaughtons are building an addition (I believe you call it) to their barn, and a child has the measles at another place, and something else is wrong somewhere else. We cannot interfere with the course of nature; but neither should we give up these charming evenings without making an effort to continue them. Our sole hope and reliance is on you, Mr. Asten."

She pronounced the words with a mock solemnity, clasping her hands, and looking into his face with bright, eager, laughing eyes.

"If it depended on myself—" Joseph began.

"O, I know the difficulty, Mr. Asten!" she exclaimed; "and really, it's unpardonable in me to propose such a thing. But isn't it possible—just possible—that Miss Miller might be persuaded by us?"

"Julia dear!" cried Anna Warriner, "I believe there's nothing you'd be afraid to undertake."

Joseph scarcely knew what to say. He looked from one to the other, coloring slightly, and ready to turn pale the next moment, as he endeavored to imagine how his aunt would receive such an astounding proposition.

"There is no reason why she should be asked," said Lucy. "It would be a great annoyance to her."

"Indeed?" said Miss Blessing; "then I should be *so* sorry! But I caught a glimpse of your lovely place the other day as we were driving up the valley. It was a perfect picture,—and I have such a desire to see it nearer!"

"Why will you not come, then?" Joseph eagerly asked. Lucy's words seemed to him blunt and unfriendly, although he knew they had been intended for his relief.

"It would be a great pleasure; yet, if I thought your aunt would be annoyed—"

"I am sure she will be glad to make your acquaintance," said Joseph, with a reproachful side-glance at Lucy.

Miss Blessing noticed the glance. "*I* am more sure," she said, playfully, "that she will be very much amused at my ignorance and inexperience. And I don't believe Lucy meant to frighten me. As for the party, we won't think of that now; but you will go with us, Lucy, won't you,—with Anna and myself, to make a neighborly afternoon call?"

Lucy felt obliged to accede to a request so amiably made, after her apparent rudeness. Yet she could not force herself to affect a hearty acquiescence, and Joseph thought her singularly cold.

He did not doubt but that Miss Blessing, whose warm, impulsive nature seemed to him very much what his own might be if he dared to show it, would fulfil her promise. Neither did he doubt that so much innocence and sweetness as she possessed would make a favorable impression upon his aunt; but he judged it best not to inform the latter of the possible visit.

CHAPTER IV
MISS BLESSING CALLS ON RACHEL MILLER

On the following Saturday afternoon, Rachel Miller sat at the front window of the sitting-room, and arranged her light task of sewing and darning, with a feeling of unusual comfort. The household work of the week was over; the weather was fine and warm, with a brisk drying breeze for the hay on the hill-field, the last load of which Joseph expected to have in the barn before his five o'clock supper was ready. As she looked down the valley, she noticed that the mowers were still swinging their way through Hunter's grass, and that Cunningham's corn sorely needed working. There was a different state of things on the Asten place. Everything was done, and well done, up to the front of the season. The weather had been fortunate, it was true; but Joseph had urged on the work with a different spirit. It seemed to her that he had taken a new interest in the farm; he was here and there, even inspecting with his own eyes the minor duties which had been formerly intrusted to his man Dennis. How could she know that this activity was the only outlet for a restless heart?

If any evil should come of his social recreation, she had done her duty; but no evil seemed likely. She had always separated his legal from his moral independence; there was no enactment establishing the period when the latter commenced, and it could not be made manifest by documents, like the former. She would have admitted, certainly, that her guardianship must cease at some time, but the thought of making preparation for that time had never entered her head. She only understood conditions, not the adaptation of characters to them. Going back over her own life, she could recall but little difference between the girl of eighteen and the woman of thirty. There was the same place in her home, the same duties, the same subjection to the will of her parents—no exercise of independence or self-reliance anywhere, and no growth of those virtues beyond what a passive maturity brought with it.

Even now she thought very little about any question of life in connection with Joseph. Her parents had trained her in the discipline of a rigid sect, and she could not dissociate the idea of morality from that of solemn renunciation. She could not say that social pleasures were positively wrong, but they always seemed to her to be enjoyed on the outside of an open door labelled "Temptation;" and who could tell what lay beyond? Some very good people, she knew, were fond of company, and made merry in an innocent fashion; they were of mature years and settled characters, and Joseph was only a boy. The danger, however, was not so imminent: no fault could be found with his attention to duty, and a chance so easily escaped was a comfortable guaranty for the future.

In the midst of this mood (we can hardly say train of thought), she detected the top of a carriage through the bushes fringing the lane. The vehicle presently came into view: Anna Warriner was driving, and there were two other ladies on the back seat. As they drew up at the hitching-post on the green, she recognized Lucy Henderson getting out; but the airy creature who sprang after her,—the girl with dark, falling ringlets,—could it be the stranger from town? The plain, country-made gingham dress, the sober linen collar, the work-bag on her arm—could they belong to the stylish young lady whose acquaintance had turned Anna's head?

A proper spirit of hospitality required her to meet the visitors at the gate; so there was no time left for conjecture. She was a little confused, but not dissatisfied at the chance of seeing the stranger.

"We thought we could come for an hour this afternoon, without disturbing you," said Anna Warriner. "Mother has lost your receipt for pickling cherries, and Bob said you were already through with the hay-harvest; and so we brought Julia along—this is Julia Blessing."

"How do you do?" said Miss Blessing, timidly extending her hand, and slightly dropping her eyelids. She then fell behind Anna and Lucy, and spoke no more until they were all seated in the sitting-room.

"How do you like the country by this time?" Rachel asked, feeling that a little attention was necessary to a new guest.

"So well that I think I shall never like the city again," Miss Blessing answered. "This quiet, peaceful life is such a rest; and I really never before knew what order was, and industry, and economy."

She looked around the room as she spoke, and glanced at the barn through the eastern window.

"Yes, your ways in town are very different," Rachel remarked.

"It seems to me, *now*, that they are entirely artificial. I find myself so ignorant of the proper way of living that I should be embarrassed among you, if you were not all so very kind. But I am trying to learn a little."

"O, we don't expect too much of town's-folks," said Rachel, in a much more friendly tone, "and we're always glad to see them willing to put up with our ways. But not many are."

"Please don't count *me* among those!" Miss Blessing exclaimed.

"No, indeed, Miss Rachel!" said Anna Warriner; "you'd be surprised to know how Julia gets along with everything—don't she, Lucy?"

"Yes, she's very quick," Lucy Henderson replied.

Miss Blessing cast down her eyes, smiled, and shook her head.

Rachel Miller asked some questions which opened the sluices of Miss Warriner's gossip—and she had a good store of it. The ways and doings of various individuals were discussed, and Miss Blessing's occasional remarks showed a complete familiarity with them. Her manner was grave and attentive, and Rachel was surprised to find so much unobtrusive good sense in her views. The reality was so different from her previously assumed impression, that she felt bound to make some reparation. Almost before she was aware of it, her manner became wholly friendly and pleasant.

"May I look at your trees and flowers?" Miss Blessing asked, when the gossip had been pretty well exhausted.

They all arose and went out on the lawn. Rose and woodbine, phlox and verbena, passed under review, and then the long, rounded walls of box attracted Miss Blessing's eye. This was a feature of the place in which Rachel Miller felt considerable pride, and she led the way through the garden gate. Anna Warriner, however, paused, and said:—

"Lucy, let us go down to the spring-house. We can get back again before Julia has half finished her raptures."

Lucy hesitated a moment. She looked at Miss Blessing, who laughed and said, "O, don't mind me!" as she took her place at Rachel's side.

The avenue of box ran the whole length of the garden, which sloped gently to the south. At the bottom the green walls curved outward, forming three-fourths of a circle, spacious enough to contain several seats. There was a delightful view of the valley through the opening.

"The loveliest place I ever saw!" exclaimed Miss Blessing, taking one of the rustic chairs. "How pleasant it must be, when you have all your neighbors here together!"

Rachel Miller was a little startled; but before she could reply, Miss Blessing continued:—

"There is such a difference between a company of young people here in the country, and what is called 'a party' in the city. There it is all dress and flirtation and vanity, but here it is only neighborly visiting on a larger scale. I have enjoyed the quiet company of all your folks *so* much the more, because I felt that it was so very innocent. Indeed, I don't see how anybody *could* be led into harmful ways here."

"I don't know," said Rachel: "we must learn to mistrust our own hearts."

"You are right! The best are weak—of themselves; but there is more safety where all have been brought up unacquainted with temptation. Now, you will perhaps wonder at me when I say that I could trust the young men—for instance, Mr. Asten, your nephew—as if they were my brothers. That is, I feel a positive certainty of their excellent character. What they say they mean: it is otherwise in the city. It is delightful to see them all together, like members of one family. You must enjoy it, I should think, when they meet here."

Rachel Miller's eyes opened wide, and there was both a puzzled and a searching expression in the look she gave Miss Blessing. The latter, with an air of almost infantine simplicity, her lips slightly parted, accepted the scrutiny with a quiet cheerfulness which seemed the perfection of candor.

"The truth is," said Rachel, slowly, "this is a new thing. I hope the merry-makings are as innocent as you think; but I'm afraid they unsettle the young people, after all."

"Do you, really?" exclaimed Miss Blessing. "What have you seen in them which leads you to think so? But no—never mind my question; you may have reasons which I have no right to ask. Now, I remember Mr. Asten telling Anna and Lucy and myself, how much he should like to invite his friends here, if it were not for a duty which prevented it; and a duty, he said, was more important to him than a pleasure."

"Did Joseph say that?" Rachel exclaimed.

"O, perhaps I oughtn't to have told it," said Miss Blessing, casting down her eyes and blushing in confusion: "in that case, *please* don't say anything about it! Perhaps it was a duty towards you, for he told me that he looked upon you as a second mother."

Rachel's eyes softened, and it was a little while before she spoke. "I've tried to do my duty by him," she faltered at last, "but it sometimes seems an unthankful business, and I can't always tell how he takes it. And so he wanted to have a company here?"

"I am so sorry I said it!" cried Miss Blessing. "I never thought you were opposed to company, on principle. Miss Chaffinch, the minister's daughter, you know, was there the last time; and, really, if you could see it—But it is presumptuous in me to say anything. Indeed, I am not a fair judge, because these little gatherings have enabled me to make such pleasant acquaintances. And the young men tell me that they work all the better after them."

"It's only on *his* account," said Rachel.

"Nay, I'm sure that the last thing Mr. Asten would wish would be your giving up a principle for his sake! I know, from his face, that his own character is founded on principle. And, besides, here in the country, you don't keep count of hospitality, as they do in the city, and feel obliged to return as much as you receive. So, if you will try to forget what I have said—"

Rachel interrupted her. "I meant something different. Joseph knows why I objected to parties. He must not feel under obligations which I stand in the way of his repaying. If he tells me that he should like to invite his friends to this place, I will help him to entertain them."

"You *are* his second mother, indeed," Miss Blessing murmured, looking at her with a fond admiration. "And now I can hope that you will forgive my thoughtlessness. I should feel humiliated in his presence, if he knew that I had repeated his words. But he will not ask you, and this is the end of any harm I may have done."

"No," said Rachel, "he will not ask me; but won't I be an offence in his mind?"

"I can understand how you feel—only a woman can judge a woman's heart. Would you think me too forward if I tell you what might be done, this once?"

She stole softly up to Rachel as she spoke, and laid her hand gently upon her arm.

"Perhaps I am wrong—but if *you* were first to suggest to your nephew that if he wished to make some return for the hospitality of his neighbors,—or put it in whatever form you think best,—would not that remove the 'offence' (though he surely cannot look at it in that light), and make him grateful and happy?"

"Well," said Rachel, after a little reflection, "if anything is done, that would be as good a way as any."

"And, of course, you won't mention me?"

"There is no call to do it—as I can see."

"Julia, dear!" cried Anna from the gate; "come and see the last load of hay hauled into the barn!"

"I should like to see it, if you will excuse me," said Miss Blessing to Rachel; "I have taken quite an interest in farming."

As they were passing the porch, Rachel paused on the step and said to Anna: "You'll bide and get your suppers?"

"I don't know," Anna replied: "we didn't mean to; but we stayed longer than we intended—"

"Then you can easily stay longer still."

There was nothing unfriendly in Rachel's blunt manner. Anna laughed, took Miss Blessing by the arm, and started for the barn. Lucy Henderson quietly turned and entered the house, where, without any offer of services, she began to assist in arranging the table.

The two young ladies took their stand on the green, at a safe distance, as the huge fragrant load approached. The hay overhung and concealed the wheels, as well as the hind quarters of the oxen, and on the summit stood Joseph, in his shirt-sleeves and leaning on a pitch-fork. He bent forward as he saw them, answering their greetings with an eager, surprised face.

"O, take care, take care!" cried Miss Blessing, as the load entered the barn-door; but Joseph had already dropped upon his knees and bent his shoulders. Then the wagon stood upon the barn-floor; he sprang lightly upon a beam, descended the upright ladder, and the next moment was shaking hands with them.

"We have kept our promise, you see," said Miss Blessing.

"Have you been in the house yet?" Joseph asked, looking at Anna.

"O, for an hour past, and we are going to take supper with you."

"Dennis!" cried Joseph, turning towards the barn, "we will let the load stand to-night."

"How much better a man looks in shirt-sleeves than in a dress-coat!" remarked Miss Blessing aside to Anna Warriner, but not in so low a tone as to prevent Joseph from hearing it.

"Why, Julia, you are perfectly countrified! I never saw anything like it!" Anna replied.

Joseph turned to them again, with a bright flush on his face. He caught Miss Blessing's eyes, full of admiration, before the lids fell modestly over them.

"So you've seen my home, already?" he said, as they walked slowly towards the house.

"O, not the half yet!" she answered, in a low, earnest tone. "A place so lovely and quiet as this cannot be appreciated at once. I almost wish I had not seen it: what shall I do when I must go back to the hot pavements, and the glaring bricks, and the dust, and the hollow, artificial life?" She tried to check a sigh, but only partially succeeded; then, with a sudden effort, she laughed lightly, and added: "I wonder if everybody doesn't long for something else? Now, Anna, here, would think it heavenly to change places with me."

"Such privileges as you have!" Anna protested.

"Privileges?" Miss Blessing echoed. "The privilege of hearing scandal, of being judged by your dress, of learning the forms and manners, instead of the good qualities, of men and women? No! give me an independent life."

"Alone?" suggested Miss Warriner.

Joseph looked at Miss Blessing, who made no reply. Her head was turned aside, and he could well understand that she must feel hurt at Anna's indelicacy.

In the house Rachel Miller and Lucy had, in the mean time, been occupied with domestic matters. The former, however, was so shaken out of her usual calm by the conversation in the garden, that in spite of prudent resolves to keep quiet, she could not restrain herself from asking a question or two.

"Lucy," said she, "how do you find these evening parties you've been attending?"

"They are lively and pleasant,—at least every one says so."

"Are you going to have any more?"

"It seems to be the wish," said Lucy, suddenly hesitating, as she found Rachel's eyes intently fixed upon her face.

The latter was silent for a minute, arranging the tea-service; but she presently asked again: "Do you think Joseph would like to invite the young people here?"

"She has told you!" Lucy exclaimed, in unfeigned irritation. "Miss Rachel, don't let it trouble you a moment: nobody expects it of you!"

Lucy felt, immediately, that her expression had been too frankly positive; but even the consciousness thereof did not enable her to comprehend its effect.

Rachel straightened herself a little, and said "Indeed?" in anything but an amiable tone. She went to the cupboard and returned before speaking again. "I didn't say anybody told me," she continued; "it's likely that Joseph might think of it, and I don't see why people should expect me to stand in the way of his wishes."

Lucy was so astonished that she could not immediately reply; and the entrance of Joseph and the two ladies cut off all further opportunity of clearing up what she felt to be an awkward misunderstanding.

"I must help, too!" cried Miss Blessing, skipping into the kitchen after Rachel. "That is one thing, at least, which we can learn in the city. Indeed, if it wasn't for housekeeping, I should feel terribly useless."

Rachel protested against her help, but in vain. Miss Blessing had a laugh and a lively answer for every remonstrance, and flitted about in a manner which conveyed the impression that she was doing a great deal.

Joseph could scarcely believe his eyes, when he came down from his room in fresh attire, and beheld his aunt not only so assisted, but seeming to enjoy it. Lucy, who appeared to be ill at ease, had withdrawn from the table, and was sitting silently beside the window. Recalling their conversation a few evenings before, he suspected that she might be transiently annoyed on his aunt's account; she had less confidence, perhaps, in Miss Blessing's winning, natural manners. So Lucy's silence threw no shadow upon his cheerfulness: he had never felt so happy, so free, so delighted to assume the character of a host.

After the first solemnity which followed the taking of seats at the table, the meal proceeded with less than the usual decorum. Joseph, indeed, so far forgot his duties, that his aunt was obliged to remind him of them from time to time. Miss Blessing was enthusiastic over the cream and butter and marmalade, and Rachel Miller found it exceedingly pleasant to have her handiwork appreciated. Although she always did her best, for Joseph's sake, she knew that men have very ignorant, indifferent tastes in such matters.

When the meal was over, Anna Warriner said: "We are going to take Lucy on her way as far as the cross-roads; so there will not be more than time to get home by sunset."

Before the carriage was ready, however, another vehicle drove up the lane. Elwood Withers jumped out, gave Joseph a hearty grip of his powerful hand, greeted the others rapidly, and then addressed himself specially to Lucy: "I was going to a township-meeting at the Corner," said he; "but Bob Warriner told me you were here with Anna, so I thought I could save her a roundabout drive by taking you myself."

"Thank you; but I'm sorry you should go so far out of your road," said Lucy. Her face was pale, and there was an evident constraint in the smile which accompanied the words.

"O, he'd go twice as far for company," Anna Warriner remarked. "You know I'd take you, and welcome, but Elwood has a good claim on you, now."

"I have no *claim*, Lucy," said Elwood, rather doggedly.

"Let us go, then," were Lucy's words.

She rose, and the four were soon seated in the two vehicles. They drove away in the low sunshine, one pair chatting and laughing merrily as long as they were within hearing, the other singularly grave and silent.

CHAPTER V
ELWOOD'S EVENING, AND JOSEPH'S

For half a mile Elwood Withers followed the carriage containing Anna Warriner and her friend; then, at the curve of the valley, their roads parted, and Lucy and he were alone. The soft light of the delicious summer evening was around them; the air, cooled by the stream which broadened and bickered beside their way, was full of all healthy meadow odors, and every farm in the branching dells they passed was a picture of tranquil happiness. Yet Lucy had sighed before she was aware of it,—a very faint, tremulous breath, but it reached Elwood's sensitive ear.

"You don't seem quite well, Lucy," he said.

"Because I have talked so little?" she asked.

"Not just that, but—but I was almost afraid my coming for you was not welcome. I don't mean—" But here he grew confused, and did not finish the sentence.

"Indeed, it was very kind of you," said she. This was not an answer to his remark, and both felt that it was not.

Elwood struck the horse with his whip, then as suddenly drew the reins on the startled animal. "Pshaw!" he exclaimed, in a tone that was almost fierce, "what's the use o' my beating about the bush in this way?"

Lucy caught her breath, and clenched her hands under her shawl for one instant. Then she became calm, and waited for him to say more.

"Lucy!" he continued, turning towards her, "you have a right to think me a fool. I can talk to anybody else more freely than to you, and the reason is, I want to say more to you than to any other woman! There's no use in my being a coward any longer; it's a desperate venture I'm making, but it must be made. Have you never guessed how I feel towards you?"

"Yes," she answered, very quietly.

"Well, what do you say to it?" He tried to speak calmly, but his breath came thick and hard, and the words sounded hoarsely.

"I will say this, Elwood," said she, "that because I saw your heart, I have watched your ways and studied your character. I find you honest and manly in everything, and so tender and faithful that I wish I could return your affection in the same measure."

A gleam, as of lightning, passed over his face.

"O, don't misunderstand me!" she cried, her calmness forsaking her, "I esteem, I honor you, and that makes it harder for me to seem ungrateful, unfeeling,—as I must. Elwood, if I could, I would answer you as you wish, but I cannot."

"If I wait?" he whispered.

"And lose your best years in a vain hope! No, Elwood, my friend,—let me always call you so,—I have been cowardly also. I knew an explanation must come, and I shrank from the pain I should feel in giving you pain. It is hard; and better for both of us that it should not be repeated!"

"There's something wrong in this world!" he exclaimed, after a long pause. "I suppose you could no more force yourself to love me than I could force myself to love Anna Warriner or that Miss Blessing. Then what put it into my heart to love you? Was it God or the Devil!"

"Elwood!"

"How can I help myself? Can I help drawing my breath? Did I set about it of my own will? Here I see a life that belongs to my own life,—as much a part of it as my head or heart; but I can't reach it,—it draws away from me, and maybe joins itself to some one else forever! O my God!"

Lucy burst into such a violent passion of weeping, that Elwood forgot himself in his trouble for her. He had never witnessed such grief, as it seemed to him, and his honest heart was filled with self-reproach at having caused it.

"Forgive me, Lucy!" he said, very tenderly encircling her with his arm, and drawing her head upon his shoulder; "I spoke rashly and wickedly, in my disappointment. I thought only of myself, and forgot that I might hurt you by my words. I'm not the only man who has this kind of trouble to bear; and perhaps if I could see clearer—but I don't know; I can only see one thing."

She grew calmer as he spoke. Lifting her head from his shoulder, she took his hand, and said: "You are a true and a noble man, Elwood. It is only a grief to me that I cannot love you as a wife should love her husband. But my will is as powerless as yours."

"I believe you, Lucy," he answered, sadly. "It's not your fault,—but, then, it isn't mine, either. You make me feel that the same rule fits both of us, leastways so far as helping the matter is concerned. You needn't tell me I may find another woman to love; the very thought of it makes me sick at heart. I'm rougher than you are, and awkward in my ways—"

"It is not that! O, believe me, it is not that!" cried Lucy, interrupting him. "Have you ever sought for reasons to account for your feeling toward me? Is it not something that does not seem to depend upon what I am,— upon any qualities that distinguish me from other women?"

"How do you know so much?" Elwood asked. "Have you—" He commenced, but did not finish the question. He leaned silently forward, urged on the horse, and Lucy could see that his face was very stern.

"They say," she began, on finding that he was not inclined to speak,— "they say that women have a natural instinct which helps them to understand many things; and I think it must be true. Why can you not spare me the demand for reasons which I have not? If I were to take time, and consider it, and try to explain, it would be of no help to you: it would not change the fact. I suppose a man feels humiliated when this trouble comes upon him. He shows his heart, and there seems to be a claim upon the woman of his choice to show hers in return. The sense of injustice is worse than humiliation, Elwood. Though I cannot, cannot do otherwise, I shall always have the feeling that I have wronged you."

"O Lucy," he murmured, in a very sad, but not reproachful voice, "every word you say, in showing me that I must give you up, only makes it more impossible to me. And it is just impossible,—that's the end of the matter! I know how people talk about trials being sent us for our good, and its being the will of God, and all that. It's a trial, that's true: whether it's for my good or not, I shall learn after a while; but I can find out God's will only by trying the strength of my own. Don't be afeared, Lucy! I've no notion of saying or doing anything from this time on to disturb you, but *here* you are" (striking his breast with his clenched hand), "and here you will be when the day comes, as I feel that it must and *shall* come, to bring us together!"

She could see the glow of his face in the gathering dusk, as he turned towards her and offered his hand. How could she help taking it? If some pulse in her own betrayed the thrill of admiring recognition of the man's powerful and tender nature, which suddenly warmed her oppressed blood, she did not fear that he would draw courage from the token. She wished to speak, but found no words which, coming after his, would not have seemed either cold and unsympathetic, or too near the verge of the hope which she would gladly have crushed.

Elwood was silent for a while, and hardly appeared to be awaiting an answer. Meanwhile the road left the valley, climbing the shoulders of its enclosing hills, where the moist meadow fragrance was left behind, and dry, warm breezes, filled with the peculiar smell of the wheat-fields, blew over them. It was but a mile farther to the Corner, near which Lucy's parents resided.

"How came you three to go to Joseph's place this afternoon?" he asked. "Wasn't it a dodge of Miss Blessing's?"

"She proposed it,—partly in play, I think; and when she afterwards insisted on our going, there seemed to be no good reason for refusing."

"O, of course not," said Elwood; "but tell me now, honestly, Lucy, what do you make out of her?"

Lucy hesitated a moment. "She is a little wilful in her ways, perhaps, but we mustn't judge too hastily. We have known her such a short time. Her manner is very amiable."

"I don't know about that," Elwood remarked. "It reminds me of one of her dresses,—so ruffled, and puckered, and stuck over with ribbons and things, that you can't rightly tell what the stuff is. I'd like to be sure whether she has an eye to Joseph."

"To *him*!" Lucy exclaimed.

"Him first and foremost! He's as innocent as a year-old baby. There isn't a better fellow living than Joseph Asten, but his bringing up has been fitter for a girl than a boy. He hasn't had his eye-teeth cut yet, and it's my opinion that *she* has."

"What do you mean by that?"

"No harm. Used to the world, as much as anything else. He don't know how to take people; he thinks th' outside color runs down to the core. So it does with him; but *I* can't see what that girl is, under her pleasant ways, and he won't guess that there's anything else of her. Between ourselves, Lucy,—you don't like her. I saw that when you came away, though you were kissing each other at the time."

"What a hypocrite I must be!" cried Lucy, rather fiercely.

"Not a bit of it. Women kiss as men shake hands. You don't go around, saying, 'Julia dear!' like Anna Warriner."

Lucy could not help laughing. "There," she said, "that's enough, Elwood! I'd rather you would think yourself in the right than to say anything more about her this evening."

She sighed wearily, not attempting to conceal her fatigue and depression.

"Well, well!" he replied; "I'll pester you no more with disagreeable subjects. There's the house, now, and you'll soon be rid of me. I won't tell you, Lucy, that if you ever want for friendly service, you must look to me,—because I'm afeared you won't feel free to do it; but you'll take all I can find to do without your asking."

Without waiting for an answer he drew up his horse at the gate of her home, handed her out, said "Good night!" and drove away.

Such a singular restlessness took possession of Joseph, after the departure of his guests, that the evening quiet of the farm became intolerable. He saddled his horse and set out for the village, readily inventing an errand which explained the ride to himself as well as to his aunt.

The regular movements of the animal did not banish the unquiet motions of his mind, but it relieved him by giving them a wider sweep and a more definite form. The man who walks is subject to the power of his Antæus of a body, moving forwards only by means of the weight which holds it to the earth. There is a clog upon all his thoughts, an ever-present sense of restriction and impotence. But when he is lifted above the soil, with the air under his foot-soles, swiftly moving without effort, his mind, a poising Mercury, mounts on winged heels. He feels the liberation of new and nimble powers; wider horizons stretch around his inward vision; obstacles are measured or overlooked; the brute strength under him charges his whole nature with a more vigorous electricity.

The fresh, warm, healthy vital force which filled Joseph's body to the last embranchment of every nerve and vein—the hum of those multitudinous spirits of life, which, while building their glorious abode, march as if in triumphant procession through its secret passages, and summon all the fairest phantoms of sense to their completed chambers—constituted, far more than he suspected, an element of his disturbance. This was the strong pinion on which his mind and soul hung balanced, above the close atmosphere which he seemed to ride away from, as he rode. The great joy of human life filled and thrilled him; all possibilities of action and pleasure and emotion swam before his sight; all he had read or heard of individual careers in all ages, climates, and conditions of the race—dazzling pictures of the myriad-sided earth, to be won by whosoever dared arbitrarily to seize the freedom waiting for his grasp—floated through his brain.

Hitherto a conscience not born of his own nature,—a very fair and saintly-visaged jailer of thought, but a jailer none the less,—had kept strict guard over every outward movement of his mind, gently touching hope and desire and conjecture when they reached a certain line, and saying, "No; no farther: it is prohibited." But now, with one strong, involuntary throb, he found himself beyond the line, with all the ranges ever trodden by man stretching forward to a limitless horizon. He rose in his stirrups, threw out his arms, lifted his face towards the sky, and cried, "God! I see what I am!"

It was only a glimpse,—like that of a landscape struck in golden fire by lightning, from the darkness. "What is it," he mused, "that stands between me and this vision of life? Who built a wall of imaginary law around these needs, which are in themselves inexorable laws? The World, the Flesh, and the Devil, they say in warning. Bright, boundless world, my home, my play-ground, my battle-field, my kingdom to be conquered! And this body they tell me to despise,—this perishing house of clay, which is so intimately myself that its comfort and delight cheer me to the inmost soul: it is a dwelling fit for an angel to inhabit! Shall not its hungering senses all be fed? Who shall decide for me—if not myself—on their claims?—who can judge for me what strength requires to be exercised, what pleasure to be enjoyed, what growth to be forwarded? All around me, everywhere, are the means of gratification,—I have but to reach forth my hand and grasp; but a narrow cell, built ages ago, encloses me wherever I go!"

Such was the vague substance of his thoughts. It was the old struggle between life—primitive, untamed life, as the first man may have felt it—and its many masters: assertion, and resistance, all the more fierce because so many influences laid their hands upon its forces. As he came back to his usual self, refreshed by this temporary escape, Joseph wondered whether other men shared the same longing and impatience; and this turned his musings into another channel. "Why do men so carefully conceal what is deepest and strongest in their natures? Why is so little of spiritual struggle and experience ever imparted? The convert publicly admits his sinful experience, and tries to explain the entrance of grace into his regenerated nature; the reformed drunkard seems to take a positive delight in making his former condition degraded and loathsome; but the opening of the individual life to the knowledge of power and passion and all the possibilities of the world is kept more secret than sin. Love is hidden as if it were a reproach; friendship watched, lest it express its warmth too frankly; joy and grief and doubt and anxiety repressed as much as possible. A great lid is shut down upon the human race. They must painfully stoop and creep, instead of standing erect with only God's heaven over their heads. I am lonely, but I know not how to cry for companionship; my words would not be understood, or, if they were, would not be answered. Only one gate is free to me,—that leading to the love of woman. There, at least, must be such an intense, intimate sympathy as shall make the reciprocal revelation of the lives possible!"

Full of this single certainty, which, the more he pondered upon it, seemed to be his nearest chance of help, Joseph rode slowly homewards. Rachel Miller, who had impatiently awaited his coming, remarked the abstraction of his face, and attributed it to a very different cause. She was thereby wonderfully strengthened to make her communication in regard to the evening company; nevertheless, the subject was so slowly approached and so ambiguously alluded to, that Joseph could not immediately understand it.

"That is something! That is a step!" he said to himself; then turning towards her with a genuine satisfaction in his face, added: "Aunt, do you know that I have never really felt until now that I am the owner of this property? It will be more of a home to me after I have received the neighborhood as my guests. It has always controlled me, but now it must serve me."

He laughed in great good-humor, and Rachel Miller, in her heart, thanked Miss Julia Blessing.

CHAPTER VI
IN THE GARDEN

Rachel Miller was not a woman to do a thing by halves. As soon as the question was settled, she gave her heart and mind to the necessary preparations. There might have been a little surprise in some quarters, when the fact became known in the neighborhood through Joseph's invitation, but no expression of it reached the Asten place. Mrs. Warriner, Anna's mother, called to inquire if she could be of service, and also to suggest, indirectly, *her* plan of entertaining company. Rachel detected the latter purpose, and was a little more acquiescent than could have been justified to her own conscience, seeing that at the very moment when she was listening with much apparent meekness, she was mentally occupied with plans for outdoing Mrs. Warriner. Moreover, the Rev. Mr. Chaffinch had graciously signified his willingness to be present, and the stamp of strictest orthodoxy was thus set upon the entertainment. She was both assured and stimulated, as the time drew near, and even surprised Joseph by saying: "If I was better acquainted with Miss Blessing, she might help me a good deal in fixing everything just as it should be. There are times, it seems, when it's an advantage to know something of the world."

"I'll ask her!" Joseph exclaimed.

"You! And a mess you'd make of it, very likely; men think they've only to agree to invite a company, and that's all! There's a hundred things to be thought of that women must look to; you couldn't even understand 'em. As for speaking to her, —she's one of the *invites,* and it would never do in the world."

Joseph said no more, but he silently determined to ask Miss Blessing on her arrival; there would still be time. She, with her wonderful instinct, her power of accommodating people to each other, and the influence which she had already acquired with his aunt, would certainly see at a glance how the current was setting, and guide it in the proper direction.

But, as the day drew near, he grew so restless and uneasy that there seemed nothing better to do than to ride over to Warriner's in the hope of catching a moment's conference with her, in advance of the occasion.

He was entirely fortunate. Anna was apparently very busy with household duties, and after the first greetings left him alone with Miss Blessing. He had anticipated a little difficulty in making his message known, and was therefore much relieved when she said: "Now, Mr. Asten, I see by your face that you have something particular to say. It's about to-morrow night, isn't it? You must let me help you, if I can, because I am afraid I have been, without exactly intending it, the cause of so much trouble to you and your aunt."

Joseph opened his heart at once. All that he had meant to say came easily and naturally to his lips, because Miss Blessing seemed to feel and understand the situation, and met him half-way in her bright, cheerful acquiescence. Almost before he knew it, he had made her acquainted with what had been said and done at home. How easily she solved the absurd doubts and difficulties which had so unnecessarily tormented him! How clearly, through her fine female instinct, she grasped little peculiarities of his aunt's nature, which he, after years of close companionship, had failed to define! Miss Rachel, she said, was both shy and inexperienced, and it was only the struggle to conceal these conscious defects which made her seem—not unamiable, exactly, but irregular in her manner. Her age, and her character in the neighborhood, did not permit her to appear incompetent to any emergency; it was a very natural pride, and must be treated very delicately and tenderly.

Would Joseph trust the matter entirely to her, Miss Blessing? It was a great deal to ask, she knew, comparative stranger as she was; but she believed that a woman, when her nature had not been distorted by the conventionalities of life, had a natural talent for smoothing difficulties, and removing obstacles for others. Her friends had told her that she possessed this power; and it was a great happiness to think so. In the present case, she was *sure* she should make no mistake. She would endeavor not to seem to suggest anything, but merely to assist in such a way that Miss Rachel would of herself see what else was necessary to be done.

"Now," she remarked, in conclusion, "this sounds like vanity in me; but I really hope it is not. You must remember that in the city we are obliged to know all the little social arts,—and artifices, I am afraid. It is not always to our credit, but then, the heart *may* be kept fresh and uncorrupted."

She sighed, and cast down her eyes. Joseph felt the increasing charm of a nature so frank and so trustful, constantly luring to the surface the maiden secrets of his own. The confidence already established between them was wholly delightful, because their sense of reciprocity increased as it deepened. He felt so free to speak that he could not measure the fitness of his words, but exclaimed, without a pause for thought:—

"Tell me, Miss Julia, did you not suggest this party to Aunt Rachel?"

"Don't give me too much credit!" she answered; "it was talked about, and I couldn't help saying Ay. I longed so much to see you—all—again before I go away."

"And Lucy Henderson objected to it?"

"Lucy, I think, wanted to save your aunt trouble. Perhaps she did not guess that the real objection was inexperience, and not want of will to entertain company. And very likely she helped to bring it about, by seeming to oppose it; so you must not be angry with Lucy,—promise me!"

She looked at him with an irresistibly entreating expression, and extended her hand, which he seized so warmly as to give her pain. But she returned the pressure, and there was a moment's silence, which Anna Warriner interrupted at the right time.

The next day, on the Asten farm, all the preparations were quietly and successfully made long in advance of the first arrivals. The Rev. Mr. Chaffinch and a few other specially chosen guests made their appearance in the afternoon. To Joseph's surprise, the Warriners and Miss Blessing speedily joined them. It was, in reality, a private arrangement which his aunt had made, in order to secure at the start the very assistance which he had been plotting to render. One half the secret of the ease and harmony which he felt was established was thus unknown to him. He looked for hints or indications of management on Miss Blessing's part, but saw none. The two women, meeting each other half-way, needed no words in order to understand each other, and Miss Rachel, gradually made secure in her part of hostess, experienced a most unaccustomed sense of triumph.

At the supper-table Mr. Chaffinch asked a blessing with fervor; a great, balmy dish of chickens stewed in cream was smoking before his nostrils, and his fourth cup of tea made Rachel Miller supremely happy. The meal was honored in silence, as is the case where there is much to eat and a proper desire and capacity to do it; only towards its close were the tongues of the guests loosened, and content made them cheerful.

"You have entertained us almost too sumptuously, Miss Miller," said the clergyman. "And now let us go out on the portico, and welcome the young people as they arrive."

"I need hardly ask you, then, Mr. Chaffinch," said she, "whether you think it right for them to come together in this way."

"Decidedly!" he answered; "that is, so long as their conversation is modest and becoming. It is easy for the vanities of the world to slip in, but we must watch,—we must watch."

Rachel Miller took a seat near him, beholding the gates of perfect enjoyment opened to her mind. Dress, the opera, the race-course, literature, stocks, politics, have their fascination for so many several classes of the human race; but to her there was nothing on this earth so delightful as to be told of temptation and backsliding and sin, and to feel that she was still secure. The fact that there was always danger added a zest to the feeling; she gave herself credit for a vigilance which had really not been exercised.

The older guests moved their chairs nearer, and listened, forgetting the sweetness of sunset which lay upon the hills down the valley. Anna Warriner laid her arm around Miss Chaffinch's waist, and drew her towards the mown field beyond the barn; and presently, by a natural chance, as it seemed, Joseph found himself beside Miss Blessing, at the bottom of the lawn.

All the western hills were covered with one cool, broad shadow. A rich orange flush touched the tops of the woods to the eastward, and brightened as the sky above them deepened into the violet-gray of coming dusk. The moist, delicious freshness which filled the bed of the valley slowly crept up the branching glen, and already tempered the air about them. Now and then a bird chirped happily from a neighboring bush, or the low of cattle was heard from the pasture-fields.

"Ah!" sighed Miss Blessing, "this is too sweet to last: I must learn to do without it."

She looked at him swiftly, and then glanced away. It seemed that there were tears in her eyes.

Joseph was about to speak, but she laid her hand on his arm. "Hush!" she said; "let us wait until the light has faded."

The glow had withdrawn to the summits of the distant hills, fringing them with a thin, wonderful radiance. But it was only momentary. The next moment it broke on the irregular topmost boughs, and then disappeared, as if blown out by a breeze which came with the sudden lifting of the sky. She turned away in silence, and they walked slowly together towards the house. At the garden gate she paused.

"That superb avenue of box!" she exclaimed; "I must see it again, if only to say farewell."

They entered the garden, and in a moment the dense green wall, breathing an odor seductive to heart and senses, had hidden them from the sight—and almost from the hearing—of the guests on the portico. Looking down through the southern opening of the avenue, they seemed alone in the evening valley.

Joseph's heart was beating fast and strong; he was conscious of a wild fear, so interfused with pleasure, that it was impossible to separate the sensations. Miss Blessing's hand was on his arm, and he fancied that it trembled.

"If life were as beautiful and peaceful as this," she whispered, at last, "we should not need to seek for truth and—and—sympathy: we should find them everywhere."

"Do you not think they are to be found?" he asked.

"O, in how few hearts! I can say it to *you*, and you will not misunderstand me. Until lately I was satisfied with life as I found it: I thought it meant diversion, and dress, and gossip, and common daily duties, but now—now I see that it is the union of kindred souls!"

She clasped both her hands over his arm as she spoke, and leaned slightly towards him, as if drawing away from the dreary, homeless world. Joseph felt all that the action expressed, and answered in an unsteady voice:—

"And yet—with a nature like yours—you must surely find them."

She shook her head sadly, and answered: "Ah, a woman cannot seek. I never thought I should be able to say—to any human being—that I have sought, or waited for recognition. I do not know why I should say it now. I try to be myself—my true self—with all persons; but it seems impossible: my nature shrinks from some and is drawn towards others. Why is this? What is the mystery that surrounds us?"

"Do you believe," Joseph asked, "that two souls may be so united that they shall dare to surrender all knowledge of themselves to each other, as we do, helplessly, before God?"

"O," she murmured, "it is my dream! I thought I was alone in cherishing it! Can it ever be realized?"

Joseph's brain grew hot: the release he had invoked sprang to life and urged him forward. Words came to his lips, he knew not how.

"If it is my dream and yours,—if we both have come to the faith and the hope we find in no others, and which alone will satisfy our lives, is it not a sign that the dream is over and the reality has begun?"

She hid her face in her hands. "Do not tempt me with what I had given up, unless you can teach me to believe again?" she cried.

"I do not tempt you," he answered breathlessly. "I tempt myself. I believe."

She turned suddenly, laid a hand upon his shoulder, lifted her face and looked into his eyes with an expression of passionate eagerness and joy. All her attitude breathed of the pause of the wave that only seems to hesitate an instant before throwing itself upon the waiting strand. Joseph had no defence, knew of none, dreamed of none. The pale-brown eyes, now dark, deep, and almost tearful, drew him with irresistible force: the sense of his own shy reticent self was lost, dissolved in the strength of an instinct which possessed him body and soul,—which bent him nearer to the slight form, which stretched his arms to answer its appeal, and left him, after one dizzy moment, with Miss Blessing's head upon his breast.

"I should like to die now," she murmured: "I never can be so happy again."

"No, no," said he, bending over her; "live for me!"

She raised herself, and kissed him again and again, and this frank, almost childlike betrayal of her heart seemed to claim from Joseph the full surrender of his own. He returned her caresses with equal warmth, and the twilight deepened around them as they stood, still half-embracing.

"Can I make you happy, Joseph?"

"Julia, I am already happier than I ever thought it possible to be."

With a sudden impulse she drew away from him. "Joseph!" she whispered, "will you always bear in mind what a cold, selfish, worldly life mine has been? You do not know me; you cannot understand the school in which I have been taught. I tell you, now, that I have had to learn cunning and artifice and equivocation. I am dark beside a nature so pure and good as yours! If you must ever learn to hate me, begin now! Take back your love: I have lived so long without the love of a noble human heart, that I can live so to the end!"

She again covered her face with her hands, and her frame shrank, as if dreading a mortal blow. But Joseph caught her back to his breast, touched and even humiliated by such sharp self-accusation. Presently she looked up: her eyes were wet, and she said, with a pitiful smile:—

"I believe you *do* love me."

"And I will not give you up," said Joseph, "though you should be full of evil as I am, myself."

She laughed, and patted his cheek: all her frank, bright, winning manner returned at once. Then commenced those reciprocal expressions of bliss, which are so inexhaustibly fresh to lovers, so endlessly monotonous to everybody else; and Joseph, lost to time, place, and circumstance, would have prolonged them far into the night, but for Miss Julia's returning self-possession.

"I hear wheels," she warned; "the evening guests are coming, and they will expect you to receive them, Joseph. And your dear, good old aunt will be looking for *me*. O, the world, the world! We must give ourselves up to it, and be as if we had never found each other. I shall be wild unless you set me an example of self-control. Let me look at you once, — one full, precious, perfect look, to carry in my heart through the evening!"

Then they looked in each other's faces; and looking was not enough; and their lips, without the use of words, said the temporary farewell. While Joseph hurried across the bottom of the lawn, to meet the stream of approaching guests which filled the lane, Miss Julia, at the top of the garden, plucked amaranth leaves for a wreath which would look well upon her dark hair, and sang, in a voice loud enough to be heard from the portico: —

"Ever be happy, light as thou art,
Pride of the pirate's heart!"

Everybody who had been invited — and quite a number who had not been, availing themselves of the easy habits of country society — came to the Asten farm that evening. Joseph, as host, seemed at times a little confused and flurried, but his face bloomed, his blue eyes sparkled, and even his nearest acquaintances were astonished at the courage and cordiality with which he performed his duties. The presence of Mr. Chaffinch kept the gayety of the company within decorous bounds; perhaps the number of detached groups appeared to form too many separate circles, or atmospheres of talk, but they easily dissolved, or gave to and took from each other. Rachel Miller was not inclined to act the part of a moral detective in the house which she managed; she saw nothing which the strictest sense of propriety could condemn.

Early in the evening, Joseph met Lucy Henderson in the hall. He could not see the graver change in her face; he only noticed that her manner was not so quietly attractive as usual. Yet on meeting her eyes he felt the absurd blood rushing to his cheeks and brow, and his tongue hesitated and stammered. This want of self-possession vexed him; he could not account for it; and he cut short the interview by moving abruptly away.

Lucy half turned, and looked after him, with an expression rather of surprise than of pain. As she did so she felt that there was an eye upon her, and by a strong effort entered the room without encountering the face of Elwood Withers.

When the company broke up, Miss Blessing, who was obliged to leave with the Warriners, found an opportunity to whisper to Joseph: "Come *soon!*" There was a long, fervent clasp of hands under her shawl, and then the carriage drove away. He could not see how the hand was transferred to that of Anna Warriner, which received from it a squeeze conveying an entire narrative to that young lady's mind.

Joseph's duties to his many guests prevented him from seeing much of Elwood during the evening; but, when the last were preparing to leave, he turned to the latter, conscious of a tenderer feeling of friendship than he had ever before felt, and begged him to stay for the night. Elwood held up the lantern, with which he had been examining the harness of a carriage that had just rolled away, and let its light fall upon Joseph's face.

"Do you really mean it?" he then asked.

"I don't understand you, Elwood."

"Perhaps I don't understand myself." But the next moment he laughed, and then added, in his usual tone: "Never mind; I'll stay."

They occupied the same room; and neither seemed inclined to sleep. After the company had been discussed, in a way which both felt to be awkward and mechanical, Elwood said: "Do you know anything more about love, by this time?"

Joseph was silent, debating with himself whether he should confide the wonderful secret. Elwood suddenly rose up in his bed, leaned forward, and whispered: "I see,—you need not answer. But tell me this one thing: is it Lucy Henderson?"

"No; O, no!"

"Does she know of it? Your face told some sort of a tale when you met her to-night."

"Not to her,—surely not to her!" Joseph exclaimed.

"I hope not," Elwood quietly said: "I love her."

With a bound Joseph crossed the room and sat down on the edge of his friend's bed. "Elwood!" he cried; "and you are happy, too! O, now I can tell you all,—it is Julia Blessing!"

"Ha! ha!" Elwood laughed,—a short, bitter laugh, which seemed to signify anything but happiness. "Forgive me, Joseph!" he presently added, "but there's a deal of difference between a mitten and a ring. You will have one and I have the other. I did think for a little while that you stood between Lucy and me; but I suppose disappointment makes men fools."

Something in Joseph's breast seemed to stop the warm flood of his feelings. He could only stammer, after a long pause: "But I am not in your way."

"So I see,—and perhaps nobody is, except myself. We won't talk of this any more; there's many a roundabout road that comes out into the straight one at last. But you,—I can't understand the thing at all. How did she—did you come to love her?"

"I don't know; I hardly guessed it until this evening."

"Then, Joseph, go slowly, and feel your way. I'm not the one to advise, after what has happened to me; but maybe I know a little more of womankind than you. It's best to have a longer acquaintance than yours has been; a fellow can't always tell a sudden fancy from a love that has the grip of death."

"Now I might turn your own words against you, Elwood, for you tried to tell me what love is."

"I did; and before I knew the half. But come, Joseph: promise me that you won't let Miss Blessing know how much you feel until—"

"Elwood," Joseph breathlessly interrupted, "she knows it now! We were together this evening."

Elwood fell back on the pillow with a groan. "I'm a poor friend to you," he said: "I want to wish you joy, but I can't,—not to-night. The way things are fixed in this world stumps me, out and out. Nothing fits as it ought, and if I didn't take my head in my own hands and hold it towards the light by main force, I'd only see blackness, and death, and hell."

Joseph stole back to his bed, and lay there silently. There was a subtle chill in the heart of his happiness, which all the remembered glow of that tender scene in the garden could not thaw.

CHAPTER VII
THE BLESSING FAMILY

Joseph's secret was not suspected by any of the company. Elwood's manner towards him next morning was warmer and kinder than ever; the chill of the past night had been forgotten, and the betrothal, which then almost seemed like a fetter upon his future, now gave him a sense of freedom and strength. He would have gone to Warriner's at once, but for the fear lest he should betray himself. Miss Blessing was to return to the city in three days more, and a single farewell call might be made with propriety; so he controlled his impatience and allowed another day to intervene.

When, at last, the hour of meeting came, Anna Warriner proved herself an efficient ally. Circumstances were against her, yet she secured the lovers a few minutes in which they could hold each other's hands, and repeat their mutual delight, with an exquisite sense of liberty in doing so. Miss Blessing suggested that nothing should be said until she had acquainted her parents with the engagement; there might be some natural difficulties to overcome; it was so unexpected, and the idea of losing her would possibly be unwelcome, at first. She would write in a few days, and then Joseph must come and make the acquaintance of her family.

"*Then,*" she added, "I shall have no fear. When they have once seen you all difficulties will vanish. There will be no trouble with ma and sister Clementina; but pa is sometimes a little peculiar, on account of his connections. There! don't look so serious, all at once; it is my duty, you know, to secure you a loving reception. You must try to feel already that you have two homes, as I do."

Joseph waited very anxiously for the promised letter, and in ten days it came; it was brief, but satisfactory. "Would you believe it, dear Joseph," she commenced, "pa makes no difficulty! he only requires some assurances which you can very easily furnish. Ma, on the other hand, don't like the idea of giving me up. I can hardly say it without seeming to praise myself; but Clementina never took very kindly to housekeeping and managing, and even if I were only indifferent in those branches, I should be missed. It really went to my heart when ma met me at the door, and cried out, 'Now I shall have a little rest!' You may imagine how hard it was to tell her. But she is a dear, good mother, and I know she will be *so* happy to find a son in you—as she certainly will. Come, soon,—soon! They are all anxious to know you."

The city was not so distant as to make a trip thither an unusual event for the young farmers of the neighborhood. Joseph had frequently gone there for a day in the interest of his sales of stock and grain, and he found no difficulty in inventing a plausible reason for the journey. The train at the nearest railway station transported him in two or three hours to the commencement of the miles of hot, dusty, rattling pavements, and left him free to seek for the brick nest within which his love was sheltered.

Yet now, so near the point whence his new life was to commence, a singular unrest took possession of him. He distinctly felt the presence of two forces, acting against each other with nearly equal power, but without neutralizing their disturbing influence. He was developing faster than he guessed, yet, to a nature like his, the last knowledge that comes is the knowledge of self. Some occult instinct already whispered that his life thenceforth would be stronger, more independent, but also more disturbed; and this was what he had believed was wanting. If the consciousness of loving and being loved were not quite the same in experience as it had seemed to his ignorant fancy, it was yet a positive happiness, and wedlock would therefore be its unbroken continuance. Julia had prepared for his introduction into her family; he must learn to accept her parents and sister as his own; and now the hour and the opportunity were at hand.

What was it, then, that struck upon his breast almost like a physical pressure, and mysteriously resisted his errand? When he reached the cross-street, in which, many squares to the northward, the house was to be found, he halted for some minutes, and then, instead of turning, kept directly onward toward the river. The sight of the water, the gliding sails, the lusty life and labor along the piers, suddenly refreshed him. Men were tramping up and down the gangways of the clipper-ships; derricks were slowly swinging over the sides the bales and boxes which had been brought up from the holds; drays were clattering to and fro: wherever he turned he saw a picture of strength, courage, reality, solid work. The men that went and came took life simply as a succession of facts, and if these did not fit smoothly into each other, they either gave themselves no trouble about the rough edges, or drove them out of sight with a few sturdy blows. What Lucy Henderson had said about going to school was recalled to Joseph's mind. Here was a class where he would be apt to stand at the foot for many days. Would any of those strapping forms comprehend the disturbance of his mind?—they would probably advise him to go to the nearest apothecary-shop and purchase a few blue-pills. The longer he watched them, the more he felt the contagion of their unimaginative, face to face grapple with life; the manly element in him, checked so long, began to push a vigorous shoot towards the light.

"It is only the old cowardice, after all," he thought. "I am still shrinking from the encounter with new faces! A lover, soon to be a husband, and still so much of a green youth! It will never do. I must learn to handle my duty as that stevedore handles a barrel,—take hold with both hands, push and trundle and guide, till the weight becomes a mere plaything. There!—he starts a fresh one,—now for mine!"

Therewith he turned about, walked sternly back to the cross-street, and entered it without pausing at the corner. It was still a long walk; and the street, with its uniform brick houses, with white shutters, green interior blinds, and white marble steps, grew more silent and monotonous. There was a mixed odor of salt-fish, molasses, and decaying oranges at every corner; dark wenches lowered the nozzles of their jetting hose as he passed, and girls in draggled calico frocks turned to look at him from the entrances of gloomy tunnels leading into the back yards. A man with something in a cart uttered from time to time a piercing unintelligible cry; barefooted youngsters swore over their marbles on the sidewalk; and, at rare intervals, a marvellous moving fabric of silks and colors and glosses floated past him. But he paused for none of these. His heart beat faster, and the strange resistance seemed to increase with the increasing numbers of houses, now rapidly approaching The One—then it came!

There was an entire block of narrow three-storied dwellings, with crowded windows and flat roofs. If Joseph had been familiar with the city, he would have recognized the air of cheap gentility which exhaled from them, and which said, as plainly as if the words had been painted on their fronts, "Here we keep up appearances on a very small capital." He noticed nothing, however, except the marble steps and the front doors, all of which were alike to him until he came upon a brass plate inscribed "B. Blessing." As he looked up a mass of dark curls vanished with a start from the window. The door suddenly opened before he could touch the bell-pull, and two hands upon his own drew him into the diminutive hall.

The door instantly closed again, but softly: then two arms were flung around his neck, and his willing lips received a subdued kiss. "Hush!" she said; "it is delightful that you have arrived, though we didn't expect you so immediately. Come into the drawing-room, and let us have a minute together before I call ma."

She tripped lightly before him, and they were presently seated side by side, on the sofa.

"What could have brought me to the window just at that moment?" she whispered; "it must have been presentiment."

Joseph's face brightened with pleasure. "And I was long on the way," he answered. "What will you think of me, Julia? I was a little afraid."

"I know you were, Joseph," she said. "It is only the cold, insensible hearts that are never agitated."

Their eyes met, and he remarked, for the first time, their peculiar pale-brown, almost tawny clearness. The next instant her long lashes slowly fell and half concealed them; she drew away slightly from him, and said: "I should like to be beautiful, for your sake; I never cared about it before."

Without giving him time to reply, she rose and moved towards the door, then looked back, smiled, and disappeared.

Joseph, left alone, also rose and walked softly up and down the room. To his eyes it seemed an elegant, if rather chilly apartment. It was long and narrow, with a small, delusive fireplace of white marble (intended only for hot air) in the middle, a carpet of many glaring colors on the floor, and a paper brilliant with lilac-bunches on the walls. There was a centre-table, with some lukewarm literature cooling itself on the marble top; an *étagère*, with a few nondescript cups and flagons, and a cottage piano, on which lay several sheets of music by Verdi and Balfe. The furniture, not very abundant, was swathed in a nankeen summer dress. There were two pictures on the walls, portraits of a gentleman and lady, and when once Joseph had caught the fixed stare of their lustreless eyes, he found it difficult to turn away. The imperfect light which came through the bowed window-shutters revealed a florid, puffy-faced young man, whose head was held up by a high black satin stock. He was leaning against a fluted pillar, apparently constructed of putty, behind which fell a superb crimson curtain, lifted up at one corner to disclose a patch of stormy sky. The long locks, tucked in at the temples, the carefully-delineated whiskers, and the huge signet-ring on the second finger of the one exposed hand, indicated that a certain "position" in society was either possessed or claimed of right by the painted person. Joseph could hardly doubt that this was a representation of "B. Blessing," as he appeared twenty or thirty years before.

He turned to the other picture. The lady was slender, and meant to be graceful, her head being inclined so that the curls on the left side rolled in studied disorder upon her shoulder. Her face was thin and long, with well-marked and not unpleasant features. There was rather too positive a bloom upon her cheeks, and the fixed smile on the narrow mouth scarcely harmonized with the hard, serious stare of the eyes. She was royally attired in purple, and her bare white arm—much more plumply rounded than her face would have given reason to suspect—hung with a listless grace over the end of a sofa.

Joseph looked from one face to the other with a curious interest, which the painted eyes seemed also to reflect, as they followed him. They were strangers, out of a different sphere of life, yet they must become, nay, were already, a part of his own! The lady scrutinized him closely, in spite of her smile; but the indifference of the gentleman, blandly satisfied with himself, seemed less assuring to his prospects.

Footsteps in the hall interrupted his revery, and he had barely time to slip into his seat when the door opened and Julia entered, followed by the original of one of the portraits. He recognized her, although the curls had disappeared, the dark hair was sprinkled with gray, and deep lines about the mouth and eyes gave them an expression of care and discontent. In one respect she differed from her daughter: her eyes were gray.

She bent her head with a stately air as Joseph rose, walked past Julia, and extended her hand, with the words,—

"Mr. Asten, I am glad to see you. Pray be seated."

When all had taken seats, she resumed: "Excuse me if I begin by asking a question. You must consider that I have only known you through Julia, and her description could not, under the circumstances, be very clear. What is your age?"

"I shall be twenty-three next birthday," Joseph replied.

"Indeed! I am happy to hear it. You do not look more than nineteen. I have reason to dread *very* youthful attachments, and am therefore reassured to know that you are fully a man and competent to test your feelings. I trust that you *have* so tested them. Again I say, excuse me if the question seems to imply a want of confidence. A mother's anxiety, you know—"

Julia clasped her hands and bent down her head.

"I am quite sure of myself," Joseph said, "and would try to make you as sure, if I knew how to do it."

"If you were one of us,—of the city, I mean,—I should be able to judge more promptly. It is many years since I have been outside of our own select circle, and I am therefore not so competent as once to judge of men in general. While I will never, without the most sufficient reason, influence my daughters in their choice, it is my duty to tell you that Julia is exceedingly susceptible on the side of her affections. A wound *there* would be incurable to her. We are alike in that; I know her nature through my own."

Julia hid her face upon her mother's shoulder: Joseph was moved, and vainly racked his brain for some form of assurance which might remove the maternal anxiety.

"There," said Mrs. Blessing; "we will say no more about it now. Go and bring your sister!"

"There are some other points, Mr. Asten," she continued, "which have no doubt already occurred to your mind. Mr. Blessing will consult with you in relation to them. I make it a rule never to trespass upon his field of duty. As you were not positively expected to-day, he went to the Custom-House as usual; but it will soon be time for him to return. Official labors, you understand, cannot be postponed. If you have ever served in a government capacity, you will appreciate his position. I have sometimes wished that we had not become identified with political life; but, on the other hand, there are compensations."

Joseph, impressed more by Mrs. Blessing's important manner than the words she uttered, could only say, "I beg that my visit may not interfere in any way with Mr. Blessing's duties."

"Unfortunately," she replied, "they cannot be postponed. His advice is more required by the Collector than his special official services. But, as I said, he will confer with you in regard to the future of our little girl. I call her so, Mr. Asten, because she is the youngest, and I can hardly yet realize that she is old enough to leave me. Yes: the youngest, and the first to go. Had it been Clementina, I should have been better prepared for the change. But a mother should always be ready to sacrifice herself, where the happiness of a child is at stake."

Mrs. Blessing gently pressed a small handkerchief to the corner of each eye, then heaved a sigh, and resumed her usual calm dignity of manner. The door opened, and Julia re-entered, followed by her sister.

"This is Miss Blessing," said the mother.

The young lady bowed very formally, and therewith would have finished her greeting, but Joseph had already risen and extended his hand. She thereupon gave him the tips of four limp fingers, which he attempted to grasp and then let go.

Clementina was nearly a head taller than her sister, and amply proportioned. She had a small, petulant mouth, small gray eyes, a low, narrow forehead, and light brown hair. Her eyelids and cheeks had the same puffy character as her father's, in his portrait on the wall; yet there was a bloom and brilliancy about her complexion which suggested beauty. A faint expression of curiosity passed over her face, on meeting Joseph, but she uttered no word of welcome. He looked at Julia, whose manner was suddenly subdued, and was quick enough to perceive a rivalry between the sisters. The stolidity of Clementina's countenance indicated that indifference which is more offensive than enmity. He disliked her from the first moment.

Julia kept modestly silent, and the conversation, in spite of her mother's capacity to carry it on, did not flourish. Clementina spoke only in monosyllables, which she let fall from time to time with a silver sweetness which startled Joseph, it seemed so at variance with her face and manner. He felt very much relieved when, after more than one significant glance had been exchanged with her mother, the two arose and left the room. At the door Mrs. Blessing said: "Of course you will stay and take a family tea with us, Mr. Asten. I will order it to be earlier served, as you are probably not accustomed to our city hours."

Julia looked up brightly after the door had closed, and exclaimed: "Now! when ma says *that*, you may be satisfied. Her housekeeping is like the laws of the Medes and Persians. She probably seemed rather formal to you, and it is true that a certain amount of form has become natural to her; but it always gives way when she is strongly moved. Pa is to come yet, but I am sure you will get on very well with him; men always grow acquainted in a little while. I'm afraid that Clementina did not impress you very—very genially; she is, I may confess it to you, a little peculiar."

"She is very quiet," said Joseph, "and very unlike you."

"Every one notices that. And we seem to be unlike in character, as much so as if there were no relationship between us. But I must say for Clementina, that she is above personal likings and dislikings; she looks at people abstractly. You are only a future brother-in-law to her, and I don't believe she can tell whether your hair is black or the beautiful golden brown that it is."

Joseph smiled, not ill-pleased with Julia's delicate flattery. "I am all the more delighted," he said, "that you are different. I should not like you, Julia, to consider me an abstraction."

"You are very real, Joseph, and very individual," she answered, with one of her loveliest smiles.

Not ten minutes afterwards, Julia, whose eyes and ears were keenly on the alert, notwithstanding her gay, unrestrained talk, heard the click of a latch-key. She sprang up, laid her forefinger on her lips, gave Joseph a swift, significant glance, and darted into the hall. A sound of whispering followed, and there was no mistaking the deep, hoarse murmur of one of the voices.

Mr. Blessing, without the fluted pillar and the crimson curtain, was less formidable than Joseph had anticipated. The years had added to his body and taken away from his hair; yet his face, since high stocks were no longer in fashion, had lost its rigid lift, and expressed the chronic cordiality of a popular politician. There was a redness about the rims of his eyes, and a fulness of the under lid, which also denoted political habits. However, despite wrinkles, redness, and a general roughening and coarsening of the features, the resemblance to the portrait was still strong; and Joseph, feeling as if the presentation had already been made, offered his hand as soon as Mr. Blessing entered the room.

"Very happy to see you, Mr. Asten," said the latter. "An unexpected pleasure, sir."

He removed the glove from his left hand, pulled down his coat and vest, felt the tie of his cravat, twitched at his pantaloons, ran his fingers through his straggling gray locks, and then threw himself into a chair, exclaiming: "After business, pleasure, sir! My duties are over for the day. Mrs. Blessing probably informed you of my official capacity; but you can have no conception of the vigilance required to prevent evasion of the revenue laws. We are the country's watch-dogs, sir."

"I can understand," Joseph said, "that an official position carries with it much responsibility."

"Quite right, sir, and without adequate remuneration. Figuratively speaking, we handle millions, and we are paid by dimes. Were it not for the consciousness of serving and saving for the nation—but I will not pursue the subject. When we have become better acquainted, you can judge for yourself whether preferment always follows capacity. Our present business is to establish a mutual understanding,—as we say in politics, to prepare a platform,—and I think you will agree with me that the circumstances of the case require frank dealing, as between man and man."

"Certainly!" Joseph answered; "I only ask that, although I am a stranger to you, you will accept my word until you have the means of verifying it."

"I may safely do that with you, sir. My associations—duties, I may say—compel me to know many persons with whom it would *not* be safe. We will forget the disparity of age and experience between us. I can hardly ask you to imagine yourself placed in my situation, but perhaps we can make the case quite as clear if I state to you, without reserve, what *I* should be ready to do, if our present positions were reversed: Julia, will you look after the tea?"

"Yes, pa," said she, and slipped out of the drawing-room.

"If I were a young man from the country, and had won the affections of a young lady of—well, I may say it to you—of an old family, whose parents were ignorant of my descent, means, and future prospects in life, I should consider it my first duty to enlighten those parents upon all these points. I should reflect that the lady must be removed from their sphere to mine; that, while the attachment was, in itself, vitally important to her and to me, those parents would naturally desire to compare the two spheres, and assure themselves that their daughter would lose no material advantages by the transfer. You catch my meaning?"

"I came here," said Joseph, "with the single intention of satisfying you—at least, I came hoping that I shall be able to do so—in regard to myself. It will be easy for you to test my statements."

"Very well. We will begin, then, with the subject of Family. Understand me, I mention this solely because, in our old communities, Family is the stamp of Character. An established name represents personal qualities, virtues. It is indifferent to me whether my original ancestor was a De Belsain (though beauty and health have always been family characteristics); but it *is* important that he transmitted certain traits which—which others, perhaps, can better describe. The name of Asten is not usual; it has, in fact, rather a distinguished sound; but I am not acquainted with its derivation."

Joseph restrained a temptation to smile, and replied: "My great-grandfather came from England more than a hundred years ago: that is all I positively know. I have heard it said that the family was originally Danish."

"You must look into the matter, sir: a good pedigree is a bond for good behavior. The Danes, I have been told, were of the same blood as the Normans. But we will let that pass. Julia informs me you are the owner of a handsome farm, yet I am so ignorant of values in the country,—and my official duties oblige me to measure property by such a different standard,—that, really, unless you could make the farm evident to me in figures, I—"

He paused, but Joseph was quite ready with the desired intelligence. "I have two hundred acres," he said, "and a moderate valuation of the place would be a hundred and thirty dollars an acre. There is a mortgage of five thousand dollars on the place, the term of which has not yet expired; but I have nearly an equal amount invested, so that the farm fairly represents what I own."

"H'm," mused Mr. Blessing, thrusting his thumbs into the arm-holes of his waistcoat, "that is not a great deal here in the city, but I dare say it is a handsome competence in the country. It doubtless represents a certain annual income!"

"It is a very comfortable home, in the first place," said Joseph; "the farm ought to yield, after supplying nearly all the wants of a family, an annual return of a thousand to fifteen hundred dollars, according to the season."

"Twenty-six thousand dollars!—and five per cent!" Mr. Blessing exclaimed. "If you had the farm in money, and knew how to operate with it, you might pocket ten—fifteen—twenty per cent. Many a man, with less than that to set him afloat, has become a millionnaire in five years' time. But it takes pluck and experience, sir!"

"More of both than I can lay claim to," Joseph remarked; "but what there is of my income is certain. If Julia were not so fond of the country, and already so familiar with our ways, I might hesitate to offer her such a plain, quiet home, but—"

"O, I know!" Mr. Blessing interrupted. "We have heard of nothing but cows and spring-houses and willow-trees since she came back. I hope, for your sake, it may last; for I see that you are determined to suit each other. I have no inclination to act the obdurate parent. You have met me like a man, sir: here's my hand; I feel sure that, as my son-in-law, you will keep up the reputation of the family!"

CHAPTER VIII
A CONSULTATION

The family tea was served in a small dining-room in the rear. Mr. Blessing, who had become more and more cordial with Joseph after formally accepting him, led the way thither, and managed to convey a rapid signal to his wife before the family took their seats at the table. Joseph was the only one who did not perceive the silent communication of intelligence; but its consequences were such as to make him speedily feel at ease in the Blessing mansion. Even Clementina relented sufficiently to say, in her most silvery tones, "May I offer you the butter, Mr. Asten?"

The table, it is true, was very unlike the substantial suppers of the country. There was a variety of diminutive dishes, containing slices so delicate that they mocked rather than excited the appetite; yet Julia, (of course it was she!) had managed to give the repast an air of elegance which was at least agreeable to a kindred sense. Joseph took the little cup, the thin tea, the five drops of milk, and the fragment of sugar, without asking himself whether the beverage were palatable: he divided a leaf-like piece of flesh and consumed several wafers of bread, blissfully unconscious whether his stomach were satisfied. He felt that he had been received into The Family. Mr. Blessing was magnificently bland, Mrs. Blessing was maternally interested, Clementina recognized his existence, and Julia,—he needed but one look at her sparkling eyes, her softly flushed cheeks, her bewitching excitement of manner, to guess the relief of her heart. He forgot the vague distress which had preceded his coming, and the embarrassment of his first reception, in the knowledge that Julia was so happy, and through the acquiescence of her parents, in his love.

It was settled that he should pass the night there. Mrs. Blessing would take no denial; he must now consider their house as his home. She would also call him "Joseph," but not now,—not until she was entitled to name him "son." It had come suddenly upon her, but it was her duty to be glad, and in a little while she would become accustomed to the change.

All this was so simply and cordially said, that Joseph quite warmed to the stately woman, and unconsciously decided to accept his fortune, whatever features it might wear. Until the one important event, at least; after that it would be in his own hands—and Julia's.

After tea, two or three hours passed away rather slowly. Mr. Blessing sat in the pit of a back yard and smoked until dusk; then the family collected in the "drawing-room," and there was a little music, and a variety of gossip, with occasional pauses of silence, until Mrs. Blessing said: "Perhaps you had better show Mr. Asten to his room, Mr. Blessing. We may have already passed over his accustomed hour for retiring. If so, I know he will excuse us; we shall soon become familiar with each other's habits."

When Mr. Blessing returned, he first opened the rear window, drew an arm-chair near it, took off his coat, seated himself, and lit another cigar. His wife closed the front shutters, slipped the night-bolts of the door, and then seated herself beside him. Julia whirled around on her music-stool to face the coming consultation, and Clementina gracefully posed herself in the nearest corner of the sofa.

"How do you like him, Eliza?" Mr. Blessing asked, after several silent, luxurious whiffs.

"He is handsome, and seems amiable, but younger than I expected. Are you sure of his—his feelings, Julia?"

"O ma!" Julia exclaimed; "what a question! I can only judge them by my own."

Clementina curled her lip in a singular fashion, but said nothing.

"It seems like losing Julia entirely," Mrs. Blessing resumed. "I don't know how she will be able to retain her place in our circle, unless they spend a part of the winter in the city, and whether he has means enough—"

She paused, and looked inquisitively at her husband.

"You always look at the establishment," said he, "and never consider the chances. Marriage is a deal, a throw, a sort of kite-flying, in fact (except in *our* case, my dear), and, after all I've learned of our future son-in-law, I must say that Julia hasn't a bad hand."

"I knew you'd like him, pa!" cried the delighted Julia.

Mr. Blessing looked at her steadily a moment, and then winked; but she took no notice of it.

"There is another thing," said his wife. "If the wedding comes off this fall, we have but two months to prepare; and how will you manage about the—the money? We can save afterwards, to be sure, but there will be an immediate and fearful expense. I've thought, perhaps, that a simple and private ceremony,—married in travelling-dress, you know, just before the train leaves, and no cards,—it is sometimes done in the highest circles."

"It won't do!" exclaimed Mr. Blessing, waving his right hand. "Julia's husband must have an opportunity of learning our standing in society. I will invite the Collector, and the Surveyor, and the Appraiser. The money *must* be raised. I should be willing to pawn—"

He looked around the room, inspecting the well-worn carpet, the nankeen-covered chairs, the old piano, and finally the two pictures.

"—Your portrait, my dear; but, unless it were a Stuart, I couldn't get ten dollars on it. We must take your set of diamonds, and Julia's rubies, and Clementina's pearls."

He leaned back, and laughed with great glee. The ladies became rigid and grave.

"It is wicked, Benjamin," Mrs. Blessing severely remarked, "to jest over our troubles at such a time as this. I see nothing else to do, but to inform Mr. Asten, frankly, of our condition. He is yet too young, I think, to be repelled by poverty."

"Ma, it would break my heart," said Julia. "I could not bear to be humiliated in his eyes."

"Decidedly the best thing to do," warbled Clementina, speaking for the first time.

"That's the way with women,—flying from one extreme to the other. If you can't have white, you turn around and say there's no other color than black. When all devices are exhausted, a man of pluck and character goes to work and constructs a new one. Upon my soul, I don't know where the money is to come from; but give me ten days, and Julia shall have her white satin. Now, girls, you had better go to bed."

Mr. Blessing smoked silently until the sound of his daughters' footsteps had ceased on the stairs; then, bringing down his hand emphatically upon his thigh, he exclaimed, "By Jove, Eliza, if I were as sharp as that girl, I'd have had the Collectorship before this!"

"What do you mean? She seems to be strongly attached to him."

"O, no doubt! But she has a wonderful talent for reading character. The young fellow is pretty green wood still; what he'll season into depends on her. Honest as the day,—there's nothing like a country life for that. But it's a pity that such a fund for operations should lie idle; he has a nest-egg that might hatch out millions!"

"I hope, Benjamin, that after all your unfortunate experience—"

"Pray don't lament in advance, and especially now, when a bit of luck comes to us. Julia has done well, and I'll trust her to improve her opportunities. Besides, this will help Clementina's chances; where there is one marriage in a family, there is generally another. Poor girl! she has waited a long while. At thirty-three, the market gets v-e-r-y flat."

"And yet Julia is thirty," said Mrs. Blessing; "and Clementina's complexion and manners have been considered superior."

"There's just her mistake. A better copy of Mrs. Halibut's airs and attitudes was never produced, and it was all very well so long as Mrs. Halibut gave the tone to society; but since she went to Europe, and Mrs. Bass has somehow crept into her place, Clementina is quite—I may say— obsolete. I don't object to her complexion, because that is a standing fashion, but she is expected to be chatty, and witty, and instead of that she stands about like a Venus of Milo. She looks like me, and she can't lack intelligence and tact. Why couldn't she unbend a little more to Asten, whether she likes him or not?"

"You know I never seemed to manage Clementina," his wife replied; "if she were to dispute my opinion sometimes, I might, perhaps, gain a little influence over her: but she won't enter into a discussion."

"Mrs. Halibut's way. It was new, then, and, with her husband's money to back it, her 'grace' and 'composure' and 'serenity' carried all before her. Give me fifty thousand a year, and I'll put Clementina in the same place! But, come,—to the main question. I suppose we shall need five hundred dollars!"

"Three hundred, I think, will be ample," said Mrs. Blessing.

"Three or five, it's as hard to raise one sum as the other. I'll try for five, and if I have luck with the two hundred over—small, careful operations, you know, which always succeed—I may have the whole amount on hand, long before it's due."

Mrs. Blessing smiled in a melancholy, hopeless way, and the consultation came to an end.

When Joseph was left alone in his chamber, he felt no inclination to sleep. He sat at the open window, and looked down into the dim, melancholy street, the solitude of which was broken about once every quarter of an hour by a forlorn pedestrian, who approached through gloom and lamplight, was foreshortened to his hat, and then lengthened away on the other side. The new acquaintances he had just made remained all the more vividly in his thoughts from their nearness; he was still within their atmosphere. They were unlike any persons he knew, and therefore he felt that he might do them injustice by a hasty estimate of their character. Clementina, however, was excluded from this charitable resolution. Concentrating his dislike on her, he found that her parents had received him with as much consideration as a total stranger could expect. Moreover, whatever they might be, Julia was the same here, in her own home, as when she was a guest in the country. As playful, as winning, and as natural; and he began to suspect that her present life was not congenial to such a nature. If so, her happiness was all the more assured by their union.

This thought led him into a pictured labyrinth of anticipation, in which his mind wandered with delight. He was so absorbed in planning the new household, that he did not hear the sisters entering the rear room on the same floor, which was only separated by a thin partition from his own.

"White satin!" he suddenly heard Clementina say: "of course I shall have the same. It will become *me* better than you."

"I should think you might be satisfied with a light silk," Julia said; "the expenses will be very heavy."

"We'll see," Clementina answered shortly, pacing up and down the room.

After a long pause, he heard Julia's voice again. "Never mind," she said, "I shall soon be out of your way."

"I wonder how much he knows about you!" Clementina exclaimed. "Your arts were new there, and you played an easy game." Here she lowered her voice, and Joseph only distinguished a detached word now and then. He rose, indignant at this unsisterly assault, and wishing to hear no more; but it seemed that the movement was not noticed, for Julia replied, in smothered, excited tones, with some remark about "complexion."

"Well, there is one thing," Clementina continued, —"one thing you will keep very secret, and that is your birthday. Are you going to tell him that you are—"

Joseph had seized the back of a chair and with a sudden impulse tilted it and let it fall on the floor. Then he walked to the window, closed it, and prepared to go to rest,—all with more noise than was habitual with him. There were whispers and hushed movements in the next room, but not another audible word was spoken. Before sleeping he came to the conclusion that he was more than Julia's lover: he was her deliverer. The idea was not unwelcome: it gave a new value and significance to his life.

However curious Julia might have been to discover how much he had overheard, she made no effort to ascertain the fact. She met him next morning with a sweet unconsciousness of what she had endured, which convinced him that such painful scenes must have been frequent, or she could not have forgotten so easily. His greeting to Clementina was brief and cold, but she did not seem to notice it in the least.

It was decided, before he left, that the wedding should take place in October.

CHAPTER IX
JOSEPH AND HIS FRIEND

The train moved slowly along through the straggling and shabby suburbs, increasing its speed as the city melted gradually into the country; and Joseph, after a vain attempt to fix his mind upon one of the volumes he had procured for his slender library at home, leaned back in his seat and took note of his fellow-travellers. Since he began to approach the usual destiny of men, they had a new interest for him. Hitherto he had looked upon strange faces very much as on a strange language, without a thought of interpreting them; but now their hieroglyphics seemed to suggest a meaning. The figures around him were so many sitting, silent histories, so many locked-up records of struggle, loss, gain, and all the other forces which give shape and color to human life. Most of them were strangers to each other, and as reticent (in their railway conventionality) as himself; yet, he reflected, the whole range of passion, pleasure, and suffering was probably illustrated in that collection of existences. His own troublesome individuality grew fainter, so much of it seemed to be merged in the common experience of men.

There was the portly gentleman of fifty, still ruddy and full of unwasted force. The keenness and coolness of his eyes, the few firmly marked lines on his face, and the color and hardness of his lips, proclaimed to everybody: "I am bold, shrewd, successful in business, scrupulous in the performance of my religious duties (on the Sabbath), voting with my party, and not likely to be fooled by any kind of sentimental nonsense." The thin, not very well-dressed man beside him, with the irregular features and uncertain expression, announced as clearly, to any who could read: "I am weak, like others, but I never consciously did any harm. I just manage to get along in the world, but if I only had a chance, I might make something better of myself." The fresh, healthy fellow, in whose lap a child was sleeping, while his wife nursed a younger one,—the man with ample mouth, large nostrils, and the hands of a mechanic,—also told his story: "On the whole, I find life a comfortable thing. I don't know much about it, but I take it as it comes, and never worry over what I can't understand."

The faces of the younger men, however, were not so easy to decipher. On them life was only beginning its plastic task, and it required an older eye to detect the delicate touches of awakening passions and hopes. But Joseph consoled himself with the thought that his own secret was as little to be discovered as any they might have. If they were still ignorant, of the sweet experience of love, he was already their superior; if they were sharers in it, though strangers, they were near to him. Had he not left the foot of the class, after all?

All at once his eye was attracted by a new face, three or four seats from his own. The stranger had shifted his position, so that he was no longer seen in profile. He was apparently a few years older than Joseph, but still bright with all the charm of early manhood. His fair complexion was bronzed from exposure, and his hands, graceful without being effeminate, were not those of the idle gentleman. His hair, golden in tint, thrust its short locks as it pleased about a smooth, frank forehead; the eyes were dark gray, and the mouth, partly hidden by a mustache, at once firm and full. He was moderately handsome, yet it was not of that which Joseph thought; he felt that there was more of developed character and a richer past history expressed in those features than in any other face there. He felt sure—and smiled at himself, notwithstanding, for the impression—that at least some of his own doubts and difficulties had found their solution in the stranger's nature. The more he studied the face, the more he was conscious of its attraction, and his instinct of reliance, though utterly without grounds, justified itself to his mind in some mysterious way.

It was not long before the unknown felt his gaze, and, turning slowly in his seat, answered it. Joseph dropped his eyes in some confusion, but not until he had caught the full, warm, intense expression of those that met them. He fancied that he read in them, in that momentary flash, what he had never before found in the eyes of strangers,—a simple, human interest, above curiosity and above mistrust. The usual reply to such a gaze is an unconscious defiance: the unknown nature is on its guard: but the look which seems to answer, "We are men, let us know each other!" is, alas! too rare in this world.

While Joseph was fighting the irresistible temptation to look again, there was a sudden thud of the car-wheels. Many of the passengers started from their seats, only to be thrown into them again by a quick succession of violent jolts. Joseph saw the stranger springing towards the bell-rope; then he and all others seemed to be whirling over each other; there was a crash, a horrible grinding and splintering sound, and the end of all was a shock, in which his consciousness left him before he could guess its violence.

After a while, out of some blank, haunted by a single lost, wandering sense of existence, he began to awaken slowly to life. Flames were still dancing in his eyeballs, and waters and whirlwinds roaring in his ears; but it was only a passive sensation, without the will to know more. Then he felt himself partly lifted and his head supported, and presently a soft warmth fell upon the region of his heart. There were noises all about him, but he did not listen to them; his effort to regain his consciousness fixed itself on that point alone, and grew stronger as the warmth calmed the confusion of his nerves.

"Dip this in water!" said a voice, and the hand (as he now knew it to be) was removed from his heart.

Something cold came over his forehead, and at the same time warm drops fell upon his cheek.

"Look out for yourself: your head is cut!" exclaimed another voice.

"Only a scratch. Take the handkerchief out of my pocket and tie it up; but first ask yon gentleman for his flask!"

Joseph opened his eyes, knew the face that bent over his, and then closed them again. Gentle and strong hands raised him, a flask was set to his lips, and he drank mechanically, but a full sense of life followed the draught. He looked wistfully in the stranger's face.

"Wait a moment," said the latter; "I must feel your bones before you try to move. Arms and legs all right,—impossible to tell about the ribs. There! now put your arm around my neck, and lean on me as much as you like, while I lift you."

Joseph did as he was bidden, but he was still weak and giddy, and after a few steps, they both sat down together upon a bank. The splintered car lay near them upside down; the passengers had been extricated from it, and were now busy in aiding the few who were injured. The train had stopped and was waiting on the track above. Some were very pale and grave, feeling that Death had touched without taking them; but the greater part were concerned only about the delay to the train.

"How did it happen?" asked Joseph: "where was I? how did you find me?"

"The usual story,—a broken rail," said the stranger. "I had just caught the rope when the car went over, and was swung off my feet so luckily that I somehow escaped the hardest shock. I don't think I lost my senses for a moment. When we came to the bottom you were lying just before me; I thought you dead until I felt your heart. It is a severe shock, but I hope nothing more."

"But you,—are you not badly hurt?"

The stranger pushed up the handkerchief which was tied around his head, felt his temple, and said: "It must have been one of the splinters; I know nothing about it. But there is no harm in a little blood-letting except"— he added, smiling—"except the spots on your face."

By this time the other injured passengers had been conveyed to the train; the whistle sounded a warning of departure.

"I think we can get up the embankment now," said the stranger. "You must let me take care of you still: I am travelling alone."

When they were seated side by side, and Joseph leaned his head back on the supporting arm, while the train moved away with them, he felt that a new power, a new support, had come to his life. The face upon which he looked was no longer strange; the hand which had rested on his heart was warm with kindred blood. Involuntarily he extended his own; it was taken and held, and the dark gray, courageous eyes turned to him with a silent assurance which he felt needed no words.

"It is a rough introduction," he then said: "my name is Philip Held. I was on my way to Oakland Station; but if you are going farther—"

"Why, that is my station also!" Joseph exclaimed, giving his name in return.

"Then we should have probably met, sooner or later, in any case. I am bound for the forge and furnace at Coventry, which is for sale. If the company who employ me decide to buy it,—according to the report I shall make,—the works will be placed in my charge."

"It is but six miles from my farm," said Joseph, "and the road up the valley is the most beautiful in our neighborhood. I hope you can make a favorable report."

"It is only too much to my own interest to do so. I have been mining and geologizing in Nevada and the Rocky Mountains for three or four years, and long for a quiet, ordered life. It is a good omen that I have found a neighbor in advance of my settlement. I have often ridden fifty miles to meet a friend who cared for something else than horse-racing or *monte*; and your six miles,—it is but a step!"

"How much you have seen!" said Joseph. "I know very little of the world. It must be easy for you to take your own place in life."

A shade passed over Philip Held's face. "It is only easy to a certain class of men," he replied,—"a class to which I should not care to belong. I begin to think that nothing is very valuable, the light to which a man don't earn,—except human love, and that seems to come by the grace of God."

"I am younger than you are,—not yet twenty-three," Joseph remarked. "You will find that I am very ignorant."

"And I am twenty-eight, and just beginning to get my eyes open, like a nine-days' kitten. If I had been frank enough to confess my ignorance, five years ago, as you do now, it would have been better for me. But don't let us measure ourselves or our experience against each other. That is one good thing we learn in Rocky Mountain life; there is no high or low, knowledge or ignorance, except what applies to the needs of men who come together. So there are needs which most men have, and go all their lives hungering for, because they expect them to be supplied in a particular form. There is something," Philip concluded, "deeper than that in human nature."

Joseph longed to open his heart to this man, every one of whose words struck home to something in himself. But the lassitude which the shock left behind gradually overcame him. He suffered his head to be drawn upon Philip Held's shoulder, and slept until the train reached Oakland Station. When the two got upon the platform, they found Dennis waiting for Joseph, with a light country vehicle. The news of the accident had reached the station, and his dismay was great when he saw the two bloody faces. A physician had already been summoned from the neighboring village, but they had little need of his services. A prescription of quiet and sedatives for Joseph, and a strip of plaster for his companion, were speedily furnished, and they set out together for the Asten place.

It is unnecessary to describe Rachel Miller's agitation when the party arrived; or the parting of the two men who had been so swiftly brought near to each other; or Philip Held's farther journey to the forge that evening. He resisted all entreaty to remain at the farm until morning, on the ground of an appointment made with the present proprietor of the forge. After his departure Joseph was sent to bed, where he remained for a day or two, very sore and a little feverish. He had plenty of time for thought,—not precisely of the kind which his aunt suspected, for out of pure, honest interest in his welfare, she took a step which proved to be of doubtful benefit. If he had not been so innocent,—if he had not been quite as unconscious of his inner nature as he was over-conscious of his external self,—he would have perceived that his thoughts dwelt much more on Philip Held than on Julia Blessing. His mind seemed to run through a swift, involuntary chain of reasoning, to account to himself for his feeling towards her, and her inevitable share in his future; but towards Philip his heart sprang with an instinct beyond his control. It was impossible to imagine that the latter also would not be shot, like a bright thread, through the web of his coming days.

On the third morning, when he had exchanged the bed for an arm-chair, a letter from the city was brought to him. "Dearest Joseph," it ran, "what a fright and anxiety we have had! When pa brought the paper home, last night, and I read the report of the accident, where it said, 'J. Asten, severe contusions,' my heart stopped beating for a minute, and I can only write now (as you see) with a trembling hand. My first thought was to go directly to you; but ma said we had better wait for intelligence. Unless our engagement were generally known, it would give rise to remarks,—in short, I need not repeat to you all the *worldly* reasons with which she opposed me; but, oh, how I longed for *the right* to be at your side, and assure myself that the dreadful, dreadful danger has passed! Pa was quite shaken with the news: he felt hardly able to go to the Custom-House this morning. But he sides with ma about my going, and now, when my time as a daughter with them is growing so short, I dare not disobey. I know you will understand my position, yet, dear and true as you are, you cannot guess the anxiety with which I await a line from your hand, the hand that was so nearly taken from me forever!"

Joseph read the letter twice and was about to commence it for the third time, when a visitor was announced. He had barely time to thrust the scented sheet into his pocket; and the bright eyes and flushed face with which he met the Rev. Mr. Chaffinch convinced both that gentleman and his aunt, as she ushered the latter into the room, that the visit was accepted as an honor and a joy.

On Mr. Chaffinch's face the air of authority which he had been led to believe belonged to his calling had not quite succeeded in impressing itself; but melancholy, the next best thing, was strongly marked. His dark complexion and his white cravat intensified each other; and his eyes, so long uplifted above the concerns of this world, had ceased to vary their expression materially for the sake of any human interest. All this had been expected of him, and he had simply done his best to meet the requirements of the flock over which he was placed. Any of the latter might have easily been shrewd enough to guess, in advance, very nearly what the pastor would say, upon a given occasion; but each and all of them would have been both disappointed and disturbed if he had not said it.

After appropriate and sympathetic inquiries concerning Joseph's bodily condition, he proceeded to probe him spiritually.

"It was a merciful preservation. I hope you feel that it is a solemn thing to look Death in the face."

"I am not afraid of death," Joseph replied.

"You mean the physical pang. But death includes what comes after it,— judgment. That is a very awful thought."

"It may be to evil men; but I have done nothing to make me fear it."

"You have never made an open profession of faith; yet it may be that grace has reached you," said Mr. Chaffinch. "Have you found your Saviour?"

"I believe in him with all my soul!" Joseph exclaimed; "but you mean something else by 'finding' him. I will be candid with you, Mr. Chaffinch. The last sermon I heard you preach, a month ago, was upon the nullity of all good works, all Christian deeds; you called them 'rags, dust, and ashes,' and declared that man is saved by faith alone. I *have* faith, but I can't accept a doctrine which denies merit to works; and you, unless I accept it, will you admit that I have 'found' Christ?"

"There is but One Truth!" exclaimed Mr. Chaffinch, very severely.

"Yes," Joseph answered, reverently, "and that is only perfectly known to God."

The clergyman was more deeply annoyed than he cared to exhibit. His experience had been confined chiefly to the encouragement of ignorant souls, willing to accept *his* message, if they could only be made to comprehend it, or to the conflict with downright doubt and denial. A nature so seemingly open to the influences of the Spirit, yet inflexibly closed to certain points of doctrine, was something of a problem to him. He belonged to a class now happily becoming scarce, who, having been taught to pace a reasoned theological round, can only efficiently meet those antagonists who voluntarily come inside of their own ring.

His habit of control, however, enabled him to say, with a moderately friendly manner, as he took leave: "We will talk again when you are stronger. It is my duty to give spiritual help to those who seek it."

To Rachel Miller he said: "I cannot say that he is dark. His mind is cloudy, but we find that the vanities of youth often obscure the true light for a time."

Joseph leaned back in his arm-chair, closed his eyes, and meditated earnestly for half an hour. Rachel Miller, uncertain whether to be hopeful or discouraged by Mr. Chaffinch's words, stole into the room, but went about on tiptoe, supposing him to be asleep. Joseph was fully conscious of all her movements, and at last startled her by the sudden question:—

"Aunt, why do you suppose I went to the city?"

"Goodness, Joseph! I thought you were sound asleep. I suppose to see about the fall prices for grain and cattle."

"No, aunt," said he, speaking with determination, though the foolish blood ran rosily over his face, "I went to get a wife!"

She stood pale and speechless, staring at him. But for the rosy sign on his cheeks and temples she could not have believed his words.

"Miss Blessing?" she finally uttered, almost in a whisper.

Joseph nodded his head. She dropped into the nearest chair, drew two or three long breaths, and in an indescribable tone ejaculated, "Well!"

"I knew you would be surprised," said he; "because it is almost a surprise to myself. But you and she seemed to fall so easily into each other's ways, that I hope —"

"Why, you're hardly acquainted with her!" Rachel exclaimed. "It is so hasty! And you are so young!"

"No younger than father was when he married mother; and I have learned to know her well in a short time. Isn't it so with you, too, aunt? — you certainly liked her?"

"I'll not deny that, nor say the reverse now: but a farmer's wife should be a farmer's daughter."

"But suppose, aunt, that the farmer doesn't happen to love any farmer's daughter, and *does* love a bright, amiable, very intelligent girl, who is delighted with country life, eager and willing to learn, and very fond of the farmer's aunt (who can teach her everything)?"

"Still, it seems to me a risk," said Rachel; but she was evidently relenting.

"There is none to you," he answered, "and I am not afraid of mine. You will be with us, for Julia couldn't do without you, if she wished. If she were a farmer's daughter, with different ideas of housekeeping, it might bring trouble to both of us. But now you will have the management in your own hands until you have taught Julia, and afterwards she will carry it on in your way."

She did not reply; but Joseph could see that she was becoming reconciled to the prospect. After awhile she came across the room, leaned over him, kissed him upon the forehead, and then silently went away.

CHAPTER X
APPROACHING FATE

Only two months intervened until the time appointed for the marriage, and the days rolled swiftly away. A few lines came to Joseph from Philip Held, announcing that he was satisfied with the forge and furnace, and the sale would doubtless be consummated in a short time. He did not, however, expect to take charge of the works before March, and therefore gave Joseph his address in the city, with the hope that the latter would either visit or write to him.

On the Sunday after the accident Elwood Withers came to the farm. He seemed to have grown older in the short time which had elapsed since they had last met; after his first hearty rejoicing over Joseph's escape and recovery, he relapsed into a silent but not unfriendly mood. The two young men climbed the long hill behind the house and seated themselves under a noble pin-oak on the height, whence there was a lovely view of the valley for many miles to the southward.

They talked mechanically, for a while, of the season, and the crops, and the other usual subjects which farmers never get to the end of discussing; but both felt the impendence of more important themes, and, nevertheless, were slow to approach them. At last Elwood said: "Your fate is settled by this time, I suppose?"

"It is arranged, at least," Joseph replied. "But I can't yet make clear to myself that I shall be a married man in two months from now."

"Does the time seem long to you?"

"No," Joseph innocently answered; "it is very short."

Elwood turned away his head to conceal a melancholy smile; it was a few minutes before he spoke again.

"Joseph," he then said, "are you sure, quite sure, you love her?"

"I am to marry her."

"I meant nothing unfriendly," Elwood remarked, in a gentle tone. "My thought was this,—if you should ever find a still stronger love growing upon you,—something that would make the warmth you feel now seem like ice compared to it,—how would you be able to fight it? I asked the question of myself for you. I don't think I'm much different from most soft-hearted men,—except that I keep the softness so well stowed away that few persons know of it,—but if I were in your place, within two months of marriage to the girl I love, I should be miserable!"

Joseph turned towards him with wide, astonished eyes.

"Miserable from hope and fear," Elwood went on; "I should be afraid of fever, fire, murder, thunderbolts! Every hour of the day I should dread lest something might come between us; I should prowl around her house day after day, to be sure that she was alive! I should lengthen out the time into years; and all because I'm a great, disappointed, soft-hearted fool!"

The sad, yearning expression of his eyes touched Joseph to the heart. "Elwood," he said, "I see that it is not in my power to comfort you; if I give you pain unknowingly, tell me how to avoid it! I meant to ask you to stand beside me when I am married; but now you must consider your own feeling in answering, not mine. Lucy is not likely to be there."

"That would make no difference," Elwood answered. "Do you suppose it is a pain for me to see her, because she seems lost to me? No; I'm always a little encouraged when I have a chance to measure myself with her, and to guess—sometimes this and sometimes that—what it is that she needs to find in me. Force of will is of no use; as to faithfulness,—why, what it's worth can't be shown unless something turns up to try it. But you had better not ask me to be your groomsman. Neither Miss Blessing nor her sister would be overly pleased."

"Why so?" Joseph asked; "Julia and you are quite well acquainted, and she was always friendly towards you."

Elwood was silent and embarrassed. Then, reflecting that silence, at that moment, might express even more than speech, he said: "I've got the notion in my head; maybe it's foolish, but there it is. I talked a good deal with Miss Blessing, it's true, and yet I don't feel the least bit acquainted. Her manner to me was very friendly, and yet I don't think she likes me."

"Well!" exclaimed Joseph, forcing a laugh, though he was much annoyed, "I never gave you credit for such a lively imagination. Why not be candid, and admit that the dislike is on your side? I am sorry for it, since Julia will so soon be in the house there as my wife. There is no one else whom I can ask, unless it were Philip Held—"

"Held! To be sure, he took care of you. I was at Coventry the day after, and saw something of him." With these words, Elwood turned towards

Joseph and looked him squarely in the face. "He'll have charge there in a few months, I hear," he then said, "and I reckon it as a piece of good luck for you. I've found that there are men, all, maybe, as honest and outspoken as they need be; yet two of 'em will talk at different marks and never fully understand each other, and other two will naturally talk right straight at the same mark and never miss. Now, Held is the sort that can hit the thing in the mind of the man they're talking to; it's a gift that comes o' being knocked about the world among all classes of people. What we learn here, always among the same folks, isn't a circumstance."

"Then you think I might ask him?" said Joseph, not fully comprehending all that Elwood meant to express.

"He's one of those men that you're safe in asking to do anything. Make him spokesman of a committee to wait on the President, arbitrator in a crooked lawsuit, overseer of a railroad gang, leader in a prayer-meeting (if he'd consent), or whatever else you choose, and he'll do the business as if he was used to it! It's enough for you that I don't know the town ways, and he does; it's considered worse, I've heard, to make a blunder in society than to commit a real sin."

He rose, and they loitered down the hill together. The subject was quietly dropped, but the minds of both were none the less busy. They felt the stir and pressure of new experiences, which had come to one through disappointment and to the other through success. Not three months had passed since they rode together through the twilight to Warriner's, and already life was opening to them,—but how differently! Joseph endeavored to make the most kindly allowance for his friend's mood, and to persuade himself that his feelings were unchanged. Elwood, however, knew that a shadow had fallen between. It was nothing beside the cloud of his greater trouble: he also knew the cost of his own justification to Joseph, and prayed that it might never come.

That evening, on taking leave, he said: "I don't know whether you meant to have the news of your engagement circulated; but I guess Anna Warriner has heard, and that amounts to—"

"To telling it to the whole neighborhood, doesn't it?" Joseph answered. "Then the mischief is already done, if it is a mischief. It is well, therefore, that the day is set: the neighborhood will have little time for gossip."

He smiled so frankly and cheerfully, that Elwood seized his hand, and with tears in his eyes, said: "Don't remember anything against me, Joseph. I've always been honestly your friend, and mean to stay so."

He went that evening to a homestead where he knew he should find Lucy Henderson. She looked pale and fatigued, he thought; possibly his presence had become a restraint. If so, she must bear his unkindness: it was the only sacrifice he could not make, for he felt sure that his intercourse with her must either terminate in hate or love. The one thing of which he was certain was, that there could be no calm, complacent friendship between them.

It was not long before one of the family asked him whether he had heard the news; it seemed that they had already discussed it, and his arrival revived the flow of expression. In spite of his determination, he found it impossible to watch Lucy while he said, as simply as possible, that Joseph Asten seemed very happy over the prospect of the marriage; that he was old enough to take a wife; and if Miss Blessing could adapt herself to country habits, they might get on very well together. But later in the evening he took a chance of saying to her: "In spite of what I said, Lucy, I don't feel quite easy about Joseph's marriage. What do you think of it?"

She smiled faintly, as she replied: "Some say that people are attracted by mutual unlikeness. This seems to me to be a case of the kind; but they are free choosers of their own fates."

"Is there no possible way of persuading him—them—to delay?"

"No!" she exclaimed, with unusual energy; "none whatever!"

Elwood sighed, and yet felt relieved.

Joseph lost no time in writing to Philip Held, announcing his approaching marriage, and begging him—with many apologies for asking such a mark of confidence on so short an acquaintance—to act the part of nearest friend, if there were no other private reasons to prevent him.

Four or five days later the following answer arrived:—

> My dear Asten:—Do you remember that curious whirling, falling sensation, when the car pitched over the edge of the embankment? I felt a return of it on reading your letter; for you have surprised me beyond measure. Not by your request, for that is just what I should have expected of you; and as well now, as if we had known each other for twenty years; so the apology is the only thing objectionable—But I am tangling my sentences; I want to say how heartily I return the feeling which prompted you to ask me, and yet how embarrassed I am that I cannot unconditionally say, "Yes, with all my heart!" My great, astounding surprise is, to find you about to be married to Miss Julia Blessing,—a

young lady whom I once knew. And the embarrassment is this: I knew her under circumstances (in which she was not personally concerned, however) which might possibly render my presence now, as your groomsman, unwelcome to the family: at least, it is my duty—and yours, if you still desire me to stand beside you—to let Miss Blessing and her family decide the question. The circumstances to which I refer concern them rather than myself. I think your best plan will be simply to inform them of your request and my reply, and add that I am entirely ready to accept whatever course they may prefer.

Pray don't consider that I have treated your first letter to me ungraciously. I am more grieved than you can imagine that it happens so. You will probably come to the city a day before the wedding, and I insist that you shall share my bachelor quarters, in any case.

Always your friend,

Philip Held.

This letter threw Joseph into a new perplexity. Philip a former acquaintance of the Blessings! Formerly, but not now; and what could those mysterious "circumstances" have been, which had so seriously interrupted their intercourse? It was quite useless to conjecture; but he could not resist the feeling that another shadow hung over the aspects of his future. Perhaps he had exaggerated Elwood's unaccountable dislike to Julia, which had only been implied, not spoken; but here was a positive estrangement on the part of the man who was so suddenly near and dear to him. He never thought of suspecting Philip of blame; the candor and cheery warmth of the letter rejoiced his heart. There was evidently nothing better to do than to follow the advice contained in it, and leave the question to the decision of Julia and her parents.

Her reply did not come by the return mail, nor until nearly a week afterwards; during which time he tormented himself by imagining the wildest reasons for her silence. When the letter at last arrived, he had some difficulty in comprehending its import.

"Dearest Joseph," she said, "you must *really* forgive me this long trial of your patience. Your letter was *so* unexpected,—I mean its contents,—and it seems as if ma and pa and Clementina would never agree what was best to be done. For that matter, I cannot say that they agree now; we had *no idea* that you were an intimate friend of Mr. Held, (I can't think how ever you should have become acquainted!) and it seems to break open old wounds,—none of mine, fortunately, for I have none. As Mr. Held leaves the question in our hands, there is, you will understand, all the more necessity that we should be careful. Ma thinks he has said nothing to you about the unfortunate occurrence, or you would have expressed an opinion. You never can know how happy your fidelity makes me; but I felt that, the first moment we met.

"Ma says that at *very private* (what pa calls informal) weddings there need not be bridesmaids or groomsmen. Miss Morrisey was married that way, not long ago; it is true that she is not of our circle, nor strictly a *first* family (this is ma's view, not mine, for I understand the hollowness of society); but we could very well do the same. Pa would be satisfied with a reception afterwards; he wants to ask the Collector, and the Surveyor, and the Appraiser. Clementina won't say anything now, but I know what she thinks, and so does ma; however, Mr. Held has so dropped out of city life that it is not important. I suppose everything must be dim in his memory now; you do not write to me much that he related. How strange that he should be your friend! They say my dress is lovely, but I am sure I should like a plain muslin just as well. I shall only breathe freely when I get back to the quiet of the country, (and your—*our* charming home, and dear, good Aunt Rachel!) and away from all these conventional forms. Ma says if there is one groomsman there ought to be two; either very simple, or according to custom. In a matter so delicate, perhaps, Mr. Held would be as competent to decide as we are; at least *I* am quite willing to leave it to *his* judgment. But how trifling is all this discussion, compared with the importance of the day to us! It is now drawing very near, but I have no misgivings, for I confide in you wholly and forever!"

After reading the letter with as much coolness as was then possible to him, Joseph inferred three things: that his acquaintance with Philip Held was not entirely agreeable to the Blessing family; that they would prefer the simplest style of a wedding, and this was in consonance with his own tastes; and that Julia clung to him as a deliverer from conditions with which her nature had little sympathy. Her incoherence, he fancied, arose from an agitation which he could very well understand, and his answer was intended to soothe and encourage her. It was difficult to let Philip know that his services would not be required, without implying the existence of an unfriendly feeling towards him; and Joseph, therefore, all the more readily accepted his invitation. He was assured that the mysterious difficulty did not concern Julia; even if it were so, he was not called upon to do violence, without cause, to so welcome a friendship.

The September days sped by, not with the lingering, passionate uncertainty of which Elwood Withers spoke, but almost too swiftly. In the hurry of preparation, Joseph had scarcely time to look beyond the coming event and estimate its consequences. He was too ignorant of himself to doubt: his conscience was too pure and perfect to admit the possibility of changing the course of his destiny. Whatever the gossip of the neighborhood might have been, he heard nothing of it that was not agreeable. His aunt was entirely reconciled to a wife who would not immediately, and probably not for a long time, interfere with her authority; and the shadows raised by the two men whom he loved best seemed, at last, to be accidentally thrown from clouds beyond the horizon of his life. This was the thought to which he clung, in spite of a vague, utterly formless apprehension, which he felt lurking somewhere in the very bottom of his heart.

Philip met him on his arrival in the city, and after taking him to his pleasant quarters, in a house looking on one of the leafy squares, good-naturedly sent him to the Blessing mansion, with a warning to return before the evening was quite spent. The family was in a flutter of preparation, and though he was cordially welcomed, he felt that, to all except Julia, he was subordinate in interest to the men who came every quarter of an hour, bringing bouquets, and silver spoons with cards attached, and pasteboard boxes containing frosted cakes. Even Julia's society he was only allowed to enjoy by scanty instalments; she was perpetually summoned by her mother or Clementina, to consult about some indescribable figment of dress. Mr. Blessing was occupied in the basement, with the inspection of various hampers. He came to the drawing-room to greet Joseph, whom he shook by both hands, with such incoherent phrases that Julia presently interposed. "You must not forget, pa," she said, "that the man is waiting: Joseph will excuse you, I know." She followed him to the basement, and he returned no more.

Joseph left early in the evening, cheered by Julia's words: "We can't complain of all this confusion, when it's for our sakes; but we'll be happier when it's over, won't we?"

He gave her an affirmative kiss, and returned to Philip's room. That gentleman was comfortably disposed in an arm-chair, with a book and a cigar. "Ah!" he exclaimed, "you find that a house is more agreeable any evening than that before the wedding?"

"There is one compensation," said Joseph; "it gives me two or three hours with you."

"Then take that other arm-chair, and tell me how this came to pass. You see I have the curiosity of a neighbor, already."

He listened earnestly while Joseph related the story of his love, occasionally asking a question or making a suggestive remark, but so gently that it seemed to come as an assistance. When all had been told, he rose and commenced walking slowly up and down the room. Joseph longed to ask, in turn, for an explanation of the circumstances mentioned in Philip's letter; but a doubt checked his tongue.

As if in response to his thought, Philip stopped before him and said: "I owe you my story, and you shall have it after a while, when I can tell you more. I was a young fellow of twenty when I knew the Blessings, and I don't attach the slightest importance, now, to anything that happened. Even if I did, Miss Julia had no share in it. I remember her distinctly; she was then about my age, or a year or two older; but hers is a face that would not change in a long while."

Joseph stared at his friend in silence. He recalled the latter's age, and was startled by the involuntary arithmetic which revealed Julia's to him. It was unexpected, unwelcome, yet inevitable.

"Her father had been lucky in some of his 'operations,'" Philip continued, "but I don't think he kept it long. I hardly wonder that she should come to prefer a quiet country life to such ups and downs as the family has known. Generally, a woman don't adapt herself so readily to a change of surroundings as a man: where there is love, however, everything is possible."

"There is! there is!" Joseph exclaimed, certifying the fact to himself as much as to his friend. He rose and stood beside him.

Philip looked at him with grave, tender eyes.

"What can I do?" he said.

"What should you do?" Joseph asked.

"This!" Philip exclaimed, laying his hands on Joseph's shoulders,— "this, Joseph! I can be nearer than a brother. I know that I am in your heart as you are in mine. There is no faith between us that need be limited, there is no truth too secret to be veiled. A man's perfect friendship is rarer than a woman's love, and most hearts are content with one or the other: not so with yours and mine! I read it in your eyes, when you opened them on my knee: I see it in your face now. Don't speak: let us clasp hands."

But Joseph could not speak.

CHAPTER XI
A CITY WEDDING

There was not much of the happy bridegroom to be seen in Joseph's face when he arose the next morning. To Philip's eyes he appeared to have suddenly grown several years older; his features had lost their boyish softness and sweetness, which would thenceforth never wholly come back again. He spoke but little, and went about his preparation with an abstracted, mechanical air, which told how much his mind was preoccupied. Philip quietly assisted, and when all was complete, led him before the mirror.

"There!" he said; "now study the general effect; I think nothing more is wanting."

"It hardly looks like myself," Joseph remarked, after a careless inspection.

"In all the weddings I have seen," said Philip, "the bridegrooms were pale and grave, the brides flushed and trembling. You will not make an exception to the rule; but it is a solemn thing, and I—don't misunderstand me, Joseph—I almost wish you were not to be married to-day."

"Philip!" Joseph exclaimed, "let me think, now, at least,—now, at the last moment,—that it is best for me! If you knew how cramped, restricted, fettered, my life has been, and how much emancipation has already come with this—this love! Perhaps my marriage is a venture, but it is one which must be made; and no consequence of it shall ever come between us!"

"No; and I ought not to have spoken a word that might imply a doubt. It may be that your emancipation, as you rightly term it, can only come in this way. My life has been so different, that I am unconsciously putting myself in your place, instead of trying to look with your eyes. When I next go to Coventry Forge, I shall drive over and dine with you, and I hope your Julia will be as ready to receive me as a friend as I am to find one in her. There is the carriage at the door, and you had better arrive a little before the appointed hour. Take only my good wishes, my prayers for your happiness, along with you,—and now, God bless you, Joseph!"

The carriage rolled away. Joseph, in full wedding costume, was painfully conscious of the curious glances which fell upon him, and presently pulled down the curtains. Then, with an impatient self-reprimand, he pulled them up again, lowered the window, and let the air blow upon his hot cheeks. The house was speedily reached, and he was admitted by a festive waiter (hired for the occasion) before he had been exposed for more than five seconds to the gaze of curious eyes in all the windows around.

Mrs. Blessing, resplendent in purple, and so bedight that she seemed almost as young as her portrait, swept into the drawing-room. She inspected him rapidly, and approved, while advancing; otherwise he would scarcely have received the thin, dry kiss with which she favored him.

"It lacks half an hour," she said; "but you have the usual impatience of a bridegroom. I am accustomed to it. Mr. Blessing is still in his room; he has only just commenced arranging his cambric cravat, which is a work of time. He cannot forget that he was distinguished for an elegant tie in his youth. Clementina,"—as that young lady entered the room,—"is the bride completely attired?"

"All but her gloves," replied Clementina, offering three-fourths of her hand to Joseph. "And she don't know what ear-rings to wear."

"I think we might venture," Mrs. Blessing remarked, "as there seems to be no rule applicable to the case, to allow Mr. Asten a sight of his bride. Perhaps his taste might assist her in the choice."

Thereupon she conducted Joseph up stairs, and, after some preliminary whispering, he was admitted to the room. He and Julia were equally surprised at the change in each other's appearance: he older, paler, with a grave and serious bearing; she younger, brighter, rounder, fresher, and with the loveliest pink flush on her cheeks. The gloss of her hair rivalled that of the white satin which draped her form and gave grace to its outlines; her neck and shoulders were slight, but no one could have justly called them lean; and even the thinness of her lips was forgotten in the vivid coral of their color, and the nervous life which hovered about their edges. At that moment she was certainly beautiful, and a stranger would have supposed her to be young.

She looked into Joseph's face with a smile in which some appearance of maiden shyness yet lingered. A shrewder bridegroom would have understood its meaning, and would have said, "How lovely you are!" Joseph, it is true, experienced a sense of relief, but he knew not why, and could not for his life have put it into words. His eyes dwelt upon and followed her, and she seemed to be satisfied with that form of recognition. Mrs. Blessing inspected the dress with a severe critical eye, pulling out a fold here and smoothing a bit of lace there, until nothing further could be detected. Then, the adornment of the victim being completed, she sat down and wept moderately.

"O ma, try to bear up!" Julia exclaimed, with the very slightest touch of impatience in her voice; "it is all to come yet."

There was a ring at the door.

"It must be your aunt," said Mrs. Blessing, drying her eyes. "My sister," she added, turning to Joseph,—Mrs. Woollish, with Mr. Woollish and their two sons and one daughter. He's in the—the leather trade, so to speak, which has thrown her into a very different circle; but, as we have no nearer relations in the city, they will be present at the ceremony. He is said to be wealthy. I have no means of knowing; but one would scarcely think so, to judge from his wedding-gift to Julia."

"Ma, why should you mention it?"

"I wish to enlighten Mr. Asten. Six pairs of shoes!—of course all of the same pattern; and the fashion may change in another year!"

"In the country we have no fashions in shoes," Joseph suggested.

"Certainly!" said Julia. "*I* find Uncle Woollish's present very practical indeed."

Mrs. Blessing looked at her daughter, and said nothing.

Mr. Blessing, very red in the face, but with triumphant cambric about his throat, entered the room, endeavoring to get his fat hands into a pair of No. 9 gloves. A strong smell of turpentine or benzine entered with him.

"Eliza," said he, "you must find me some eau de cologne. The odor left from my—my rheumatic remedy is still perceptible. Indeed, patchouly would be better, if it were not the scent peculiar to *parvenus*."

Clementina came to say that the clergyman's carriage had just reached the door, and Mr. Blessing was hurried down stairs, mopping his gloves and the collar of his coat with liquid fragrance by the way. Mrs. Blessing and Clementina presently followed.

"Julia," said Joseph when they were quite alone, "have you thought that this is for life?"

She looked up with a tender smile, but something in his face arrested it on her lips.

"I have lived ignorantly until now," he continued,—"innocently and ignorantly. From this time on I shall change more than you, and there may be, years hence, a very different Joseph Asten from the one whose name you will take to-day. If you love me with the love I claim from you,—the love that grows with and through all new knowledge and experience,—there will be no discord in our lives. We must both be liberal and considerate towards each other; it has been but a short time since we met, and we have still much to learn."

"O, Joseph!" she murmured, in a tone of gentle reproach, "I knew your nature at first sight."

"I hope you did," he answered gravely, "for then you will be able to see its needs, and help me to supply them. But, Julia, there must not the shadow of concealment come between us: nothing must be reserved. I understand no love that does not include perfect trust. I must draw nearer, and be drawn nearer to you, constantly, or—"

He paused; it was no time to utter the further sentence in his mind. Julia glided to him, clasped her arms about his waist, and laid her head against his shoulder. Although she said nothing, the act was eloquent. It expressed acquiescence, trust, fidelity, the surrender of her life to his, and no man in his situation could have understood it otherwise. A tenderness, which seemed to be the something hitherto lacking to his love, crept softly over his heart, and the lurking unrest began to fade from his face.

There was a rustle on the stairs; Clementina and Miss Woollish made their appearance. "Mr. Bogue has arrived," whispered the former, "and ma thinks you should come down soon. Are you entirely ready? I don't think you need the salts, Julia; but you might carry the bottle in your left hand: brides are expected to be nervous."

She gave a light laugh, like the purl and bubble of a brook; but Joseph shrank, with an inward chill, from the sound.

"So! shall we go? Fanny and I—(I beg pardon; Mr. Asten—Miss Woollish)—will lead the way. We will stand a little in the rear, not beside you, as there are no groomsmen. Remember, the farther end of the room!"

They rustled slowly downward, in advance, and the bridal pair followed. The clergyman, Mr. Bogue, suddenly broke off in the midst of an oracular remark about the weather, and, standing in the centre of the room, awaited them. The other members of the two families were seated, and very silent.

Joseph heard the introductory remarks, the ceremony, and the final benediction, as in a dream. His lips opened mechanically, and a voice which did not exactly seem to be his own uttered the "I will!" at the proper time; yet, in recalling the experience afterwards, he was unable to decide whether any definite thought or memory or hope had passed through his mind. From his entrance into the room until his hand was violently shaken by Mr. Blessing, there was a blank.

Of course there were tears, but the beams of congratulation shone through them, and they saddened nobody. Miss Fanny Woollish assured the bridal pair, in an audible whisper, that she had never seen a *sweeter* wedding; and her mother, a stout, homely little body, confirmed the opinion with, "Yes, you both did beautifully!" Then the marriage certificate was produced and signed, and the company partook of wine and refreshments to strengthen them for the reception.

Until there had been half a dozen arrivals, Mrs. Blessing moved about restlessly, and her eyes wandered to the front window. Suddenly three or four carriages came rattling together up the street, and Joseph heard her whisper to her husband: "There they are! it will be a success!" It was not long before the little room was uncomfortably crowded, and the presentations followed so rapidly that Joseph soon became bewildered. Julia, however, knew and welcomed every one with the most bewitching grace, being rewarded with kisses by the gorgeous young ladies and compliments by the young men with weak mouths and retreating chins.

In the midst of the confusion Mr. Blessing, with a wave of his hand, presented "Mr. Collector Twining" and "Mr. Surveyor Knob" and "Mr. Appraiser Gerrish," all of whom greeted Joseph with a bland, almost affectionate, cordiality. The door of the dining-room was then thrown open, and the three dignitaries accompanied the bridal pair to the table. Two servants rapidly whisked the champagne-bottles from a cooling-tub in the adjoining closet, and Mr. Blessing commenced stirring and testing a huge bowl of punch. Collector Twining made a neat little speech, proposing the health of bride and bridegroom, with a pun upon the former's name, which was received with as much delight as if it had never been heard before. Therefore Mr. Surveyor Knob repeated it in giving the health of the bride's parents. The enthusiasm of the company not having diminished, Mr. Appraiser Gerrish improved the pun in a third form, in proposing "the Ladies." Then Mr. Blessing, although his feelings overcame him, and he was obliged to use a handkerchief smelling equally of benzine and eau de cologne, responded, introducing the collector's and surveyor's names with an ingenuity which was accepted as the inspiration of genius. His peroration was especially admired.

"On this happy occasion," he said, "the elements of national power and prosperity are represented. My son-in-law, Mr. Asten, is a noble specimen of the agricultural population,—the free American yeomanry; my daughter, if I may be allowed to say it in the presence of so many bright eyes and blooming cheeks, is a representative child of the city, which is the embodiment of the nation's action and enterprise. The union of the two is the movement of our life. The city gives to the country as the ocean gives the cloud to the mountain-springs: the country gives to the city as the streams flow back to the ocean. ["Admirable!" Mr. Collector Twining exclaimed.] Then we have, as our highest honor, the representatives of the political system under which city and country flourish alike. The wings of our eagle must be extended over this fortunate house to-day, for here are the strong Claws which seize and guard its treasures!"

The health of the Claws was drunk enthusiastically. Mr. Blessing was congratulated on his eloquence; the young gentlemen begged the privilege of touching their glasses to his, and every touch required that the contents be replenished; so that the bottom of the punch-bowl was nearly reached before the guests departed.

When Joseph came down in his travelling-dress, he found the drawing-room empty of the crowd; but leaves, withered flowers, crumbs of cake, and crumpled cards scattered over the carpet, indicated what had taken place. In the dining-room Mr. Blessing, with his cravat loosened, was smoking a cigar at the open window.

"Come, son-in-law!" he cried, "take another glass of punch before you start."

Joseph declined, on the plea that he was not accustomed to the beverage.

"Nothing could have gone off better!" said Mr. Blessing. "The collector was delighted: by the by, you're to go to the St. Jerome, when you get to New York this evening. He telegraphed to have the bridal-chamber reserved for you. Tell Julia: she won't forget it. That girl has a deuced sharp intellect: if you'll be guided by her in your operations—"

"Pa, what are you saying about me?" Julia, asked, hastily entering the room.

"Only that you have a deuced sharp intellect, and to-day proves it. Asten is one of us now, and I may tell him of his luck."

He winked and laughed stupidly, and Joseph understood and obeyed his wife's appealing glance. He went to his mother-in-law in the drawing-room.

Julia lightly and swiftly shut the door. "Pa," she said, in a strong, angry whisper; "if you are not able to talk coherently, you must keep your tongue still. What will Joseph think of *me*, to hear you?"

"What he'll think anyhow, in a little while," he doggedly replied. "Julia, you have played a keen game, and played it well; but you don't know much of men yet. He'll not always be the innocent, white-nosed lamb he is now, nibbling the posies you hold out to him. Wait till he asks for stronger feed, and see whether he'll follow you!"

She was looking on the floor, pale and stern. Suddenly one of her gloves burst, across the back of the hand. "Pa," she then said, "it's very cruel to say such things to me, now when I'm leaving you."

"So it is!" he exclaimed, tearfully contrite; "I am a wretch! They flattered my speech so much,—the collector was so impressed by me,—and said so many pleasant things, that—I don't feel quite steady. Don't forget the St. Jerome; the bridal-chamber is ordered, and I'll see that Mumm writes a good account for the 'Evening Mercury.' I wish you could be here to remember my speech for me. O, I shall miss you! I shall miss you!"

With these words, and his arm lovingly about his daughter, they joined the family. The carriage was already at the door, and the coachman was busy with the travelling-trunks. There were satchels, and little packages,—an astonishing number it seemed to Joseph,—to be gathered together, and then the farewells were said.

As they rolled through the streets towards the station, Julia laid her head upon her husband's shoulder, drew a long, deep breath, and said, "Now all our obligations to society are fulfilled, and we can rest awhile. For the first time in my life I am a free woman,—and you have liberated me!"

He answered her in glad and tender words; he was equally grateful that the exciting day was over. But, as they sped away from the city through the mellow October landscapes, Philip's earnest, dark gray eyes, warm with more than brotherly love, haunted his memory, and he knew that Philip's faithful thoughts followed him.

CHAPTER XII
CLOUDS

There are some days when the sun comes slowly up, filling the vapory air with diffused light, in advance of his coming; when the earth grows luminous in the broad, breezeless morning; when nearer objects shine and sparkle, and the distances melt into dim violet and gold; when the vane points to the southwest, and the blood of man feels neither heat nor cold, but only the freshness of that perfect temperature wherein the limits of the body are lost, and the pulses of its life beat in all the life of the world. But ere long the haze, instead of thinning into blue, gradually thickens into gray; the vane creeps southward, swinging to southeast in brief, rising flaws of the air; the horizon darkens; the enfranchised life of the spirit creeps back to its old isolation, shorn of all its rash delight, and already foreboding the despondency which comes with the east wind and the chilly rains.

Some such variation of the atmospheric influences attended Joseph Asten's wedding-travel. The mellow, magical glory of his new life diminished day by day; the blue of his sky became colder and grayer. Yet he could not say that his wife had changed: she was always ready with her smiles, her tender phrases, her longings for quiet and rest, and simple, natural life, away from the conventionalities and claims of Society. But, even as, looking into the pale, tawny-brown of her eyes, he saw no changing depth below the hard, clear surface, so it also seemed with her nature; he painfully endeavored to penetrate beyond expressions, the repetition of which it was hard not to find tiresome, and to reach some spring of character or feeling; yet he found nothing. It was useless to remember that he had been content with those expressions before marriage had given them his own eager interpretation, independent of her will and knowledge; that his duty to her remained the same, for she had not deceived him.

On the other hand, she was as tender and affectionate as he could desire. Indeed, he would often have preferred a less artless manifestation of her fondness; but she playfully insisted on his claiming the best quarters at every stopping-place, on the ground of their bridal character, and was sometimes a little petulant when she fancied that they had not been sufficiently honored. Joseph would have willingly escaped the distinction, allowing himself to be confounded with the prosaic multitude, but she would not permit him to try the experiment.

"The newly married are always detected," she would say, "and they are only laughed at when they try to seem like old couples. Why not be frank and honest, and meet half-way the sympathy which I am sure everybody has for us?"

To this he could make no reply, except that it was not agreeable to exact a special attention.

"But it is our right!" was her answer.

In every railway-car they entered she contrived, in a short time, to impress the nature of their trip upon the other travellers; yet it was done with such apparent unconsciousness, such innocent, impulsive manifestations of her happiness in him, that he could not, in his heart, charge her with having intentionally brought upon him the discomfort of being curiously observed. He could have accustomed himself to endure the latter, had it been inevitable; the suspicion that he owed it to her made it an increasing annoyance. Yet, when the day's journey was over, and they were resting together in their own private apartment, she would bring a stool to his feet, lay her head on his knee, and say: "Now we can talk as we please,—there are none watching and listening."

At such times he was puzzled to guess whether some relic of his former nervous shyness were not remaining, and had made him over-sensitive to her ways. The doubt gave him an additional power of self-control; he resolved to be more slow and cautious of judgment, and observe men and women more carefully than he had been wont to do. Julia had no suspicion of what was passing in his mind: she took it for granted that his nature was still as shallow and transparent as when she first came in contact with it.

After nearly a fortnight this flying life came to an end. They returned to the city for a day, before going home to the farm. The Blessing mansion received them with a hearty welcome; yet, in spite of it, a depressing atmosphere seemed to fill the house. Mrs. Blessing looked pinched and care-worn, Clementina discontented, and Mr. Blessing as melancholy as was possible to so bouyant a politician.

"What's the matter? I hope pa hasn't lost his place," Julia remarked in an undertone to her mother.

"Lost my place!" Mr. Blessing exclaimed aloud; "I'd like to see how the collection of customs would go on without me. But a man may keep his place, and yet lose his house and home."

Clementina vanished, Mrs. Blessing followed, with her handkerchief to her eyes, and Julia hastened after them, crying: "Ma! dear ma!"

"It's only on *their* account," said Mr. Blessing, pointing after them and speaking to Joseph. "A plucky man never desponds, sir; but women, you'll find, are upset by every reverse."

"May I ask what has happened?"

"A delicate regard for you," Mr. Blessing replied, "would counsel me to conceal it, but my duty as your father-in-law leaves me no alternative. Our human feelings prompt us to show only the bright side of life to those whom we love; principle, however,—conscience, commands us not to suppress the shadows. I am but one out of the many millions of victims of mistaken judgment. The case is simply this; I will omit certain legal technicalities touching the disposition of property, which may not be familiar to you, and state the facts in the most intelligible form; securities which I placed as collaterals for the loan of a sum, not a very large amount, have been very unexpectedly depreciated, but only temporarily so, as all the market knows. If I am forced to sell them at such an untoward crisis, I lose the largest part of my limited means; if I retain them, they will ultimately recover their full value."

"Then why not retain them?" Joseph asked.

"The sum advanced upon them must be repaid, and it so happens—the market being very tight—that every one of my friends is short. Of course, where their own paper is on the street, I can't ask them to float mine for three months longer, which is all that is necessary. A good indorsement is the extent of my necessity; for any one who is familiar with the aspects of the market can see that there must be a great rebound before three months."

"If it were not a very large amount," Joseph began.

"Only a thousand! I know what you were going to say it is perfectly natural: I appreciate it, because, if our positions were reversed, I should have done the same thing. But, although it is a mere form, a temporary fiction, which has the force of reality, and, therefore, so far as you are concerned, I should feel entirely easy, yet it might subject me to very dishonoring suspicions! It might be said that I had availed myself of your entrance into my family to beguile you into pecuniary entanglements; the amount might be exaggerated, the circumstance misrepresented,—no, no! rather than that, let me make the sacrifice like a man! I'm no longer young, it is true; but the feeling that I stand on principle will give me strength to work."

"On the other hand, Mr. Blessing," said Joseph, "very unpleasant things might be said of me, if I should permit you to suffer so serious a loss, when my assistance would prevent it."

"I don't deny it. You have made a two-horned dilemma out of a one-sided embarrassment. Would that I had kept the secret in my own breast! The temptation is strong, I confess, for the mere use of your name for a few months is all I should require. Either the securities will rise to their legitimate value, or some of the capitalists with whom I have dealings will be in a position to accommodate me. I have frequently tided over similar snags and sand-bars in the financial current; they are familiar even to the most skilful operators,—navigators, I might say, to carry out the figure,—and this is an instance where an additional inch of water will lift me from wreck to flood-tide. The question is, should I allow what I feel to be a just principle, a natural suggestion of delicacy, to intervene between my necessity and your generous proffer of assistance?"

"Your family—" Joseph began.

"I know! I know!" Mr. Blessing cried, leaning his head upon his hand. "There is my vulnerable point,—my heel of Achilles! There would be no alternative,—better sell this house than have my paper dishonored! Then, too, I feel that this is a turning-point in my fortunes: if I can squeeze through this narrow pass, I shall find a smooth road beyond. It is not merely the sum which is at stake, but the future possibilities into which it expands. Should I crush the seed while it is germinating? Should I tear up the young tree, with an opening fruit-bud on every twig? You see the considerations that sway me: unless you withdraw your most generous proffer, what can I do but yield and accept it?"

"I have no intention of withdrawing it," Joseph answered, taking his words literally; "I made the offer freely and willingly. If my indorsement is all that is necessary now, I can give it at once."

Mr. Blessing grasped him by the hand, winked hard three or four times, and turned away his head without speaking. Then he drew a large leather pocket-book from his breast, opened it, and produced a printed promissory note.

"We will make it payable at your county bank," said he, "because your name is known there, and upon acceptance—which can be procured in two days—the money will be drawn here. Perhaps we had better say four months, in order to cover all contingencies."

He went to a small writing-desk, at the farther end of the room, and filled the blanks in the note, which Joseph then endorsed. When it was safely lodged in his breast-pocket, he said: "We will keep this entirely to ourselves. My wife, let me whisper to you, is very proud and sensitive, although the De l'Hotels (Doolittles now) were never quite the equals of the De Belsains;

but women see matters in a different light. They can't understand the accommodation of a name, but fancy that it implies a kind of humiliation, as if one were soliciting charity."

He laughed and rubbed his hands. "I shall soon be in a position," he said, "to render you a favor in return. My long experience, and, I may add, my intimate knowledge of the financial field, enables me to foresee many splendid opportunities. There are, just now, some movements which are not yet perceptible on the surface. Mark my words! we shall shortly have a new excitement, and a cool, well-seasoned head is a fortune at such times."

"In the country," Joseph replied, "we only learn enough to pay off our debts and invest our earnings. We are in the habit of moving slowly and cautiously. Perhaps we miss opportunities; but if we don't see them, we are just as contented as if they had not been. I have enough for comfort, and try to be satisfied."

"Inherited ideas! They belong to the community in which you live. Are you satisfied with your neighbors' ways of living and thinking? I do not mean to disparage them, but have you no desire to rise above their level? Money,—as I once said at a dinner given to a distinguished railroad man,—money is the engine which draws individuals up the steepest grades of society; it is the lubricating oil which makes the truck of life run easy; it is the safety-break which renders collision and wreck impossible! I have long been accustomed to consider it in the light of power, not of property, and I classify men according as they take one or the other view. The latter are misers; but the former, sir, are philosophers!"

Joseph scarcely knew how to answer this burst of eloquence. But there was no necessity for it; the ladies entered the room at that moment, each one, in her own way, swiftly scrutinizing the two gentlemen. Mrs. Blessing's face lost its woe-worn expression, while a gleam of malicious satisfaction passed over Clementina's.

The next day, on their journey to the country, Julia suddenly said, "I am sure, Joseph, that pa made use of your generosity; pray don't deny it!"

There was the faintest trace of hardness in her voice, which he interpreted as indicating dissatisfaction with his failure to confide the matter to her.

"I have no intention of denying anything, Julia," he answered. "I was not called upon to exercise generosity; it was simply what your father would term an 'accommodation.'"

"I understand. How much?"

"An endorsement of his note for a thousand dollars, which is little, when it will prevent him from losing valuable securities."

Julia was silent for at least ten minutes; then, turning towards him with a sternness which she vainly endeavored to conceal under a "wreathed smile," she said: "In future, Joseph, I hope you will always consult me in any pecuniary venture. I may not know much about such matters, but it is my duty to learn. I have been obliged to hear a great deal of financial talk from pa and his friends, and could not help guessing some things which I think I can apply for your benefit. We are to have no secrets from each other, you know."

His own words! After all, what she said was just and right, and he could not explain to himself why he should feel annoyed. Perhaps he missed a frank expression of delight in the assistance he had so promptly given; but why should he suspect that it was unwelcome to her? He tried to banish the feeling, to hide it under self-reproach and shame, but it clung to him most uncomfortably.

Nevertheless, he forgot everything in the pleasure of the homeward drive from the station. The sadness of late autumn lay upon the fields, but spring already said, "I am coming!" in the young wheat; the houses looked warm and cosey behind their sheltering fir-trees; cattle still grazed on the meadows, and the corn was not yet deserted by the huskers. The sun gave a bright edge to the sombre colors of the landscape, and to Joseph's eyes it was beautiful as never before. Julia leaned back in the carriage, and complained of the cold wind.

"There!" cried Joseph, as a view of the valley opened below them, with the stream flashing like steel between the leafless sycamores,—"there is home-land! Do you know where to look for our house?"

Julia made an effort, leaned forward, smiled, and pointed silently across the shoulder of a hill to the eastward. "You surely didn't suppose I *could* forget," she murmured.

Rachel Miller awaited them at the gate, and Julia had no sooner alighted than she flung herself into her arms. "Dear Aunt Rachel!" she cried: "you must now take my mother's place; I have *so* much to learn from you! It is doubly a home since you are here. I feel that we shall all be happy together!"

Then there were kisses, of which Joseph received his share, and the first evening lapsed away in perfect harmony. Everything was delightful: the room, the furniture, the meal, even the roar of the wind in the dusky trees. While Julia lay in the cushioned rocking-chair, Rachel gave her nephew an account of all that had been done on the farm; but Joseph only answered her from the surface of his mind. Under the current of his talk ran a graver thought, which said: "You wanted independence and a chance of growth for your life; you fancied they would come in this form. Lo, now! here are the conditions which you desired to establish; from this hour begins the new life of which you dreamed. Whether you have been wise or rash, you can change nothing. You are limited, as before, though within a different circle. You may pace it to its fullest extent, but all the lessons you have yet learned require you to be satisfied within it."

CHAPTER XIII
PRESENTIMENTS

The autumn lapsed into winter, and the household on the Asten farm began to share the isolation of the season. There had been friendly visits from all the nearest neighbors and friends, followed by return visits, and invitations which Julia willingly accepted. She was very amiable, and took pains to confirm the favorable impression which she knew she had made in the summer. Everybody remarked how she had improved in appearance, how round and soft her neck and shoulders, how bright and fresh her complexion. She thanked them, with many grateful expressions to which they were not accustomed, for their friendly reception, which she looked upon as an adoption into their society; but at home, afterwards, she indulged in criticisms of their manners and habits which were not always friendly. Although these were given in a light, playful tone, and it was sometimes impossible not to be amused, Rachel Miller always felt uncomfortable when she heard them.

Then came quiet, lonely days, and Julia, weary of her idle life, undertook to master the details of the housekeeping. She went from garret to cellar, inspecting every article in closet and pantry, wondering much, censuring occasionally, and only praising a little when she found that Rachel was growing tired and irritable. Although she made no material changes, it was soon evident that she had very stubborn views of her own upon many points, and possessed a marked tendency for what the country people call "nearness." Little by little she diminished the bountiful, free-handed manner of provision which had been the habit of the house. One could not say that anything needful was lacking, and Rachel would hardly have been dissatisfied, had she not felt that the innovation was an indirect blame.

In some directions Julia seemed the reverse of "near," persuading Joseph into expenditures which the people considered very extravagant. When the snow came, his new and elegant sleigh, with the wolf-skin robe, the silver-mounted harness, and the silver-sounding bells, was the envy of all the young men, and an abomination to the old. It was a splendor which he could easily afford, and he did not grudge her the pleasure; yet it seemed to change his relation to the neighbors, and some of them were very free in hinting that they felt it so. It would be difficult to explain why they should resent this or any other slight departure from their fashions, but such had always been their custom.

In a few days the snow vanished and a tiresome season of rain and thaw succeeded. The south-eastern winds, blowing from the Atlantic across the intervening lowlands, rolled interminable gray masses of fog over the hills and blurred the scenery of the valley; dripping trees, soaked meadows, and sodden leaves were the only objects that detached themselves from the general void, and became in turn visible to those who travelled the deep, quaking roads. The social intercourse of the neighborhood ceased perforce, though the need of it were never so great: what little of the main highway down the valley was visible from the windows appeared to be deserted.

Julia, having exhausted the resources of the house, insisted on acquainting herself with the barn and everything thereto belonging. She laughingly asserted that her education as a farmer's wife was still very incomplete; she must know the amount of the crops, the price of grain, the value of the stock, the manner of work, and whatever else was necessary to her position. Although she made many pretty blunders, it was evident that her apprehension was unusually quick, and that whatever she acquired was fixed in her mind as if for some possible future use. She never wearied of the most trivial details, while Joseph, on the other hand, would often have willingly shortened his lessons. His mind was singularly disturbed between the desire to be gratified by her curiosity, and the fact that its eager and persistent character made him uncomfortable.

When an innocent, confiding nature begins to suspect that its confidence has been misplaced, the first result is a preternatural stubbornness to admit the truth. The clearest impressions are resisted, or half-consciously misinterpreted, with the last force of an illusion which already foresees its own overthrow. Joseph eagerly clung to every look and word and action which confirmed his sliding faith in his wife's sweet and simple character, and repelled—though a deeper instinct told him that a day would come when it *must* be admitted—the evidence of her coldness and selfishness. Yet, even while almost fiercely asserting to his own heart that he had every reason to be happy, he was consumed with a secret fever of unrest, doubt, and dread.

The horns of the growing moon were still turned downwards, and cold, dreary rains were poured upon the land. Julia's patience, in such straits, was wonderful, if the truth had been known, but she saw that some change was necessary for both of them. She therefore proposed, not what she most desired, but what her circumstances prescribed,—a visit from her sister

Clementina. Joseph found the request natural enough: it was an infliction, but one which he had anticipated; and after the time had been arranged by letter, he drove to the station to meet the westward train from the city.

Clementina stepped upon the platform, so cloaked and hooded that he only recognized her by the deliberate grace of her movements. She extended her hand, giving his a cordial pressure, which was explained by the brass baggage-checks thus transferred to his charge.

"I will wait in the ladies' room," was all she said.

At the same moment Joseph's arm was grasped.

"What a lucky chance!" exclaimed Philip: then, suddenly pausing in his greeting, he lifted his hat and bowed to Clementina, who nodded slightly as she passed into the room.

"Let me look at you!" Philip resumed, laying his hands on Joseph's shoulders. Their eyes met and lingered, and Joseph felt the blood rise to his face as Philip's gaze sank more deeply into his heart and seemed to fathom its hidden trouble; but presently Philip smiled and said: "I scarcely knew, until this moment, that I had missed you so much, Joseph!"

"Have you come to stay?" Joseph asked.

"I think so. The branch railway down the valley, which you know was projected, is to be built immediately; but there are other reasons why the furnaces should be in blast. If it is possible, the work—and my settlement with it—will begin without any further delay. Is she your first family visit?"

He pointed towards the station.

"She will be with us a fortnight; but you will come, Philip?"

"To be sure!" Philip exclaimed. "I only saw her face indistinctly through the veil, but her nod said to me, 'A nearer approach is not objectionable.' Certainly, Miss Blessing; but with all the conventional forms, if you please!"

There was something of scorn and bitterness in the laugh which accompanied these words, and Joseph looked at him with a puzzled air.

"You may as well know now," Philip whispered, "that when I was a spoony youth of twenty, I very nearly imagined myself in love with Miss Clementina Blessing, and she encouraged my greenness until it spread as fast as a bamboo or a gourd-vine. Of course, I've long since congratulated myself that she cut me up, root and branch, when our family fortune was lost. The awkwardness of our intercourse is all on her side. Can she still have faith in her charms and my youth, I wonder? Ye gods! that would be a lovely conclusion of the comedy!"

Joseph could only join in the laugh as they parted. There was no time to reflect upon what had been said. Clementina, nevertheless, assumed a new interest in his eyes; and as he drove her towards the farm, he could not avoid connecting her with Philip in his thoughts. She, too, was evidently preoccupied with the meeting, for Philip's name soon floated to the surface of their conversation.

"I expect a visit from him soon," said Joseph. As she was silent, he ventured to add: "You have no objections to meeting with him, I suppose?"

"Mr. Held is still a gentleman, I believe," Clementina replied, and then changed the subject of conversation.

Julia flew at her sister with open arms, and showered on her a profusion of kisses, all of which were received with perfect serenity, Clementina merely saying, as soon as she could get breath: "Dear me, Julia, I scarcely recognize you! You are already so countrified!"

Rachel Miller, although a woman, and notwithstanding her recent experience, found herself greatly bewildered by this new apparition. Clementina's slow, deliberate movements and her even-toned, musical utterance impressed her with a certain respect; yet the qualities of character they suggested never manifested themselves. On the contrary, the same words, in any other mouth, would have often expressed malice or heartlessness. Sometimes she heard her own homely phrases repeated, as if by the most unconscious purposeless imitation, and had Julia either smiled or appeared annoyed her suspicions might have been excited; as it was, she was constantly and sorely puzzled.

Once only, and for a moment, the two masks were slightly lifted. At dinner, Clementina, who had turned the conversation upon the subject of birthdays, suddenly said to Joseph: "By the way, Mr. Asten, has Julia told you her age?"

Julia gave a little start, but presently looked up, with an expression meant to be artless.

"I knew it before we were married," Joseph quietly answered.

Clementina bit her lip. Julia, concealing her surprise, flashed a triumphant glance at her sister, then a tender one at Joseph, and said: "We will both let the old birthdays go; we will only have one and the same anniversary from this time on!"

Joseph felt, through some natural magnetism of his nature rather than from any perceptible evidence, that Clementina was sharply and curiously watching the relation between himself and his wife. He had no fear of her detecting misgivings which were not yet acknowledged to himself, but was instinctively on his guard in her presence.

It was not many days before Philip called. Julia received him cordially, as the friend of her husband, while Clementina bowed with an impassive face, without rising from her seat. Philip, however, crossed the room and gave her his hand, saying cheerily: "We used to be old friends, Miss Blessing. You have not forgotten me?"

"We cannot forget when we have been asked to do so," she warbled.

Philip took a chair. "Eight years!" he said: "I am the only one who has changed in that time."

Julia, looked at her sister, but the latter was apparently absorbed in comparing some zephyr tints.

"The whirligig of time!" he exclaimed: "who can foresee anything? Then I was an ignorant, petted young aristocrat,—an expectant heir; now behold me, working among miners and puddlers and forgemen! It's a rough but wholesome change. Would you believe it, Mrs. Asten, I've forgotten the mazurka!"

"I wish to forget it," Julia replied: "the spring-house is as important to me as the furnace to you."

"Have you seen the Hopetons lately?" Clementina asked.

Joseph saw a shade pass over Philip's face, and he seemed to hesitate a moment before answering: "I hear they will be neighbors of mine next summer. Mr. Hopeton is interested in the new branch down the valley, and has purchased the old Calvert property for a country residence."

"Indeed? Then you will often see them."

"I hope so: they are very agreeable people. But I shall also have my own little household: my sister will probably join me."

"Not Madeline!" exclaimed Julia.

"Madeline," Philip answered. "It has long been her wish, as well as mine. You know the little cottage on the knoll, at Coventry, Joseph! I have taken it for a year."

"There will be quite a city society," murmured Clementina, in her sweetest tones. "You will need no commiseration, Julia. Unless, indeed, the country people succeed in changing you all into their own likeness. Mrs. Hopeton will certainly create a sensation. I am told that she is very extravagant, Mr. Held?"

"I have never seen her husband's bank account," said Philip, dryly.

He rose presently, and Joseph accompanied him to the lane. Philip, with the bridle-rein over his arm, delayed to mount his horse, while the mechanical commonplaces of speech, which, somehow, always absurdly come to the lips when graver interests have possession of the heart, were exchanged by the two. Joseph felt, rather than saw, that Philip was troubled. Presently the latter said: "Something is coming over both of us,—not between us. I thought I should tell you a little more, but perhaps it is too soon. If I guess rightly, neither of us is ready. Only this, Joseph, let us each think of the other as a help and a support!"

"I do, Philip!" Joseph answered. "I see there is some influence at work which I do not understand, but I am not impatient to know what it is. As for myself, I seem to know nothing at all; but you can judge,—you see all there is."

Even as he pronounced these words Joseph felt that they were not strictly sincere, and almost expected to find an expression of reproof in Philip's eyes. But no: they softened until he only saw a pitying tenderness. Then he knew that the doubts which he had resisted with all the force of his nature were clearly revealed to Philip's mind.

They shook hands, and parted in silence; and Joseph, as he looked up to the gray blank of heaven, asked himself: "Is this all? Has my life already taken the permanent imprint of its future?"

CHAPTER XIV
THE AMARANTH

Clementina returned to the city without having made any very satisfactory discovery. Her parting was therefore conventionally tender: she even thanked Joseph for his hospitality, and endeavored to throw a little natural emphasis into her words as she expressed the hope of being allowed to renew her visit in the summer.

During her stay it seemed to Joseph that the early harmony of his household had been restored. Julia's manner had been so gentle and amiable, that, on looking back, he was inclined to believe that the loneliness of her new life was alone responsible for any change. But after Clementina's departure his doubts were reawakened in a more threatening form. He could not guess, as yet, the terrible chafing of a smiling mask; of a restraint which must not only conceal itself, but counterfeit its opposite; of the assumption by a narrow, cold, and selfish nature of virtues which it secretly despises. He could not have foreseen that the gentleness, which had nearly revived his faith in her, would so suddenly disappear. But it was gone, like a glimpse of the sun through the winter fog. The hard, watchful expression came back to Julia's face; the lowered eyelids no longer gave a fictitious depth to her shallow, tawny pupils; the soft roundness of her voice took on a frequent harshness, and the desire of asserting her own will in all things betrayed itself through her affected habits of yielding and seeking counsel.

She continued her plan of making herself acquainted with all the details of the farm business. When the roads began to improve, in the early spring, she insisted in driving to the village alone, and Joseph soon found that she made good use of these journeys in extending her knowledge of the social and pecuniary standing of all the neighboring families. She talked with farmers, mechanics, and drovers; became familiar with the fluctuations in the prices of grain and cattle; learned to a penny the wages paid for every form of service; and thus felt, from week to week, the ground growing more secure under her feet.

Joseph was not surprised to see that his aunt's participation in the direction of the household gradually diminished. Indeed, he scarcely noticed the circumstance at all, but he was at last forced to remark her increasing silence and the trouble of her face. To all appearance the domestic harmony was perfect, and if Rachel Miller felt some natural regret at being obliged to divide her sway, it was a matter, he thought, wherein he had best not interfere. One day, however, she surprised him by the request:—

"Joseph, can you take or send me to Magnolia to-morrow?"

"Certainly, Aunt!" he replied. "I suppose you want to visit Cousin Phebe; you have not seen her since last summer."

"It was that,—and something more." She paused a moment, and then added, more firmly: "She has always wished that I should make my home with her, but I couldn't think of any change so long as I was needed here. It seems to me that I am not really needed now."

"Why, Aunt Rachel!" Joseph exclaimed, "I meant this to be your home always, as much as mine! Of course you are needed,—not to do all that you have done heretofore, but as a part of the family. It is your right."

"I understand all that, Joseph. But I've heard it said that a young wife should learn to see to everything herself, and Julia, I'm sure, doesn't need either my help or my advice."

Joseph's face became very grave. "Has she—has she—?" he stammered.

"No," said Rachel, "she has not said it—in words. Different persons have different ways. She is quick, O very quick!—and capable. You know I could never sit idly by, and look on; and it's hard to be directed. I seem to belong to the place and everything connected with it; yet there's times when what a body ought to do is plain."

In endeavoring to steer a middle course between her conscience and her tender regard for her nephew's feelings Rachel only confused and troubled him. Her words conveyed something of the truth which she sought to hide under them. She was both angered and humiliated; the resistance with which she had attempted to meet Julia's domestic innovations was no match for the latter's tactics; it had gone down like a barrier of reeds and been contemptuously trampled under foot. She saw herself limited, opposed, and finally set aside by a cheerful dexterity of management which evaded her grasp whenever she tried to resent it. Definite acts, whereon to base her indignation, seemed to slip from her memory, but the atmosphere of the house became fatal to her. She felt this while she spoke, and felt also that Joseph must be spared.

"Aunt Rachel," said he, "I know that Julia is very anxious to learn everything which she thinks belongs to her place,—perhaps a little more than is really necessary. She's an enthusiastic nature, you know. Maybe you are not fully acquainted yet; maybe you have misunderstood her in some things: I would like to think so."

"It is true that we are different, Joseph,—*very* different. I don't say, therefore, that I'm always right. It's likely, indeed, that any young wife and any old housekeeper like myself would have their various notions. But where there can be only one head, it's the wife's place to be that head. Julia has not asked it of me, but she has the right. I can't say, also, that I don't need a little rest and change, and there seems to be some call on me to oblige Phebe. Look at the matter in the true light," she continued, seeing that Joseph remained silent, "and you must feel that it's only natural."

"I hope so," he said at last, repressing a sigh; "all things are changing."

"What can we do?" Julia asked, that evening, when he had communicated to her his aunt's resolution; "it would be so delightful if she would stay, and yet I have had a presentiment that she would leave us—for a little while only, I hope. Dear, good Aunt Rachel! I couldn't help seeing how hard it was for her to allow the least change in the order of housekeeping. She would be perfectly happy if I would sit still all day and let her tire herself to death; but how can I do that, Joseph? And no two women have exactly the same ways and habits. I've tried to make everything pleasant for her: if she would only leave many little matters entirely to me, or at least not think of them,—but I fear she cannot. She manages to see the least that I do, and secretly worries about it, in the very kindness of her heart. Why can't women carry on partnerships in housekeeping as men do in business? I suppose we are too particular; perhaps I am just as much so as Aunt Rachel. I have no doubt she thinks a little hardly of me, and so it would do her good—we should really come nearer again—if she had a change. If she *will* go, Joseph, she must at least leave us with the feeling that our home is always hers, whenever she chooses to accept it."

Julia bent over Joseph's chair, gave him a rapid kiss, and then went off to make her peace with Aunt Rachel. When the two women came to the tea-table the latter had an uncertain, bewildered air, while the eyelids of the former were red,—either from tears or much rubbing.

A fortnight afterwards Rachel Miller left the farm and went to reside with her widowed niece, in Magnolia.

The day after her departure another surprise came to Joseph in the person of his father-in-law. Mr. Blessing arrived in a hired vehicle from the station. His face was so red and radiant from the March winds, and perhaps some private source of satisfaction, that his sudden arrival could not possibly be interpreted as an omen of ill-fortune. He shook hands with the Irish groom who had driven him over, gave him a handsome gratuity in addition to the hire of the team, extracted an elegant travelling-satchel from under the seat, and met Joseph at the gate, with a breezy burst of feeling:—

"God bless you, son-in-law! It does my heart good to see you again! And then, at last, the pleasure of beholding your ancestral seat; really, this is quite—quite manorial!"

Julia, with a loud cry of "O pa!" came rushing from the house.

"Bless me, how wild and fresh the child looks!" cried Mr. Blessing, after the embrace. "Only see the country roses on her cheeks! Almost too young and sparkling for Lady Asten, of Asten Hall, eh? As Dryden says, 'Happy, happy, happy pair!' It takes me back to the days when *I* was a gay young lark; but I must have a care, and not make an old fool of myself. Let us go in and subside into soberness: I am ready both to laugh and cry."

When they were seated in the comfortable front room, Mr. Blessing opened his satchel and produced a large leather-covered flask. Julia was probably accustomed to his habits, for she at once brought a glass from the sideboard.

"I am still plagued with my old cramps," her father said to Joseph, as he poured out a stout dose. "Physiologists, you know, have discovered that stimulants diminish the wear and tear of life, and I find their theories correct. You, in your pastoral isolation and pecuniary security, can form no conception of the tension under which we men of office and of the world live, *Beatus ille*, and so forth,—strange that the only fragment of Latin which I remember should be so appropriate! A little water, if you please, Julia."

In the evening, when Mr. Blessing, slippered, sat before the open fireplace, with a cigar in his mouth, the object of his sudden visit crept by slow degrees to the light. "Have you been dipping into oil?" he asked Joseph.

Julia made haste to reply. "Not yet, but almost everybody in the neighborhood is ready to do so now, since Clemson has realized his fifty thousand dollars in a single year. They are talking of nothing else in the village. I heard yesterday, Joseph, that Old Bishop has taken three thousand dollars' worth of stock in a new company."

"Take my advice, and don't touch 'em!" exclaimed Mr. Blessing.

"I had not intended to," said Joseph.

"There is this thing about these excitements," Mr. Blessing continued: "they never reach the rural districts until the first sure harvest is over. The sharp, intelligent operators in the large cities—the men who are ready to take up soap, thimbles, hand-organs, electricity, or hymn-books, at a moment's notice—always cut into a new thing before its value is guessed by the multitude. Then the smaller fry follow and secure their second crop, while your quiet men in the country are shaking their heads and crying 'humbug!' Finally, when it really gets to be a humbug, in a speculative sense, they just begin to believe in it, and are fair game for the bummers and camp-followers of the financial army. I respect Clemson, though I never heard of him before; as for Old Bishop, he may be a very worthy man, but he'll never see the color of his three thousand dollars again."

"Pa!" cried Julia, "how clear you do make everything. And to think that I was wishing—O, wishing so much!—that Joseph would go into oil."

She hung her head a little, looking at Joseph with an affectionate, penitent glance. A quick gleam of satisfaction passed over Mr. Blessing's face; he smiled to himself, puffed rapidly at his cigar for a minute, and then resumed: "In such a field of speculation everything depends on being initiated. There are men in the city—friends of mine—who know every foot of ground in the Alleghany Valley. They can smell oil, if it's a thousand feet deep. They never touch a thing that isn't safe,—but, then, they know *what's* safe. In spite of the swindling that's going on, it takes years to exhaust the good points; just so sure as your honest neighbors here will lose, just so sure will these friends of mine gain. There are millions in what they have under way, at this moment."

"What is it?" Julia breathlessly asked, while Joseph's face betrayed that his interest was somewhat aroused.

Mr. Blessing unlocked his satchel, and took from it a roll of paper, which he began to unfold upon his knee. "Here," he said, "you see this bend of the river, just about the centre of the oil region, which is represented by the yellow color. These little dots above the bend are the celebrated Fluke Wells; the other dots below are the equally celebrated Chowder Wells. The distance between the two is nearly three miles. Here is an untouched portion of the treasure,—a pocket of Pactolus waiting to be rifled. A few of us have acquired the land, and shall commence boring immediately."

"But," said Joseph, "it seems to me that either the attempt must have been made already, or that the land must command such an enormous price as to lessen the profits."

"Wisely spoken! It is the first question which would occur to any prudent mind. But what if I say that neither is the case? And you, who are familiar with the frequent eccentricities of old farmers, can understand the explanation. The owner of the land was one of your ignorant, stubborn men, who took such a dislike to the prospectors and speculators, that he refused to let them come near him. Both the Fluke and Chowder Companies tried their best to buy him out, but he had a malicious pleasure in leading them on to make immense offers, and then refusing. Well, a few months ago he died, and his heirs were willing enough to let the land go; but before it could be regularly offered for sale, the Fluke and Chowder Wells began to flow less and less. Their shares fell from 270 to 95; the supposed value of the land fell with them, and finally the moment arrived when we could purchase for a very moderate sum. I see the question in your mind; why should we wish to buy when the other wells were giving out? There comes in the secret, which is our veritable success. Consider it whispered in your ears, and locked in your bosoms,—torpedoes! It was not then generally exploded (to carry out the image), so we bought at the low figure, in the very nick of time. Within a week the Fluke and Chowder Wells were torpedoed, and came back to more than their former capacity; the shares rose as rapidly as they had fallen, and the central body we hold—to which they are, as it were, the two arms—could now be sold for ten times what it cost us!"

Here Mr. Blessing paused, with his finger on the map, and a light of merited triumph in his eyes. Julia clapped her hands, sprang to her feet, and cried: "Trumps at last!"

"Ay," said he, "wealth, repose for my old days,—wealth for us all, if your husband will but take the hand I hold out to him. You now know, son-in-law, why the endorsement you gave me was of such vital importance; the note, as you are aware, will mature in another week. Why should you not charge yourself with the payment, in consideration of the transfer to you of shares of the original stock, already so immensely appreciated in value? I have delayed making any provision, for the sake of offering you the chance."

Julia was about to speak, but restrained herself with an apparent effort.

"I should like to know," Joseph said, "who are associated with you in the undertaking?"

"Well done, again! Where did you get your practical shrewdness? The best men in the city!—not only the Collector and the Surveyor, but Congressman Whaley, E. D. Stokes, of Stokes, Pirricutt and Company, and even the Reverend Doctor Lellifant. If I had not been an old friend of Kanuck, the agent who negotiated the purchase, my chance would have been impalpably small. I have all the documents with me. There has been no more splendid opportunity since oil became a power! I hesitate to advise even one so near to me in such matters; but if you knew the certainties as I know them, you would go in with all your available capital. The excitement, as you say, has reached the country communities, which are slow to rise and equally slow to subside; all oil stock will be in demand, but the Amaranth,—'The Blessing,' they wished to call it, but I was obliged to decline, for official reasons,—the Amaranth shares will be the golden apex of the market!"

Julia looked at Joseph with eager, hungry eyes. He, too, was warmed and tempted by the prospect of easy profit which the scheme held out to him; only the habit of his nature resisted, but with still diminishing force. "I might venture the thousand," he said.

"It is no venture!" Julia cried. "In all the speculations I have heard discussed by pa and his friends, there was nothing so admirably managed as this. Such a certainty of profit may never come again. If you will be advised by me, Joseph, you will take shares to the amount of five or ten thousand."

"Ten thousand is exactly the amount I hold open," Mr. Blessing gravely remarked. "That, however, does not represent the necessary payment, which can hardly amount to more than twenty-five per cent. before we begin to realize. Only ten per cent. has yet been called, so that your thousand at present will secure you an investment of ten thousand. Really, it seems like a fortunate coincidence."

He went on, heating himself with his own words, until the possibilities of the case grew so splendid that Joseph felt himself dazzled and bewildered. Mr. Blessing was a master in the art of seductive statement. Even where he was only the mouthpiece of another, a few repetitions led him to the profoundest belief. Here there could be no doubt of his sincerity, and, moreover, every movement from the very inception of the scheme, every statistical item, all collateral influences, were clear in his mind and instantly accessible. Although he began by saying, "I will make no estimate of the profits, because it is not prudent to fix our hopes on a positive sum," he was soon carried far away from this resolution, and most luxuriously engaged, pencil in hand, in figuring out results which drove Julia wild with desire, and almost took away Joseph's breath. The latter finally said, as they rose from the session, late at night:—

"It is settled that I take as much as the thousand will cover; but I would rather think over the matter quietly for a day or two before venturing further."

"You must," replied Mr. Blessing, patting him on the shoulder. "These things are so new to your experience, that they disturb and—I might almost say—alarm you. It is like bringing an increase of oxygen into your mental atmosphere. (Ha! a good figure: for the result will be, a richer, fuller life. I must remember it.) But you are a healthy organization, and therefore you are certain to see clearly: I can wait with confidence."

The next morning Joseph, without declaring his purpose, drove to Coventry Forge to consult Philip. Mr. Blessing and Julia, remaining at home, went over the shining ground again, and yet again, confirming each other in the determination to secure it. Even Joseph, as he passed up the valley in the mild March weather, taking note of the crimson and gold of the flowering spice-bushes and maple-trees, could not prevent his thoughts from dwelling on the delights of wealth, — society, books, travel, and all the mellow, fortunate expansion of life. Involuntarily, he hoped that Philip's counsel might coincide with his father-in-law's offer.

But Philip was not at home. The forge was in full activity, the cottage on the knoll was repainted and made attractive in various ways, and Philip would soon return with his sister to establish a permanent home. Joseph found the sign-spiritual of his friend in numberless little touches and changes; it seemed to him that a new soul had entered into the scenery of the place.

A mile or two farther up the valley, a company of mechanics and laborers were apparently tearing the old Calvert mansion inside out. House, barn, garden, and lawn were undergoing a complete transformation. While he paused at the entrance of the private lane, to take a survey of the operations, Mr. Clemson rode down to him from the house. The Hopetons, he said, would migrate from the city early in May: work had already commenced on the new railway, and in another year a different life would come upon the whole neighborhood.

In the course of the conversation Joseph ventured to sound Mr. Clemson in regard to the newly formed oil companies. The latter frankly confessed that he had withdrawn from further speculation, satisfied with his fortune; he preferred to give no opinion, further than that money was still to be made, if prudently placed. Tho Fluke and Chowder Wells, he said, were old, well known, and profitable. The new application of torpedoes had restored their failing flow, and the stock had recovered from its temporary depreciation. His own venture had been made in another part of the region.

The atmosphere into which Joseph entered, on returning home, took away all further power of resistance. Tempted already, and impressed by what he had learned, he did what his wife and father-in-law desired.

CHAPTER XV
A DINNER PARTY

Having assumed the payment of Mr. Blessing's note, as the first instalment upon his stock, Joseph was compelled to prepare himself for future emergencies. A year must still elapse before the term of the mortgage upon his farm would expire, but the sums he had invested for the purpose of meeting it when due must be held ready for use. The assurance of great and certain profit in the mean time rendered this step easy; and, even at the worst, he reflected, there would be no difficulty in procuring a new mortgage whereby to liquidate the old. A notice which he received at this time, that a second assessment of ten per cent. on the Amaranth stock had been made, was both unexpected and disquieting. Mr. Blessing, however, accompanied it with a letter, making clear not only the necessity, but the admirable wisdom of a greater present outlay than had been anticipated. So the first of April—the usual business anniversary of the neighborhood— went smoothly by. Money was plenty, the Asten credit had always been sound, and Joseph tasted for the first time a pleasant sense of power in so easily receiving and transferring considerable sums.

One result of the venture was the development of a new phase in Julia's nature. She not only accepted the future profit as certain, but she had apparently calculated its exact amount and framed her plans accordingly. If she had been humiliated by the character of Joseph's first business transaction with her father, she now made amends for it. "Pa" was their good genius. "Pa" was the agency whereby they should achieve wealth and social importance. Joseph now had the clearest evidence of the difference between a man who knew the world and was of value in it, and their slow, dull-headed country neighbors. Indeed, Julia seemed to consider the Asten property as rather contemptible beside the splendor of the Blessing scheme. Her gratitude for a quiet home, her love of country life, her disparagement of the shams and exactions of "society," were given up as suddenly and coolly as if she had never affected them. She gave herself no pains to make the transition gradual, and thus lessen its shock. Perhaps she supposed that Joseph's fresh, unsuspicious nature was so plastic that it had already sufficiently taken her impress, and that he would easily forget the mask she had worn. If so, she was seriously mistaken.

He saw, with a deadly chill of the heart, the change in her manner,—a change so complete that another face confronted him at the table, even as another heart beat beside his on the dishallowed marriage-bed. He saw the gentle droop vanish from the eyelids, leaving the cold, flinty pupils unshaded; the soft appeal of the half-opened lips was lost in the rigid, almost cruel compression which now seemed habitual to them; all the slight dependent gestures, the tender airs of reference to his will or pleasure, had rapidly transformed themselves into expressions of command or obstinate resistance. But the patience of a loving man is equal to that of a loving woman: he was silent, although his silence covered an ever-increasing sense of outrage.

Once it happened, that after Julia had been unusually eloquent concerning "what pa is doing for us," and what use they should make of "pa's money, as I call it," Joseph quietly remarked:—

"You seem to forget, Julia, that without my money not much could have been done."

An angry color came into her face; but, on second thought, she bent her head, and murmured in an offended voice: "It is very mean and ungenerous in you to refer to our temporary poverty. You might forget, by this time, the help pa was compelled to ask of you."

"I did not think of that!" he exclaimed. "Besides, you did not seem entirely satisfied with my help, at the time."

"O, how you misunderstand me!" she groaned. "I only wished to know the extent of his need. He is so generous, so considerate towards us, that we only guess his misfortune at the last moment."

The possibility of being unjust silenced Joseph. There were tears in Julia's voice, and he imagined they would soon rise to her eyes. After a long, uncomfortable pause, he said, for the sake of changing the subject: "What can have become of Elwood Withers? I have not seen him for months."

"I don't think you need care to know," she remarked. "He's a rough, vulgar fellow: it's just as well if he keeps away from us."

"Julia! he is my friend, and must always be welcome to me. You were friendly enough towards him, and towards all the neighborhood, last summer: how is it that you have not a good word to say now?"

He spoke warmly and indignantly. Julia, however, looked at him with a calm, smiling face. "It is very simple," she said. "You will agree with me, in another year. A guest, as I was, must try to see only the pleasant side of people: that's our duty; and so I enjoyed—as much as I could—the rusticity, the awkwardness, the ignorance, the (now, don't be vexed, dear!)—the vulgarity of your friend. As one of the society of the neighborhood, as a resident, I am not bound by any such delicacy. I take the same right to judge and select as I should take anywhere. Unless I am to be hypocritical, I cannot—towards you, at least—conceal my real feelings. How shall I ever get you to see the difference between yourself and these people, unless I continually point it out? You are modest, and don't like to acknowledge your own superiority."

She rose from the table, laughing, and went out of the room humming a lively air, leaving Joseph to make the best of her words.

A few days after this the work on the branch railway, extending down the valley, reached a point where it could be seen from the Asten farm. Joseph, on riding over to inspect the operations, was surprised to find Elwood, who had left his father's place and become a sub-contractor. The latter showed his hearty delight at their meeting.

"I've been meaning to come up," he said, "but this is a busy time for me. It's a chance I couldn't let slip, and now that I've taken hold I must hold on. I begin to think this is the thing I was made for, Joseph."

"I never thought of it before," Joseph answered, "and yet I'm sure you are right. How did you hit upon it?"

"*I* didn't; it was Mr. Held."

"Philip?"

"Him. You know I've been hauling for the Forge, and so it turned up by degrees, as I may say. He's at home, and, I expect, looking for you. But how are you now, really?"

Elwood's question meant a great deal more than he knew how to say. Suddenly, in a flash of memory, their talk of the previous year returned to Joseph's mind; he saw his friend's true instincts and his own blindness as never before. But he must dissemble, if possible, with that strong, rough, kindly face before him.

"O," he said, attempting a cheerful air, "I am one of the old folks now. You must come up—"

The recollection of Julia's words cut short the invitation upon his lips. A sharp pang went through his heart, and the treacherous blood crowded to his face all the more that he tried to hold it back.

"Come, and I'll show you where we're going to make the cutting," Elwood quietly said, taking him by the arm. Joseph fancied, thenceforth, that there was a special kindness in his manner, and the suspicion seemed to rankle in his mind as if he had been slighted by his friend.

As before, to vary the tedium of his empty life, so now, to escape from the knowledge which he found himself more and more powerless to resist, he busied himself beyond all need with the work of the farm. Philip had returned with his sister, he knew, but after the meeting with Elwood he shrank with a painful dread from Philip's heart-deep, intimate eye. Julia, however, all the more made use of the soft spring weather to survey the social ground, and choose where to take her stand. Joseph scarcely knew, indeed, how extensive her operations had been, until she announced an invitation to dine with the Hopetons, who were now in possession of the renovated Calvert place. She enlarged, more than was necessary, on the distinguished city position of the family, and the importance of "cultivating" its country members. Joseph's single brief meeting with Mr. Hopeton—who was a short, solid man, in ripe middle age, of a thoroughly cosmopolitan, though not a remarkably intellectual stamp—had been agreeable, and he recognized the obligation to be neighborly. Therefore he readily accepted the invitation on his own grounds.

When the day arrived, Julia, after spending the morning over her toilet, came forth resplendent in rosy silk, bright and dazzling in complexion, and with all her former grace of languid eyelids and parted lips. The void in Joseph's heart grew wider at the sight of her; for he perceived, as never before, her consummate skill in assuming a false character. It seemed incredible that he should have been so deluded. For the first time a feeling of repulsion, which was almost disgust, came upon him as he listened to her prattle of delight in the soft weather, and the fragrant woods, and the blossoming orchards. Was not, also, this delight assumed? he asked himself: false in one thing, false in all, was the fatal logic which then and there began its torment.

The most that was possible in such a short time had been achieved on the Calvert place. The house had been brightened, surrounded by light, airy verandas, and the lawn and garden, thrown into one and given into the hands of a skilful gardener, were scarcely to be recognized. A broad, solid gravel-walk replaced the old tan-covered path; a pretty fountain tinkled before the door; thick beds of geranium in flower studded the turf, and veritable thickets of rose-trees were waiting for June. Within the house, some rooms had been thrown together, the walls richly yet harmoniously colored, and the sumptuous furniture thus received a proper setting. In contrast to the houses of even the wealthiest farmers, which expressed a nicely reckoned sufficiency of comfort, the place had an air of joyous profusion, of a wealth which delighted in itself.

Mr. Hopeton met them with the frank, offhand manner of a man of business. His wife followed, and the two guests made a rapid inspection of her as she came down the hall. Julia noticed that her crocus-colored dress was high in the neck, and plainly trimmed; that she wore no ornaments, and that the natural pallor of her complexion had not been corrected by art. Joseph remarked the simple grace of her movement, the large, dark, inscrutable eyes, the smooth bands of her black hair, and the pure though somewhat lengthened oval of her face. The gentle dignity of her manner more than refreshed, it soothed him. She was so much younger than her husband that Joseph involuntarily wondered how they should have come together.

The greetings were scarcely over before Philip and Madeline Held arrived. Julia, with the least little gush of tenderness, kissed the latter, whom Philip then presented to Joseph for the first time. She had the same wavy hair as her brother, but the golden hue was deepened nearly into brown, and her eyes were a clear hazel. It was also the same frank, firm face, but her woman's smile was so much the sweeter as her lips were lovelier than the man's. Joseph seemed to clasp an instant friendship in her offered hand.

There was but one other guest, who, somewhat to his surprise, was Lucy Henderson. Julia concealed whatever she might have felt, and made so much reference to their former meetings as might satisfy Lucy without conveying to Mrs. Hopeton the impression of any special intimacy. Lucy looked thin and worn, and her black silk dress was not of the latest fashion: she seemed to be the poor relation of the company. Joseph learned that she had taken one of the schools in the valley, for the summer. Her manner to him was as simple and friendly as ever, but he felt the presence of some new element of strength and self-reliance in her nature.

His place at dinner was beside Mrs. Hopeton, while Lucy—apparently by accident—sat upon the other side of the hostess. Philip and the host led the conversation, confining it too exclusively to the railroad and iron interests; but those finally languished, and gave way to other topics in which all could take part. Joseph felt that while the others, except Lucy and himself, were fashioned under different aspects of life, some of which they shared in common, yet that their seeming ease and freedom of communication touched, here and there, some invisible limit, which they were careful not to pass. Even Philip appeared to be beyond his reach, for the time.

The country and the people, being comparatively new to them, naturally came to be discussed.

"Mr. Held, or Mr. Asten,—either of you know both,"—Mr. Hopeton asked, "what are the principal points of difference between society in the city and in the country?"

"Indeed, I know too little of the city," said Joseph.

"And I know too little of the country,—here, at least," Philip added. "Of course the same passions and prejudices come into play everywhere. There are circles, there are jealousies, ups and downs, scandals, suppressions, and rehabilitations: it can't be otherwise."

"Are they not a little worse in the country," said Julia, "because—I may ask the question here, among *us*—there is less refinement of manner?"

"If the external forms are ruder," Philip resumed, "it may be an advantage, in one sense. Hypocrisy cannot be developed into an art."

Julia bit her lip, and was silent.

"But are the country people, hereabouts, so rough?" Mrs. Hopeton asked. "I confess that they don't seem so to me. What do you say, Miss Henderson?"

"Perhaps I am not an impartial witness," Lucy answered. "We care less about what is called 'manners' than the city people. We have no fixed rules for dress and behavior,—only we don't like any one to differ too much from the rest of us."

"That's it!" Mr. Hopeton cried; "the tyrannical levelling sentiment of an imperfectly developed community! Fortunately, I am beyond its reach."

Julia's eyes sparkled: she looked across the table at Joseph, with a triumphant air.

Philip suddenly raised his head. "How would you correct it? Simply by resistance?" he asked.

Mr. Hopeton laughed. "I should no doubt get myself into a hornet's-nest. No; by indifference!"

Then Madeline Held spoke. "Excuse me," she said; "but is indifference possible, even if it were right? You seem to take the levelling spirit for granted, without looking into its character and causes; there must be some natural sense of justice, no matter how imperfectly society is developed. We are members of this community,—at least, Philip and I certainly consider ourselves so,—and I am determined not to judge it without knowledge, or to offend what may be only mechanical habits of thought, unless I can see a sure advantage in doing so."

Lucy Henderson looked at the speaker with a bright, grateful face. Joseph's eyes wandered from her to Julia, who was silent and watchful.

"But I have no time for such conscientious studies," Mr. Hopeton resumed. "One can be satisfied with half a dozen neighbors, and let the mass go. Indifference, after all, is the best philosophy. What do you say, Mr. Held?"

"Indifference!" Philip echoed. A dark flush came into his face, and he was silent a moment. "Yes: our hearts are inconvenient appendages. We suffer a deal from unnecessary sympathies, and from imagining, I suppose, that others feel them as we do. These uneasy features of society are simply the effort of nature to find some occupation for brains otherwise idle—or empty. Teach the people to think, and they will disappear."

Joseph stared at Philip, feeling that a secret bitterness was hidden under his careless, mocking air. Mrs. Hopeton rose, and the company left the table. Madeline Held had a troubled expression, but there was an eager, singular brightness in Julia's eyes.

"Emily, let us have coffee on the veranda," said Mr. Hopeton, leading the way. He had already half forgotten the subject of conversation: his own expressions, in fact, had been made very much at random, for the sole purpose of keeping up the flow of talk. He had no very fixed views of any kind, beyond the sphere of his business activity.

Philip, noticing the impression he had made on Joseph, drew him to one side. "Don't seriously remember my words against me," he said; "you were sorry to hear them, I know. All I meant was, that an over-sensitive tenderness towards everybody is a fault. Besides, I was provoked to answer him in his own vein."

"But, Philip!" Joseph whispered, "such words tempt me! What if they were true?"

Philip grasped his arm with a painful force. "They never can be true to you, Joseph," he said.

Gay and pleasant as the company seemed to be, each one felt a secret sense of relief when it came to an end. As Joseph drove homewards, silently recalling what had been said, Julia interrupted his reflections with: "Well, what do you think of the Hopetons?"

"She is an interesting woman," he answered.

"But reserved; and she shows very little taste in dress. However, I suppose you hardly noticed anything of the kind. She kept Lucy Henderson beside her as a foil: Madeline Held would have been damaging."

Joseph only partly guessed her meaning; it was repugnant, and he determined to avoid its further discussion.

"Hopeton is a shrewd business man," Julia continued, "but he cannot compare with her for shrewdness—either with her or—Philip Held!"

"What do you mean?"

"I made a discovery before the dinner was over, which you—innocent, unsuspecting man that you are—might have before your eyes for years, without seeing it. Tell me now, honestly, did you notice nothing?"

"What should I notice, beyond what was said?" he asked.

"That was the least!" she cried; "but, of course, I knew you couldn't. And perhaps you won't believe me, when I tell you that Philip Held,—your particular friend, your hero, for aught I know your pattern of virtue and character, and all that is manly and noble,—that Philip Held, I say, is furiously in love with Mrs. Hopeton!"

Joseph started as if he had been shot, and turned around with an angry red on his brow. "Julia!" he said, "how dare you speak so of Philip!"

She laughed. "Because I dare to speak the truth, when I see it. I thought I should surprise you. I remembered a certain rumor I had heard before she was married,—while she was Emily Marrable,—and I watched them closer than they guessed. I'm certain of Philip: as for her, she's a deep creature, and she was on her guard; but they are near neighbors."

Joseph was thoroughly aroused and indignant. "It is your own fancy!" he exclaimed. "You hate Philip on account of that affair with Clementina; but you ought to have some respect for the woman whose hospitality you have accepted!"

"Bless me! I have any quantity of respect both for her and her furniture. By the by, Joseph, our parlor would furnish better than hers; I have been thinking of a few changes we might make, which would wonderfully improve the house. As for Philip, Clementina was a fool. She'd be glad enough to have him now, but in these matters, once gone is gone for good. Somehow, people who marry for love very often get rich afterwards,—ourselves, for instance."

It was some time before Joseph's excitement subsided. He had resented Julia's suspicion as dishonorable to Philip, yet he could not banish the conjecture of its possible truth. If Philip's affected cynicism had tempted him, Julia's unblushing assumption of the existence of a passion which was forbidden, and therefore positively guilty, seemed to stain the pure texture of his nature. The lightness with which she spoke of the matter was even more abhorrent to him than the assertion itself; the malicious satisfaction in the tones of her voice had not escaped his ear.

"Julia," he said, just before they reached home, "do not mention your fancy to another soul than me. It would reflect discredit on you."

"You *are* innocent," she answered. "And you are not complimentary. If I have any remarkable quality, it is tact. Whenever I speak, I shall know the effect before-hand; even pa, with all his official experience, is no match for me in this line. I see what the Hopetons are after, and I mean to show them that we were first in the field. Don't be concerned, you good, excitable creature, you are no match for such well-drilled people. Let me alone, and before the summer is over *we* will give the law to the neighborhood!"

CHAPTER XVI
JOSEPH'S TROUBLE, AND PHILIP'S

The bare, repulsive, inexorable truth was revealed at last. There was no longer any foothold for doubt, any possibility of continuing his desperate self-deceit. From that day all the joy, the trust, the hope, seemed to fade out of Joseph's life. What had been lost was irretrievable: the delusion of a few months had fixed his fate forever.

His sense of outrage was so strong and keen—so burned upon his consciousness as to affect him like a dull physical pain—that a just and temperate review of his situation was impossible. False in one thing, false in all: that was the single, inevitable conclusion. Of course she had never even loved him. Her coy maiden airs, her warm abandonment to feeling, her very tears and blushes, were artfully simulated: perhaps, indeed, she had laughed in her heart, yea, sneered, at his credulous tenderness! Her assumption of rule, therefore, became an arrogance not to be borne. What right had she, guilty of a crime for which there is no name and no punishment, to reverse the secret justice of the soul, and claim to be rewarded?

So reasoned Joseph to himself, in his solitary broodings; but the spell was not so entirely broken as he imagined. Sternly as he might have resolved in advance, there was a glamour in her mask of cheerfulness and gentleness, which made his resolution seem hard and cruel. In her presence he could not clearly remember his wrongs: the past delusion had been a reality, nevertheless; and he could make no assertion which did not involve his own miserable humiliation. Thus the depth and vital force of his struggle could not be guessed by Julia. She saw only irritable moods, the natural male resistance which she had often remarked in her father,—perhaps, also, the annoyance of giving up certain "romantic" fancies, which she believed to be common to all young men, and never permanent. Even an open rupture could not have pushed them apart so rapidly as this hollow external routine of life.

Joseph took the earliest opportunity of visiting Philip, whom he found busy in forge and foundry. "This would be the life for you!" he said: "we deal only with physical forces, human and elemental: we direct and create power, yet still obey the command to put money in our purses."

"Is that one secret of your strength?" Joseph asked.

"Who told you that I had any?"

"I feel it," said Joseph; and even as he said it he remembered Julia's unworthy suspicion.

"Come up and see Madeline a moment, and the home she has made for me. We get on very well, for brother and sister—especially since her will is about as stubborn as mine."

Madeline was very bright and cheerful, and Joseph, certainly, saw no signs of a stubborn will in her fair face. She was very simply dressed, and busy with some task of needle-work, which she did not lay aside.

"You might pass already for a member of our community," he could not help saying.

"I think your most democratic farmers will accept me," she answered, "when they learn that I am Philip's housekeeper. The only dispute we have had, or are likely to have, is in relation to the salary."

"She is an inconsistent creature, Joseph," said Philip. "I was obliged to offer her as much as she earned by her music-lessons before she would come at all, and now she can't find work enough to balance it."

"How can I, Philip, when you tempt me every day with walks and rides, botany, geology, and sketching from nature?"

So much frank, affectionate confidence showed itself through the playful gossip of the two, that Joseph was at once comforted and pained. "If I had only had a sister!" he sighed to Philip, as they walked down the knoll.

The friends took the valley road, Joseph leading his horse by the bridle. The stream was full to its banks, and crystal clear: shoals of young fishes passed like drifted leaves over the pebbly ground, and the fragrant water-beetles skimmed the surface of the eddies. Overhead the vaults of the great elms and sycamores were filled with the green, delicious illumination of the tender foliage. It was a scene and a season for idle happiness.

Yet the first words Philip spoke, after a long silence, were: "May I speak now?" There was infinite love and pity in his voice. He took Joseph by the hand.

"Yes," the latter whispered.

"It has come," Philip continued; "you cannot hide it from yourself any longer. My pain is that I did not dare to warn you, though at the risk of losing your friendship. There was so little time—"

"You *did* try to warn me, Philip! I have recalled your words, and the trouble in your face as you spoke, a thousand times. I was a fool, a blind, miserable fool, and my folly has ruined my life!"

"Strange," said Philip, musingly, "that only a perfectly good and pure nature can fall into such a wretched snare. And yet 'Virtue is its own reward,' is dinned into our ears! It is Hell for a single fault: nay, not even a fault, an innocent mistake! But let us see what can be done: is there no common ground whereon your natures can stand together? If there should be a child—"

Joseph shuddered. "Once it seemed too great, too wonderful a hope," he said, "but now, I don't dare to wish for it. Philip, I am too sorely hurt to think clearly: there is nothing to do but to wait. It is a miserable kind of comfort to me to have your sympathy, but I fear you cannot help me."

Philip saw that he could bear no more: his face was pale to the lips and his hands trembled. He led him to the bank, sat down beside him, and laid his arm about his neck. The silence and the caress were more soothing to Joseph than any words; he soon became calm, and remembered an important part of his errand, which was to acquaint Philip with the oil speculation, and to ask his advice.

They discussed the matter long and gravely. With all his questions, and the somewhat imperfect information which Joseph was able to give, Philip could not satisfy himself whether the scheme was a simple swindle or a well-considered business venture. Two or three of the names were respectable, but the chief agent, Kanuck, was unknown to him; moreover, Mr. Blessing's apparent prominence in the undertaking did not inspire him with much confidence.

"How much have you already paid on the stock?" he asked.

"Three instalments, which, Mr. Blessing thinks, is all that will be called for. However, I have the money for a fourth, should it be necessary. He writes to me that the stock has already risen a hundred per cent. in value."

"If that is so," said Philip, "let me advise you to sell half of it, at once. The sum received will cover your liabilities, and the half you retain, as a venture, will give you no further anxiety."

"I had thought of that; yet I am sure that my father-in-law will oppose such a step with all his might. You must know him, Philip; tell me, frankly, your opinion of his character."

"Blessing belongs to a class familiar enough to me," Philip answered; "yet I doubt whether you will comprehend it. He is a swaggering, amiable, magnificent adventurer; never purposely dishonest, I am sure, yet sometimes engaged in transactions that would not bear much scrutiny. His life has been one of ups and downs. After a successful speculation, he is luxurious, open-handed, and absurdly self-confident; his success is soon flung away: he then good-humoredly descends to poverty, because he never believes it can last long. He is unreliable, from his over-sanguine temperament; and yet this very temperament gives him a certain power and influence. Some of our best men are on familiar terms with him. They are on their guard against his pecuniary approaches, they laugh at his extravagant schemes, but they now and then find him useful. I heard Gray, the editor, once speak of him as a man 'filled with available enthusiasms,' and I guess that phrase hits both his strength and his weakness."

On the whole, Joseph felt rather relieved than disquieted. The heart was lighter in his breast as he mounted his horse and rode homewards.

Philip slowly walked forwards, yielding his mind to thoughts wherein Joseph was an important but not the principal figure. Was there a positive strength, he asked himself, in a wider practical experience of life? Did such experience really strengthen the basis of character which must support a man, when some unexpected moral crisis comes upon him? He knew that he seemed strong, to Joseph; but the latter, so far, was bearing his terrible test with a patience drawn from some source of elemental power. Joseph had simply been ignorant: *he* had been proud, impatient, and—he now confessed to himself—weakly jealous. In both cases, a mistake had passed beyond the plastic stage where life may still be remoulded: it had hardened into an inexorable fate. What was to be the end of it all?

A light footstep interrupted his reflections. He looked up, and almost started, on finding himself face to face with Mrs. Hopeton.

Her face was flushed from her walk and the mellow warmth of the afternoon. She held a bunch of wild-flowers,—pink azaleas, delicate sigillarias, valerian, and scarlet painted-cup. She first broke the silence by asking after Madeline.

"Busy with some important sewing,—curtains, I fancy. She is becoming an inveterate housekeeper," Philip said.

"I am glad, for her sake, that she is here. And it must be very pleasant for you, after all your wanderings."

"I must look on it, I suppose," Philip answered, "as the only kind of a home I shall ever have,—while it lasts. But Madeline's life must not be mutilated because mine happens to be."

The warm color left Mrs. Hopeton's face. She strove to make her voice cold and steady, as she said: "I am sorry to see you growing so bitter, Mr. Held."

"I don't think it is my proper nature, Mrs. Hopeton. But you startled me out of a retrospect which had exhausted my capacity for self-reproach, and was about to become self-cursing. There is no bitterness quite equal to that of seeing how weakly one has thrown away an irrecoverable fortune."

She stood before him, silent and disturbed. It was impossible not to understand, yet it seemed equally impossible to answer him. She gave one glance at his earnest, dark gray eyes, his handsome manly face, and the sprinkled glosses of sunshine on his golden hair, and felt a chill strike to her heart. She moved a step, as if to end the interview.

"Only one moment, Mrs. Hopeton—Emily!" Philip cried. "We may not meet again—thus—for years. I will not needlessly recall the past. I only mean to speak of my offence,—to acknowledge it, and exonerate you from any share in the misunderstanding which—made us what we are. You cannot feel the burden of an unpardoned fault; but will you not allow me to lighten mine?"

A softer change came over her stately form. Her arm relaxed, and the wild-flowers fell upon the ground.

"I was wrong, first," Philip went on, "in not frankly confiding to you the knowledge of a boyish illusion and disappointment. I had been heartlessly treated: it was a silly affair, not worth the telling now; but the leaven of mistrust it left behind was not fully worked out of my nature. Then, too, I had private troubles, which my pride—sore, just then, from many a trifling prick, at which I should now laugh—led me to conceal. I need not go over the appearances which provoked me into a display of temper as unjust as it was unmanly,—it is enough to say that all circumstances combined to make me impatient, suspicious, fiercely jealous. I never paused to reflect that you could not know the series of aggravations which preceded our misunderstanding. I did not guess how far I was giving expression to *them*, and unconsciously transferring to you the offences of others. Nay, I exacted a completer surrender of your woman's pride, because a woman had already chosen to make a plaything of my green boy-love. There is no use in speaking of any of the particulars of our quarrel; for I confess to you that I was recklessly, miserably wrong. But the time has come when you can afford to be generous, when you can allow yourself to speak my forgiveness. Not for the sake of anything I might have been to you, but as a true woman, dealing with her brother-man, I ask your pardon!"

Mrs. Hopeton could not banish the memory of the old tenderness which pleaded for Philip in her heart. He had spoken no word which could offend or alarm her: they were safely divided by a gulf which might never be bridged, and perhaps it was well that a purely human reconciliation should now clarify what was turbid in the past, and reunite them by a bond pure, though eternally sad. She came slowly towards him, and gave him her hand.

"All is not only pardoned, Philip," she said, "but it is now doubly my duty to forget it. Do not suppose, however, that I have had no other than reproachful memories. My pride was as unyielding as yours, for it led me to the defiance which you could not then endure. I, too, was haughty and imperious. I recall every word I uttered, and I know that you have not forgotten them. But let there be equal and final justice between us: forget my words, if you can, and forgive me!"

Philip took her hand, and held it softly in his own. No power on earth could have prevented their eyes from meeting. Out of the far-off distance of all dead joys, over all abysses of fate, the sole power which time and will are powerless to tame, took swift possession of their natures. Philip's eyes were darkened and softened by a film of gathering tears: he cried in a broken voice: —

"Yes, pardon! — but I thought pardon might be peace. Forget? Yes, it would be easy to forget the past, if, —O Emily, we have never been parted until now!"

She had withdrawn her hand, and covered her face. He saw, by the convulsive tremor of her frame, that she was fiercely suppressing her emotion. In another moment she looked up, pale, cold, and almost defiant.

"Why should you say more?" she asked. "Mutual forgiveness is our duty, and there the duty ends. Leave me now!"

Philip knew that he had betrayed himself. Not daring to speak another word he bowed and walked rapidly away. Mrs. Hopeton stood, with her hand pressed upon her bosom, until he had disappeared among the farther trees: then she sat down, and let her withheld tears flow freely.

Presently the merry whoops and calls of children met her ear. She gathered together the fallen flowers, rose and took her way across the meadows towards a little stone schoolhouse, at the foot of the nearest hill. Lucy Henderson already advanced to meet her. There was still an hour or two of sunshine, but the mellow, languid heat of the day was over, and the breeze winnowing down the valley brought with it the smell of the blossoming vernal grass.

The two women felt themselves drawn towards each other, though neither had as yet divined the source of their affectionate instinct. Now, looking upon Lucy's pure, gently firm, and reliant face, Mrs. Hopeton, for the second or third time in her life, yielded to a sudden, powerful impulse, and said: "Lucy, I foresee that I shall need the love and the trust of a true woman: where shall I find it if not in you?"

"If mine will content you," said Lucy.

"O my dear!" Mrs. Hopeton cried; "none of us can stand alone. God has singular trials for us, sometimes, and the use and the conquest of a trouble may both become clear in the telling of it. The heart can wear itself out with its own bitterness. You see, I force my confidence upon you, but I know you are strong to receive it."

"At least," Lucy answered, gravely, "I have no claim to strength unless I am willing to have it tested."

"Then let me make the severest test at once: I shall have less courage if I delay. Can you comprehend the nature of a woman's trial, when her heart resists her duty?"

A deep blush overspread Lucy's face, but she forced herself to meet Mrs. Hopeton's gaze. The two women were silent a moment; then the latter threw her arms around Lucy's neck and kissed her.

"Let us walk!" she said. "We shall both find the words we need."

They moved away over the fragrant, shining meadows. Down the valley, at the foot of the blue cape which wooed their eyes, and perhaps suggested to their hearts that mysterious sense of hope which lies in landscape distances, Elwood Withers was directing his gang of workmen. Over the eastern hill, Joseph Asten stood among his fields, hardly recognizing their joyous growth. The smoke of Philip's forge rose above the trees to the northward. So many disappointed hearts, so many thwarted lives! What strand stall be twisted out of the broken threads of these destinies, thus drawn so near to each other? What new forces—fatal or beneficent—shall be developed from these elements?

Mr. Hopeton, riding homewards along the highway, said to himself: "It's a pleasant country, but what slow, humdrum lives the people lead!"

CHAPTER XVII
A STORM

"I have a plan," said Julia, a week or two later. "Can you guess it? No, I think not; yet you *might*! O, how lovely the light falls on your hair: it is perfect satin!"

She had one hand on his shoulder, and ran the fingers of the other lightly through his brown locks. Her face, sparkling all over with a witching fondness, was lifted towards his. It was the climax of an amiable mood which had lasted three days.

What young man can resist a playful, appealing face, a soft, caressing touch? Joseph smiled as he asked,—

"Is it that I shall wear my hair upon my shoulders, or that we shall sow plaster on the clover-field, as old Bishop advised you the other day?"

"Now you are making fun of my interest in farming; but wait another year! I am trying earnestly to understand it, but only so that ornament—beauty—what was the word in those lines you read last night?—may grow out of use. That's it—Beauty out of Use! I know I've bored you a little sometimes——just a little, now, confess it!—with all my questions; but this is something different. Can't you think of anything that would make our home, O so much more beautiful?"

"A grove of palm-trees at the top of the garden? Or a lake in front, with marble steps leading down to the water?"

"You perverse Joseph! No: something possible, something practicable, something handsome, something profitable! Or, are you so old-fashioned that you think we must drudge for thirty years, and only take our pleasure after we grow rheumatic?"

Joseph looked at her with a puzzled, yet cheerful face.

"You don't understand me yet!" she exclaimed. "And indeed, indeed, I dread to tell you, for one reason: you have such a tender regard for old associations,—not that I'd have it otherwise, if I could. I like it: I trust I have the same feeling; yet a little sentiment sometimes interferes practically with the improvement of our lives."

Joseph's curiosity was aroused. "What do you mean, Julia?" he asked.

"No!" she cried; "I will not tell you until I have read part of pa's letter, which came this afternoon. Take the arm-chair, and don't interrupt me."

She seated herself on the window-sill and opened the letter. "I saw," she said, "how uneasy you felt when the call came for the fourth instalment of ten per cent. on the Amaranth shares, especially after I had so much difficulty in persuading you not to sell the half. It surprised *me*, although I knew that, where pa is concerned, there's a good reason for everything. So I wrote to him the other day, and this is what he says,—you remember, Kanuck is the company's agent on the spot:—

"'Tell Joseph that in matters of finance there's often a wheel within a wheel. Blenkinsop, of the Chowder Company, managed to get a good grab of our shares through a third party, of whom we had not the slightest suspicion. I name no name at present, from motives of prudence. We only discovered the circumstance after the third party left for Europe. Looking upon the Chowder as a rival, it is our desire, of course, to extract this entering wedge before it has been thrust into our vitals, and we can only accomplish the end by still keeping secret the discovery of the torpedoes (an additional expense, I might remark), and calling for fresh instalments from *all* the stockholders. Blenkinsop, not being within the inside ring,— and no possibility of *his* getting in!—will naturally see only the blue of disappointment where we see the rose of realized expectations. Already, so Kanuck writes to me, negotiations are on foot which will relieve our Amaranth of this parasitic growth, and a few weeks—days—hours, in fact, may enable us to explode and triumph! I was offered, yesterday, by one of our shrewdest operators, who has been silently watching us, ten shares of the Sinnemahoning Hematite for eight of ours. Think of that,—the Sinnemahoning Hematite! No better stock in the market, if you remember the quotations! Explain the significance of the figures to your husband, and let him see that he has—but no, I will restrain myself and make no estimate. I will only mention, under the seal of the profoundest secrecy, that the number of shafts now sinking (or being sunk) will give an enormous flowing capacity when the electric spark fires the mine, and I should not wonder if our shares then soared high over the pinnacles of all previous speculation!'

"No, nor I!" Julia exclaimed, as she refolded the letter; "it is certain,— positively certain! I have never known the Sinnemahoning Hematite to be less than 147. What do you say, Joseph?"

"I hope it may be true," he answered. "I can't feel so certain, while an accident—the discovery of the torpedo-plan, for instance—might change the prospects of the Amaranth. It will be a great relief when the time comes to 'realize,' as your father says."

"You only feel so because it is your first experience; but for your sake I will consent that it shall be the last. We shall scarcely need any more than this will bring us; for, as pa says, a mere competence in the city is a splendid fortune in the country. You need leisure for books and travel and society, and you shall have it. Now, let us make a place for both!"

Thereupon she showed him how the parlor and rear bed-room might be thrown into one; where there were alcoves for bookcases and space for a piano; how a new veranda might be added to the western end of the house; how the plastering might be renewed, a showy cornice supplied, and an air of elegant luxury given to the new apartment. Joseph saw and listened, conscious at once of a pang at changing the ancient order of things, and a temptation to behold a more refined comfort in its place. He only asked to postpone the work; but Julia pressed him so closely, with such a multitude of unanswerable reasons, that he finally consented to let a mechanic look at the house, and make an estimate of the expense.

In such cases, the man who deliberates is lost.

His consent once reluctantly exacted, Julia insisting that she would take the whole charge of directing the work, a beginning was made without delay, and in a few days the ruin was so complete that the restoration became a matter of necessity.

Julia kept her word only too faithfully. With a lively, playful manner in the presence of the workmen, but with a cold, inflexible obstinacy when they were alone, she departed from the original plan, adding showy and expensive features, every one of which, Joseph presently saw, was devised to surpass the changes made by the Hopetons in their new residence. His remonstrances produced no effect, and he was precluded from a practical interference by the fear of the workmen guessing his domestic trouble. Thus the days dragged on, and the breach widened without an effort on either side to heal it.

The secret of her temporary fondness gave him a sense of positive disgust when it arose in his memory. He now suspected a selfish purpose in her caresses, and sought to give her no chance of repeating them, but in the company of others he was forced to endure a tenderness which, he was surprised to find, still half deceived him, as it wholly deceived his neighbors. He saw, too,—and felt himself powerless to change the impression,—that Julia's popularity increased with her knowledge of the people, while their manner towards him was a shade less frank and cordial than formerly. He knew that the changes in his home were so much needless extravagance, to them; and that Julia's oft-repeated phrase (always accompanied with a loving look), "Joseph is making the old place so beautiful for me!" increased their mistrust, while seeming to exalt him as a devoted husband.

It is not likely that she specially intended this result; while, on the other hand, he somewhat exaggerated its character. Her object was simply to retain her growing ascendency: within the limits where her peculiar faculties had been exercised she was nearly perfect; but she was indifferent to tracing the consequences of her actions beyond those limits. When she ascertained Mr. Chaffinch's want of faith in Joseph's entire piety, she became more regular in her attendance at his church, not so much to prejudice her husband by the contrast, as to avoid the suspicion which he had incurred. To Joseph, however, in the bitterness of his deception, these actions seemed either hostile or heartless; he was repelled from the clearer knowledge of a nature so foreign to his own. So utterly foreign: yet how near beyond all others it had once seemed!

It was not a jealousy of the authority she assumed which turned his heart from her: it was the revelation of a shallowness and selfishness not at all rare in the class from which she came, but which his pure, guarded youth had never permitted him to suspect in any human being. A man familiar with men and women, if he had been caught in such toils, would have soon discovered some manner of controlling her nature, for the very shrewdest and falsest have their vulnerable side. It gave Joseph, however, so much keen spiritual pain to encounter her in her true character, that such a course was simply impossible.

Meanwhile the days went by; the expense of labor and material had already doubled the estimates made by the mechanics; bills were presented for payment, and nothing was heard from the Amaranth. Money was a necessity, and there was no alternative but to obtain a temporary loan at a county town, the centre of transactions for all the debtors and creditors of the neighboring country. It was a new and disagreeable experience for Joseph to appear in the character of a borrower, and he adopted it most reluctantly; yet the reality was a greater trial than he had suspected. He found that the most preposterous stories of his extravagance were afloat. He was transforming his house into a castle: he had made, lost, and made again a large fortune in petroleum; he had married a wealthy wife and squandered her money; he drove out in a carriage with six white horses; he was becoming irregular in his habits and heretical in his religious views; in short, such marvellous powers of invention had been exercised that the Arab story-tellers were surpassed by the members of that quiet, sluggish community.

It required all his self-control to meet the suspicions of the money-agents, and convince them of the true state of his circumstances. The loan was obtained, but after such a wear and tear of flesh and spirit as made it seem a double burden.

When he reached home, in the afternoon, Julia instantly saw, by his face, that all had not gone right. A slight effort, however, enabled her to say carelessly and cheerfully,—

"Have you brought me my supplies, dear?"

"Yes," he answered curtly.

"Here is a letter from pa," she then said. "I opened it, because I knew what the subject must be. But if you're tired, pray don't read it now, for then you may be impatient. There's a little more delay."

"Then I'll not delay to know it," he said, taking the letter from her hand. A printed slip, calling upon the stockholders of the Amaranth to pay a *fifth* instalment, fell out of the envelope. Accompanying it there was a hasty note from B. Blessing: "Don't be alarmed, my dear son-in-law! Probably a mere form. Blenkinsop still holds on, but we think this will bring him at once. If it don't, we shall very likely have to go on *with* him, even if it obliges us to unite the Amaranth and the Chowder. In any case, we shall ford or bridge this little Rubicon within a fortnight. Have the money ready, if convenient, but do not forward unless I give the word. We hear, through third parties, that Clementina (who is now at Long Branch) receives much attention from Mr. Spelter, a man of immense wealth, but, I regret to say, no refinement."

Joseph smiled grimly when he finished the note. "Is there never to be an end of humbug?" he exclaimed.

"There, now!" cried Julia; "I knew you'd be impatient. You are so unaccustomed to great operations. Why, the Muchacho Land Grant—I remember it, because pa sold out just at the wrong time—hung on for seven years!"

"D——curse the Muchacho Land Grant, and the Amaranth too!"

"Aren't you ashamed!" exclaimed Julia, taking on a playful air of offence; "but you're tired and hungry, poor fellow!" Therewith she put her hands on his shoulders, and raised herself on tiptoe to kiss him.

Joseph, unable to control his sudden instinct, swiftly turned away his head.

"O you wicked husband, you deserve to be punished!" she cried, giving him what was meant to be a light tap on the cheek.

It was a light tap, certainly; but perhaps a little of the annoyance which she banished from her face had lodged, unconsciously, in her fingers. They left just sting enough to rouse Joseph's heated blood. He started back a step, and looked at her with flaming eyes.

"No more of that, Julia! I know, *now*, how much your arts are worth. I am getting a vile name in the neighborhood,—losing my property,—losing my own self-respect,—because I have allowed you to lead me! Will you be content with what you have done, or must you go on until my ruin is complete?"

Before he had finished speaking she had taken rapid counsel with herself, and decided. "Oh, oh! such words to me!" she groaned, hiding her face between her hands. "I never thought *you* could be so cruel! I had *such* pleasure in seeing you rich and free, in trying to make your home beautiful; and now this little delay, which no business man would think anything of, seems to change your very nature! But I will not think it's your true self: something has worried you to-day,—you have heard some foolish story—"

"It is not the worry of to-day," he interrupted, in haste to state his whole grievance, before his weak heart had time to soften again,—"it is the worry of months past! It is because I thought you true and kind-hearted, and I find you selfish and hypocritical! It is very well to lead me into serious expenses, while so much is at stake, and now likely to be lost,—it is very well to make my home beautiful, especially when you can outshine Mrs. Hopeton! It is easy to adapt yourself to the neighbors, and keep on the right side of them, no matter how much your husband's character may suffer in the process!"

"That will do!" said Julia, suddenly becoming rigid. She lifted her head, and apparently wiped the tears from her eyes. "A little more and it would be too much for even *me*! What do I care for 'the neighbors'? persons whose ideas and tastes and habits of life are so different from mine? I have endeavored to be friendly with them for *your* sake: I have taken special pains to accommodate myself to their notions, just because I intended they should justify *you* in choosing me! I believed—for you told me so—that there was no calculation in love, that money was dross in comparison; and how could I imagine that you would so soon put up a balance and begin to weigh the two? Am I your wife or your slave? Have I an equal share in what is yours, or am I here merely to increase it? If there is to be a question of dollars and cents between us, pray have my allowance fixed, so that I may not overstep it, and may save myself from such reproaches! I knew you would be disappointed in pa's letter: I have been anxious and uneasy since it came, through my sympathy with you, and was ready to make any sacrifice that might relieve your mind; and now you seem to be full of unkindness and injustice! What shall I do, O what shall I do?

She threw herself upon a sofa, weeping hysterically.

"Julia!" he cried, both shocked and startled by her words, "you purposely misunderstand me. Think how constantly I have yielded to you, against my own better judgment! When have you considered my wishes?"

"When?" she repeated: then, addressing the cushion with a hopeless, melancholy air, "he asks, when! How could I misunderstand you? your words were as plain as daggers. If you were not aware how sharp they were, call them back to your mind when these mad, unjust suspicions have left you! I trusted you so perfectly, I was looking forward to such a happy future, and now—now, all seems so dark! It is like a flash of lightning: I am weak and giddy: leave me,—I can bear no more!"

She covered her face, and sobbed wretchedly.

"I am satisfied that you are not as ignorant as you profess to be," was all Joseph could say, as he obeyed her command, and left the room. He was vanquished, he knew, and a little confused by his wife's unexpected way of taking his charges in flank instead of meeting them in front, as a man would have done. *Could* she be sincere? he asked himself. Was she really so ignorant of herself, as to believe all that she had uttered? There seemed to be not the shadow of hypocrisy in her grief and indignation. Her tears were real: then why not her smiles and caresses? Either she was horribly, incredibly false,—worse than he dared dream her to be,—or so fatally unconscious of her nature that nothing short of a miracle could ever enlighten her. One thing only was certain: there was now no confidence between them, and there might never be again.

He walked slowly forth from the house, seeing nothing, and unconscious whither his feet were leading him.

CHAPTER XVIII
ON THE RAILROAD TRACK

Still walking, with bent head, and a brain which vainly strove to work its way to clearness through the perplexities of his heart, Joseph went on. When, wearied at last, though not consciously calmer, he paused and looked about him, it was like waking from a dream. Some instinct had guided him on the way to Philip's forge: the old road had been moved to accommodate the new branch railway, and a rapid ring of hammers came up from the embankment below. It was near the point of the hill where Lucy's schoolhouse stood, and even as he looked she came, accompanied by her scholars, to watch the operation of laying the track. Elwood Withers, hale, sunburnt, full of lusty life, walked along the sleepers directing the workmen.

"He was right,—only too right!" muttered Joseph to himself. "Why could I not see with his eyes? 'It's the bringing up,' he would say; but that is not all. I have been an innocent, confiding boy, and thought that years and acres had made me a man. O, *she* understood me—she understands me now; but in spite of her, God helping me, I shall yet be a man."

Elwood ran down the steep side of the embankment, greeted Lucy, and helped her to the top, the children following with whoops and cries.

"Would it have been different," Joseph further soliloquized, "if Lucy and I had loved and married? It is hardly treating Elwood fairly to suppose such a thing, yet—a year ago—I might have loved her. It is better as it is: I should have stepped upon a true man's heart. Have they drawn nearer? and if so, does he, with his sturdier nature, his surer knowledge, find no flaw in her perfections?"

A morbid curiosity to watch the two suddenly came upon him. He clambered over the fence, crossed the narrow strip of meadow, and mounted the embankment. Elwood's back was towards him, and he was just saying: "It all comes of taking an interest in what you're doing. The practical part is easy enough, when you once have the principles. I can manage the theodolite already, but I need a little showing when I come to the calculations. Somehow, I never cared much about study before, but here it's all applied as soon as you've learned it, and that fixes it, like, in your head."

Lucy was listening with an earnest, friendly interest on her face. She scarcely saw Joseph until he stood before her. After the first slight surprise, her manner towards him was quiet and composed: Elwood's eyes were bright, and there was a fresh intelligence in his appearance. The habit of command had already given him a certain dignity.

"How can I get knowledge which may be applied as soon as learned?" Joseph asked, endeavoring to assume the manner furthest from his feelings. "I'm still at the foot of the class, Lucy," he added, turning to her.

"How?" Elwood replied. "I should say by going around the world alone. That would be about the same for you as what these ten miles I'm overseeing are to me. A little goes a great way with me, for I can only pick up one thing at a time."

"What kind of knowledge are you looking for, Joseph?" Lucy gravely asked.

"Of myself," said he, and his face grew dark.

"That's a true word!" Elwood involuntarily exclaimed. He then caught Lucy's eye, and awkwardly added: "It's about what we all want, I take it."

Joseph recovered himself in a moment, and proposed looking over the work. They walked slowly along the embankment, listening to Elwood's account of what had been done and what was yet to do, when the Hopeton carriage came up the highway, near at hand. Mrs. Hopeton sat in it alone.

"I was looking for you, Lucy," she called. "If you are going towards the cutting, I will join you there."

She sent the coachman home with the carriage, and walked with them on the track. Joseph felt her presence as a relief, but Elwood confessed to himself that he was a little disturbed by the steady glance of her dark eyes. He had already overcome his regret at the interruption of his rare and welcome chance of talking with Lucy, but then Joseph knew his heart, while this stately lady looked as if she were capable of detecting what she had no right to know. Nevertheless, she was Lucy's friend, and that fact had great weight with Elwood.

"It's rather a pity to cut into the hills and bank up the meadows in this way, isn't it?" he asked.

"And to disturb my school with so much hammering," Lucy rejoined; "when the trains come I must retreat."

"None too soon," said Mrs. Hopeton. "You are not strong, Lucy, and the care of a school is too much for you."

Elwood thanked her with a look, before he knew what he was about.

"After all," said Joseph, "why shouldn't nature be cut up? I suppose everything was given up to us to use, and the more profit the better the use, seems to be the rule of the world. 'Beauty grows out of Use,' you know."

His tone was sharp and cynical, and grated unpleasantly on Lucy's sensitive ear.

"I believe it is a rule in art," said Mrs. Hopeton, "that mere ornament, for ornament's sake, is not allowed. It must always seem to answer some purpose, to have a necessity for its existence. But, on the other hand, what is necessary should be beautiful, if possible."

"A loaf of bread, for instance," suggested Elwood.

They all laughed at this illustration, and the conversation took a lighter turn. By this time they had entered the narrower part of the valley, and on passing around a sharp curve of the track found themselves face to face with Philip and Madeline Held.

If Mrs. Hopeton's heart beat more rapidly at the unexpected meeting, she preserved her cold, composed bearing. Madeline, bright and joyous, was the unconscious agent of unconstraint, in whose presence each of the others felt immediately free.

"Two inspecting committees at once!" cried Philip. "It is well for you, Withers, that you didn't locate the line. My sister and I have already found several unnecessary curves and culverts."

"And *we* have found a great deal of use and no beauty," Lucy answered.

"Beauty!" exclaimed Madeline. "What is more beautiful than to see one's groceries delivered at one's very door? Or to have the opera and the picture-gallery brought within two hours' distance? How far are we from a lemon, Philip?"

"You were a lemon, Mad, in your vegetable, pre-human state; and you are still acid and agreeable."

"Sweets to the sweet!" she gayly cried. "And what, pray, was Miss Henderson?"

"Don't spare me, Mr. Held," said Lucy, as he looked at her with a little hesitation.

"An apple."

"And Mrs. Hopeton?"

"A date-palm," said Philip, fixing his eyes upon her face.

She did not look up, but an expression which he could not interpret just touched her lips and faded.

"Now, it's your turn, Miss Held," Elwood remarked: "what were we men?"

"O, Philip a prickly pear, of course; and you, well, some kind of a nut; and Mr. Asten—"

"A cabbage," said Joseph.

"What vanity! Do you imagine that you are all head,—or that your heart is in your head? Or that you keep the morning dew longer than the rest of us?"

"It might well be," Joseph answered; and Madeline felt her arm gently pinched by Philip, from behind. She had tact enough not to lower her pitch of gayety too suddenly, but her manner towards Joseph became grave and gentle. Mrs. Hopeton said but little: she looked upon the circling hills, as if studying their summer beauty, while the one desire in her heart was to be away from the spot,—away from Philip's haunting eyes.

After a little while, Philip seemed to be conscious of her feeling. He left his place on the opposite side of the track, took Joseph's arm and led him a little aside from the group.

"Philip, I want you!" Joseph whispered; "but no, not quite yet. There is no need of coming to you in a state of confusion. In a day or two more I shall have settled a little."

"You are right," said Philip: "there is no opiate like time, be there never so little of it. I felt the fever of your head in your hand. Don't come to me, until you feel that it is the one thing which must be done! I think you know why I say so."

"I do!" Joseph exclaimed. "I am just now more of an ostrich than anything else; I should like to stick my head in the sand, and imagine myself invisible. But—Philip—here are six of us together. One other, I know, has a secret wound, perhaps two others: is it always so in life? I think I am selfish enough to be glad to know that I am not specially picked out for punishment."

Philip could not help smiling. "Upon my soul," he said, "I believe Madeline is the only one of the six who is not busy with other thoughts than those we all seem to utter. Specially picked out? There is no such thing as special picking out, in this world! Joseph, it may seem hard and schoolmaster-like in me again to say 'wait!' yet that is the only word I can say."

"Good evening, all!" cried Elwood. "I must go down to my men; but I'd be glad of such an inspection as this, a good deal oftener."

"I'll go that far with you," said Joseph.

Mrs. Hopeton took Lucy's arm with a sudden, nervous movement. "If you are not too tired, let us walk over the hill," she said; "I want to find the right point of view for sketching our house."

The company dissolved. Philip, as he walked up the track with his sister, said to himself: "Surely she was afraid of me. And what does her fear indicate? What, if not that the love she once bore for me still lives in her heart, in spite of time and separated fates? I should not, *dare* not think of her; I shall never again speak a word to her which her husband might not hear; but I cannot tear from me the dream of what she might be, the knowledge of what she is, false, hopeless, fatal, as it all may be!"

"Elwood," said Joseph, when they had walked a little distance in silence, "do you remember the night you spent with me, a year ago?"

"I'm not likely to forget it."

"Let me ask you one question, then. Have you come nearer to Lucy Henderson?"

"If no further off means nearer, and it almost seems so in my case,—yes!"

"And you see no difference in her,—no new features of character, which you did not guess, at first?"

"Indeed, I do!" Elwood emphatically answered. "To me she grows less and less like any other woman,—so right, so straightforward, so honest in all her ways and thoughts! If I am ever tempted to do anything—well, not exactly mean, you know, but such as a man might as well leave undone, I have only to say to myself: 'If you're not thoroughly good, my boy, you'll lose her!' and that does the business, right away. Why, Joseph, I'm proud of myself, that I mean to deserve her!"

"Ah!" A sigh, almost a groan, came from Joseph's lips. "What will you think of me?" he said. "I was about to repeat your own words,—to warn you to be cautious, and take time, and test your feelings, and not to be too sure of *her* perfection! What can a young man know about women? He can only discover the truth after marriage, and then—they are indifferent how it affects him—*their* fortunes are made!"

"I know," answered Elwood, turning his head away slightly; "but there's a difference between the women you seek, and work to get, and the women who seek, and work to get you."

"I understand you."

"Forgive me for saying it!" Elwood cried, instantly repenting his words. "I couldn't help seeing and feeling what you know now. But what man—leastways, what friend—could ha' said it to you with any chance of being believed? You were like a man alone in a boat above a waterfall; only *you* could bring yourself to shore. If I stood on the bank and called, and you didn't believe me, what then? The Lord knows, I'd give this right arm, strong as it is, to put you back where you were a year ago."

"I've been longing for frankness, and I ought to bear it better," said Joseph. "Put the whole subject out of your thoughts, and come and see me as of old. It is quite time I should learn to manage my own life."

He grasped Elwood's hand convulsively, sprang down the embankment, and took to the highway. Elwood looked after him a minute, then slowly shook his head and walked onward towards the men.

Meanwhile, Mrs. Hopeton and Lucy had climbed the hill, and found themselves on the brow of a rolling upland, which fell on the other side towards the old Calvert place. The day was hot. Mrs. Hopeton's knees trembled under her, and she sank on the soft grass at the foot of a tree. Lucy took a seat beside her.

"You know so much of my trouble," said the former, when the coolness and rest had soothed her, "and I trust you so perfectly, that I can tell you all, Lucy. Can you guess the man whom I loved, but must never love again?"

"I have sometimes thought—" but here Lucy hesitated.

"Speak the name in your mind, or, let me say 'Philip Held' for you! Lucy, what am I to do? he loves me still: he told me so, just now, where we were all together below there!"

Lucy turned with a start, and gazed wonderingly upon her friend's face.

"Why does he continue telling me what I must not hear? with his eyes, Lucy! in the tones of his voice, in common words which I am forced to interpret by *his* meaning! I had learned to bear my inevitable fate, for it is not an unhappy one; I can bear even his presence, if he were generous enough to close his heart as I do,—either that, or to avoid me; for I now dread to meet him again."

"Is it not," Lucy asked, "because the trial is new, and takes you by surprise and unprepared? May you not be fearing more than Mr. Held has expressed, or, at least, intended?"

"The speech that kills, or makes alive, needs no words. What I mean is, there is no *resistance* in his face. I blush for myself, I am indignant at my own pitiful weakness, but something in his look to-day made me forget everything that has passed since we were parted. While it lasted, I was under a spell,—a spell which it humiliates me to remember. Your voices sounded faint and far-off; all that I have, and hold, seemed to be slipping from me. It was only for a moment, but, Lucy, it frightened me. My will is strong, and I think I can depend upon it; yet what if some influence beyond my control were to paralyze it?"

"Then you must try to win the help of a higher will; our souls always win something of that which they wrestle and struggle to reach. Dear Mrs. Hopeton, have you never thought that we are still as children who cannot have all they cry for? Now that you know what you fear, do not dread to hold it before your mind and examine what it is: at least, I think that would be my instinct,—to face a danger at once when I found I could not escape it."

"I have no doubt you are right, Lucy," said Mrs. Hopeton; but her tone was sad, as if she acquiesced without clearly believing.

"It seems very hard," Lucy continued, "when we cannot have the one love of all others that we need, harder still when we must put it forcibly from our hearts. But I have always felt that, when we can bring ourselves to renounce cheerfully, a blessing will follow. I do not know how, but I must believe it. Might it not come at last through the love that we have, though it now seems imperfect?"

Mrs. Hopeton lifted her head from her knees, and sat erect. "Lucy," she said, "I do not believe you are a woman who would ask another to bear what is beyond your own strength. Shall I put you to the test?"

Lucy, though her face became visibly paler, replied: "I did not mean to compare my burden with yours; but weigh me, if you wish. If I am found wanting, you will show me wherein."

"Your one love above all others is lost to you. Have you conquered the desire for it?"

"I think I have. If some soreness remains, I try to believe that it is the want of the love which I know to be possible, not that of the—the person."

"Then could you be happy with what you call an imperfect love?"

Lucy blushed a little, in spite of herself. "I am still free," she answered, "and not obliged to accept it. If I were bound, I hope I should not neglect my duty."

"What if another's happiness depended on your accepting it? Lucy, my eyes have been made keen by what I have felt. I saw to-day that a man's heart follows you, and I guess that you know it. Here is no imperfect love on his part: were you his wife, could you learn to give him so much that your life might become peaceful and satisfied?"

"You do, indeed, test me!" Lucy murmured. "How can I know? What answer can I make? I have shrunk from thinking of that, and I cannot feel that my duty lies there. Yet, if it were so, if I were already bound, irrevocably, surely all my present faith must be false if happiness in some form did not come at last!"

"I believe it would, to you!" cried Mrs. Hopeton. "Why not to me? Do you think I have ever looked for *love* in my husband? It seems, now, that I have been content to know that he was proud of me. If I seek, perhaps I may find more than I have dreamed of; and if I find,—if indeed and truly I find,—I shall never more lack self-possession and will!"

She rose to her full height, and a flush came over the pallor of her cheeks. "Yes," she continued, "rather than feel again the humiliation of to-day, I will trample all my nature down to the level of an imperfect love!"

"Better," said Lucy, rising also,—"better to bend only for a while to the imperfect, that you may warm and purify and elevate it, until it shall take the place of the perfect in your heart."

The two women kissed each other, and there were tears on the cheeks of both.

CHAPTER XIX
THE "WHARF-RAT"

On his way home Joseph reviewed the quarrel with a little more calmness, and, while admitting his own rashness and want of tact, felt relieved that it had occurred. Julia now knew, at least, how sorely he had been grieved by her selfishness, and she had thus an opportunity, if she really loved him, of showing whether her nature were capable of change. He determined to make no further reference to the dissension, and to avoid what might lead to a new one. He did not guess, as he approached the house, that his wife had long been watching at the front window, in an anxious, excited state, and that she only slipped back to the sofa and covered her head just before he reached the door.

For a day or two she was silent, and perhaps a little sullen; but the payment of the most pressing bills, the progress of the new embellishments, and the necessity of retaining her affectionate playfulness in the presence of the workmen, brought back her customary manner. Now and then a sharp, indirect allusion showed that she had not forgotten, and had not Joseph closed his teeth firmly upon his tongue, the household atmosphere might have been again disturbed.

Not many days elapsed before a very brief note from Mr. Blessing announced that the fifth instalment would be needed. He wrote in great haste, he said, and would explain everything by a later mail.

Joseph was hardly surprised now. He showed the note to Julia, merely saying: "I have not the money, and if I had, he could scarcely expect me to pay it without knowing the necessity. My best plan will be to go to the city at once."

"I think so, too," she answered. "You will be far better satisfied when you have seen pa, and he can also help you to raise the money temporarily, if it is really inevitable. He knows all the capitalists."

"I shall do another thing, Julia. I shall sell enough of the stock to pay the instalment; nay, I shall sell it all, if I can do so without loss."

"Are you—" she began fiercely, but, checking herself, merely added, "see pa first, that's all I stipulate."

Mr. Blessing had not returned from the Custom-House when Joseph reached the city. He had no mind to sit in the dark parlor and wait; so he plunged boldly into the labyrinth of clerks, porters, inspectors, and tide-waiters. Everybody knew Blessing, but nobody could tell where he was to be found. Finally some one, more obliging than the rest, said: "Try the Wharf-Rat!"

The Wharf-Rat proved to be a "saloon" in a narrow alley behind the Custom-House. On opening the door, a Venetian screen prevented the persons at the bar from being immediately seen, but Joseph recognized his father-in-law's voice, saying, "Straight, if you please!" Mr. Blessing was leaning against one end of the bar, with a glass in his hand, engaged with an individual of not very prepossessing appearance. He remarked to the latter, almost in a whisper (though the words reached Joseph's ears), "You understand, the collector can't be seen every day; it takes time, and—more or less capital. The doorkeeper and others expect to be fed."

As Joseph approached, he turned towards him with an angry, auspicious look, which was not changed into one of welcome so soon that a flash of uncomfortable surprise did not intervene. But the welcome once there, it deepened and mellowed, and became so warm and rich that only a cold, contracted nature could have refused to bathe in its effulgence.

"Why!" he cried, with extended hands, "I should as soon have expected to see daisies growing in this sawdust, or to find these spittoons smelling like hyacinths! Mr. Tweed, one of our rising politicians, Mr. Asten, my son-in-law! Asten, of Asten Hall, I might almost say, for I hear that your mansion is assuming quite a palatial aspect. Another glass, if you please: your throat must be full of dust, Joseph,—*pulvis faucibus hæsit*, if I might be allowed to change the classic phrase."

Joseph tried to decline, but was forced to compromise on a moderate glass of ale; while Mr. Blessing, whose glass was empty, poured something into it from a black bottle, nodded to Mr. Tweed, and saying, "Always straight!" drank it off.

"You would not suppose," he then said to Joseph, "that this little room, dark as it is, and not agreeably fragrant, has often witnessed the arrangement of political manœuvres which have decided the City, and through the City the State. I have seen together at that table, at midnight, Senator Slocum, and the Honorables Whitstone, Hacks, and Larruper. Why, the First Auditor of the Treasury was here no later than last week! I frequently transact some of the confidential business of the Custom-House within these precincts, as at present."

"Shall I wait for you outside?" Joseph asked.

"I think it will not be necessary. I have stated the facts, Mr. Tweed, and if you accept them, the figures can be arranged between us at any time. It is a simple case of algebra: by taking x, you work out the unknown quantity."

With a hearty laugh at his own smartness, he shook the "rising politician's" hand, and left the Wharf-Rat with Joseph.

"We can talk here as well as in the woods," he said. "Nobody ever hears anything in this crowd. But perhaps we had better not mention the Amaranth by name, as the operation has been kept so very close. Shall we say 'Paraguay' instead, or—still better—'Reading,' which is a very common stock? Well, then, I guess you have come to see me in relation to the Reading?"

Joseph, as briefly as possible, stated the embarrassment he suffered, on account of the continued calls for payment, the difficulty of raising money for the fifth instalment, and bluntly expressed his doubts of the success of the speculation. Mr. Blessing heard him patiently to the end, and then, having collected himself, answered:—

"I understand, most perfectly, your feeling in the matter. Further, I do not deny that in respect to the time of realizing from the Am—Reading, I should say—I have also been disappointed. It has cost me no little trouble to keep my own shares intact, and my stake is so much greater than yours, for it is my *all*! I am ready to unite with the Chowder, at once: indeed, as one of the directors, I mentioned it at our last meeting, but the proposition, I regret to say, was not favorably entertained. We are dependent, in a great measure, on Kanuck, who is on the spot superintending the Reading; he has been telegraphed to come on, and promises to do so as soon as the funds now called for are forthcoming. My faith, I hardly need intimate, is firm."

"My only resource, then," said Joseph, "will be to sell a portion of my stock, I suppose?"

"There is one drawback to that course, and I am afraid you may not quite understand my explanation. The—Reading has not been introduced in the market, and its *real* value could not be demonstrated without betraying the secret lever by which we intend hoisting it to a fancy height. We could only dispose of a portion of it to capitalists whom we choose to take into our confidence. The same reason would be valid against hypothecation."

"Have *you* paid this last instalment?" Joseph suddenly asked.

"N—no; not wholly; but I anticipate a temporary accommodation. If Mr. Spelter deprives me of Clementina, as I hear (through third parties) is daily becoming more probable, my family expenses will be so diminished that I shall have an ample margin; indeed, I shall feel like a large paper copy, with my leaves uncut!"

He rubbed his hands gleefully; but Joseph was too much disheartened to reply.

"*This* might be done," Mr. Blessing continued. "It is not certain that all the stockholders have yet paid. I will look over the books, and if such be the case, your delay would not be a sporadic delinquency. If otherwise, I will endeavor to gain the consent of my fellow-directors to the introduction of a new capitalist, to whom a small portion of your interest may be transferred. I trust you perceive the relevancy of this caution. We do not mean that our flower shall always blush unseen, and waste its sweetness on the oleaginous air; we only wish to guard against its being 'untimely ripped' (as Shakespeare says) from its parent stalk. I can well imagine how incomprehensible all this may appear to you. In all probability much of *your* conversation at home, relative to crops and the like, would be to me an unknown dialect. But I should not, therefore, doubt your intelligence and judgment in such matters."

Joseph began to grow impatient. "Do I understand you to say, Mr. Blessing," he asked, "that the call for the fifth instalment *can* be met by the sale of a part of my stock?"

"In an ordinary case it might not—under the peculiar circumstances of our operation—be possible. But I trust I do not exaggerate my own influence when I say that it is within *my* power to arrange it. If you will confide it to my hands, you understand, of course, that a slight formality is necessary,—a power of attorney?"

Joseph, in his haste and excitement, had not considered this, or any other legal point: Mr. Blessing was right.

"Then, supposing the shares to be worth only their par value," he said, "the power need not apply to more than one-tenth of my stock?"

Mr. Blessing came into collision with a gentleman passing him. Mutual wrath was aroused, followed by mutual apologies. "Let us turn into the other street," he said to Joseph; "really, our lives are hardly safe in this crowd; it is nearly three o'clock, and the banks will soon be closed."

"It would be prudent to allow a margin," he resumed, after their course had been changed: "the money market is very tight, and if a *necessity* were suspected, most capitalists are unprincipled enough to exact according to the urgency of the need. I do not say—nor do I at all anticipate—that it would be so in your case; still, the future is a sort of dissolving view, and my suggestion is that of the merest prudence. I have no doubt that double the amount—say one-fifth of your stock—would guard us against all contingencies. If you prefer not to intrust the matter to my hands, I will introduce you to Honeyspoon Brothers, the bankers,—the elder Honeyspoon being a director,—who will be very ready to execute your commission."

What could Joseph do? It was impossible to say to Mr. Blessing's face that he mistrusted him: yet he certainly did not trust! He was weary of plausible phrases, the import of which he was powerless to dispute, yet which were so at variance with what seemed to be the facts of the case. He felt that he was lifted aloft into a dazzling, secure atmosphere, but as often as he turned to look at the wings which upheld him, their plumage shrivelled into dust, and he fell an immense distance before his feet touched a bit of reality.

The power of attorney was given. Joseph declined Mr. Blessing's invitation to dine with him at the Universal Hotel, the Blessing table being "possibly a little lean to one accustomed to the bountiful profusion of the country," on the plea that he must return by the evening train; but such a weariness and disgust came over him that he halted at the Farmers' Tavern, and took a room for the night. He slept until long into the morning, and then, cheered in spirit through the fresh vigor of all his physical functions, started homewards.

CHAPTER XX
A CRISIS

Joseph had made half the distance between Oakland Station and his farm, walking leisurely, when a buggy, drawn by an aged and irreproachable gray horse, came towards him. The driver was the Reverend Mr. Chaffinch. He stopped as they met.

"Will you turn back, as far as that tree?" said the clergyman, after greetings had been exchanged. "I have a message to deliver."

"Now," he continued, reining up his horse in the shade, "we can talk without interruption. I will ask you to listen to me with the spiritual, not the carnal ear. I must not be false to my high calling, and the voice of my own conscience calls me to awaken yours."

Joseph said nothing, but the flush upon his face was that of anger, not of confusion, as Mr. Chaffinch innocently supposed.

"It is hard for a young man, especially one wise in his own conceit, to see how the snares of the Adversary are closing around him. We cannot plead ignorance, however, when the Light is there, and we wilfully turn our eyes from it. You are walking on a road, Joseph Asten, it may seem smooth and fair to you, but do you know where it leads? I will tell you: to Death and Hell!"

Still Joseph was silent.

"It is not too late! Your fault, I fear, is that you attach merit to works, as if works could save you! You look to a cold, barren morality for support, and imagine that to do what is called 'right' is enough for God! You shut your eyes to the blackness of your own sinful heart, and are too proud to acknowledge the vileness and depravity of man's nature; but without this acknowledgment your morality (as you call it) is corrupt, your good works (as you suppose them to be) will avail you naught. You are outside the pale of Grace, and while you continue there, knowing the door to be open, there is no Mercy for you!"

The flush on Joseph's face faded, and he became very pale, but he still waited. "I hope," Mr. Chaffinch continued, after a pause, "that your silence is the beginning of conviction. It only needs an awakening, an opening of the eyes in them that sleep. Do you not recognize your guilt, your miserable condition of sin?"

"No!"

Mr. Chaffinch started, and an ugly, menacing expression came into his face.

"Before you speak again," said Joseph, "tell me one thing! Am I indebted for this Catechism to the order—perhaps I should say the request—of my wife?"

"I do not deny that she has expressed a Christian concern for your state; but I do not wait for a request when I see a soul in peril. If I care for the sheep that willingly obey the shepherd, how much more am I commanded to look after them which stray, and which the wolves and bears are greedy to devour!"

"Have you ever considered, Mr. Chaffinch," Joseph rejoined, lifting his head and speaking with measured clearness, "that an intelligent man may possibly be aware that he has an immortal soul,—that the health and purity and growth of that soul may possibly be his first concern in life,—that no other man can know, as he does, its imperfections its needs, its aspirations which rise directly towards God; and that the attempt of a stranger to examine and criticise, and perhaps blacken, this most sacred part of his nature, may possibly be a pious impertinence?"

"Ah, the natural depravity of the heart!" Mr. Chaffinch groaned.

"It is not the depravity, it is the only pure quality which the hucksters of doctrine, the money-changers in God's temple of Man, cannot touch! Shall I render a reckoning to *you* on the day when souls are judged? Are *you* the infallible agent of the Divine Mercy? What blasphemy!"

Mr. Chaffinch shuddered. "I wash my hands of you!" he cried. "I have had to deal with many sinners in my day, but I have found no sin which came so directly from the Devil as the pride of the mind. If you were rotten in all your members from the sins of the flesh, I might have a little hope. Verily, it shall go easier with the murderer and the adulterer on that day than with such as ye!"

He gave the horse a more than saintly stroke, and the vehicle rattled away. Joseph could not see the predominance of routine in all that Mr. Chaffinch had said. He was too excited to remember that certain phrases are transmitted, and used without a thought of their tremendous character; he applied every word personally, and felt it as an outrage in all the sensitive fibres of his soul. And who had invoked the outrage? His wife: Mr. Chaffinch had confessed it. What representations had she made?—he could only measure them by the character of the clergyman's charges. He sat down on the bank, sick at heart; it was impossible to go home and meet her in his present frame of mind.

Presently he started up, crying aloud: "I will go to Philip! He cannot help me, I know, but I must have a word of love from a friend, or I shall go mad!"

He retraced his steps, took the road up the valley, and walked rapidly towards the Forge. The tumult in his blood gradually expended its force, but it had carried him along more swiftly than he was aware. When he reached the point where, looking across the valley, now narrowed to a glen, he could see the smoke of the Forge near at hand, and even catch a glimpse of the cottage on the knoll, he stopped. Up to this moment he had felt, not reflected; and a secret instinct told him that he should not submit his trouble to Philip's riper manhood until it was made clear and coherent in his own mind. He must keep Philip's love, at all hazards; and to keep it he must not seem simply a creature of moods and sentiments, whom his friend might pity, but could not respect.

He left the road, crossed a sloping field on the left, and presently found himself on a bank overhanging the stream. Under the wood of oaks and hemlocks the laurel grew in rich, shining clumps; the current, at this point deep, full, and silent, glimmered through the leaves, twenty feet below; the opposite shore was level, and green with an herbage which no summer could wither. He leaned against a hemlock bole, and tried to think, but it was not easy to review the past while his future life overhung him like a descending burden which he had not the strength to lift. Love betrayed, trust violated, aspiration misinterpreted, were the spiritual aspects; a divided household, entangling obligations, a probability of serious loss, were the material evils which accompanied them. He was so unprepared for the change that he could only rebel, not measure, analyze, and cast about for ways of relief.

It was a miserable strait in which he found himself; and the more he thought—or, rather, seemed to think—the less was he able to foresee any other than an unfortunate solution. What were his better impulses, if men persisted in finding them evil? What was life, yoked to such treachery and selfishness? Life had been to him a hope, an inspiration, a sound, enduring joy; now it might never be so again! Then what a release were death!

He walked forward to the edge of the rock. A few pebbles, dislodged by his feet, slid from the brink, and plunged with a bubble and a musical tinkle into the dark, sliding waters. One more step, and the release which seemed so fair might be attained. He felt a morbid sense of delight in playing with the thought. Gathering a handful of broken stones, he let them fall one by one, thinking, "So I hold my fate in my hand." He leaned over and saw a shifting, quivering image of himself projected against the reflected sky, and a fancy, almost as clear as a voice, said: "This is your present self: what will you do with it beyond the gulf, where only the soul superior to circumstances here receives a nobler destiny?"

He was still gazing down at the flickering figure, when a step came upon the dead leaves. He turned and saw Philip, moving stealthily towards him, pale, with outstretched hand. They looked at each other for a moment without speaking.

"I guess your thought, Philip," Joseph then said. "But the things easiest to do are sometimes the most impossible."

"The bravest man may allow a fancy to pass through his mind, Joseph, which only the coward will carry into effect."

"I am not a coward!" Joseph exclaimed.

Philip took his hand, drew him nearer, and flinging his arms around him, held him to his heart.

Then they sat down, side by side.

"I was up the stream, on the other side, trolling for trout," said Philip, "when I saw you in the road. I was welcoming your coming, in my heart: then you stopped, stood still, and at last turned away. Something in your movements gave me a sudden, terrible feeling of anxiety: I threw down my rod, came around by the bridge at the Forge, and followed you here. Do not blame me for my foolish dread."

"Dear, dear friend," Joseph cried, "I did not mean to come to you until I seemed stronger and more rational in my own eyes. If that were a vanity, it is gone now: I confess my weakness and ignorance. Tell me, if you can, why this has come upon me? Tell me why nothing that I have been taught, why no atom of the faith which I still must cling to, explains, consoles, or remedies any wrong of my life!"

"Faiths, I suspect," Philip answered, "are, like laws, adapted to the average character of the human race. You, in the confiding purity of your nature, are not an average man: you are very much above the class, and if virtue were its own reward, you would be most exceptionally happy. Then the puzzle is, what's the particular use of virtue?"

"I don't know, Philip, but I don't like to hear you ask the question. I find myself so often on the point of doubting all that was my Truth a little while ago; and yet, why should my misfortunes, as an individual, make the truth a lie? I am only one man among millions who *must* have faith in the efficacy of virtue. Philip, if I believed the faith to be false, I think I should still say, 'Let it be preached!'"

Joseph related to Philip the whole of his miserable story, not sparing himself, nor concealing the weakness which allowed him to be entangled to such an extent. Philip's brow grew dark as he listened, but at the close of the recital his face was calm, though stern.

"Now," said he,—"now put this aside for a little while, and give your ear (and your heart too, Joseph) to *my* story. Do not compare my fortune with yours, but let us apply to both the laws which seem to govern life, and see whether justice is possible."

Joseph had dismissed his wife's suspicion, after the dinner at Hopeton's, so immediately from his memory, that he had really forgotten it; and he was not only startled, but also a little shocked, by Philip's confession. Still, he saw that it was only the reverse form of his own experience, not more strange, perhaps not more to be condemned, yet equally inevitable.

"Is there no way out of this labyrinth of wrong?" Philip exclaimed. "Two natures, as far apart as Truth and Falsehood, monstrously held together in the most intimate, the holiest of bonds,—two natures destined for each other monstrously kept apart by the same bonds! Is life to be so sacrificed to habit and prejudice? I said that Faith, like Law, was fashioned for the average man: then there must be a loftier faith, a juster law, for the men— and the women—who cannot shape themselves according to the common-place pattern of society,—who were born with instincts, needs, knowledge, and rights—ay, *rights*!—of their own!"

"But, Philip," said Joseph, "we were both to blame: you through too little trust, I through too much. We have both been rash and impatient: I cannot forget that; and how are we to know that the punishment, terrible as it seems, is disproportioned to the offence?"

"We know this, Joseph,—and who can know it and be patient?—that the power which controls our lives is pitiless, unrelenting! There is the same punishment for an innocent mistake as for a conscious crime. A certain Nemesis follows ignorance, regardless how good and pure may be the individual nature. Had you even guessed your wife's true character just before marriage, your very integrity, your conscience, and the conscience of the world, would have compelled the union, and Nature would not have mitigated her selfishness to reward you with a tolerable life. O no! You would still have suffered as now. Shall a man with a heart feel this horrible injustice, and not rebel? Grant that I am rightly punished for my impatience, my pride, my jealousy, how have *you* been rewarded for your stainless youth, your innocent trust, your almost miraculous goodness? Had you known the world better, even though a part of your knowledge might have been evil, you would have escaped this fatal marriage. Nothing can be more certain; and will you simply groan and bear? What compensating fortune have you, or can you ever expect to find?"

Joseph was silent at first; but Philip could see, from the trembling of his hands, and his quick breathing, that he was profoundly agitated. "There is something within me," he said, at last, "which accepts everything you say; and yet, it alarms me. I feel a mighty temptation in your words: they could lead me to snap my chains, break violently away from my past and present life, and surrender myself to will and appetite. O Philip, if we could make our lives wholly our own! If we could find a spot—"

"I know such a spot!" Philip cried, interrupting him,—"a great valley, bounded by a hundred miles of snowy peaks; lakes in its bed; enormous hillsides, dotted with groves of ilex and pine; orchards of orange and olive; a perfect climate, where it is bliss enough just to breathe, and freedom from the distorted laws of men, for none are near enough to enforce them! If there is no legal way of escape for you, here, at least, there is no force which can drag you back, once you are there: I will go with you, and perhaps— perhaps—"

Philip's face glowed, and the vague alarm in Joseph's heart took a definite form. He guessed what words had been left unspoken.

"If we could be sure!" he said.

"Sure of what? Have I exaggerated the wrong in your case? Say we should be outlaws there, in our freedom!—here we are fettered outlaws."

"I have been trying, Philip, to discover a law superior to that under which we suffer, and I think I have found it. If it be true that ignorance is equally punished with guilt; if causes and consequences, in which there is neither pity nor justice, govern our lives,—then what keeps our souls from despair but the infinite pity and perfect justice of God? Yes, here is the difference between human and divine law! This makes obedience safer than rebellion. If you and I, Philip, stand above the level of common natures, feeling higher needs and claiming other rights, let us shape them according to the law which is above, not that which is below us!"

Philip grew pale. "Then you mean to endure in patience, and expect me to do the same?" he asked.

"If I can. The old foundations upon which my life rested are broken up, and I am too bewildered to venture on a random path. Give me time;

nay, let us both strive to wait a little. I see nothing clearly but this: there is a Divine government, on which I lean now as never before. Yes, I say again, the very wrong that has come upon us makes God necessary!"

It was Philip's turn to be agitated. There was a simple, solemn conviction in Joseph's voice which struck to his heart. He had spoken from the heat of his passion, it is true, but he had the courage to disregard the judgment of men, and make his protest a reality. Both natures shared the desire, and were enticed by the daring of his dream; but out of Joseph's deeper conscience came a whisper, against which the cry of passion was powerless.

"Yes, we will wait," said Philip, after a long pause. "You came to me, Joseph, as you said, in weakness and confusion: I have been talking of your innocence and ignorance. Let us not measure ourselves in this way. It is not experience alone which creates manhood. What will become of us I cannot tell, but I will not, I dare not, say you are wrong!"

They took each other's hands. The day was fading, the landscape was silent, and only the twitter of nesting birds was heard in the boughs above them. Each gave way to the impulse of his manly love, rarer, alas! but as tender and true as the love of woman, and they drew nearer and kissed each other. As they walked back and parted on the highway, each felt that life was not wholly unkind, and that happiness was not yet impossible.

CHAPTER XXI
UNDER THE WATER

Joseph said nothing that evening concerning the result of his trip to the city, and Julia, who instantly detected the signs which a powerful excitement had left upon his face, thought it prudent to ask no immediate questions. She was purposely demonstrative in little arrangements for his comfort, but spared him her caresses; she did not intend to be again mistaken in choosing the time and occasion of bestowing them.

The next morning, when he felt that he could speak calmly, Joseph told her what he had done, carefully avoiding any word that might seem to express disappointment, or even doubt.

"I hope you are satisfied that pa will make it easy for you?" she ventured to say.

"He thinks so." Then Joseph could not help adding: "He depends, I imagine, upon your sister Clementina marrying a Mr. Spelter,—'a man of immense wealth, but, I regret to say, no refinement.'"

Julia bit her lip, and her eyes assumed that hard, flinty look which her husband knew so well. "If Clementina marries immense wealth," she exclaimed, with a half-concealed sneer, "she will become simply insufferable! But what difference can that make in pa's business affairs?"

The answer tingled on Joseph's tongue: "Probably he expects Mr. Spelter to indorse a promissory note"; but he held it back. "What *I* have resolved to do is this," he said. "In a day or two—as soon as I can arrange to leave—I shall make a journey to the oil region, and satisfy myself where and what the Amaranth is. Your own practical instincts will tell you, Julia, that this intention of mine must be kept secret, even from your father."

She leaned her head upon her hand, and appeared to reflect. When she looked up her face had a cheerful, confiding expression.

"I think you are right," she then said. "If—if things should not happen to be *quite* as they are represented, you can secure yourself against any risk—and pa, too—before the others know of it. You will have the inside track; that is, if there is one. On the other hand, if all is right, pa can easily manage, if some of the others are shaky in their faith, to get their stock at a bargain. I am sure he would have gone out there himself, if his official services were not so important to the government."

It was a hard task for Joseph to keep his feelings to himself.

"And now," she continued,—"now I know you will agree to a plan of mine, which I was going to propose. Lucy Henderson's school closes this week, and Mrs. Hopeton tells me she is a little overworked and ailing. It would hardly help her much to go home, where she could not properly rest, as her father is a hard, avaricious man, who can't endure idleness, except, I suppose, in a corpse (so these people seem to me). I want to ask Lucy to come here. I think you always liked her" (here Julia shot a swift, stealthy glance at Joseph), "and so she will be an agreeable guest for both of us. She shall just rest and grow strong. While you are absent, I shall not seem quite so lonely. You may be gone a week or more, and I shall find the separation very hard to bear, even with her company."

"Why has Mrs. Hopeton not invited her?" Joseph asked.

"The Hopetons are going to the sea-shore in a few days. She would take Lucy as a guest, but there is one difficulty in the way. She thinks Lucy would accept the trip and the stay there as an act of hospitality, but that she cannot (or thinks she cannot) afford the dresses that would enable her to appear in Mrs. Hopeton's circle. But it is just as well: I am sure Lucy would feel more at home *here*."

"Then by all means ask her!" said Joseph. "Lucy Henderson is a noble girl, for she has forced a true-hearted man to love her, without return."

"Ind-e-e-d!"

Julia's drawl denoted surprise and curiosity, but Joseph felt that once more he had spoken too quickly. He endeavored to cover his mistake by a hearty acquiescence in the plan, which was speedily arranged between them, in all its details, Lucy's consent being taken for granted.

It required, however, the extreme of Julia's powers of disguise, aided by Joseph's frank and hearty words and Mrs. Hopeton's influence, to induce Lucy to accept the invitation. Unable to explain wholly to herself, much less mention to any other, the instinct which held her back, she found herself, finally, placed in a false position, and then resolved to blindly trust that she was doing right, inasmuch as she could not make it clear that she was doing wrong. Her decision once taken, she forcibly banished all misgivings, and determined to find nothing but a cheerful and restful holiday before her.

And, indeed, the first day or two of her residence at the farm, before Joseph's departure, brought her a more agreeable experience than she had imagined. Both host and hostess were busy, the latter in the household and the former in the fields, and when they met at meals or in the evening, her presence was an element which compelled an appearance of harmony. She was surprised to find so quiet and ordered a life in two persons whom she had imagined to be miserably unfitted for each other, and began to suspect that she had been seriously mistaken.

After Joseph left, the two women were much together. Julia insisted that she should do nothing, and amiably protested at first against Lucy giving her so much of her society; but, little by little, the companionship was extended and became more frank and intimate. Lucy was in a charitable mood, and found it very easy to fancy that Julia's character had been favorably affected by the graver duties which had come with her marriage. Indeed, Julia found many indirect ways of hinting as much: she feared she had seemed flighty (perhaps a little shallow); looking back upon her past life she could see that such a charge would not be unjust. Her education had been so superficial; all city education of young women was false; they were taught to consider external appearances, and if they felt a void in their nature which these would not fill, whither could they turn for counsel or knowledge?

Her face was sad and thoughtful while she so spoke; but when, shaking her dark curls with a pretty impatience, she would lift her head and ask, with a smile: "But it is not too late, in my case, is it? I'm really an older child, you know,"—Lucy could only answer: "Since you know what you need, it can never be too late. The very fact that you *do* know, proves that it will be easy for you."

Then Julia would shake her head again, and say, "O, you are too kind, Lucy; you judge my nature by your own."

When the friendly relation between them had developed a little further, Julia became—though still with a modest reticence—more confiding in relation to Joseph.

"He is so good, so very, very true and good," she said, one day, "that it grieves me, more than I can tell, to be the cause of a little present anxiety of his. As it is only a business matter, some exaggerated report of which you have probably heard (for I know there have been foolish stories afloat in the neighborhood), I have no hesitation about confiding it to you. Perhaps you can advise me how to atone for my error; for, if it was an error, I fear it cannot be remedied now; if not, it will be a relief to me to confess it."

Thereupon she gave a minute history of the Amaranth speculation, omitting the energy of her persuasion with Joseph, and presenting very strongly her father's views of a sure and splendid success soon to follow. "It was for Joseph's sake," she concluded, "rather than my own, that I advised the investment; though, knowing his perfect unselfishness, I fear he complied only for mine. He had guessed already, it seems to me now, that we women like beauty as well as comfort about our lives; otherwise, he would hardly have undertaken these expensive improvements of our home. But, Lucy, it terrifies me to think that pa and Joseph and I may have been deceived! The more I shut my mind against the idea the more it returns to torment me. I, who brought so little to him, to be the instrument of such a loss! O, if you were not here, how could I endure the anxiety and the absence?"

She buried her face in her handkerchief, and sobbed.

"I know Joseph to be good and true," said Lucy, "and I believe that he will bear the loss cheerfully, if it should come. But it is never good to 'borrow trouble,' as we say in the country. Neither the worst nor the best things which we imagine ever come upon us."

"You are wrong!" cried Julia, starting up and laughing gleefully; "I *have* the best thing, in my husband! And yet, you are right, too: no worst thing can come to me, while I keep him!"

Lucy wished to visit the Hopetons before their departure for the sea-shore, and Julia was quite ready to accompany her. Only, with the wilfulness common to all selfish natures, she determined to arrange the matter in her own way. She drove away alone the next morning to the post-office, with a letter for Joseph, but never drew rein until she had reached Coventry Forge. Philip being absent, she confided to Madeline Held her wish (and Lucy's) that they should all spend an afternoon together, on the banks of the stream,—a free society in the open air instead of a formal one within doors. Madeline entered into the plan with joyous readiness, accepting both for herself and for Philip. They all met together too rarely, she said: a lunch or a tea under the trees would be delightful: there was a little skiff which might be borrowed, and they might even catch and cook their own fish, as the most respectable people did in the Adirondacks.

Julia then drove to the Hopetons in high spirits. Mr. Hopeton found the proposed party very pleasant, and said at once to his wife: "We have still three days, my dear: we can easily spare to-morrow?"

"Mrs. Asten is very kind," she replied; "and her proposition is tempting: but I should not like to go without you, and I thought your business might—"

"O, there is nothing pressing," he interrupted. "I shall enjoy it exceedingly, especially the boat, and the chance of landing a few trout."

So it was settled. Lucy, it is true, felt a dissatisfaction which she could scarcely conceal, and possibly did not, to Julia's eyes; but it was not for her own sake. She must seem grateful for a courtesy meant to favor both herself and her friend, and a little reflection reconciled her to the plan. Mrs. Hopeton dared not avoid Philip Held, and it might be well if she carried away with her to the sea-shore a later and less alarming memory of him. Lucy's own desire for a quiet talk with the woman in whom she felt such a loving interest was of no consequence, if this was the result.

They met in the afternoon, on the eastern side of the stream, just below the Forge, where a little bay of level shore, shaded by superb trees, was left between the rocky bluffs. Stumps and a long-fallen trunk furnished them with rough tables and seats; there was a natural fireplace among some huge tumbled stones; a spring of icy crystal gushed out from the foot of the bluff; and the shimmering, murmuring water in front, with the meadows beyond burning like emerald flame in the sunshine, offered a constant delight to the senses.

All were enchanted with the spot, which Philip and Madeline claimed as their discovery. The gypsy spirit awoke in them, and while they scattered here and there, possessed with the influences of the place, and constantly stumbling upon some new charm or convenience, Lucy felt her heart grow light for her friend, and the trouble of her own life subside. For a time no one seemed to think of anything but the material arrangements. Mr. Hopeton's wine-flasks were laid in the spring to cool; Philip improvised a rustic table upon two neighboring stumps; rough seats were made comfortable, dry sticks collected for fire-wood, stores unpacked and placed in readiness, and every little preliminary of labor, insufferable in a kitchen, took on its usual fascination in that sylvan nook.

Then they rested from their work. Mr. Hopeton and Philip lighted cigars and sat to leeward, while the four ladies kept their fingers busy with bunches of maiden-hair and faint wildwood blossoms, as they talked. It really seemed as if a peace and joy from beyond their lives had fallen upon them. Madeline believed so, and Lucy hoped so: let us hope so, too, and not lift at once the veil which was folded so closely over two restless hearts!

Mr. Hopeton threw away the stump of his cigar, adjusted his fishing-tackle, and said: "If we are to have a trout supper, I must begin to troll at once."

"May I go with you?" his wife asked.

"Yes," he answered, smiling, "if you will not be nervous. But I hardly need to make that stipulation with you, Emily."

Philip assisted her into the unsteady little craft, which was fastened to a tree. Mr. Hopeton seated himself carefully, took the two light, short oars, and held himself from the shore, while Philip loosened the rope.

"I shall row up stream," he said, "and then float back to you, trolling as I come. When I see you again, I hope I can ask you to have the coals ready."

Slowly, and not very skilfully, he worked his way against the current, and passed out of sight around a bend in the stream. Philip watched Mrs. Hopeton's slender figure as she sat in the stern, listlessly trailing one hand in the water. "Does she feel that my eyes, my thoughts, are following her?" he asked; but she did not once turn her head.

"Philip!" cried Madeline, "here are three forlorn maidens, and you the only Sir Isumbras, or whoever is the proper knight! Are you looking into the stream, expecting the 'damp woman' to arise? She only rises for fishermen: she will come up and drag Mr. Hopeton down. Let me invoke the real nymph of this stream!" She sang: —

"Sabrina fair,

Listen where thou art sitting

Under the glassy, cool, translucent wave,

In twisted braids of lilies knitting

The loose train of thy amber-dropping hair;

Listen for dear honor's sake,

Goddess of the silver lake,

Listen and save!"

Madeline did not know what she was doing. She could not remark Philip's paleness in the dim green light where they sat, but she was struck by the startled expression of his eyes.

"One would think you really expected Sabrina to come," she laughed. "Miss Henderson, too, looks as if I had frightened her. You and I, Mrs. Asten, are the only cool, unimaginative brains in the party. But perhaps it was all owing to my poor voice? Come now, confess it! I don't expect you to say, —

'Can any mortal mixture of earth's mould

Breathe such divine, enchanting ravishment?'"

"I was trying to place the song," said Lucy; "I read it once."

"If any one could evoke a spirit, Madeline," Philip replied, "it would be you. But the spirit would be no nymph; it would have little horns and hoofs, and you would be glad to get rid of it again."

They all laughed at this, and presently, at Julia's suggestion, arranged the wood they had collected, and kindled a fire. It required a little time and patience to secure a strong blaze, and in the great interest which the task called forth the Hopetons were forgotten.

At last Philip stepped back, heated and half stifled, for a breath of fresher air, and, turning, saw the boat between the trees gliding down the stream. "There they are!" he cried; "now, to know our luck!"

Tho boat was in midstream, not far from a stony strip which rose above the water. Mrs. Hopeton sat musing with her hands in her lap, while her husband, resting on his knees and one hand, leaned over the bow, watching the fly which trailed at the end of his line. He seemed to be quite unconscious that an oar, which had slowly loosened itself from the lock, was floating away behind the boat.

"You are losing your oars!" Philip cried.

Mr. Hopeton started, as from a dream of trout, dropped his line and stretched forward suddenly to grasp the oar. The skiff was too light and unbalanced to support the motion. It rocked threateningly; Mrs. Hopeton, quite forgetting herself, started to her feet, and, instantly losing her equilibrium, was thrown headlong into the deeper water. The skiff whirled back, turned over, and before Mr. Hopeton was aware of what had happened, he plunged full length, face downwards, into the shallower current.

It was all over before Madeline and Lucy reached the bank, and Philip was already in the stream. A few strokes brought him to Mrs. Hopeton, who struggled with the current as she rose to the surface, but made no outcry. No sooner had she touched Philip than she seized and locked him in her arms, and he was dragged down again with her. It was only the physical clinging to life: if some feeble recognition at that moment told her whose was the form she held and made powerless, it could not have abated an atom of her frantic, instinctive force.

Philip felt that they had drifted into water beyond his depth. With great exertion he freed his right arm and sustained himself and her a moment at the surface. Mrs. Hopeton's head was on his shoulder; her hair drifted against his face, and even the desperation of the struggle could not make him insensible to the warmth of her breast upon his own. A wild thought flashed upon and stung his brain: she was his at last—his in death, if not in life!

His arm slackened, and they sank slowly together. Heart and brain were illuminated with blinding light, and the swift succession of his thoughts compressed an age into the fragment of a second. Yes, she was his now: clasping him as he clasped, their hearts beating against each other, with ever slower pulsations, until they should freeze into one. The world, with its wrongs and prejudices, lay behind them; the past was past, and only a short and painless atonement intervened between the immortal possession of souls! Better that it should end thus: he had not sought this solution, but he would not thrust it from him.

But, even as his mind accepted it, and with a sense of perfect peace, He heard Joseph's voice, saying, "We must shape our lives according to the law which is above, not that which is below us." Through the air and the water, on the very rock which now overhung his head, he again saw Joseph bending, and himself creeping towards him with outstretched hand. Ha! who was the coward now? And again Joseph spake, and his words were: "The very wrong that has come upon us makes God necessary." God? Then how would God in his wisdom fashion their future life? Must they sweep eternally, locked in an unsevering embrace, like Paolo and Francesca, around some dreary circle of hell? Or must the manner of entering that life together be the act to separate them eternally? Only the inevitable act dare ask for pardon; but here, if not will or purpose, was at least submission without resistance! Then it seemed to him that Madeline's voice came again to him, ringing like a trumpet through the waters, as she sang:—

"Listen for dear honor's sake,

Goddess of the silver lake,

Listen and save!"

He pressed his lips to Mrs. Hopeton's unconscious brow, his heart saying, "Never, never again!" released himself by a sudden, powerful effort, seized her safely, as a practised swimmer, shot into light and air, and made for the shallower side of the stream. The upturned skiff was now within reach, and all danger was over.

Who could guess that the crisis of a soul had been reached and passed in that breath of time under the surface? Julia's long, shrill scream had scarcely come to an end; Mr. Hopeton, bewildered by his fall, was trying to run towards them through water up to his waist, and Lucy and Madeline looked on, holding their breath in an agony of suspense. In another moment Philip touched bottom, and raising Mrs. Hopeton in his arms, carried her to the opposite bank.

She was faint and stunned, but not unconscious. She passively allowed Philip to support her until Mr. Hopeton, struggling through the shallows, drew near with an expression of intense terror and concern on his broad face. Then, breaking from Philip, she half fell, half flung herself into his arms, laid her head upon his shoulder, and burst into a fit of hysterical weeping.

Tears began to run down the honest man's cheeks, and Philip, turning away, busied himself with righting the boat and recovering the oars.

"O, my darling!" said Mr. Hopeton, "what should I do if I had lost you?"

"Hold me, keep me, love me!" she cried. "I must not leave you!"

He held her in his arms, he kissed her, he soothed her with endearing words. She grew calm, lifted her head, and looked in his eyes with a light which he had never yet seen in them. The man's nature was moved and stirred: his lips trembled, and the tears still slowly trickled from his eyes.

"Let me set you over!" Philip called from the stream. "The boat is wet, but then neither of us is dry. We have, fortunately, a good fire until the carriage can be brought for Mrs. Hopeton, and your wine will be needed at once."

They had no trout, nor indeed any refreshment, except the wine. Philip tried to rally the spirits of the party, but Julia was the only one who at all seconded his efforts; the others had been too profoundly agitated. Mr. and Mrs. Hopeton were grave; it seemed scarcely possible for them to speak, and yet, as Lucy remarked with amazement, the faces of both were bright and serene.

"I shall never invoke another water-nymph," said Madeline, as they were leaving the spot.

"Yes!" Philip cried, "always invoke Sabrina, and the daughter of Locrine will arise for you, as she arose to-day."

"That is, not at all?"

"No," said Philip, "she arose."

CHAPTER XXII
KANUCK

When he set forth upon his journey, Joseph had enough of natural shrewdness to perceive that his own personal interest in the speculation were better kept secret. The position of the Amaranth property, inserted like a wedge between the Fluke and Chowder Companies, was all the geography he needed; and he determined to assume the character of a curious traveller,—at least for a day or two,—to keep his eyes and ears open, and learn as much as might be possible to one outside the concentric "rings" of oil operations.

He reached Corry without adventure, and took passage in the train to Oil City, intending to make the latter place the starting-point of his investigations. The car was crowded, and his companion on the seat was a keen, witty, red-faced man, with an astonishing diamond pin and a gold watch-chain heavy enough to lift an anchor. He was too restless, too full of "operative" energy, to travel in silence, as is the universal and most dismal American habit; and before they passed three stations he had extracted from Joseph the facts that he was a stranger, that he intended visiting the principal wells, and that he might possibly (Joseph allowing the latter point to be inferred) be tempted to invest something, if the aspects were propitious.

"You must be sure to take a look at *my* wells," said the stranger; "not that any of our stock is in the market,—it is never offered to the public, unless accidentally,—but they will give you an illustration of the magnitude of the business. All wells, you know, sink after a while to what some people call the normal flowing capacity (we oilers call it 'the everidge run'), and so it was reported of ourn. But since we've begun to torpedo them, it's almost equal to the first tapping, though I don't suppose it'll hold out so long."

"Are the torpedoes generally used?" Joseph asked, in some surprise.

"They're generally *tried*, anyhow. The cute fellow who first hit upon the idea meant to keep it dark, but the oilers, you'll find, have got their teeth skinned, and what they can't find out isn't worth finding out! Lord! I torpedoed my wells at midnight, and it wasn't a week before the Fluke was at it, bustin' and bustin' all their dry auger-holes!"

"The *what!*" Joseph exclaimed.

"Fluke. Queer name, isn't it? But that's nothing: we have the Crinoline, the Pipsissaway, the Mud-Lark, and the Sunburst, between us and Tideoute."

"What is the name of your company, if I may ask?"

"About as queer as any of 'em, — the Chowder."

Joseph started, in spite of himself. "It seems to me I have heard of that company," he managed to say.

"O no doubt," replied the stranger. "'T isn't often quoted in the papers, but it's *known.* I'm rather proud of it, for I got it up. I was boring—boss, though—at three dollars a day, two years ago, and now I have my forty thousand a year, 'free of income tax,' as the Insurance Companies say. But then, where one is lucky like the Chowder, a hundred busts."

Joseph rapidly collected himself while the man was speaking. "I should very much like to see your wells," he said. "Will you be there a day or two from now? My name is Asten, — not that you have ever heard of it before."

"Shall be glad to hear it again, though, and to see you," said the man. "My name is Blenkinsop."

Again it was all that Joseph could do to restrain his astonishment.

"I suppose you are the President of the Chowder?" he ventured to say.

"Yes," Mr. Blenkinsop answered, "since it's a company. It was all mine at the start, but I wanted capital, and I had to work 'em."

"What other important companies are there near you?"

"None of any account, except the Fluke and the Depravity. *They* flow tolerable now, after torpedoing. To be sure, there are kites and catches with all sorts o' names, — the Penny-royal, the Ruby, the Wallholler (whatever *that* is), and the Amaranth, — ha, ha!"

"I think I have heard of the Amaranth," Joseph mildly remarked.

"Lord! are you *bit* already?" Mr. Blenkinsop exclaimed, fixing his small, sharp eyes on Joseph's face.

"I—I really don't know what you mean."

"No offence: I thought it likely, that's all. The Amaranth is Kanuck's last dodge. He keeps mighty close, but if he don't feather his nest in a hurry, at somebody's expense, *I* ain't no judge o' men!"

Joseph did not dare to mention the Amaranth again. He parted with Mr. Blenkinsop at Tarr Farm, and went on to Oil City, where he spent a day in unprofitable wanderings, and then set out up the river, first to seek the Chowder wells, and afterwards to ascertain whether there was any perennial beauty in the Amaranth.

The first thing which he remarked was the peculiar topography of the region. The Chowder property was a sloping bottom, gradually rising from the river to a range of high hills a quarter of a mile in the rear. Just above this point the river made a sharp horseshoe bend, washing the foot of the hills for a considerable distance, and then curving back again, with a second tract of bottom-land beyond. On the latter, he was informed, the Fluke wells were located. The inference was therefore irresistible that the Amaranth Company must be the happy possessor of the lofty section of hills dividing the two.

"Do they get oil up there?" he asked of Blenkinsop's foreman, pointing to the ragged, barren heights.

"They may get skunk oil, or rattlesnake oil," the man answered. "Them'll do to peddle, but you can't fill tanks with 'em. I hear they've got a company for that place,—th' Amaranth, they call it,—but any place'll do for derned fools. Why, look 'ee here! *We*'ve got seven hundred feet to bore: now, jest put twelve hundred more atop o' that, and guess whether they can even pump oil, with the Chowder and Fluke both sides of 'em! But it does for green 'uns, as well as any other place."

Joseph laughed,—a most feeble, unnatural, ridiculous laugh.

"I'll walk over that way to the Fluke," he said. "I should like to see how such things are managed."

"Then be a little on your guard with Kanuck, if you meet him," the man good-naturedly advised. "Don't ask him too many questions."

It was a hot, wearisome climb to the timber-skeletons on the summit (more like gibbets than anything else), which denoted shafts to the initiated as well as the ignorant eye. There were a dozen or more, but all were deserted.

Joseph wandered from one to the other, asking himself, as he inspected each, "Is this the splendid speculation?" What was there in that miserable, shabby, stony region, a hundred acres of which would hardly pasture a cow, whence wealth should come? Verily, as stony and as barren were the natures of the men, who on this wretched basis built their cheating schemes!

A little farther on he came to a deep ravine, cleaving the hills in twain. There was another skeleton in its bed, but several shabby individuals were gathered about it,—the first sign of life or business he had yet discovered.

He hastened down the steep declivity, the warning of the Chowder foreman recurring to his mind, yet it seemed so difficult to fix his policy in advance that he decided to leave everything to chance. As he approached he saw that the men were laborer's, with the exception of a tall, lean individual, who looked like an unfortunate clergyman. He had a sallow face, lighted by small, restless, fiery eyes, which reminded Joseph, when they turned upon him, of those of a black snake. His greeting was cold and constrained, and his manner said plainly, "The sooner you leave the better I shall be satisfied."

"This is a rough country for walking," said Joseph; "how much farther is it to the Fluke wells?"

"Just a bit," said one of the workmen.

Joseph took a seat on a stone, with the air of one who needed rest. "This well, I suppose," he remarked, "belongs to the Amaranth?"

"Who told you so?" asked the lean, dark man.

"They said below, at the Chowder, that the Amaranth was up here."

"Did Blenkinsop send you this way?" the man asked again.

"Nobody sent me," Joseph replied. "I am a stranger, taking a look at the oil country. I have never before been in this part of the State."

"May I ask your name?"

"Asten," said Joseph, unthinkingly.

"Asten! I think I know where that name belongs. Let me see."

The man pulled out a large dirty envelope from his breast-pocket, ran over several papers, unfolded one, and presently asked,—

"Joseph Asten?"

"Yes." (Joseph set his teeth, and silently cursed his want of forethought.)

"Proprietor of ten thousand dollars' worth of stock in the Amaranth! Who sent you here?"

His tone, though meant to be calm, was fierce and menacing. Joseph rose, scanned the faces of the workmen, who listened with a malicious curiosity, and finally answered, with a candor which seemed to impress, while it evidently disappointed the questioner:—

"No one sent me, and no one, beyond my own family, knows that I am here. I am a farmer, not a speculator. I was induced to take the stock from representations which have not been fulfilled, and which, I am now convinced, never will be fulfilled. My habit is, when I cannot get the truth from others, to ascertain it for myself. I presume you are Mr. Kanuck?"

The man did not answer immediately, but the quick, intelligent glance of one of the workmen showed Joseph that his surmise was correct. Mr. Kanuck conversed apart with the men, apparently giving private orders, and then, said, with a constrained civility:—

"If you are bound for the Fluke, Mr. Asten, I will join you. I am also going in that direction, and we can talk on the way."

They toiled up the opposite side of the ravine in silence. When they had reached the top and taken breath, Mr. Kanuck commenced:—

"I must infer that you have little faith in anything being realized from the Amaranth. Any man, ignorant of the technicalities of boring, might be discouraged by the external appearance of things; and I shall therefore not endeavor to explain to you my grounds of hope, unless you will agree to join me for a month or two and become practically acquainted with the locality and the modes of labor."

"That is unnecessary," Joseph replied.

"You being a farmer, of course I could not expect it. On the other hand, I think I can appreciate your,—disappointment, if we must call it so, and I should be willing, under certain conditions, to save you, not from positive loss, because I do not admit the possibility of that, but from what, at present, may seem loss to you. Do I make my meaning clear?"

"Entirely," Joseph replied, "except as to the conditions."

"We are dealing on the square, I take it?"

"Of course."

"Then," said Mr. Kanuck, "I need only intimate to you how important it is that I should develop our prospects. To do this, the faith of the principal stockholders must not be disturbed, otherwise the funds without which the prospects cannot be developed may fail me at the critical moment. Your hasty and unintelligent impressions, if expressed in a reckless manner, might do much to bring about such a catastrophe. I must therefore stipulate that you keep such impressions to yourself. Let me speak to you as man to man, and ask you if your expressions, not being founded on knowledge, would be honest? So far from it, you will be bound in all fairness, in consideration of my releasing you and restoring you what you have ventured, to adopt and disseminate the views of an expert,—namely, mine."

"Let me put it into fewer words," said Joseph. "You will buy my stock, repaying me what I have disbursed, if, on my return, I say nothing of what I have seen, and express my perfect faith (adopting your views) in the success of the Amaranth?"

"You have stated the conditions a little barely, perhaps, but not incorrectly. I only ask for perfect fairness, as between man and man."

"One question first, Mr. Kanuck. Does Mr. Blessing know the *real* prospects of the Amaranth?"

"No man more thoroughly, I assure you, Mr. Asten. Indeed, without Mr. Blessing's enthusiastic concurrence in the enterprise, I doubt whether we could have carried the work so far towards success. His own stock, I may say to you,—since we understand each other,—was earned by his efforts. If you know him intimately, you know also that he has no visible means of support. But he has what is much more important to us,—a thorough knowledge of men and their means."

He rubbed his hands, and laughed softly. They had been walking rapidly during the conversation, and now came suddenly upon the farthest crest of the hills, where the ridge fell away to the bottom occupied by the Fluke wells. Both paused at this point.

"On the square, then!" said Mr. Kanuck, offering his hand. "Tell me where you will be to-morrow morning, and our business can be settled in five minutes. You will carry out your part of the bargain, as man to man, when you find that I carry out mine."

"Do you take me for an infernal scoundrel?" cried Joseph, boiling over with disgust and rage.

Mr. Kanuck stepped back a pace or two. His sallow face became livid, and there was murder in his eyes. He put his hand into his breast, and Joseph, facing him, involuntarily did the same. Not until long afterwards, when other experiences had taught him the significance of the movement, did he remember what it then meant.

"So! that's your game, is it?" his antagonist said, hissing the words through his teeth. "A spy, after all! Or a detective, perhaps? I was a fool to trust a milk-and-water face: but one thing I tell you,—you may get away, but come back again if you dare!"

Joseph said nothing, but gazed steadily in the man's eyes, and did not move from his position so long as he was within sight. Then, breathing deeply, as if relieved from the dread of an unknown danger, he swiftly descended the hill.

That evening, as he sat in the bar-room of a horrible shanty (called a hotel), farther up the river, he noticed a pair of eyes fixed intently upon him: they belonged to one of the workmen in the Amaranth ravine. The man made an almost imperceptible signal, and left the room. Joseph followed him.

"Hush!" whispered the former. "Don't come back to the hill; and get away from here to-morrow morning, if you can!" With these words he darted off and disappeared in the darkness.

The counsel was unnecessary. Joseph, with all his inexperience of the world, saw plainly that his only alternatives were loss—or connivance. Nothing was to be gained by following the vile business any further. He took the earliest possible train, and by the afternoon of the following day found himself again in the city.

He was conscious of no desire to meet Mr. Blessing, yet the pressure of his recent experience seemed to drive him irresistibly in that direction. When he rang the bell, it was with the hope that he should find nobody at home. Mr. Blessing, however, answered the summons, and after the first expression of surprise, ushered him into the parlor.

"I am quite alone," he said; "Mrs. Blessing is passing the evening with her sister, Mrs. Woollish, and Clementina is still at Long Branch. I believe it is as good as settled that we are to lose her; at least she has written to inquire the extent of my available funds, which, in her case, is tantamount to—very much more."

Joseph determined to avoid all digressions, and insist on the Amaranth speculation, once for all, being clearly discussed. He saw that his father-in-law became more uneasy and excited as he advanced in the story of his journey, and, when it was concluded, did not seem immediately prepared to reply. His suspicions, already aroused by Mr. Kanuck's expressions, were confirmed, and a hard, relentless feeling of hostility took possession of his heart.

"I—I really must look into this," Mr. Blessing stammered, at last. "It seems incredible: pardon me, but I would doubt the statements, did they come from other lips than yours. It is as if I had nursed a dove in my bosom, and unexpectedly found it to be a—a basilisk!"

"It can be no serious loss to you," said Joseph, "since you received your stock in return for services."

"That is true: I was not thinking of myself. The real sting of the cockatrice is, that I have innocently misled you."

"Yet I understood you to say you had ventured your all?"

"My all of hope—my all of expectation!" Mr. Blessing cried. "I dreamed I had overtaken the rainbow at last; but this—this is senna—quassia—aloes! My nature is so confiding that I accept the possibilities of the future as present realities, and build upon them as if they were Quincy granite. And yet, with all my experience, my acknowledged sagacity, my acquaintance with the hidden labyrinths of finance, it seems impossible that I can be so deceived! There must be some hideous misunderstanding: I have calculated all the elements, prognosticated all the planetary aspects, so to speak, and have not found a whisper of failure!"

"You omitted one very important element," Joseph said.

"What is that? I might have employed a detective, it is true—"

"No!" Joseph replied. "Honesty!"

Mr. Blessing fell back in his chair, weeping bitterly.

"I deserve this!" he exclaimed. "I will not resent it. I forgive you in advance of the time when you shall recognize my sincere, my heartfelt wish to serve you! Go, go: let me not recriminate! I meant to be, and still mean to be, your friend: but spare my too confiding child!"

Without a word of good-by, Joseph took his hat and hastened from the house. At every step the abyss of dishonesty seemed to open deeper before his feet. Spare the too confiding child! Father and daughter were alike: both mean, both treacherous, both unpardonably false to him.

With such feelings he left the city next morning, and made his way homewards.

CHAPTER XXIII
JULIA'S EXPERIMENT

In the mean time the Hopetons had left for the sea-shore, and the two women, after a drive to Magnolia, remained quietly on the farm. Julia employed the days in studying Lucy with a soft, stealthy, unremitting watchfulness which the latter could not suspect, since, in the first place, it was a faculty quite unknown to her, and, secondly, it would have seemed absurd because inexplicable. Neither could she guess with what care Julia's manner and conversation were adapted to her own. She was only surprised to find so much earnest desire to correct faults, such artless transparency of nature. Thus an interest quite friendly took the place of her former repulsion of feeling, of which she began to be sincerely ashamed.

Moreover, Julia's continual demonstration of her love for Joseph, from which Lucy at first shrank with a delicate tremor of the heart, soon ceased to affect her. Nay, it rather seemed to interpose a protecting barrier between her present and the painful memory of her past self. She began to suspect that all regret was now conquered, and rejoiced in the sense of strength which could only thus be made clear to her mind. Her feeling towards Joseph became that of a sister or a dear woman friend; there could be no harm in cherishing it; she found a comfort in speaking to Julia of his upright, unselfish character, his guilelessness and kindness of heart.

The work upon the house was nearly finished, but new and more alarming bills began to come in; and worse was in store. There was a chimney-piece, "the loveliest ivory veins through the green marble," Julia said, which she had ordered from the city; there were boxes and packages of furniture already on hand, purchased without Joseph's knowledge and with entire faith in the virtues of the Amaranth. Although she still clung to that faith with a desperate grip, the sight of the boxes did not give her the same delight as she had felt in ordering them. She saw the necessity of being prepared, in advance, for either alternative. It was not in her nature to dread any scene or circumstance of life (although she had found the *appearance* of timidity very available, and could assume it admirably); the question which perplexed her was, how to retain and strengthen her ascendency over Joseph?

It is needless to say that the presence of Lucy Henderson was a part of her plan, although she held a more important service in reserve. Lucy's warm, frank expressions of friendship for Joseph gave her great satisfaction, and she was exhaustless in inventing ways to call them forth.

"You look quite like another person, Lucy," she would say; "I really think the rest has done you good."

"I am sure of it," Lucy answered.

"Then you must be in no hurry to leave. We must build you up, as the doctors say; and, besides, if—if this speculation *should* be unfortunate—O, I don't dare to think of it!—there will be such a comfort to me, and I am sure to Joseph also, in having you here until we have learned to bear it. We should not allow our minds to dwell on it so much, you know; we should make an exertion to hide our disappointment in your presence, and that would be *such* a help! Now you will say I am borrowing trouble, but do, pray, make allowances for me, Lucy! Think how everything has been kept from me that I ought to have known!"

"Of course, I will stay a little while for your sake," Lucy answered; "but Joseph is a man, and most men bear bad luck easily. He would hardly thank me for condoling with him."

"O, no, no!" Julia cried; "he thinks *everything* of you! He was *so* anxious for you to come here! he said to me, 'Lucy Henderson is a noble, true-hearted girl, and you will love her at once,' as I did, Lucy, when I first saw you, but without knowing why, as I now do."

A warm color came into Lucy's face, but she only shook her head and said nothing.

The two women had just risen from the breakfast-table the next morning, when a shadow fell into the room through the front window, and a heavy step was heard on the stone pavement of the veranda. Julia gave a little start and shriek, and seized Lucy's arm. The door opened and Joseph was there. He had risen before daybreak and taken the earliest train from the city. He had scarcely slept for two nights; his face was stern and haggard, and the fatigue, instead of exhausting, had only added to his excitement.

Julia sprang forward, threw her arm around, him, and kissed him repeatedly. He stood still and passively endured the caress, without returning it; then, stepping forward, he gave his hand to Lucy. She felt that it was cold and moist; and she did not attempt to repress the quick sympathy which came into her face and voice.

Julia guessed something of the truth instantly, and nothing but the powerful necessity of continuing to play her part enabled her to conceal the bitter anger which the contrast between Joseph's greeting to her and to Lucy aroused in her heart. She stood for a moment as if paralyzed, but in reality to collect herself; then, approaching her husband, she stammered forth: "O, Joseph—I'm afraid—I don't dare to ask you what—what news you bring. You didn't write—I've been so uneasy—and now I see from your face—that something is wrong."

He did not answer.

"Don't tell me all at once, if it's very bad!" she then cried: "but, no! it's my duty to hear it, my duty to bear it,—Lucy has taught me that,—tell me all, tell me *all*, this moment!"

"You and your father have ruined me: that is all."

"Joseph!" The word sounded like the essence of tender protest, of heartbreaking reproach. Lucy rose quietly and moved towards the door.

"Don't leave me, Lucy!" was Julia's appeal.

"It is better that I should go," Lucy answered, in a faint voice, and left the room.

"But, Joseph," Julia resumed, with a wild, distracted air, "why do you say such terrible things? I really do not know what you mean. What have you learned? what have you seen?"

"I have seen the Amaranth!"

"Well! Is there no oil?"

"O yes, plenty of oil!" he laughed; "skunk oil and rattlesnake oil! It is one of the vilest cheats that the Devil ever put into the minds of bad men."

"O, poor pa!" Julia cried; "what a terrible blow to him!"

"'Poor pa!' Yes, my discovery of the cheat *is* a terrible blow to 'poor pa,'—he did not calculate on its being found out so soon. When I learned from Kanuck that all the stock he holds was given to him for services,—that is, for getting the money out of the pockets of innocents like myself,—you may judge how much pity I feel for poor pa! I told him the fact to his face, last night, and he admitted it."

"Then," said Julia, "if the others know nothing, he may be able to sell his stock to-day,—his and yours; and we may not lose much after all."

"I should have sent *you* to the oil region, instead of going myself," Joseph answered, with a sneer. "You and Kanuck would soon have come to terms. He offered to take my stock off my hands, provided I would go back to the city and make such a report of the speculation as he would dictate."

"*And you didn't do it?*" Julia's voice rose almost to a scream, as the words burst involuntarily from her lips.

The expression on Joseph's face showed her that she had been rash; but the words were said, and she could only advance, not recede.

"It is *perfectly* legitimate in business," she continued. "Every investment in the Amaranth was a venture,—every stockholder knew that he risked losing his money! There is not one that would not save himself in that way, if he had the chance. But you pride yourself on being so much better than other men! Mr. Chaffinch is right; you have what he calls a 'moral pride'! You—"

"Stop!" Joseph interrupted. "Who was it that professed such concern about my faith? Who sent Mr. Chaffinch to insult me?"

"Faith and business are two different things: all the churches know that. There was Mr. Sanctus, in the city: he subscribed ten thousand dollars to the Church of the Acceptance: he couldn't pay it, and they levied on his property, and sold him out of house and home! Really, you are as ignorant of the world as a baby!"

"God keep me so, then!" he exclaimed.

"However," she resumed, after a pause, "since you insist on our bearing the loss, I shall expect of your moral pride that you bear it patiently, if not cheerfully. It is far from being ruin to us. The rise in property will very likely balance it, and you will still be worth what you were."

"That is not all," he said. "I will not mention my greatest loss, for you are incapable of understanding it; but how much else have you saddled me with? Let me have a look at it!"

He crossed the hall and entered the new apartment, Julia following. Joseph inspected the ceiling, the elaborate and overladen cornices, the marble chimney-piece, and finally peered into the boxes and packages, not trusting himself to speak while the extent of the absurd splendor to which she had committed him grew upon his mind. Finally he said, striving to make his voice calm, although it trembled in his throat: "Since you were so free to make all these purchases, perhaps you will tell me how they are to be paid for?"

"Let me manage it, then," she answered. "There is no hurry. These country mechanics are always impatient,—*I* should call them impertinent, and I should like to teach them a lesson. Sellers are under obligations to the buyers, and they are bound to be accommodating. They have so many bills which are never paid, that an extension of time is the least they can do. Why, they will always wait a year, two years, three years, rather than lose."

"I suppose so."

"Then," said Julia, deceived by Joseph's quiet tone, "their profits are so enormous, that it would only be fair to reduce the bills. I am sure, that if I were to mention that you were embarrassed by heavy losses, and press them hard, they would compromise with me on a moderate amount. You know they allow what is called a margin for losses,—pa told me, but I forget how much,—they always expect to lose a certain percentage; and, of course, it can make no difference by whom they lose it. You understand, don't you?"

"Yes: it is very plain."

"Pa could help me to get both a reduction and an extension of time. The bills have not all been sent, and it will be better to wait two or three months after they have come in. If the dealers are a little uneasy in advance, they will be all the readier to compromise afterwards."

Joseph walked up and down the hollow room, with his hands clasped behind his back and his eyes fixed upon the floor. Suddenly he stopped before her and said: "There is another way."

"Not a better one, I am certain."

"The furniture has not yet been unpacked, and can be returned to them uninjured. Then the bills need not be paid at all."

"And we should be the laughing-stock of the neighborhood!" she cried, her eyes flashing. "I *never* heard of anything so ridiculous! If the worst comes to the worst, you can sell Bishop those fifty acres over the hill, which he stands ready to take, any day. But you'd rather have a dilapidated house,—no parlor,—guests received in the dining-room and the kitchen,—the Hopetons and your friends, the Helds, sneering at us behind our backs! And what would your credit be worth? We shall not even get trusted for groceries at the village store, if you leave things as they are!"

Joseph groaned, speaking to himself rather than answering her: "Is there no way out of this? What is done is done; shall I submit to it, and try to begin anew? or—"

He did not finish the sentence. Julia turned her head, so that only the chimney-piece and the furniture could see the sparkle of triumph in her eyes. She felt that she had maintained her position; and, what was far more, she now clearly saw the course by which she could secure it.

She left the room, drawing a full breath of relief as the door closed behind her. The first shock of the evil news was over, and it had not fallen quite so heavily as she had feared. There were plenty of devices in store whereby all that was lost might be recovered. Had not her life at home been an unbroken succession of devices? Was she not seasoned to all manner of ups and downs, and wherefore should this first failure disconcert her? The loss of the money was, in reality, much less important to her than the loss of her power over Joseph. Weak as she had supposed him to he, he had shown a fierce and unexpected resistance, which must be suppressed *now*, or it might crush her whole plan of life. It seemed to her that he was beginning to waver: should she hasten a scheme by which she meant to entrap him into submission,—a subtle and dangerous scheme, which must either wholly succeed, or, wholly failing, involve her in its failure?

Rapidly turning over the question in her mind, she entered her bedroom. Locking the door, she walked directly to the looking-glass; the curtain was drawn from the window, and a strong light fell upon her face.

"This will never do!" she said to herself. "The anxiety and excitement have made me thin again, and I seem to have no color." She unfastened her dress, bared her neck, and pushed the ringlets behind her ears. "I look pinched; a little more, and I shall look old. If I were a perfect brunette or a perfect blonde, there would be less difficulty; but I have the most provoking, unmanageable complexion! I must bring on the crisis at once, and then see if I can't fill out these hollows."

She heard the front door opening, and presently saw Joseph on the lawn. He looked about for a moment, with a heavy, bewildered air, and then slowly turned towards the garden. She withdrew from the window, hesitated a moment, murmured to herself, "I will try, there cannot be a better time!" and then, burying her face in her hands and sobbing, rushed to Lucy's room.

"O Lucy!" she cried, "help me, or I am lost! How can I tell you? it is harder than I ever dreamed!"

"Is the loss so very serious,—so much more than you feared?" Lucy asked.

"Not that—O, if that were all! But Joseph—" Here Julia's sobs became almost hysterical. "He is so cruel; I *did* advise him, as I told you, for *his* sake, and now he says that pa and I have combined to cheat him! I don't think he knows how dreadful his words are. I would sooner die than hear any more of them! Go to him, Lucy; he is in the garden; perhaps he will listen to you. I am afraid, and I never thought I should be afraid of *him*!"

"It is very, very sad," said Lucy. "But if he is in such an excited condition he will surely resent my coming. What can I say?"

"Say only what you heard me speak! Tell him of my anxiety, my self-reproach! Tell him that even if he *will* believe that pa meant to deceive him, he must not believe it of me! You know, Lucy, how he wrongs me in his thoughts; if you knew how hard it is to be wronged by a husband, you would pity me!"

"I do pity you, Julia, from my very heart; and the proof of it is, that I will try to do what you ask, against my own sense of its prudence. If Joseph repels my interference, I shall not blame him."

"Heaven bless you, Lucy! He will not repel you, he cannot!" Julia sobbed. "I will lie down and try to grow calm." She rose from the bed, upon which she had flung herself, and tottered through the door. When she had reached her own room, she again looked at her image in the glass, nodded and smiled.

Lucy walked slowly along the garden paths, plucking a flower or two, and irresolute how to approach Joseph. At last, descending the avenue of box, she found him seated in the semicircular enclosure, gazing steadfastly down the valley, but (she was sure) not seeing the landscape. As he turned his head at her approach, she noticed that his eyelids were reddened and his lips compressed with an expression of intense pain.

"Sit down, Lucy; I am a grim host, to-day," he said, with a melancholy attempt at a smile.

Lucy had come to him with a little womanly indignation, for Julia's sake, in her heart; but it vanished utterly, and the tears started into her eyes. For a moment she found it impossible to speak.

"I shall not talk of my ignorance any more, as I once did," Joseph continued. "If there is a class in the school of the world, graded according to experience of human meanness and treachery and falsehood, I ought to stand at the head."

Lucy stretched out her hand in protest. "Do not speak so bitterly, Joseph; it pains me to hear you."

"How would you have me speak?"

"As a man who will not see ruin before him because a part of his property happens to slip from him,—nay, if all were lost! I always took you to be liberal, Joseph, never careful of money for money's sake, and I cannot understand how your nature should be changed now, even though you have been the victim of some dishonesty."

"'Some dishonesty'! You are thinking only of money: what term would you give to the betrayal of a heart, the ruin of a life?"

"Surely, Joseph, you do not, you cannot mean—"

"My wife, of course. It needed no guessing."

"Joseph!" Lucy cried, seizing the opportunity, "indeed you do her wrong! I know what anxiety she has suffered during your absence. She blamed herself for having advised you to risk so much in an uncertain speculation, dreaded your disappointment, resolved to atone for it, if she could! She may have been rash and thoughtless, but she never meant to deceive you. If you are disappointed in some qualities, you should not shut your eyes and refuse to see others. I know, now, that I have myself not been fair in my judgment of Julia. A nearer acquaintance has led me to conceive what disadvantages of education, for which she is not responsible, she is obliged to overcome: she sees, she admits them, and she *will* overcome them. You, as her husband, are bound to show her a patient kindness—"

"Enough!" Joseph interrupted; "I see that you have touched pitch, also. Lucy, your first instinct was right. The woman whom I am bound to look upon as my wife is false and selfish in every fibre of her nature; how false and selfish I only can know, for to *me* she takes off her mask!"

"Do you believe *me*, then?" Lucy's words were slightly defiant. She had not quite understood the allusion to touching pitch, and Joseph's indifference to her advocacy seemed to her unfeeling.

"I begin to fear that Philip was right," said Joseph, not heeding her question. "Life is relentless: ignorance or crime, it is all the same. And if God cares less about our individual wrongs than we flatter ourselves He does, what do we gain by further endurance? Here is Lucy Henderson, satisfied that my wife is a suffering angel; thinks *my* nature is changed, that I am cold-hearted and cruel, while I know Lucy to be true and noble, and deceived by the very goodness of her own heart!"

He lifted his head, looked in her face a moment, and then went on:—

"I am sick of masks; we all wear them. Do you want to know the truth, Lucy? When I look back I can see it very clearly, now. A little more than a year ago the one girl who began to live in my thoughts was *you*! Don't interrupt me: I am only speaking of what *was*. When I went to Warriner's, it was in the hope of meeting you, not Julia Blessing. It was not yet love that I felt, but I think it would have grown to that, if I had not been led away by the cunningest arts ever a woman devised. I will not speculate on what might have been: if I had loved you, perhaps there would have been no return: had there been, I should have darkened the life of a friend. But this I say; I honor and esteem you, Lucy, and the loss of your friendship, if I now lose it, is another evil service which my wife has done me."

Joseph little suspected how he was torturing Lucy. She must have been more than woman, had not a pang of wild regret for the lost fortune, and a sting of bitter resentment against the woman who had stolen it, wrung her heart. She became deadly pale, and felt that her whole body was trembling.

"Joseph," she said, "you should not, must not, speak so to me."

"I suppose not," he answered, letting his head sink wearily; "it is certainly not conventional; but it is true, for all that! I could tell you the whole story, for I can read it backwards, from now to the beginning, without misunderstanding a word. It would make no difference; she is simple, natural, artless, amiable, for all the rest of the world, while to me—"

There was such despondency in his voice and posture, that Lucy, now longing more than ever to cheer him, and yet discouraged by the failure of her first attempt, felt sorely troubled.

"You mistake me, Joseph," she said, at last, "if you think you have lost my friendship, my sincerest sympathy. I can see that your disappointment is a bitter one, and my prayer is that you will not make it bitterer by thrusting from you the hopeful and cheerful spirit you once showed. We all have our sore trials."

Lucy found her own words very mechanical, but they were the only ones, that came to her lips. Joseph did not answer; he still sat, stooping, with his elbows on his knees, and his forehead resting on his palms.

"If I am deceived in Julia," she began again, "it is better to judge too kindly than too harshly. I know you cannot change your sentence against her now, nor, perhaps, very soon. But you are bound to her for life, and you must labor—it is your sacred duty—to make that life smoother and brighter for both. I do not know how, and I have no right to condemn you if you fail. But, Joseph, make the attempt now, when the most unfortunate experience that is likely to come to you is over; make it, and it may chance that, little by little, the old confidence will return, and you will love her again."

Joseph started to his feet. "Love her!" he exclaimed, with suppressed passion,—"love her! I hate her!"

There was a hissing, rattling sound, like that of some fierce animal at bay. The thick foliage of two of the tall box-trees was violently parted. The branches snapped and gave way: Julia burst through, and stood before them.

CHAPTER XXIV
FATE

The face that so suddenly glared upon them was that of a Gorgon. The ringlets were still pushed behind her ears and the narrowness of the brow was entirely revealed; her eyes were full of cold, steely light; the nostrils were violently drawn in, and the lips contracted, as if in a spasm, so that the teeth were laid bare. Her hands were clenched, and there was a movement in her throat as of imprisoned words or cries; but for a moment no words came.

Lucy, who had started to her feet at the first sound, felt the blood turn chill in her veins, and fell, rather than sank, upon the seat again.

Joseph was hardly surprised, and wholly reckless. This eavesdropping was nothing worse than he already knew; indeed, there was rather a comfort in perceiving that he had not overestimated her capacity for treachery. There was now no limit; anything was possible.

"There is *one* just law, after all," he said, "the law that punishes listeners. You have heard the truth, for once. You have snared and trapped me, but I don't take to my captor more kindly than any other animal. From this moment I choose my own path, and if you still wish to appear as my wife, you must adapt your life to mine!"

"You mean to brazen it out, do you!" Julia cried, in a strange, hoarse, unnatural voice. "That's not so easy! I have not listened to no purpose: I have a hold upon your precious 'moral pride' at last!"

Joseph laughed scornfully.

"Yes, laugh, but it is in my hands to make or break you! There is enough decent sentiment in this neighborhood to crush a married man who dares to make love to an unmarried girl! As to the girl who sits still and listens to it, I say nothing; her reputation is no concern of mine!"

Lucy uttered a faint cry of horror.

"If you choose to be so despicable," said Joseph, "you will force me to set my truth against your falsehood. Wherever you tell your story, I shall follow with mine. It will be a wretched, a degrading business; but for the sake of Lucy's good name, I have no alternative. I have borne suspicion, misrepresentation, loss of credit,—brought upon me by you,—patiently, because they affected only myself; but since I am partly responsible in bringing to this house a guest for your arts to play upon and entrap, I am doubly bound to protect her against you. But I tell you, Julia, beware! I am desperate; and it is ill meddling with a desperate man! You may sneer at my moral pride, but you dare not forget that I have another quality,—manly self-respect,—which it will be dangerous to offend."

If Julia did not recognize, in that moment, that her subject had become her master, it was because the real, unassumed rage which convulsed her did not allow her to perceive anything clearly. Her first impulse was to scream and shriek, that servant and farm-hand might hear her, and then to repeat her accusation before them; but Joseph's last words, and the threatening sternness of his voice withheld her.

"So?" she said, at last; "*this* is the man who was all truth, and trust, and honor! With you the proverb seems to be reversed; it's off with the new love and on with the old. You can insult and threaten me in *her* presence! Well—go on: play out your little love-scene: I shall not interrupt you. I have heard enough to darken my life from this day!"

She walked away from them, up the avenue. Her dress was torn, her arms scratched and bleeding. She had played her stake and failed,—miserably, hopelessly failed. Her knees threatened to give way under her at every step, but she forced herself to walk erect, and thus reached the house without once looking back.

Joseph and Lucy mechanically followed her with their eyes. Then they turned and gazed at each other a moment without speaking. Lucy was very pale, and the expression of horror had not yet left her face.

"She told me to come to you," she stammered. "She begged me, with tears, to try and soften your anger against her; and then—oh, it is monstrous!"

"Now I see the plan!" Joseph exclaimed; "and I, in my selfish recklessness, saying what there was no need to utter, have almost done as she calculated,—have exposed you to this outrage! Why should I have recalled the past at all? I was not taking off a mask, I was only showing a scar—no, not even a scar, but a bruise!—which I ought to have forgotten. Forget it, too, Lucy, and, if you can, forgive me!"

"It is easy to forgive—everything but my own blindness," Lucy answered. "But there is one thing which I must do immediately: I must leave this house!"

Joseph and His Friend | 183

"I see that," said Joseph, sadly. Then, as if speaking to himself, he murmured: "Who knows what friends will come to it in the future? Well, I will hear what can be borne; and afterwards,—there is Philip's valley. A free outlaw is better than a fettered outlaw!"

Lucy feared that his mind was wandering. He straightened himself to his full height, drew a deep breath, and exclaimed: "Action is a sedative in such cases, isn't it? Dennis has gone to the mill; I will get the other horse from the field and drive you home. Or, stay! will you not go to Philip Held's cottage for a day or two? I think his sister asked you to come."

"No, no!" cried Lucy; "you must not go! I will wait for Dennis."

"No one must suspect what has happened here this morning, unless Julia compels me to make it known, and I don't think she will. It is, therefore, better that I should take you. It will put me, I hope, in a more rational frame of mind. Go quietly to your room and make your preparations. I will see Julia, and if there is no further scene now, there will be none of the kind henceforth. She is cunning when she is calm."

On reaching the house Joseph went directly to his wife's bed-room. The necessity of an immediate interview could not be avoided, since Lucy was to leave. When he opened the door, Julia, who was bending over an open drawer of her bureau, started up with a little cry of alarm. She closed the drawer hastily, and began to arrange her hair at the mirror. Her face in the glass was flushed, but its expression was sullen and defiant.

"Julia," he said, as coolly as possible, "I am going to take Lucy home. Of course you understand that she cannot stay here an hour longer. You overheard my words to her, and you know just how much they were worth. I expect now, that—for *your* sake as much as hers or mine—you will behave towards her at parting in such a way that the servants may find no suggestions of gossip or slander."

"And if I don't choose to obey you?"

"I am not commanding. I propose a course which your own mind must find sensible. You have 'a deuced sharp intellect,' as your father said, on our wedding-day."

Joseph bit his tongue: he felt that he might have omitted this sting. But he was so little accustomed to victory, that he did not guess how thoroughly he had already conquered.

"Pa loved me, nevertheless," she said, and burst into tears.

Her emotion seemed real, but he mistrusted it.

"What can I do?" she sobbed: "I will try. I thought I was your wife, but I am not much more than your slave."

The foolish pity again stole into Joseph's heart, although he set his teeth and clenched his hands against it. "I am going for the horse," he said, in a kinder tone. "When I come back from this drive, this afternoon, I hope I shall find you willing to discuss our situation dispassionately, as I mean to do. We have not known each other fairly before to-day, and our plan of life must be rearranged."

It was a relief to walk forth, across the silent, sunny fields; and Joseph had learned to accept a slight relief as a substitute for happiness. The feeling that the inevitable crisis was over, gave him, for the first time in months, a sense of liberation. There was still a dreary and painful task before him, and he hardly knew why he should be so cheerful; but the bright, sweet currents of his blood were again in motion, and the weight upon his heart was lifted by some impatient, joyous energy.

The tempting vision of Philip's valley, which had haunted him from time to time, faded away. The angry tumult through which he had passed appeared to him like a fever, and he rejoiced consciously in the beginning of his spiritual convalescence. If he could simply suspend Julia's active interference in his life, he might learn to endure his remaining duties. He was yet young; and how much strength and knowledge had come to him — through sharpest pain, it was true — in a single year! Would he willingly return to his boyish innocence of the world, if that year could be erased from his life? He was not quite sure. Yet his nature had not lost the basis of that innocent time, and he felt that he must still build his future years upon it.

Thus meditating, he caught the obedient horse, led him to the barn, and harnessed him to the light carriage which Julia was accustomed to use. His anxiety concerning her probable demeanor returned as he entered the house. The two servant-women were both engaged, in the hall, in some sweeping or scouring operation, and might prove to be very inconvenient witnesses. The workmen in the new parlor — fortunately, he thought — were absent that day.

Lucy Henderson, dressed for the journey, sat in the dining-room. "I think I will go to Madeline Held for a day or two," she said; "I made a half-promise to visit her after your return."

"Where is Julia?"

"In her bed-room. I have not seen her. I knocked at the door, but there was no answer."

Joseph's trouble returned. "I will see her myself," he said, sternly; "she forgets what is due to a guest."

"No, I will go again," Lucy urged, rising hastily; "perhaps she did not hear me."

She followed him into the hall. Scarcely had he set his foot upon the first step of the staircase, when the bed-room door above suddenly burst open, and Julia, with a shriek of mortal terror, tottered down to the landing. Her face was ashy, and the dark-blue rings around her sunken eyes made them seem almost like the large sockets of a skull. She leaned against the railing, breathing short and hard.

Joseph sprang up the steps, but as he approached her she put out her right hand, and pushed against his breast with all her force, crying out: "Go away! You have killed me!"

The next moment She fell senseless upon the landing.

Joseph knelt and tried to lift her. "Good God! she is dead!" he exclaimed.

"No," said Lucy, after taking Julia's wrist, "it is only a fainting fit. Bring some water, Susan."

The frightened woman, who had followed them, rushed down the stairs.

"But she must be ill, very ill," Lucy continued. "This is not an ordinary swoon. Perhaps the violent excitement has brought about some internal injury. You must send for a physician as soon as possible."

"And Dennis not here! I ought not to leave her; what shall I do?"

"Go yourself, and instantly! The carriage is ready. I will stay and do all that can be done during your absence."

Joseph delayed until, under the influence of air and water, Julia began to recover consciousness. Then he understood Lucy's glance,—the women were present and she dared not speak,—that he should withdraw before Julia could recognize him.

He did not spare the horse, but the hilly road tried his patience. It was between two and three miles to the house of the nearest physician, and he only arrived, anxious and breathless, to find that the gentleman had been called away to attend another patient. Joseph was obliged to retrace part of his road, and drive some distance in the opposite direction, in order to summon a second. Here, however, he was more fortunate. The physician was just sitting down to an early dinner, which he persisted in finishing, assuring Joseph, after ascertaining such symptoms of the case as the latter was able to describe, that it was probably a nervous attack, "a modified form of hysteria." Notwithstanding he violated his own theory of digestion by eating rapidly, the minutes seemed intolerably long. Then his own horse must be harnessed to his own sulky, during which time he prepared a few doses of valerian, belladonna, and other palliatives, which he supposed might be needed.

Meanwhile, Lucy and the woman had placed Julia in her own bed, and applied such domestic restoratives as they could procure, but without any encouraging effect. Julia appeared to be conscious, but she shook her head when they spoke to her, and even, so Lucy imagined, attempted to turn it away. She refused the tea, the lavender and ginger they brought, and only drank water in long, greedy draughts. In a little while she started up, with clutchings and incoherent cries, and then slowly sank back again, insensible.

The second period of unconsciousness was longer and more difficult to overcome. Lucy began to be seriously alarmed as an hour, two hours, passed by, and Joseph did not return. Dennis was despatched in search of him, carrying also a hastily pencilled note to Madeline Held, and then Lucy, finding that she could do nothing more, took her seat by the window and watched the lane, counting the seconds, one by one, as they were ticked off by the clock in the hall.

Finally a horse's head appeared above the hedge, where it curved around the shoulder of the hill: then the top of a carriage,—Joseph at last! The physician's sulky was only a short distance in the rear. Lucy hurried down and met Joseph at the gate.

"No better,—worse, I fear," she said, answering his look.

"Dr. Hartman," he replied,—"Worrall was away from home,—thinks it is probably a nervous attack. In that case it can soon be relieved."

"I hope so, but I fancy there is danger."

The doctor now arrived, and after hearing Lucy's report, shook his head. "It is not an ordinary case of hysteria," he remarked; "let me see her at once."

When they entered the room Julia opened her eyes languidly, fixed them on Joseph, and slowly lifted her hand to her head. "What has happened to me?" she murmured, in a hardly audible whisper.

"You had a fainting fit," he answered, "and I have brought the doctor. This is Dr. Hartman; you do not know him, but he will help you; tell him how you feel, Julia!"

"Cold!" she said, "cold! Sinking down somewhere! *Will* he lift me up?"

The physician made a close examination, but seemed to become more perplexed as he advanced. He administered only a slight stimulant, and then withdrew from the bedside. Lucy and the servant left the room, at his request, to prepare some applications.

"There is something unusual here," he whispered, drawing Joseph aside. "She has been sinking rapidly since the first attack. The vital force is very low: it is in conflict with some secret enemy, and it cannot resist much longer, unless we discover that enemy at once. I will do my best to save her, but I do not yet see how."

He was interrupted by a noise from the bed. Julia was vainly trying to rise: her eyes were wide and glaring. "No, no!" came from her lips, "I will not die! I heard you. Joseph, I will try—to be different—but—I must live—for that!"

Then her utterance became faint and indistinct, and she relapsed into unconsciousness. The physician re-examined her with a grave, troubled face. "She need not be conscious," he said, "for the next thing I shall do. I will not interrupt this syncope at once; it may, at least, prolong the struggle. What have they been giving her?"

He picked up, one by one, the few bottles of the household pharmacy which stood upon the bureau. Last of all, he found an empty glass shoved behind one of the supports of the mirror. He looked into it, held it against the light, and was about to set it down again, when he fancied that there was a misty appearance on the bottom, as if from some delicate sediment. Stepping to the window, he saw that he had not been mistaken. He collected a few of the minute granulations on the tip of his forefinger, touched them to his tongue, and, turning quickly to Joseph, whispered:—

"She is poisoned!"

"Impossible!" Joseph exclaimed; "she could not have been so mad!"

"It is as I tell you! This form of the operation of arsenic is very unusual, and I did not suspect it; but now I remember that it is noted in the books. Repeated syncopes, utter nervous prostration, absence of the ordinary burning and vomiting, and signs of rapid dissolution; it fits the case exactly! If I had some oxy-hydrate of iron, there might still be a possibility, but I greatly fear—"

"Do all you can!" Joseph interrupted. "She must have been insane! Do not tell me that you have *no* antidote!"

"We must try an emetic, though it will now be very dangerous. Then oil, white of egg,"—and the doctor hastened down to the kitchen.

Joseph walked up and down the room, wringing his hands. Here was a horror beyond anything he had imagined. His only thought was to save the life which she, in the madness of passion, must have resolved to take;

she must not, *must not*, die now; and yet she seemed to be already in some region on the very verge of darkness, some region where it was scarcely possible to reach and pull her back. What could be done? Human science was baffled; and would God, who had allowed him to be afflicted through her, now answer his prayer to continue that affliction? But, indeed, the word "affliction" was not formed in his mind; the only word which he consciously grasped was "Life! life!"

He paused by the bedside and gazed upon her livid skin, her sunken features: she seemed already dead. Then, sinking on his knees, he tried to pray, if that was prayer which was the single intense appeal of all his confused feelings. Presently he heard a faint sigh; she slightly moved; consciousness was evidently returning.

She looked at him with half-opened eyes, striving to fix upon something which evaded her mind. Then she said, in the faintest broken whisper: "I did love you—I *did*—and *do*—love you! But—you—you hate me!"

A pang sharper than a knife went through Joseph's heart. He cried, through his tears: "I did not know what I said! Give me your forgiveness, Julia! Pardon me, not because I ask it, but freely, from your heart, and I will bless you!"

She did not speak, but her eyes softened, and a phantom smile hovered upon her lips. It was no mask this time: she was sacredly frank and true. Joseph bent over her and kissed her.

"O Julia!" he said, "why did you do it? Why did you not wait until I could speak with you? Did you think you would take a burden off yourself or me?"

Her lips moved, but no voice came. He lifted her head, supported her, and bent his ear to her mouth. It was like the dream of a voice:—

"I—did—not—mean—"

There it stopped. The doctor entered the room, followed by Lucy.

"First the emetic," said the former.

"For God's sake, be silent!" Joseph cried, with his ear still at Julia's lips. The doctor stepped up softly and looked, at her. Then, seating himself on the bed beside Joseph, he laid his hand upon her heart. For several minutes there was silence in the room.

Then the doctor removed his hand, took Julia's head out of Joseph's arms, and laid it softly upon the pillow.

She was dead.

CHAPTER XXV
THE MOURNERS

"It cannot be!" cried Joseph, looking at the doctor with an agonized face; "it is too dreadful!"

"There is no room for doubt in relation to the cause. I suspect that her nervous system has been subjected to a steady and severe tension, probably for years past. This may have induced a condition, or at least a temporary paroxysm, during which she was—you understand me—not wholly responsible for her actions. You must have noticed whether such a condition preceded this catastrophe."

Lucy looked from one to the other, and back to the livid face on the pillow, unable to ask a question, and not yet comprehending that the end had come. Joseph arose at the doctor's words.

"That is my guilt," he said. "I was excited and angry, for I had been bitterly deceived. I warned her that her life must henceforth conform to mine: my words were harsh and violent. I told her that we had at last ascertained each other's true natures, and proposed a serious discussion for the purpose of arranging our common future, this afternoon. Can she have misunderstood my meaning? It was not separation, not divorce: I only meant to avoid the miserable strife of the last few weeks. Who could imagine that this would follow?"

Even as he spoke the words Joseph remembered the tempting fancy which had passed through his own mind,—and the fear of Philip,—as he stood on the brink of the rock, above the dark, sliding water. He covered his face with his hands and sat down. What right had he to condemn her, to pronounce her mad? Grant that she had been blinded by her own unbalanced, excitable nature rather than consciously false; grant that she had really loved him, that the love survived under all her vain and masterful ambition,—and how could he doubt it after the dying words and looks?—it was then easy to guess how sorely she had been wounded, how despair should follow her fierce excitement! Her words, "Go away! *you* have killed me!" were now explained. He groaned in the bitterness of his self-accusation. What were all the trials he had endured to this? How light seemed the burden from which he was now free! how gladly would he bear it, if the day's words and deeds could be unsaid and undone!

The doctor, meanwhile, had explained the manner of Julia's death to Lucy Henderson. She, almost overcome with this last horror, could only agree with his conjecture, for her own evidence confirmed it. Joseph had forborne to mention her presence in the garden, and she saw no need of repeating his words to her; but she described Julia's convulsive excitement, and her refusal to admit her to her room, half an hour before the first attack of the poison. The case seemed entirely clear to both.

"For the present," said the doctor, "let us say nothing about the suicide. There is no necessity for a *post-mortem* examination: the symptoms, and the presence of arsenic in the glass, are quite sufficient to establish the cause of death. You know what a foolish idea of disgrace is attached to families here in the country when such a thing happens, and Mr. Asten is not now in a state to bear much more. At least, we must save him from painful questions until after the funeral is over. Say as little as possible to him: he is not in a condition to listen to reason: he believes himself guilty of her death."

"What shall I do?" cried Lucy: "will you not stay until the man Dennis returns? Mr. Asten's aunt must be fetched immediately."

It was not a quarter of an hour before Dennis arrived, followed by Philip and Madeline Held.

Lucy, who had already despatched Dennis, with a fresh horse, to Magnolia, took Philip and Madeline into the dining-room, and hurriedly communicated to them the intelligence of Julia's death. Philip's heart gave a single leap of joy; then he compelled himself to think of Joseph and the exigencies of the situation.

"You cannot stay here alone," he said. "Madeline must keep you company. I will go up and take care of Joseph: we must think of both the living and the dead."

No face could have been half so comforting in the chamber of death as Philip's. The physician had, in the mean time, repeated to Joseph the words he had spoken to Lucy, and now Joseph said, pointing to Philip, "Tell *him* everything!"

Philip, startled as he was, at once comprehended the situation. He begged Dr. Hartman to leave all further arrangements to him, and to summon Mrs. Bishop, the wife of one of Joseph's near neighbors, on his way home. Then, taking Joseph by the arm, he said:—

"Now come with me. We will leave this room awhile to Lucy and Madeline; but neither must you be alone. If I am anything to you, Joseph, now is the time when my presence should be some slight comfort. We need not speak, but we will keep together."

Joseph clung the closer to his friend's arm, without speaking, and they passed out of the house. Philip led him, mechanically, towards the garden, but as they drew near the avenue of box-trees Joseph started back, crying out:—

"Not there!—O, not there!"

Philip turned in silence, conducted him past the barn into the grass-field, and mounted the hill towards the pin-oak on its summit. From this point the house was scarcely visible behind the fir-trees and the huge weeping-willow, but the fair hills around seemed happy under the tender sky, and the melting, vapory distance, seen through the southern opening of the valley, hinted of still happier landscapes beyond. As Joseph contemplated the scene, the long strain upon his nerves relaxed: he leaned upon Philip's shoulder, as they sat side by side, and wept passionately.

"If she had not died!" he murmured, at last.

Philip was hardly prepared for this exclamation, and he did not immediately answer.

"Perhaps it is better for me to talk," Joseph continued. "You do not know the whole truth, Philip. You have heard of her madness, but not of my guilt. What was it I said when we last met? I cannot recall it now: but I know that I feared to call my punishment unjust. Since then I have deserved it all, and more. If I am a child, why should I dare to handle fire? If I do not understand life, why should I dare to set death in motion?"

He began, and related everything that had passed since they parted on the banks of the stream. He repeated the words that had been spoken in the house and in the garden, and the last broken sentences that came from Julia's lips. Philip listened with breathless surprise and attention. The greater part of the narrative made itself clear to his mind; his instinctive knowledge of Julia's nature enabled him to read much further than was then possible to Joseph; but there was a mystery connected with the suicide which he could not fathom. Her rage he could easily understand; her apparent submission to Joseph's request, however,—her manifest desire to live, on overhearing the physician's fears,—her last incomplete sentence, "I—did—not—mean—" indicated no such fatal intention, but the reverse. Moreover, she was too inherently selfish, even in the fiercest paroxysm of disappointment, to take her own life, he believed. All the evidence justified him in this view of her nature, yet at the same time rendered her death more inexplicable.

It was no time to mention these doubts to Joseph. His only duty was to console and encourage.

"There is no guilt in accident," he said. "It was a crisis which must have come, and you took the only course possible to a man. If she felt that she was defeated, and her mad act was the consequence, think of your fate had she felt herself victorious!"

"It could have been no worse than it was," Joseph answered. "And she might have changed: I did not give her time. I have accused my own mistaken education, but I had no charity, no pity for hers!"

When they descended the hill Mrs. Bishop had arrived, and the startled household was reduced to a kind of dreary order. Dennis, who had driven with speed, brought Rachel Miller at dusk, and Philip and Madeline then departed, taking Lucy Henderson with them. Rachel was tearful, but composed; she said little to her nephew, but there was a quiet, considerate tenderness in her manner which soothed him more than any words.

The reaction from so much fatigue and excitement almost prostrated him. When he went to bed in his own guest-room, feeling like a stranger in a strange house, he lay for a long time between sleep and waking, haunted by all the scenes and personages of his past life. His mother's face, so faded in memory, came clear and fresh from the shadows; a boy whom he had loved in his school-days floated with fair, pale features just before his closed eyes; and around and between them there was woven a web of twilights and moonlights, and sweet sunny days, each linked to some grief or pleasure of the buried years. It was a keen, bitter joy, a fascinating torment, from which he could not escape. He was caught and helplessly ensnared by the phantoms, until, late in the night, the strong claim of nature drove them away and left him in a dead, motionless, dreamless slumber.

Philip returned in the morning, and devoted the day not less to the arrangements which must necessarily be made for the funeral than to standing between Joseph and the awkward and inquisitive sympathy of the neighbors. Joseph's continued weariness favored Philip's exertions, while at the same time it blunted the edge of his own feelings, and helped him over that cold, bewildering, dismal period, during which a corpse is lord of the mansion and controls the life of its inmates.

Towards evening Mr. and Mrs. Blessing, who had been summoned by telegraph, made their appearance. Clementina did not accompany them. They were both dressed in mourning: Mrs. Blessing was grave and rigid,

Mr. Blessing flushed and lachrymose. Philip conducted them first to the chamber of the dead and then to Joseph.

"It is so sudden, so shocking!" Mrs. Blessing sobbed; "and Julia always seemed so healthy! What have you done to her, Mr. Asten, that she should be cut off in the bloom of her youth?"

"Eliza!" exclaimed her husband, with his handkerchief to his eyes; "do not say anything which might sound like a reproach to our heart-broken son! There are many foes in the citadel of life: they may be undermining our—our foundations at this very moment!"

"No," said Joseph; "you, her father and mother, must hear the truth. I would give all I have in the world if I were not obliged to tell it."

It was, at the best, a painful task; but it was made doubly so by exclamations, questions, intimations, which he was forced to hear. Finally, Mrs. Blessing asked, in a tone of alarm:—

"How many persons know of this?"

"Only the physician and three of my friends," Joseph answered.

"They must be silent! It might ruin Clementina's prospects if it were generally known. To lose one daughter and to have the life of another blasted would be too much."

"Eliza," said her husband, "we must, try to accept whatever is inevitable. It seems to me that I no more recognize Julia's usually admirable intellect in her—yes, I must steel myself to say the word!—her suicide, than I recognized her features just now! unless Decay's effacing fingers have already swept the lines where beauty lingers. I warned her of the experiment, for such I felt it to be; yet in this last trying experience I do not complain of Joseph's disappointment, and his temporary—I trust it is only temporary—suspicion. We must not forget that he has lost more than we have."

"Where is—" Joseph began, endeavoring to turn the conversation from this point.

"Clementina? I knew you would find her absence unaccountable. We instantly forwarded a telegram to Long Branch; the answer said, 'My grief is great, but it is quite impossible to come.' Why impossible she did not particularize, and we can only conjecture. When I consider her age and lost opportunities, and the importance which a single day, even a fortunate situation, may possess for her at present, it seems to remove some of the sharpness of the serpent's tooth. Neither she nor we are responsible for Julia's rash taking off; yet it is always felt as a cloud which lowers upon the family. There was a similar case among the De Belsains, during the

Huguenot times, but we never mention it. For your sake silence is rigidly imposed upon us; since the preliminary—what shall I call it?—dis-harmony of views?—would probably become a part of the narrative."

"Pray do not speak of that now!" Joseph groaned.

"Pardon me; I will not do so again. Our minds naturally become discursive under the pressure of grief. It is easier for me to talk at such times than to be silent and think. My power of recuperation seems to be spiritual as well as physical; it is congenital, and therefore exposes me to misconceptions. But we can close over the great abyss of our sorrow, and hide it from view in the depth of our natures, without dancing on the platform which covers it."

Philip turned away to hide a smile, and even Mrs. Blessing exclaimed: "Really, Benjamin, you are talking heartlessly!"

"I do not mean it so," he said, melting into tears, "but so much has come upon me all at once! If I lose my buoyancy, I shall go to the bottom like a foundered ship! I was never cut out for the tragic parts of life; but there are characters who smile on the stage and weep behind the scenes. And, you know, the Lord loveth a cheerful giver."

He was so touched by the last words he spoke, that he leaned his head upon his arms and wept bitterly.

Then Mrs. Blessing, weeping also, exclaimed: "O, don't take on so, Benjamin!"

Philip put an end to the scene, which was fast becoming a torment to Joseph. But, later in the evening, Mr. Blessing again sought the latter, softly apologizing for the intrusion, but declaring that he was compelled, then and there, to make a slight explanation.

"When you called the other evening," he said, "I was worn out, and not competent to grapple with such an unexpected revelation of villany. I had been as ignorant of Kanuck's real character as you were. All our experience of the world is sometimes at fault; but where the Reverend Dr. Lellifant was first deceived, my own case does not seem so flagrant. Your early information, however, enabled me (through third parties) to secure a partial sale of the stock held by yourself and me,—at something of a sacrifice, it is true; but I prefer not to dissociate myself entirely from the enterprise. I do not pretend to be more than the merest tyro in geology; nevertheless, as I lay awake last night,—being, of course, unable to sleep after the shock of the telegram,—I sought relief in random scientific fancies. It occurred to me that since the main Chowder wells are 'spouting,' their source or reservoir must be considerably higher than the surface. Why might not that source be found under the hills of the Amaranth? If so, the Chowder would be tapped at the fountain-head and the flow of Pactolean grease would be ours! When I return to the city I shall need instantly—after the fearful revelations of to-day—some violently absorbing occupation; and what could be more appropriate? If anything could give repose to Julia's unhappy shade, it would be the knowledge that her faith in the Amaranth was at last justified! I do not presume to awaken your confidence: it has been too deeply shaken; all I ask is, that I may have the charge of your shares, in order—without calling upon you for the expenditure of another cent, you understand—to rig a jury-mast on the wreck, and, D. V., float safely into port!"

"Why should I refuse to trust you with what is already worthless?" said Joseph.

"I will admit even *that*, if you desire. '*Exitus acta probat*' was Washington's motto; but I don't consider that we have yet reached the *exitus*! Thank you, Joseph! Your question has hardly the air of returning confidence, but I will force myself to consider it as such, and my labor will be to deserve it."

He wrung Joseph's hand, shed a few more tears, and betook himself to his wife's chamber. "Eliza, let us be calm: we never know our strength until it has been tried," he said to her, as he opened his portmanteau and took from it the wicker-covered flask.

Then came the weariest and dreariest day of all,—when the house must be thrown open to the world; when in one room the corpse must be displayed for solemn stares and whispered comments, while in another the preparation of the funeral meats absorbs all the interest of half a dozen busy women; when the nearest relatives of the dead sit together in a room up stairs, hungering only for the consolations of loneliness and silence; when all talk under their voices, and uncomfortably fulfil what they believe to be their solemn duty; and when even Nature is changed to all eyes, and the mysterious gloom of an eclipse seems to fall from the most unclouded sun.

There was a general gathering of the neighbors from far and near. The impression seemed to be—and Philip was ready to substantiate it—that Julia had died in consequence of a violent convulsive spasm, which some attributed to one cause and some to another.

The Rev. Mr. Chaffinch made his way, as by right, to the chamber of the mourners. Rachel Miller was comforted in seeing him, Mr. and Mrs. Blessing sadly courteous, and Joseph strengthened himself to endure with patience what might follow. After a few introductory words, and a long prayer, the clergyman addressed himself to each, in turn, with questions or remarks which indicated a fierce necessity of resignation.

"I feel for you, brother," he said, as he reached Joseph and bent over his chair. "It is an inscrutable visitation, but I trust you submit, in all obedience?"

Joseph bowed silently.

"He has many ways of searching the heart," Mr. Chaffinch continued. "Your one precious comfort must be that *she* believed, and that she is now in glory. O, if you would but resolve to follow in her footsteps! He shows His love, in that He chastens you: it is a stretching out of His hand, a visible offer of acceptance, this on one side, and the lesson of our perishing mortality on the other! Do you not feel your heart awfully and tenderly moved to approach Him?"

Joseph sat, with bowed head, listening to the smooth, unctuous, dismal voice at his ear, until the tension of his nerves became a positive physical pain. He longed to cry aloud, to spring up and rush away; his heart was moved, but not awfully and tenderly. It had been yearning towards the pure Divine Light in which all confusions of the soul are disentangled; but now some opaque foreign substance intervened, and drove him back upon himself. How long the torture lasted he did not know. He spake no word, and made no further sign.

Then Philip took him and Rachel Miller down, for the last conventional look at the stony, sunken face. He was seated here and led there; he was dimly conscious of a crowd, of murmurs and steadfast faces; he heard some one whisper, "How dreadfully pale he looks!" and wondered whether the words could possibly refer to him. Then there was the welcome air and the sunshine, and Dennis driving them slowly down the lane, following a gloomy vehicle, in which *something*—not surely the Julia whom he knew—was carried.

He recalled but one other such stupor of the senses: it was during the performance of the marriage ceremony.

But the longest day wears out at last; and when night came only Philip was beside him. The Blessings had been sent to Oakland Station for the evening train to the city, and Joseph's shares in the Amaranth Company were in their portmanteau.

CHAPTER XXVI
THE ACCUSATION

For a few days it almost seemed to Joseph that the old order of his existence had been suddenly restored, and the year of his betrothal and marriage had somehow been intercalated into his life simply as a test and trial. Rachel Miller was back again, in her old capacity, and he did not yet see—what would have been plain to any other eyes—that her manner towards him was far more respectful and considerate than formerly. But, in fact, she made a wide distinction between the "boy" that he had been and the man and widower which he had come to be. At first, she had refused to see the dividing line: having crossed it, her new course soon became as natural and fixed as the old. She was the very type of a mechanically developed old maid,—inflexibly stern towards male youth, devotedly obedient to male maturity.

Joseph had been too profoundly moved to lose at once the sense of horror which the manner of Julia's death had left in his heart. He could not forgive himself for having, though never so ignorantly, driven her to madness. He was troubled, restless, unhappy; and the mention of his loss was so painful that he made every effort to avoid hearing it. Some of his neighbors, he imagined, were improperly curious in their inquiries. He felt bound, since the doctor had suggested it, since Philip and Lucy had acquiesced, and Mrs. Blessing had expressed so much alarm lest it might become known, to keep the suicide a secret; but he was driven so closely by questions and remarks that his task became more and more difficult.

Had the people taken offence at his reticence? It seemed so; for their manner towards him was certainly changed. Something in the look and voice; an indefinable uneasiness at meeting him; an awkward haste and lame excuses for it,—all these things forced themselves upon his mind. Elwood Withers, alone, met him as of old, with even a tenderer though a more delicately veiled affection; yet in Elwood's face he detected the signs of a grave trouble. It could not be possible, he thought, that Elwood had heard some surmise, or distorted echo, of his words to Lucy in the garden,—that there had been another listener besides Julia!

There were times, again, when he doubted all these signs, when he ascribed them to his own disturbed mind, and decided to banish them from his memory. He would stay quietly at home, he resolved, and grow into a healthier mood: he would avoid the society of men, until he should cease to wrong them by his suspicions.

First, however, he would see Philip; but on reaching the Forge he found Philip absent. Madeline received him with a subdued kindness in which he felt her sympathy; but it was also deeper, he acknowledged to himself, than he had any right to claim.

"You do not see much of your neighbors, I think, Mr. Asten?" she asked. The tone of her voice indicated a slight embarrassment.

"No," he answered; "I have no wish to see any but my friends."

"Lucy Henderson has just left us. Philip took her to her father's, and was intending to call at your place on his way home. I hope you will not miss him. That is," she added, while a sudden flush of color spread over her face, "I want you to see him to-day. I beg you won't take my words as intended for a dismissal."

"Not now, certainly," said Joseph. But he rose from his seat as he spoke.

Madeline looked both confused and pained. "I know that I spoke awkwardly," she said, "but indeed I was very anxious. It was also Lucy's wish. We have been talking about you this morning."

"You are very kind. And yet—I ought to wish you a more cheerful subject."

What was it in Madeline's face that haunted Joseph on his way home? The lightsome spirit was gone from her eyes, and they were troubled as if by the pressure of tears, held back by a strong effort. Her assumed calmness at parting seemed to cover a secret anxiety; he had never before seen her bright, free nature so clouded.

Philip, meanwhile, had reached the farm, where he was received by Rachel Miller.

"I am glad to find that Joseph is not at home," he said; "there are some things which I need to discuss with you, before I see him. Can you guess what they are? Have you heard nothing,—no stories?"

Rachel's face grew pale, yet there was a strong fire of indignation in her eyes. "Dennis told me an outrageous report he had heard in the village," she said: "if you mean the same thing, you did well to see me first. You can help me to keep this insult from Joseph's knowledge."

"If I could I would, Miss Rachel. I share your feeling about it; but suppose the report were now so extended—and of course in a more exaggerated form the farther it goes—that we cannot avoid its probable consequences? This is not like a mere slander, which can be suffered to die of itself. It is equivalent to a criminal charge, and must be faced."

She clasped her hands, and stared at him in terror.

"But why," she faltered—"why does any one *dare* to make such a charge? And against the best, the most innocent—"

"The fact of the poisoning cannot be concealed," said Philip. "It appears, moreover, that one of the women who was in the house on the day of Julia's death heard her cry out to Joseph: 'Go away,—you have killed me!' I need not take up the reports any further; there is enough in these two circumstances to excite the suspicions of those who do not know Joseph as we do. It is better, therefore, to meet those suspicions before they come to us in a legal form."

"What can we do?" cried Rachel; "it is terrible!"

"One course is clear, if it is possible. We must try to discover not only the cause of Julia's suicide, but the place where she procured the poison, and her design in procuring it. She must have had it already in the house."

"I never thought of that And her ways were so quiet and sly! How shall we ever find it out? O, to think that, dead and gone as she is, she can yet bring all this upon Joseph!"

"Try to be calm, Miss Rachel," said Philip. "I want your help, and you must have all your wits about you. First, you must make a very careful examination of her clothing and effects, even to the merest scrap of paper. A man's good name—a man's life, sometimes—hangs upon a thread, in the most literal sense. There is no doubt that Julia meant to keep a secret, and she must have had a strong reason; but we have a stronger one, now, to discover it. First, as to the poison; was there any arsenic in the house when Julia came?"

"Not a speck! I never kept it, even for rats."

"Then we shall begin with ascertaining where she bought it. Let us make our investigations secretly, and as speedily as possible. Joseph need not know, at present, what we have undertaken, but he must know the charge that hangs over him. Unless I tell him, he may learn it in a more violent way. I sent Elwood Withers to Magnolia yesterday, and his report leaves me no choice of action."

Rachel Miller felt, from the stern gravity of Philip's manner, that he had not exaggerated Joseph's danger. She consented to be guided by him in all things; and this point being settled, they arranged a plan of action and communication, which was tolerably complete by the time Joseph returned.

As gently as possible Philip broke the unwelcome news; but, lightly as he pretended to consider it, Joseph's instinct saw at once what might be the consequences. The circumstances were all burned upon his consciousness, and it needed no reflection to show him how completely he was entangled in them.

"There is no alternative," he said, at last. "It was a mistake to conceal the cause of her death from the public: it is easy to misunderstand her exclamation, and make my crime out of her madness. I see the whole connection! This suspicion will not stop where it is. It will go further; and therefore I must anticipate it. I must demand a legal inquiry before the law forces one upon me. If it is not my only method of defence, it is certainly my best!"

"You are right!" Philip exclaimed. "I knew this would be your decision; I said so to Madeline this morning."

Now Madeline's confused manner became intelligible to Joseph. Yet a doubt still lingered in his mind. "Did she, did Madeline question it?" he asked.

"Neither she nor Lucy Henderson. If you do this, I cannot see how it will terminate without a trial. Lucy may then happen to be an important witness."

Joseph started. "*Must* that be!" he cried. "Has not Lucy been already forced to endure enough for my sake? Advise me, Philip! Is there any other way than that I have proposed?"

"I see no other. But your necessity is far greater than that for Lucy's endurance. She is a friend, and there can be no sacrifice in so serving you. What are we all good for, if not to serve you in such a strait?"

"I would like to spare her, nevertheless," said Joseph, gloomily. "I meant so well towards all my friends, and my friendship seems to bring only disgrace and sorrow."

"Joseph!" Philip exclaimed, "you have saved one friend from more than disgrace and sorrow! I do not know what might have come, but you called me back from the brink of an awful, doubtful eternity! You have given me an infinite loss and an infinite gain! I only ask you, in return, to obey your first true, proud instinct of innocence, and let me, and Lucy, and Elwood be glad to take its consequences, for your sake!"

"I cannot help myself," Joseph answered. "My rash impatience and injustice will come to light, and that may be the atonement I owe. If Lucy will spare herself, and report me truly, as I must have appeared to her, she will serve me best."

"Leave that, now! The first step is what most concerns us. When will you be ready to demand a legal investigation?"

"At once!—to-morrow!"

"Then we will go together to Magnolia. I fear we cannot change the ordinary forms of procedure, and there must be bail for your appearance at the proper time."

"Already on the footing of a criminal?" Joseph murmured, with a sinking of the heart. He had hardly comprehended, up to this moment, what his position would be.

The next day they drove to the county town. The step had not been taken a moment too soon, for such representations had been made that a warrant for Joseph's arrest was in the hands of the constable, and would have been served in a few hours. Philip and Mr. Hopeton, who also happened to be in the town by a fortunate chance (though Philip knew how the chance came), offered to accept whatever amount of bail might be demanded. The matter was arranged as privately as possible, but it leaked out in some way, and Philip was seriously concerned lest the curiosity—perhaps, even, the ill-will—of a few persons might be manifested towards Joseph. He visited the offices of the county papers, and took care that the voluntary act should be stated in such a manner as to set its character properly before the people. Everything, he felt, depended on securing a fair and unprejudiced judgment of the case.

This, indeed, was far more important than even he suspected. In a country where the press is so entirely free, and where, owing to the lazy, indifferent habit of thought—or, rather, habit of *no* thought—of the people, the editorial views are accepted without scrutiny, a man's good name or life may depend on the coloring given to his acts by a few individual minds, it is especially necessary to keep the balance even, to offset one statement by another, and prevent a partial presentation of the case from turning the scales in advance. The same phenomena were as likely to present themselves here, before a small public, as in the large cities, where the whole population of the country become a more or less interested public. The result might hinge, not upon Joseph's personal character as his friends knew it, but upon the political party with which he was affiliated, the church to which he belonged,—nay, even upon the accordance of his personal sentiments with the public sentiment of the community in which he lived. If he had dared to defy the latter, asserting the sacred right of his own mind to the largest liberty, he was already a marked man. Philip did not understand the extent and power of the external influences which control what we complacently call "justice," but he knew something of the world, and acted in reality more prudently than he supposed.

He was calm and cheerful for Joseph's sake; yet, now that the matter was irrevocably committed to the decision of a new, uninterested tribunal, he began to feel the gravity of his friend's position.

"I almost wish," Joseph said, as they drove homewards, "that no bail had been granted. Since the court meets in October, a few weeks of seclusion would do me no harm; whereas now I am a suspected person to nearly all whom I may meet."

"It is not agreeable," Philip answered, "but the discipline may be useful. The bail terminates when the trial commences, you understand, and you will have a few nights alone, as it is,—quite enough, I imagine, to make you satisfied with liberty under suspicion. However I have one demand to make, Joseph! I have thought over all possible lines of defence; I have secured legal assistance for you, and we are agreed as to the course to be adopted. I do not think you can help us at all. If we find that you can, we will call upon you; in the mean time, wait and hope!"

"Why should I not?" Joseph asked. "I have nothing to fear, Philip."

"No!" But Philip's emphatic answer was intended to deceive. He was purposely false, knew himself to be so, and yet his conscience never troubled him less!

When they reached the farm, Philip saw by Rachel Miller's face that she had a communication to make. It required a little management to secure an interview with her without Joseph's knowledge; but some necessity for his presence at the barn favored his friend. No sooner were they alone than Rachel approached Philip hastily and said, in a hurried whisper:—

"Here! I have found something, at last! It took a mighty search: I thought I never *should* come upon the least bit that we could make anything of: but *this* was in the upper part of a box where she kept her rings and chains, and such likes! Take it,—it makes me uncomfortable to hold it in my fingers!"

She thrust a small paper into his hand.

It was folded very neatly, and there was an apothecary's label on the back. Philip read: "Ziba Linthicum's Drug store, No. 77 Main St., Magnolia." Under this printed address was written in large letters the word "Arsenic."

On unfolding the paper he saw that a little white dust remained in the creases: quite enough to identify the character of the drug.

"I shall go back to-morrow!" he said. "Thank Heaven, we have got one clew to the mystery! Joseph must know nothing of this until all is explained; but while I am gone make another and more thorough search! Leave no corner unexplored: I am sure we shall find something more."

"I'd rip up her dresses!" was Rachel's emphatic reply. "That is, if it would do any good. But perhaps feeling of the lining and the hems might be enough. I'll take every drawer out, and move the furniture! But I must wait for daylight: I'm not generally afeared, but there is some things, you know, which a body would as lief not do by night, with cracks and creaks all around you, which you don't seem to hear at other times."

CHAPTER XXVII
THE LABELS

The work at Coventry Forge was now so well organized that Philip could easily give the most of his time to Joseph's vindication. He had secured the services of an excellent country lawyer, but he also relied much upon the assistance of two persons,—his sister Madeline and Elwood Withers: Madeline, from her rapid, clear insight, her shrewd interpretation of circumstances; and Elwood as an active, untiring practical agent.

The latter, according to agreement, had ridden up from his section of the railway, and was awaiting Philip when he returned home.

Philip gave them the history of the day,—this time frankly, with all the signs and indications which he had so carefully kept from Joseph's knowledge. Both looked aghast; and Elwood bent an ivory paper-cutter so suddenly in his hands that it snapped in twain. He colored like a girl.

"It serves me right," he said. "Whenever my hands are idle, Satan finds mischief for 'em,—as the spelling-book says. But just so the people bend and twist Joseph Asten's character, and just so unexpectedly his life may snap in their hands!"

"May the omen be averted!" Madeline cried. "Put down the pieces, Mr. Withers! You frighten me."

"No, it is reversed!" said Philip. "Just so Joseph's friends will snap this chain of circumstances. If you begin to be superstitious, I must look out for other aids. The tracing of the poison is a more fortunate step than I hoped, at the start. I cannot at all guess to what it may lead, but there is a point beyond which even the most malignant fate has no further power over an innocent man. Thus far we have met nothing but hostile circumstances: there seems to be more than Chance in the game, and I have an idea that the finding of this paper will break the evil spell. Come now, Madeline, and you, Withers, give me your guesses as to what my discovery shall be to-morrow!"

After a pause, Madeline answered: "It must have been purchased—perhaps even by Mr. Asten—for rats or mice; and she may have swallowed the drug in a fit of passion."

"*I* think," said Elwood, "that she bought it for the purpose of poisoning Joseph! Then, may be, the glasses were changed, as I've heard tell of a man whose wife changed his coffee-cup because there was a fly in it, giving him hers, and thereby innocently killed him when *he* meant to ha' killed her."

"Ha!" Philip cried; "the most incredible things, apparently, are sometimes the most natural! I had not thought of this explanation."

"O Philip!" said Madeline, "that would be a new horror! Pray, let us not think of it: indeed, indeed, we must not guess any more."

Philip strove to put the idea from his mind: he feared lest it might warp his judgment and mislead him in investigations which it required a cool, sharp intellect to prosecute. But the idea would not stay away: it haunted him precisely on account of its enormity, and he rode again to Magnolia the next day with a foreboding sense of some tragic secret about to be revealed.

But he never could have anticipated the actual revelation.

There was no difficulty in finding Ziba Linthicum's Drug store. The proprietor was a lank, thin-faced man, with projecting, near-sighted eyes, and an exceedingly prim, pursed mouth. His words, uttered in the close, wiry twang peculiar to Southern Pennsylvania, seemed to give him a positive relish: one could fancy that his mouth watered slightly as he spoke. His long, lean lips had a settled smirk at the corner, and the skin was drawn so tightly over his broad, concave chin-bone that it shone, as if polished around the edges.

He was waiting upon a little girl when Philip entered; but he looked up from his scales, bowed, smiled, and said: "In a moment, if you please."

Philip leaned upon the glass case, apparently absorbed in the contemplation of the various soaps and perfumes under his eyes, but thinking only of the paper in his pocket-book.

"Something in this line, perhaps?"

Mr. Linthicum, with a still broader smile, began to enumerate: "These are from the Society Hygiennick—"

"No," said Philip, "my business is especially private. I take it for granted that you have many little confidential matters intrusted to you."

"Oh, undoubtedly, sir! Quite as much so as a physician."

"You are aware also that mistakes sometimes occur in making up prescriptions, or in using them afterwards?"

"Not by *me*, I should hope. I keep a record of every dangerous ingredient which goes out of my hands."

"Ah!" Philip exclaimed. Then he paused, uncertain how much to confide to Mr. Linthicum's discretion. But, on mentioning his name and residence, he found that both himself and Mr. Hopeton were known—and favorably, it seemed—to the apothecary. He knew the class of men to which the latter belonged,—prim, fussy, harmlessly vain persons, yet who take as good care of their consciences as of their cravats and shirt-bosoms. He produced the paper without further delay.

"That was bought here, certainly," said Mr. Linthicum. "The word 'Arsenic' is written in my hand. The date when, and the person by whom it was purchased, must be in my register. Will you go over it with me?"

He took a volume from a drawer, and beginning at the last entry, they went slowly backward over the names, the apothecary saying: "This is confidential: I rely upon your seeing without remembering."

They had not gone back more than two or three weeks before Philip came upon a name that made his heart stand still. There was a record in a single line:—

"*Miss Henderson. Arsenic.*"

He waited a few seconds, until he felt sure of his voice. Then he asked: "Do you happen to know Miss Henderson?"

"Not at all! A perfect stranger."

"Can you, perhaps, remember her appearance?"

"Let me see," said Mr. Linthicum, biting the end of his forefinger; "that must have been the veiled lady. The date corresponds. Yes, I feel sure of it, as all the other poison customers are known to me."

"Pray describe her then!" Philip exclaimed.

"Really, I fear that I cannot. Dressed in black, I think; but I will not be positive. A soft, agreeable voice, I am sure."

"Was she alone? Or was any one else present?"

"Now I *do* recall one thing," the apothecary answered. "There was an agent of a wholesale city firm—a travelling agent, you understand—trying to persuade me into an order on his house. He stepped on one side as she came to the counter, and he perhaps saw her face more distinctly, for he laughed as she left, and said something about a handsome girl putting her lovers out of their misery."

But Mr. Linthicum could remember neither the name of the agent nor that of the firm which he represented. All Philip's questioning elicited no further particulars, and he was obliged to be satisfied with the record of the day and probable hour of the purchase, and with the apothecary's promise of the strictest secrecy.

He rode immediately home, and after a hasty consultation with Madeline, remounted his horse and set out to find Lucy Henderson. He was fortunate enough to meet her on the highway, on her way to call upon a neighbor. Springing from his horse he walked beside her, and announced his discovery at once.

Lucy remembered the day when she had accompanied Julia to Magnolia, during Joseph's absence from home. The time of the day, also, corresponded to that given by the apothecary.

"Did you visit the drug-store?" Philip asked.

"No," she answered, "and I did not know that Julia had. I paid two or three visits to acquaintances, while she did her shopping, as she told me."

"Then try and remember, not only the order of those visits, but the time occupied by each," said Philip. "Write to your friends, and ask them to refresh their memories. It has become an important point, for—the poison was purchased in your name!"

"Impossible!" Lucy cried. She gazed at Philip with such amazement that her innocence was then fixed in his mind, if it had not been so before.

"Yes, I say 'impossible!' too," he answered. "There is only one explanation. Julia Asten gave your name instead of her own when she purchased it."

"Oh!" Lucy's voice sounded like a hopeless personal protest against the collective falsehood and wickedness of the world.

"I have another chance to reach the truth," said Philip. "I shall find the stranger,—the travelling agent,—if it obliges me to summon every such agent of every wholesale drug-house in the city! It is at least a positive fortune that we have made this discovery now."

He looked at his watch. "I have just time to catch the evening train," he said, hurriedly, "but I should like to send a message to Elwood Withers. If you pass through that wood on the right, you will see the track just below you. It is not more than half a mile from here; and you are almost sure to find him at or near the unfinished tunnel. Tell him to see Rachel Miller, and if anything further has been found, to inform my sister Madeline at once. That is all. I make no apology for imposing the service on you: good-by, and keep up your faith, Lucy!"

He pressed her hand, sprang into the saddle, and cantered briskly away.

Lucy, infected by his haste, crossed the field, struggled through the under-growth of the wild belt of wood, and descended to the railway track, without giving herself time to think. She met a workman near the mouth of the tunnel, and not daring to venture in, sent by him a summons to Elwood. It was not many minutes before he appeared.

"Something has happened, Lucy? he exclaimed.

"Philip thinks he has made a discovery," she answered, "and I come to you as his messenger." She then repeated Philip's words.

"Is that all?" Elwood asked, scanning her face anxiously. "You do not seem quite like your real self, Lucy."

She sat down upon the hank. "I am out of breath," she said; "I must have walked faster than I thought."

"Wait a minute!" said he. He ran up the track, to where a little side-glen crossed it, sprang down among the bushes, and presently reappeared with a tin cup full of cold, pure spring water.

The draught seemed to revive her at once. "It is not all, Elwood," she said. "Joseph is not the only one, now, who is implicated by the same circumstances."

"Who else?—not Philip Held!"

"No," she answered, very quietly, "it is a woman. Her name is Lucy Henderson."

Before Elwood could speak, she told him all that she had heard from Philip. He could scarcely bring his mind to accept its truth.

"Oh, the—" he began; "but, no! I will keep the words to myself. There is something deeper in this than any of us has yet looked for! Depend upon it, Lucy, she had a plan in getting you there!"

Lucy was silent. She fancied she knew Julia's plan already.

"Did she mean to poison Joseph herself, and throw the suspicion on you? And now by her own death, after all, she accomplishes her chief end! It is a hellish tangle, whichever way I look; but they say that the truth will sooner or later put down any amount of lies, and so it must be, here. We must get at the truth, the whole truth, and nothing but the truth! Do you not say so, Lucy?"

"Yes!" she answered firmly, looking him in the face.

"Ay, though *all* should come to light! We can't tell what it may be necessary to say. They may go to work and unravel Joseph's life, and yours, and mine, and hold up the stuff for everybody to look at. Well, let 'em! say

I. If there are dark streaks in mine, I guess they'll look tolerably fair beside that one black heart. We're here alone, Lucy; there may not be a chance to say it soon again, so I'll say now, that if need comes to publish what I said to you one night a year ago,—to publish it for Joseph's sake, or your sake,—don't keep back a single word! The worst would be, some men or women might think me conceited."

"No, Elwood!" she exclaimed: "that reproach would fall on me! You once offered me your help, and I—I fear I spurned it; but I will take it now. Nay, I beg you to offer it to me again, and I will accept it with gratitude!"

She rose, and stretched out her hand.

Elwood clasped it tenderly, held it a moment, and seemed about to speak. But although his lips parted, and there was a movement of the muscles of his throat, he did not utter a word. In another moment he turned, walked a few yards up the track, and then came back to her.

"No one could mistake you for Julia Asten," he said. "You are at least half a head taller than she was. Your voice is not at all the same: the apothecary will surely notice the difference! Then an *alibi*, as they call it, can be proved."

"So Philip Held thought. But if my friends should not remember the exact time,—what should I then do?"

"Lucy, don't ask yourself the question now! It seems to me that the case stands this way: one evil woman has made a trap, fallen into it herself, and taken the secret of its make away with her. There is nothing more to be invented, and so we hold all that we gain. While we are mining, where's the counter-mining to come from? Who is to lie us out of our truth? There isn't much to stand on yet, I grant; but another step—the least little thing—may give us all the ground we want!"

He spoke so firmly and cheerily that Lucy's despondent feeling was charmed away. Besides, nothing could have touched her more than Elwood's heroic self-control. After the miserable revelation which Philip had made, it was unspeakably refreshing to be brought into contact with a nature so sound and sweet and strong. When he had led her by an easier path up the hill, and they had parted at the end of the lane leading to her father's house, she felt, as never before, the comfort of relying so wholly on a faithful man friend.

Elwood took his horse and rode to the Asten farm. Joseph's face brightened at his appearance, and they talked as of old, avoiding the dark year that lay between their past intimacy and its revival. As in Philip's case, it was difficult to communicate secretly with Rachel Miller; but Elwood, with great patience, succeeded in looking his wish to speak with her, and uniting her efforts with his own. She adroitly turned the conversation upon a geological work which Joseph had been reading.

"I've been looking into the subject myself," Elwood said. "Would you let me see the book: it may be the thing I want."

"It is on the book-shelf in your bed-room, Joseph," Rachel remarked.

There was time enough for Elwood to declare his business, and for Rachel to answer: "Mr. Held said every scrap, and it is but a scrap, with half a name on it. I found it behind and mostly under the lower drawer in the same box. I'll get it before you leave, and give it to you when we shake hands. Be careful, for he may make something out of it, after all. Tell him there isn't a stitch in a dress but I've examined, and a mortal work it was!"

It was late before Elwood could leave; nevertheless, he rode to Coventry Forge. The scrap of paper had been successfully transferred, and his pressing duty was to deliver it into the hands of Madeline Held. He found her anxiously waiting, in accordance with Philip's instructions.

When they looked at the paper, it seemed, truly, to be a worthless fragment. It had the character, also, of an apothecary's label, but the only letters remaining were those forming the end of the name, apparently —*ers*, and a short distance under them —*Sts*.

"Behind and mostly under the lower drawer of her jewel-case," said Madeline, musingly. "I think I might guess how it came there. She had seen the label, which had probably been forgotten, and then, as she supposed, had snatched it away and destroyed it, without noticing that this piece, caught behind the drawer, had been torn off. But there is no evidence—and perhaps none can be had—that the paper contained poison."

"Can you make anything out of the letters?" Elwood asked.

"The '*Sts*' certainly means 'Streets'—now I see! It is a corner house! This makes the place a little mare easy to be identified. If Philip cannot find it, I am sure a detective can. I will write to him at once."

"Then I'll wait and ride to the office with the letter," said Elwood.

Madeline rose, and commenced walking up and down the room: she appeared to be suddenly and unusually excited.

"I have a new suspicion," she said, at last. "Perhaps I am in too much of a hurry to make conjectures, because Philip thinks I have a talent for it,—and yet, this grows upon me every minute! I hope—oh, I hope I am right!"

She spoke with so much energy that Elwood began to share her excitement without knowing its cause. She noticed the eager, waiting expression of his face.

"You must really pardon, me, Mr. Withers. I believe I was talking to myself rather than to you; I will not mention my fancy until Philip decides whether it is worth acting upon. There will be no harm if each of us finds a different clew, and follows it. Philip will hardly leave the city to-morrow. I shall not write, but go down with the first train in the morning!"

Elwood took his leave, feeling hopeful and yet very restless.

It was a long while before Madeline encountered Philip. He was busily employed in carrying out his plan of tracing the travelling agent,—not yet successful, but sanguine of success. He examined the scrap of paper which Madeline brought, listened to her reasons for the new suspicion which had crossed her mind, and compared them with the little evidence already collected.

"Do not let us depend too seriously on this," he then said; "there is about an even chance that you are right. We will keep it as an additional and independent test, but we dare not lose sight of the fact that the law will assume Joseph's guilt, and we must establish his innocence, first of all. Nay, if we can simply prove that Julia, and not Lucy, purchased the poison, we shall save both! But, at the same time, I will try to find this —*ers*, who lives in a corner house, and I will have a talk with old Blessing this very evening."

"Why not go now?"

"Patience, you impetuous girl! I mean to take no step without working out every possible result in advance. If I were not here in the city, I would consult with Mr. Pinkerton before proceeding further. Now I shall take you to the train: you must return to Coventry, and watch and wait there."

When Philip called at the Blessing mansion, in the evening, he found only Mrs. Blessing at home. She was rigid and dreary in her mourning, and her reception of him was almost repellant in its stiff formality.

"Mr. Blessing is absent," she explained, inviting Philip to a seat by a wave of her hand. "His own interests rendered a trip to the Oil Regions imperative; it is a mental distraction which I do not grudge him. This is a cheerless household, sir,—one daughter gone forever, and another about to leave us. How does Mr. Asten bear his loss?"

Philip thereupon, as briefly and forcibly as possible, related all that had occurred. "I wish to consult Mr. Blessing," he concluded, "in relation to the possibility of his being able to furnish any testimony on his son-in-law's side. Perhaps you, also—"

"No!" she interrupted. "I know nothing whatever! If the trial (which I think most unnecessary and shocking) gets into the city papers, it will be a terrible scandal for us. When will it come on, did you say?"

"In two or three weeks"

"There will be barely time!" she cried.

"For that reason," said he, "I wish to secure the evidence at once. All the preparations for the defence must be completed within that time."

"Clementina," Mrs. Blessing continued, without heeding his words, "will be married about the first of October. Mr. Spelter has been desirous of making a bridal tour in Europe. She did not favor the plan; but it seems to me like an inter-position of Heaven!"

Philip rose, too disgusted to speak. He bowed in silence, and left the house.

CHAPTER XXVIII
THE TRIAL

As the day of trial drew nigh, the anxiety and activity of Joseph's friends increased, so that even the quiet atmosphere wherein he lived was disturbed by it. He could not help knowing that they were engaged in collecting evidence, but inasmuch as Philip always said, "You can do nothing!" he forced himself to wait with such patience as was possible. Rachel Miller, who had partly taken the hired man, Dennis, into her confidence, hermetically sealed the house to the gossip of the neighborhood; but her greatest triumph was in concealing her alarm, as the days rolled by and the mystery was not yet unravelled.

There was not much division of opinion in the neighborhood, however. The growing discord between husband and wife had not been generally remarked: they were looked upon as a loving and satisfied couple. Joseph's integrity of character was acknowledged, and, even had it been doubted, the people saw no motive for crime. His action in demanding a legal investigation also operated favorably upon public opinion.

The quiet and seclusion were beneficial to him. His mind became calmer and clearer; he was able to survey the past without passion, and to contemplate his own faults with a sense of wholesome bitterness rather than pain. The approaching trial was not a pleasant thing to anticipate, but the worst which he foresaw was the probability of so much of his private life being laid bare to the world. Here, again, his own words returned to condemn him. Had he not said to Lucy, on the morning of that fatal day, "I am sick of masks!" Had he not threatened to follow Julia with his own miserable story? The system of checks which restrain impulse, and the whirl of currents and counter-currents which govern a man's movement through life, began to arrange themselves in his mind. True wisdom, he now felt, lay in understanding these, and so employing them as to reach individual liberty of action through law, and not outside of it. He had been shallow and reckless, even in his good impulses; it was now time to endure quietly for a season what their effect had been.

The day previous to the trial Philip had a long consultation with Mr. Pinkerton. He had been so far successful that the name and whereabouts of the travelling agent had been discovered: the latter had been summoned, but he could not possibly arrive before the next day. Philip had also seen Mr. Blessing, who entered with great readiness into his plans, promised his assistance in ascertaining the truth of Madeline's suspicion, and would give his testimony as soon as he could return from New York, whither he had gone to say farewell to Mrs. Clementina Spelter, before her departure for Paris on a bridal journey. These were the two principal witnesses for the defence, and it was yet uncertain what kind of testimony they would be able to give.

"We must finish the other witnesses," Mr. Pinkerton said, "(who, in spite of all we can do, will strengthen the prosecution), by the time you reach here. If Spenham gives us trouble, as I am inclined to suspect, we cannot well spare you the first day, but I suppose it cannot be helped."

"I will send a telegram to Blessing, in New York, to make sure," Philip answered. "Byle and Glanders answer for their agent, and I can try him with the photograph on the way out. If that succeeds, Blessing's failure will be of less consequence."

"If only they do not reach Linthicum in the mean time! I will prolong the impanelling of the jury, and use every other liberty of delay allowed me; yet I have to be cautious. This is Spenham's first important case, and he is ambitious to make capital."

Mr. Spenham was the prosecuting attorney, who had just been elected to his first term of service in that capacity. He had some shrewdness as a criminal lawyer, and a great deal of experience of the subterranean channels of party politics. This latter acquirement, in fact, was the secret of his election, for he was known to be coarse, unscrupulous, and offensive. Mr. Pinkerton was able to foresee his probable line of attack, and was especially anxious, for that reason, to introduce testimony which would shorten the trial.

When the hour came, and Joseph found that Philip was inevitably absent, the strength he had summoned to his heart seemed to waver for an instant. All his other friends were present, however: Lucy Henderson and Madeline came with the Hopetons, and Elwood Withers stood by his side so boldly and proudly that he soon recovered his composure.

The court-room was crowded, not only by the idlers of the town, but also many neighbors from the country. They were grave and silent, and Joseph's appearance in the place allotted to the accused seemed to impress them painfully. The preliminaries occupied some time, and it was nearly noon before the first witness was called.

This was the physician. He stated, in a clear, business-like manner, the condition in which he found Julia, his discovery of the poison, and the unusual character of its operation, adding his opinion that the latter was owing to a long-continued nervous tension, culminating in hysterical excitement. Mr. Spenham questioned him very closely as to Joseph's demeanor, and his expressions before and after the death. The point of attack which he selected was Julia's exclamation: "Joseph, I will try to be different, but I must live for that!"

"These words," he said, "indicate a previous threat on the part of the accused. His helpless victim—"

Mr. Pinkerton protested against the epithet. But his antagonist found numberless ways of seeming to take Joseph's guilt for granted, and thus gradually to mould the pliant minds of a not very intelligent jury. The physician was subjected to a rigid cross-examination, in the course of which he was led to state that he, himself, had first advised that the fact of the poisoning should not be mentioned until after the funeral. The onus of the secrecy was thus removed from Joseph, and this was a point gained.

The next witness was the servant-woman, who had been present in the hall when Julia fell upon the landing of the staircase. She had heard the words, "Go away! you have killed me!" spoken in a shrill, excited voice. She had already guessed that something was wrong between the two. Mr. Asten came home looking quite wild and strange; he didn't seem to speak in his usual voice; he walked about in a restless way, and then went into the garden. Miss Lucy followed him, and then Mrs. Asten; but in a little while *she* came back, with her dress torn and her arms scratched; she, the witness, noticed this as Mrs. Asten passed through the hall, tottering as she went and with her fists shut tight.

Then Mr. Asten went up stairs to her bed-room; heard them speaking, but not the words; said to Sally, who was in the kitchen, "It's a real tiff and no mistake," and Sally remarked, "They're not used to each other yet, as they will be in a year or two."

The witness was with difficulty kept to a direct narrative. She had told the tale so often that every particular had its fixed phrases of description, and all the questioning on both sides called forth only repetitions. Joseph listened with a calm, patient air; nothing had yet occurred for which he was not prepared. The spectators, however, began to be deeply interested, and a sharp observer might have noticed that they were already taking sides.

Mr. Pinkerton soon detected that, although the woman's statements told against Joseph, she possessed no friendly feeling for Julia. He endeavored to make the most of this; but it was not much.

When Lucy Henderson's name was called, there was a stir of curiosity in the audience. They knew that the conference in the garden, from which Julia had returned in such an excited condition, must now be described. Mr. Spenham pricked up his red ears, ran his hand through his stubby hair, and prepared himself for battle; while Mr. Pinkerton, already in possession of all the facts, felt concerned only regarding the manner in which Lucy might give them. This was a case where so much depended on the impression produced by the individual!

By the time Lucy was sworn she appeared to be entirely composed; her face was slightly pale, but calm, and her voice steady. Mrs. Hopeton and Madeline Held sat near her, and Elwood Withers, leaning against a high railing, was nearly opposite.

There was profound silence as she began, and the interest increased as she approached the time of Joseph's return. She described his appearance, repeated the words she had heard, reproduced the scene in her own chamber, and so came, step by step, to the interview in the garden. The trying nature of her task now became evident. She spoke slowly, and with longer pauses; but whichever way she turned in her thought, the inexorable necessity of the whole truth stared her in the face.

"Must I repeat everything?" she asked. "I am not sure of recollecting the words precisely as they were spoken."

"You can certainly give the substance," said Mr. Spenham. "And be careful that you omit nothing: you are on your oath, and you ought to know what that means."

His words were loud and harsh. Lucy looked at the impassive face of the judge, at Elwood's earnest features, at the attentive jurymen, and went on.

When she came to Joseph's expression of the love that might have been possible, she gave also his words: "Had there been, I should have darkened the life of a friend."

"Ha!" exclaimed Mr. Spenham, "we are coming upon the motive of the murder."

Again Mr. Pinkerton protested, and was sustained by the court.

"Tell the jury," said Mr. Spenham, "whether there had been any interchange of such expressions between you and the accused previous to his marriage!"

This question was objected to, but the objection was overruled.

"None whatever!" was the answer.

Julia's sudden appearance, the accusation she made, and the manner in which Joseph met it, seemed to turn the current of sympathy the other way. Lucy's recollection of this scene was very clear and complete: had she wished it, she could not have forgotten a word or a look. In spite of Mr. Spenham's angry objections, she was allowed to go on and relate the conversation between Joseph and herself after Julia's return to the house. Mr. Pinkerton made the best use of this portion of the evidence, and it seemed that his side was strengthened, in spite of all unfavorable appearances.

"This is not all!" exclaimed the prosecuting attorney. "A married man does not make a declaration of love—"

"Of a past *possible* love," Mr. Pinkerton interrupted.

"A very fine hair-splitting indeed! A 'possible' love and a 'possible' return, followed by a 'possible' murder and a 'possible' remarriage! Our duty is to remove possibilities and establish facts. The question is, Was there no previous affection between the witness and the accused? This is necessary to prove a motive. I ask, then, the woman—I beg pardon, the lady—what were her sentiments towards the husband of the poisoned before his marriage, at the time of the conversation in the garden, and now?"

Lucy started, and could not answer. Mr. Pinkerton came to her aid. He protested strongly against such a question, though he felt that there was equal danger in answering it or leaving it unanswered. A portion of the spectators, sympathizing with Lucy, felt indignant at Mr. Spenham's demand; another portion, hungry for the most private and intimate knowledge of all the parties concerned, eagerly hoped that it would be acceded to.

Lucy half turned, so that she caught a glimpse of Joseph. He was calm, but his eyes expressed a sympathetic trouble. Then she felt her gaze drawn to Elwood, who had become a shade paler, and who met her eyes with a deep, inscrutable expression. Was he thinking of his recent words to her,—"If need comes to publish what I said to you, don't keep back a single word!" She felt sure of it, for all that he said was in her mind. Her decision was made: for truth's sake, and under the eye of God, she would speak. Having so resolved, she shut her mind to all else, for she needed the greatest strength of either woman or man.

The judge had decided that she was not obliged to answer the question. There was a murmur, here and there, among the spectators.

"Then I will use my freedom of choice," said Lucy, in a firm voice, "and answer it."

She kept her eyes on Elwood as she spoke, and compelled him to face her. She seemed to forget judge, jury, and the curious public, and to speak only to his ear.

"I am here to tell the whole truth, God helping me," she said. "I do not know how what I am required to say can touch the question of Joseph Asten's guilt or innocence; but I cannot pause to consider that. It is not easy for a woman to lay bare her secret heart to the world; I would like to think that every man who hears me has a wife, a sister, or a beloved girl of his choice, and that he will try to understand my heart through his knowledge of hers. I *did* cherish a tenderness which might have been love—I cannot tell—for Joseph Asten before his betrothal. I admit that his marriage was a grief to me at the time, for, while I had not suffered myself to feel any hope, I could not keep the feeling of disappointment out of my heart. It was both my blame and shame: I wrestled with it, and with God's help I overcame it."

There was a simple pathos in Lucy's voice, which pierced directly to the hearts of her hearers. She stood before them as pure as Godiva in her helpful nakedness. She saw on Elwood's cheek the blush which did not visit hers, and the sparkle of an unconscious tear. Joseph had hidden his face in his hands for a moment, but now looked up with a sadness which no man there could misinterpret.

Lucy had paused, as if waiting to be questioned, but the effect of her words had been so powerful and unexpected that Mr. Spenham was not quite ready. She went on:—

"When I say that I overcame it, I think I have answered everything. I went to him in the garden against my own wish, because his wife begged me with tears and sobs to intercede for her: I could not guess that he had ever thought of me otherwise than as a friend. I attributed his expressions to his disappointment in marriage, and pardoned him when he asked me to forget them—"

"O, no doubt!" Mr. Spenham interrupted, looking at the jury; "after all we have heard, they could not have been very disagreeable!"

Elwood made a rapid step forward; then, recollecting himself, resumed his position against the railing. Very few persons noticed the movement.

"They were very unwelcome," Lucy replied: "under any other circumstances, it would not have been easy to forgive them."

"And this former—'tenderness,' I think you called it," Mr. Spenham persisted, "—do you mean to say that you feel nothing of it at present?"

There was a murmur of indignation all over the room. If there is anything utterly incomprehensible to a vulgar nature, it is the natural delicacy of feeling towards women, which is rarely wanting even to the roughest and most ignorant men. The prosecution had damaged itself, and now the popular sympathy was wholly and strongly with Lucy.

"I have already answered that question," she said. "For the holy sake of truth, and of my own free-will, I have opened my heart. I did it, believing that a woman's first affection is pure, and would be respected; I did it, hoping that it might serve the cause of an innocent man; but now, since it has brought upon me doubt and insult, I shall avail myself of the liberty granted to me by the judge, and speak no word more!"

The spectators broke into applause, which the judge did not immediately check. Lucy's strength suddenly left her; she dropped into her seat and burst into tears.

"I have no further question to ask the witness," said Mr. Pinkerton.

Mr. Spenham inwardly cursed himself for his blunder,—not for his vulgarity, for of that he was sublimely unconscious,—and was only too ready to be relieved from Lucy's presence.

She rose to leave the court, Mrs. Hopeton accompanying her; but Elwood Withers was already at her side, and she leaned upon his arm as they passed through the crowd. The people fell back to make a way, and not a few whispered some honest word of encouragement. Elwood breathed heavily, and the veins on his forehead were swollen.

Not a word was spoken until they reached the hotel. Then Lucy, taking Elwood's hand, said: "Thank you, true, dear friend! I can say no more now. Go back, for Joseph's sake, and when the day is over come here and tell me, if you can, that I have not injured him in trying to help him."

When Elwood returned to the court-room, Rachel Miller was on the witness stand. Her testimony confirmed the interpretation of Julia's character which had been suggested by Lucy Henderson's. The sweet, amiable, suffering wife began to recede into the background, and the cold, false, selfish wife to take her place.

All Mr. Spenham's cross-examination failed to give the prosecution any support until he asked the question:—

"Have you discovered nothing whatever, since your return to the house, which will throw any light upon Mrs. Asten's death?"

Mr. Pinkerton, Elwood, and Madeline all felt that the critical moment had come. Philip's absence threatened to be a serious misfortune.

"Yes," Rachel Miller answered.

"Ah!" exclaimed the prosecuting attorney, rubbing his hair; "what was it?"

"The paper in which the arsenic was put up."

"Will you produce that paper?" he eagerly asked.

"I cannot now," said Rachel; "I gave it to Mr. Philip Held, so that he might find out something more."

Joseph listened with a keen, undisguised interest. After the first feeling of surprise that such an important event had been kept from his knowledge, his confidence in Philip's judgment reassured him.

"Has Mr. Philip Held destroyed that paper?" Mr. Spenham asked.

"He retains it, and will produce it before this court to-morrow," Mr. Pinkerton replied.

"Was there any mark, or label, upon it, which indicated the place where the poison had been procured?"

"Yes," said Rachel Miller.

"State what it was."

"Ziba Linthicum's Drug store, No. 77 Main Street, Magnolia," she replied, as if the label were before her eyes.

"Let Ziba Linthicum be summoned at once!" Mr. Spenham cried.

Mr. Pinkerton, however, arose and stated that the apothecary's testimony required that of another person who was present when the poison was purchased. This other person had been absent in a distant part of the country, but had been summoned, and would arrive, in company with Mr. Philip Held, on the following morning. He begged that Mr. Linthicum's evidence might be postponed until then, when he believed that the mystery attending the poisoning would be wholly explained.

Mr. Spenham violently objected, but he again made the mistake of speaking for nearly half an hour on the subject, — an indiscretion into which he was led by his confirmed political habits. By the time the question was decided, and in favor of the defence, the afternoon was well advanced, and the court adjourned until the next day.

CHAPTER XXIX
NEW EVIDENCE

Elwood accompanied Joseph to the prison where he was obliged to spend the night, and was allowed to remain with him until Mr. Pinkerton (who was endeavoring to reach Philip by telegraph) should arrive.

Owing to Rachel Miller's forethought, the bare room was sufficiently furnished. There was a clean bed, a chair or two, and a table, upon which stood a basket of provisions.

"I suppose I must eat," said Joseph, "as a matter of duty. If you will sit down and join me, Elwood, I will try."

"If I could have that fellow Spenham by the throat for a minute," Elwood growled, "it would give me a good appetite. But I will take my share, as it is: I never can think rightly when I'm hungry. Why, there is enough for a picnic! sandwiches, cold chicken, pickles, cakes, cheese, and two bottles of coffee, as I live! Just think that we're in a hotel, Joseph! It's all in one's notion, leastways for a single night; for you can go where you like to-morrow!"

"I hope so," said Joseph, as he took his seat. Elwood set the provisions before him, but he did not touch them. After a moment of hesitation he stretched out his hand and laid it on Elwood's shoulder.

"Now, old boy!" Elwood cried: "I know it. What you mean is unnecessary, and I won't have it!"

"Let me speak!"

"I don't see why I should, Joseph. It's no more than I guessed. She didn't love me: you were tolerably near together once, and if you should now come nearer—"

But he could not finish the sentence; the words stuck in his throat.

"Great Heaven!" Joseph exclaimed, starting to his feet; "what are you thinking of? Don't you see that Lucy Henderson and I are parted forever by what has happened to-day? Didn't you hear her say that she overcame the tenderness which might have become love, as I overcame mine for her?

Neither of us can recall that first feeling, any more than we can set our lives again in the past. I shall worship her as one of the purest and noblest souls that breathe; but love her? make her my wife? It could never, never be! No, Elwood! I was wondering whether you could pardon me the rashness which has exposed her to to-day's trial."

Elwood began to laugh strangely. "You are foolish, Joseph," he said. "Pshaw! I can't hold my knife. These sudden downs and then ups are too much for a fellow! Pardon you? Yes, on one condition—that you empty your plate before you speak another word to me!"

They were both cheerful after this, and the narrow little room seemed freer and brighter to their eyes. It was late before Mr. Pinkerton arrived: he had waited in vain for an answer from Philip. Elwood's presence was a relief to him, for he did not wish to excite Joseph by a statement of what he expected to prove unless the two witnesses had been really secured. He adroitly managed, however, to say very little while seeming to say a great deal, and Joseph was then left to such rest as his busy memory might allow him.

Next morning there was an even greater crowd in the court-room. All Joseph's friends were there, with the exception of Lucy Henderson, who, by Mr. Pinkerton's advice, remained at the hotel. Philip had not arrived, but had sent a message saying that all was well, and he would come in the morning train.

Mr. Spenham, the evening before, had ascertained the nature of Mr. Linthicum's evidence. The apothecary, however, was only able to inform him of Philip's desire to discover the travelling agent, without knowing his purpose. In the name recorded as that of the purchaser of the poison Mr. Spenham saw a weapon which would enable him to repay Lucy for his discomfiture, and to indicate, if not prove, a complicity of crime, in which Philip Held also, he suspected, might be concerned.

The court opened at nine o'clock, and Philip could not be on hand before ten. Mr. Pinkerton endeavored to procure the examination of Dennis, and another subordinate witness, before the apothecary; but he only succeeded in gaining fifteen minutes' time by the discussion. Mr. Ziba Linthicum was then called and sworn. He carried a volume under his arm.

As Philip possessed the label, Mr. Linthicum could only testify to the fact that a veiled lady had purchased so many grains of arsenic of him on a certain day; that he kept a record of all sales of dangerous drugs; and that the lady's name was recorded in the book which he had brought with him. He then read the entry:—

"*Miss Henderson. Arsenic.*"

Although Mr. Pinkerton had whispered to Joseph, "Do not be startled when he reads the name!" it was all the latter could do to suppress an exclamation. There was a murmur and movement through the whole court.

"We have now both the motive and the co-agent of the crime," said Mr. Spenham, rising triumphantly. "After the evidence which was elicited yesterday, it will not be difficult to connect the two. If the case deepens in enormity as it advances, we may be shocked, but we have no reason to be surprised. The growth of free-love sentiments, among those who tear themselves loose from the guidance of religious influences, naturally leads to crime; and the extent to which this evil has been secretly developed is not suspected by the public. Testimony can be adduced to show that the accused, Joseph Asten, has openly expressed his infidelity; that he repelled with threats and defiance a worthy minister of the Gospel, whom his own pious murdered wife had commissioned to lead him into the true path. The very expression which the woman Lucy Henderson testified to his having used in the garden,—'I am sick of masks,'—what does it mean? What but unrestrained freedom of the passions,—the very foundation upon which the free-lovers build up their pernicious theories? The accused cannot complain if the law lifts the mask from his countenance, and shows his nature in all its hideous deformity. But another mask, also, must be raised: I demand the arrest of the woman Lucy Henderson!"

Mr. Pinkerton sprang to his feet. In a measured, solemn voice, which contrasted strongly with the loud, sharp tones of the prosecuting attorney, he stated that Mr. Linthicum's evidence was already known to him; that it required an explanation which would now be given in a few minutes, and which would completely exonerate Miss Henderson from the suspicion of having purchased the poison, or even having any knowledge of its purchase. He demanded that no conclusion should be drawn from evidence which would mislead the minds of the jury: he charged the prosecuting attorney with most unjustly assailing the characters of both Joseph Asten and Lucy Henderson, and invoked, in the name of impartial justice, the protection of the court.

He spoke both eloquently and earnestly; but the spectators noticed that he looked at his watch from minute to minute. Mr. Spenham interrupted him, but he continued to repeat his statements, until there came a sudden movement in the crowd, near the outer door of the hall. Then he sat down.

Philip led the way, pressing the crowd to right and left in his eagerness. He was followed by a tall young man, with a dark moustache and an abundance of jewelry, while Mr. Benjamin Blessing, flushed and perspiring, brought up the rear. The spectators were almost breathless in their hushed, excited interest.

Philip seized Joseph's hand, and, bending nearer, whispered, "You are free!" His eyes sparkled and his face glowed.

Room was made for the three witnesses, and after a brief whispered consultation between Philip and Mr. Pinkerton, Elwood was despatched to bring Lucy Henderson to the court.

"May it please the Court," said Mr. Pinkerton, "I am now able to fulfil that promise which I this moment made. The evidence which was necessary to set forth the manner of Mrs. Asten's death, and which will release the court from any further consideration of the present case, is in my hands. I therefore ask leave to introduce this evidence without any further delay."

After a little discussion the permission was granted, and Philip Held was placed upon the stand.

He first described Joseph's genuine sorrow at his wife's death, and his self-accusation of having hastened it by his harsh words to her in the morning. He related the interview at which Joseph, on learning of the reports concerning him, had immediately decided to ask for a legal investigation, and in a simple, straightforward way, narrated all that had been done up to the time of consulting Ziba Linthicum's poison record.

"As I knew it to be quite impossible that Miss Lucy Henderson could have been the purchaser," he began—

Mr. Spenham instantly objected, and the expression was ruled out by the Court.

"Then," Philip resumed, "I determined to ascertain who had purchased the arsenic. Mr. Linthicum's description of the lady was too vague to be recognized. It was necessary to identify the travelling agent who was present; for this purpose I went to the city, ascertained the names and addresses of all the travelling agents of all the wholesale drug firms, and after much time and correspondence discovered the man,—Mr. Case, who is here present. He was in Persepolis, Iowa, when the summons reached him, and would have been here yesterday but for an accident on the Erie Railway.

"In the mean time I had received the small fragment of another label, and by the clew which the few letters gave me I finally identified the place as the drug-store of Wallis and Erkers, at the corner of Fifth and Persimmon Streets. There was nothing left by which the nature of the drug could be ascertained, and therefore this movement led to nothing which could be offered as evidence in this court,—that is, by the druggists themselves, and they have not been summoned. It happened, however, by a coincidence which only came to light this morning, that—"

Here Philip was again interrupted. His further testimony was of less consequence. He was sharply cross-examined by Mr. Spenham as to his relations with Joseph, and his object in devoting so much time to procuring evidence for the defence; but he took occasion, in replying, to express his appreciation of Joseph's character so emphatically, that the prosecution lost rather than gained. Then the plan of attack was changed. He was asked whether he believed in the Bible, in future rewards and punishments, in the views of the so-called free-lovers, in facile divorce and polygamy. He was too shrewd, however, to lay himself open to the least misrepresentation, and the moral and mental torture which our jurisprudence has substituted for the rack, thumb-screws, and Spanish boots of the Middle Ages finally came to an end.

Then the tall young man, conscious of his own elegance, took his place. He gave his name and occupation as Augustus Fitzwilliam Case, commercial traveller for the house of Byle and Glanders, wholesale druggists.

"State whether you were in the drug-store of Ziba Linthicum, No. 77 Main Street, in this town, on the day of the entry in Mr. Linthicum's book."

"I was."

"Did you notice the person who called for arsenic?"

"I did."

"What led you specially to notice her?"

"It is my habit," said the witness. "I am impressible to beauty, and I saw at once that the lady had what I call—style. I recollect thinking, 'More style than could be expected in these little places.'"

"Keep your thoughts to yourself!" cried Mr. Spenham.

"Describe the lady as correctly as you can," said Mr. Pinkerton.

"Something under the medium size; a little thin, but not bad lines,— what I should call jimp, natty, or 'lissome,' in the Scotch dialect. A well-trained voice; no uncertainty about it,—altogether about as keen and wide-awake a woman as you'll find in a day's travel."

"You guessed all this from her figure?" Mr. Spenham asked, with a sneer.

"Not entirely. I saw her face. I suppose something in my appearance or attitude attracted her attention. While Mr. Linthicum was weighing the arsenic she leaned over the counter, let her veil fall forward slightly, and gave me a quick side-look. I bent a little at the same time, as if to examine the soaps, and saw her face in a three-quarter position, as the photographers say."

"Can you remember her features distinctly?"

"Quite so. In fact, it is difficult for me to forget a female face. Hers was just verging on the sharp, but still tolerably handsome. Hair quite dark, and worn in ringlets; eyebrows clean and straight; mouth a little too thin for my fancy; and eyes—well, I couldn't undertake to say exactly what color they were, for she seemed to have the trick—very common in the city—of letting the lids droop over them."

"Were you able to judge of her age?"

"Tolerably, I should say. There is a certain air of preservation which enables a practised eye to distinguish an old girl from a young one. She was certainly not to be called young,—somewhere between twenty-eight and thirty-five."

"You heard the name she gave Mr. Linthicum?"

"Distinctly. Mr. Linthicum politely stated that it was his custom to register the names of all those to whom he furnished either poisons or prescriptions requiring care in being administered. She said, 'You are *very* particular, sir;' and, a moment afterward, 'Pardon me, perhaps it is necessary.'—'What name, then?' he asked. I thought she hesitated a moment, but this I will not say positively; whether or not, the answer was, 'Miss Henderson.' She went out of the store with a light, brisk step."

"You are sure you would be able to recognize the lady?" Mr. Pinkerton asked.

"Quite sure." And Mr. Augustus Fitzwilliam Case smiled patronizingly, as if the question were superfluous.

Mr. Pinkerton made a sign to Lucy, and she arose.

"Look upon this lady!" he said to the witness.

The latter made a slight, graceful inclination of his head, as much as to say, "Pardon me, I am compelled to stare." Lucy quietly endured his gaze.

"Consider her well," said the lawyer, "and then tell the jury whether she is the person."

"No considerment is necessary. This lady has not the slightest resemblance to Miss Henderson. She is younger, taller, and modelled upon a wholly different style."

"Will you now look at this photograph?"

"Ah!" the witness exclaimed; "you can yourself judge of the correctness of my memory! Here is Miss Henderson herself, and in three-quarter face, as I saw her!"

"That," said Mr. Pinkerton, addressing the judge and jury, "that is the photograph of Mrs. Julia Asten."

The spectators were astounded, and Mr. Spenham taken completely aback by this revelation. Joseph and Elwood both felt that a great weight had been lifted from their hearts. The testimony established Julia's falsehood at the same time, and there was such an instant and complete revulsion of opinion that many persons present at once suspected her of a design to poison Joseph.

"Before calling upon Mr. Benjamin Blessing, the father of the late Mrs. Asten, for his testimony," said Mr. Pinkerton,—"and I believe he will be the last witness necessary,—I wish to show that, although Miss Lucy Henderson accompanied Mrs. Asten to Magnolia, she could not have visited Mr. Linthicum's Drug store at the time indicated; nor, indeed, at any time during that day. She made several calls upon friends, each of whom is now in attendance, and their joint evidence will account for every minute of her stay in the place. The base attempt to blacken her fair name imperatively imposes this duty upon me."

No objection was made, and the witnesses were briefly examined in succession. Their testimony was complete.

"One mystery still remains to be cleared up," the lawyer continued; "the purpose of Mrs. Asten in purchasing the poison, and the probable explanation of her death. I say 'probable,' because absolute certainty is impossible. But I will not anticipate the evidence. Mr. Benjamin Blessing, step forward, if you please!"

CHAPTER XXX
MR. BLESSING'S TESTIMONY

On entering the court-room Mr. Blessing had gone to Joseph, given his hand a long, significant grasp, and looked in his face with an expression of triumph, almost of exultation. The action was not lost upon the spectators or the jury, and even Joseph felt that it was intended to express the strongest faith in his innocence.

When the name was called there was a movement in the crowd, and a temporary crush in some quarters, as the people thrust forward their heads to see and listen. Mr. Blessing, bland, dignified, serene, feeling that he was the central point of interest, waited until quiet had been restored, slightly turning his head to either side, as if to summon special attention to what he should say.

After being sworn, and stating his name, he thus described his occupation:—

"I hold a position under government; nominally, it is a Deputy Inspectorship in the Custom-House, yet it possesses a confidential—I might say, if modesty did not prevent, an advisory—character."

"In other words, a Ward Politician!" said Mr. Spenham.

"I must ask the prosecuting attorney," Mr. Blessing blandly suggested, "not to define my place according to his own political experiences."

There was a general smile at these words; and a very audible chuckle from spectators belonging to the opposite party.

"You are the father of the late Mrs. Julia Asten?"

"I am—her unhappy father, whom nothing but the imperious commands of justice, and the knowledge of her husband's innocence of the crime with which he stands charged, could have compelled to appear here, and reveal the painful secrets of a family, which—"

Here Mr. Spenham interrupted him.

"I merely wish to observe," Mr. Blessing continued, with a stately wave of his hand towards the judge and jury, "that the De Belsains and their descendants may have been frequently unfortunate, but were never dishonorable. I act in their spirit when I hold duty to the innocent living higher than consideration for the unfortunate dead."

Here he drew forth a handkerchief, and held it for a moment to his eyes.

"Did you know of any domestic discords between your daughter and her husband?"

"I foresaw that such might be, and took occasion to warn my daughter, on her wedding-day, not to be too sure of her influence. There was too much disparity of age, character, and experience. It could not be called crabbed age and rosy youth, but there was difference enough to justify Shakespeare's doubts. I am aware that the court requires ocular—or auricular—evidence. The only such I have to offer is my son-in-law's own account of the discord which preceded my daughter's death."

"Did this discord sufficiently explain to you the cause and manner of her death?"

"My daughter's nature—I do not mean to digress, but am accustomed to state my views clearly—my daughter's nature was impulsive. She inherited my own intellect, but modified by the peculiar character of the feminine nervous system. Hence she might succumb to a depression which I should resist. She appeared to be sure of her control over my son-in-law's nature, and of success in an enterprise, in which—I regret to say—my son-in-law lost confidence. I assumed, at the time, that her usually capable mind was unbalanced by the double disappointment, and that she had rushed, unaneled, to her last account. This, I say, was the conclusion forced upon me; yet I cannot admit that it was satisfactory. It seemed to disparage my daughter's intellectual power: it was not the act which I should have anticipated in any possible emergency."

"Had you no suspicion that her husband might have been instrumental?" Mr. Spenham asked.

"He? he is simply incapable of that, or *any* crime!"

"We don't want assertions," said Mr. Spenham, sternly.

"I beg pardon of the court," remarked Mr. Blessing; "it was a spontaneous expression. The touch of nature cannot always be avoided."

"Go on, sir!"

"I need not describe the shock and sorrow following my daughter's death," Mr. Blessing continued, again applying his handkerchief. "In order to dissipate it, I obtained a leave of absence from my post,—the exigencies of the government fortunately admitting of it,—and made a journey to the Oil

Regions, in the interest of myself and my son-in-law. While there I received a letter from Mr. Philip Held, the contents of which—"

"Will you produce the letter?" Mr. Spenham exclaimed.

"It can be produced, if necessary. I will state nothing further, since I perceive that this would not be admissible evidence. It is enough to say that I returned to the city without delay, in order to meet Mr. Philip Held. The requirements of justice were more potent with me than the suggestions of personal interest. Mr. Held had already, as you will have noticed from his testimony, identified the fragment of paper as having emanated from the drug-store of Wallis and Erkers, corner of Fifth and Persimmon Streets. I accompanied him to that drug-store, heard the statements of the proprietors, in answer to Mr. Held's questions,—statements which, I confess, surprised me immeasurably (but I could not reject the natural deductions to be drawn from them), and was compelled, although it overwhelmed me with a sense of unmerited shame, to acknowledge that there was plausibility in Mr. Held's conjectures. Since they pointed to my elder daughter, Clementina, now Mrs. Spelter, and at this moment tossing upon the ocean-wave, I saw that Mr. Held might possess a discernment superior to my own. But for a lamentable cataclysm, he might have been my son-in-law, and I need not say that I prefer that refinement of character which comes of good blood to the possession of millions—"

Here Mr. Blessing was again interrupted, and ordered to confine himself to the simple statement of the necessary facts.

"I acknowledge the justice of the rebuke," he said. "But the sentiment of the *mens conscia recti* will sometimes obtrude through the rigid formula of Themis. In short, Mr. Philip Held's representations—"

"State those representations at once, and be done with them!" Mr. Spenham cried.

"I am coming to them presently. The Honorable Court understands, I am convinced, that a coherent narrative, although moderately prolix, is preferable to a disjointed narrative, even if the latter were terse as Tacitus. Mr. Held's representations, I repeat, satisfied me that an interview with my daughter Clementina was imperative. There was no time to be lost, for the passage of the nuptial pair had already been taken in the *Ville de Paris*. I started at once, sending a telegram in advance, and in the same evening arrived at their palatial residence in Fifth Avenue. Clementina's nature, I must explain to the Honorable Court, is very different from that of her sister,—the reappearance, I suspect, of some lateral strain of blood. She is reticent, undemonstrative,—in short, frequently inscrutable. I suspected that a direct question might defeat my object; therefore, when I was alone with her the next morning,—my son-in-law, Mr. Spelter, being called to a meeting of Erie of which he is one of the directors,—I said to her: 'My child, you are perfectly blooming! Your complexion was always admirable, but now it seems to me incomparable!'"

"This is irrelevant!" cried Mr. Spenham.

"By no means! It is the very *corpus delicti*,—the foot of Hercules,—the milk (powder would be more appropriate) in the cocoa-nut!" Clementina smiled in her serene way, and made no reply. 'How do you keep it up now?' I asked, tapping her cheek; 'you must be careful, here: all persons are not so discreet as Wallis and Erkers.' She was astounded, stupefied, I might say, but I saw that I had reached the core of truth. 'Did you suppose I was ignorant of it?' I said, still very friendly and playfully. 'Then it was Julia who told you!' she exclaimed. 'And if she did,' I answered, 'what was the harm? I have no doubt that Julia did the same thing.' 'She was always foolish,' Clementina then said; 'she envied me my complexion, and she watched me until she found out. I told her that it would not do for any except blondes, like myself, and *her* complexion was neither one thing nor the other. And I couldn't see that it improved much, afterwards.'"

Mr. Pinkerton saw that the jurymen were puzzled, and requested Mr. Blessing to explain the conversation to them.

"It is my painful duty to obey; yet a father's feelings may be pardoned if he shrinks from presenting the facts at once in their naked—unpleasantness. However, since the use of arsenic as a cosmetic is so general in our city, especially among blondes, as Wallis and Erkers assure me, my own family is not an isolated case. Julia commenced using the drug, so Clementina informed me, after her engagement with Mr. Asten, and only a short time before her marriage. To what extent she used it, after that event, I have no means of knowing; but, I suspect, less frequently, unless she feared that the disparity of age between her and her husband was becoming more apparent. I cannot excuse her duplicity in giving Miss Henderson's name instead of her own at Mr. Linthicum's Drug store, since the result might have been so fearfully fatal; yet I entreat you to believe that there may have been no inimical *animus* in the act. I attribute her death entirely to an over-dose of the drug, voluntarily taken, but taken in a moment of strong excitement."

The feeling of relief from suspense, not only among Joseph's friends, but throughout the crowded court-room, was clearly manifested: all present seemed to breathe a lighter and fresher atmosphere.

Mr. Blessing wiped his forehead and his fat cheeks, and looked benignly around. "There are a hundred little additional details," he said, "which will substantiate my evidence; but I have surely said sufficient for the ends of justice. The heavens will not fall because I have been forced to carve the emblems of criminal vanity upon the sepulchre of an unfortunate child,— but the judgment of an earthly tribunal may well be satisfied. However, I am ready," he added, turning towards Mr. Spenham; "apply all the engines of technical procedure, and I shall not wince."

The manner of the prosecuting attorney was completely changed. He answered respectfully and courteously, and his brief cross-examination was calculated rather to confirm the evidence for the defence than to invalidate it.

Mr. Pinkerton then rose and stated that he should call no other witnesses. The fact had been established that Mrs. Asten had been in the habit of taking arsenic to improve her complexion; also that she had purchased much more than enough of the drug to cause death, at the store of Mr. Ziba Linthicum, only a few days before her demise, and under circumstances which indicated a desire to conceal the purchase. There were two ways in which the manner of her death might be explained; either she had ignorantly taken an over-dose, or, having mixed the usual quantity before descending to the garden to overhear the conversation between Mr. Asten and Lucy Henderson, had forgotten the fact in the great excitement which followed, and thoughtlessly added as much more of the poison. Her last words to her husband, which could not be introduced as evidence, but might now be repeated, showed that her death was the result of accident, and not of design. She was thus absolved of the guilt of suicide, even as her husband of the charge of murder.

Mr. Spenham, somewhat to the surprise of those who were unacquainted with his true character, also stated that he should call no further witness for the prosecution. The testimonies of Mr. Augustus Fitzwilliam Case and Mr. Benjamin Blessing—although the latter was unnecessarily ostentatious and discursive—were sufficient to convince him that the prosecution could not make out a case. He had no doubt whatever of Mr. Joseph Asten's innocence. Lest the expressions which he had been compelled to use, in the performance of his duty, might be misunderstood, he wished to say that he had the highest respect for the characters of Mr. Asten and also of Miss Lucy Henderson. He believed the latter to be a refined and virtuous lady, an ornament to the community in which she resided. His language towards her had been professional,—by no means personal. It was in accordance with the usage of the most eminent lights of the bar; the ends of justice required the most searching examination, and the more a character was criminated the more brightly it would shine forth to the world after the test had been successfully endured. He was simply the agent of the law, and all respect of persons was prohibited to him while in the exercise of his functions.

The judge informed the jurymen that he did not find it necessary to give them any instructions. If they were already agreed upon their verdict, even the formality of retiring might be dispensed with.

There was a minute's whispering back and forth among the men, and the foreman then rose and stated that they were agreed.

The words "Not Guilty!" spoken loudly and emphatically, were the signal for a stormy burst of applause from the audience. In vain the court-crier, aided by the constables, endeavored to preserve order. Joseph's friends gathered around him with their congratulations; while Mr. Blessing, feeling that some recognition of the popular sentiment was required, rose and bowed repeatedly to the crowd. Philip led the way to the open air, and the others followed, but few words were spoken until they found themselves in the large parlor of the hotel.

Mr. Blessing had exchanged some mysterious whispers with the clerk, on arriving; and presently two negro waiters entered the room, bearing wine, ice, and other refreshments. When the glasses had been filled, Mr. Blessing lifted his with an air which imposed silence on the company, and thus spake: "'Out of the abundance of the heart the mouth speaketh.' There may be occasions when silence is golden, but to-day we are content with the baser metal. A man in whom we all confide, whom we all love, has been rescued from the labyrinth of circumstances; he comes to us as a new Theseus, saved from the Minotaur of the Law! Although Mr. Held, with the assistance of his fair sister, was the Ariadne who found the clew, it has been my happy lot to assist in unrolling it; and now we all stand together, like our classic models on the free soil of Crete, to chant a pæan of deliverance. While I propose the health and happiness and good-fortune of Joseph Asten, I beg him to believe that my words come *ab imo pectore,*—from my inmost heart: if any veil of mistrust, engendered by circumstances which I will not now recall, still hangs between him and myself, I entreat him to rend that veil, even as David rent his garments, and believe in my sincerity, if he cannot in my discretion!"

Philip was the only one, besides Joseph, who understood the last allusion. He caught hold of Mr. Blessing's hand and exclaimed: "Spoken like a man!"

Joseph stepped instantly forward. "I have again been unjust," he said, "and I thank you for making me feel it. You have done me an infinite service, sacrificing your own feelings, bearing no malice against me for my hasty and unpardonable words, and showing a confidence in my character which—after what has passed between us—puts me to shame. I am both penitent and grateful: henceforth I shall know you and esteem you!"

Mr. Blessing took the offered hand, held it a moment, and then stammered, while the tears started from his eyes: "Enough! Bury the past a thousand fathoms deep! I can still say: *foi de Belsain!*"

"One more toast!" cried Philip. "Happiness and worldly fortune to the man whom misfortunes have bent but cannot break,—who has been often deceived, but who never purposely deceived in turn,—whose sentiment of honor has been to-day so nobly manifested,—Benjamin Blessing!"

While the happy company were pouring out but not exhausting their feelings, Lucy Henderson stole forth upon the upper balcony of the hotel. There was a secret trouble in her heart, which grew from minute to minute. She leaned upon the railing, and looked down the dusty street, passing in review the events of the two pregnant days, and striving to guess in what manner they would affect her coming life. She felt that she had done her simple duty: she had spoken no word which she was not ready to repeat; yet in her words there seemed to be the seeds of change.

After a while the hostler brought a light carriage from the stable, and Elwood Withers stepped into the street below her. He was about to take the reins, when he looked up, saw her, and remained standing. She noticed the intensely wistful expression of his face.

"Are you going, Elwood,—and alone?" she asked.

"Yes," he said eagerly; and waited.

"Then I will go with you,—that is, if you will take me." She tried to speak lightly and playfully.

In a few minutes they were out of town, passing between the tawny fields and under the russet woods. A sweet west wind fanned them with nutty and spicy odors, and made a crisp, cheerful music among the fallen leaves.

"What a delicious change!" said Lucy, "after that stifling, dreadful room."

"Ay, Lucy—and think how Joseph will feel it! And how near, by the chance of a hair, we came of missing the truth!"

"Elwood!" she exclaimed, "while I was giving my testimony, and I found your eyes fixed on me, were you thinking of the counsel you gave me, three weeks ago, when we met at the tunnel?"

"I was!"

"I knew it, and I obeyed. Do you now say that I did right?"

"Not for that reason," he answered. "It was your own heart that told you what to do. I did not mean to bend or influence you in any way: I have no right."

"You have the right of a friend," she whispered.

"Yes," said he, "I sometimes take more upon myself than I ought. But it's hard, in my case, to hit a very fine line."

"O, you are now unjust to yourself, Elwood. You are both strong and generous."

"I am not strong! I am this minute spoiling my good luck. It *was* a luck from Heaven to me, Lucy, when you offered to ride home with me, and it *is*, now—if I could only swallow the words that are rising into my mouth!"

She whispered again: "Why should you swallow them?"

"You are cruel! when you have forbidden me to speak, and I have promised to obey!"

"After all you have heard?" she asked.

"All the more for what I have heard."

She took his hand, and cried, in a trembling voice: "*I* have been cruel, in remaining blind to your nature. I resisted what would have been—what will be, if you do not turn away—my one happiness in this life! Do not speak—let *me* break the prohibition! Elwood, dear, true, noble heart,— Elwood, I love you!"

"Lucy!"

And she lay upon his bosom.

CHAPTER XXXI
BEGINNING ANOTHER LIFE

It was hard for the company of rejoicing friends, at the hotel in Magnolia, to part from each other. Mr. Blessing had tact enough to decline Joseph's invitation, but he was sorely tempted by Philip's, in which Madeline heartily joined. Nevertheless, he only wavered for a moment; a mysterious resolution strengthened him, and taking Philip to one side, he whispered:—

"Will you allow me to postpone, not relinquish, the pleasure? Thanks! A grave duty beckons,—a task, in short, without which the triumph of to-day would be dramatically incomplete. I must speak in riddles, because this is a case in which a whisper might start the overhanging avalanche; but I am sure you will trust me."

"Of course I will!" Philip cried, offering his hand.

"*Foi de Belsain!*" was Mr. Blessing's proud answer, as he hurried away to reach the train for the city.

Joseph looked at Philip, as the horses were brought from the stable, and then at Rachel Miller, who, wrapped in her great crape shawl, was quietly waiting for him.

"We must not separate all at once," said Philip, stepping forward. "Miss Miller, will you invite my sister and myself to take tea with you this evening?"

Philip had become one of Rachel's heroes; she was sure that Mr. Blessing's testimony and Joseph's triumphant acquittal were owing to his exertions. The Asten farm could produce nothing good enough for his entertainment,—that was her only trouble.

"Do tell me the time o' day," she said to Joseph, as he drove out of town, closely followed by Philip's light carriage. "It's three days in one to me, and a deal more like day after to-morrow morning than this afternoon. Now, a telegraph would be a convenience; I could send word and have chickens killed and picked, against we got there."

Joseph answered her by driving as rapidly as the rough country roads permitted, without endangering horse and vehicle. It was impossible for him to think coherently, impossible to thrust back the single overwhelming prospect of relief and release which had burst upon his life. He dared to admit the fortune which had come to him through death, now that his own innocence of any indirect incitement thereto had been established. The future was again clear before him; and even the miserable discord of the past year began to recede and form only an indistinct background to the infinite pity of the death-scene. Mr. Blessing's testimony enabled him to look back and truly interpret the last appealing looks, the last broken words; his heart banished the remembrance of its accusations, and retained only—so long as it should beat among living men—a deep and tender commiseration. As for the danger he had escaped, the slander which had been heaped upon him, his thoughts were above the level of life which they touched. He was nearer than he suspected to that only true independence of soul which releases a man from the yoke of circumstances.

Rachel Miller humored his silence as long as she thought proper, and then suddenly and awkwardly interrupted it. "Yes," she exclaimed; "there's a little of the old currant wine in the cellar-closet! Town's-folks generally like it, and we used to think it good to stay a body's stomach for a late meal,—as it'll be apt to be. But I've not asked you how you relished the supper, though Elwood, to be sure, allowed that all was tolerable nice. And I see the Lord's hand in it, as I hope you do, Joseph; for the righteous is never forsaken. We can't help rejoice, where we ought to be humbly returning thanks, and owning our unworthiness; but Philip Held is a friend, if there ever was one; and the white hen's brood, though they are new-fashioned fowls, are plump enough by this time. I disremember whether I asked Elwood to stop—"

"There he is!" Joseph interrupted; "turning the corner of the wood before us! Lucy is with him,—and they must both come!"

He drove on rapidly, and soon overtook Elwood's lagging team. The horse, indeed, had had his own way, and the sound of approaching wheels awoke Elwood from a trance of incredible happiness. Before answering Joseph, he whispered to Lucy:—

"What shall we say? It'll be the heaviest favor I've ever been called upon to do a friend."

"Do it, then!" she said: "the day is too blessed to be kept for ourselves alone."

How fair the valley shone, as they came into it out of the long glen between the hills! What cheer there was, even in the fading leaves; what happy promise in the mellow autumn sky! The gate to the lane stood open; Dennis, with a glowing face, waited for the horse. He wanted to say something, but not knowing how, shook hands with Joseph, and then pretended to be concerned with the harness. Rachel, on entering the kitchen, found her neighbor, Mrs. Bishop, embarked on a full tide of preparation. Two plump fowls, scalded and plucked, lay upon the table!

This was too much for Rachel Miller. She had borne up bravely through the trying days, concealing her anxiety lest it might be misinterpreted, hiding even her grateful emotion, to make her faith in Joseph's innocence seem the stronger; and now Mrs. Bishop's thoughtfulness was the slight touch under which she gave way. She sat down and cried.

Mrs. Bishop, with a stew-pan in one hand, while she wiped her sympathetic eyes with the other, explained that her husband had come home an hour before, with the news; and that she just guessed help would be wanted, or leastways company, and so she had made bold to begin; for, though the truth had been made manifest, and the right had been proved, as anybody might know it would be, still it was a trial, and people needed to eat more and better under trials than at any other time. "You may not feel inclined for victuals; but there's the danger! A body's body must be supported, whether or no."

Meanwhile, Joseph and his guests sat on the veranda, in the still, mild air. He drew his chair near to Philip's, their hands closed upon each other, and they were entirely happy in the tender and perfect manly love which united them. Madeline sat in front, with a nimbus of sunshine around her hair, feeling also the embarrassment of speech at such a moment, yet bravely endeavoring to gossip with Lucy on other matters. But Elwood's face, so bright that it became almost beautiful, caught her eye: she glanced at Philip, who answered with a smile; then at Lucy, whose cheek bloomed with the loveliest color; and, rising without a word, she went to the latter and embraced her.

Then, stretching her hand to Elwood, she said: "Forgive me, both of you, for showing how glad I am!"

"Philip!" Joseph cried, as the truth flashed upon him; "life is not always unjust! It is we who are impatient."

They both arose and gave hands of congratulation; and Elwood, though so deeply moved that he scarcely trusted himself to speak, was so frankly proud and happy,—so purely and honestly *man* in such a sacred moment,— that Lucy's heart swelled with an equally proud recognition of his feeling. Their eyes met, and no memory of a mistaken Past could ever again come like a cloud across the light of their mutual faith.

"The day was blessed already," said Philip; "but this makes it perfect."

No one knew how the time went by, or could afterwards recall much that was said. Rachel Miller, with many apologies, summoned them to a sumptuous meal; and when the moon hung chill and clear above the creeping mists of the valley, they parted.

The next evening, Joseph went to Philip at the Forge. It was well that he should breathe another atmosphere, and dwell, for a little while, within walls where no ghosts of his former life wandered. Madeline, the most hospitably observant of hostesses, seemed to have planned the arrangements solely for his and Philip's intercourse. The short evening of the country was not half over, before she sent them to Philip's room, where a genial wood-fire prattled and flickered on the hearth, with two easy-chairs before it.

Philip lighted a pipe and they sat down. "Now, Joseph," said he, "I'll answer 'Yes!' to the question in your mind."

"You have been talking with Bishop, Philip?"

"No; but I won't mystify you. As I rode up the valley, I saw you two standing on the hill, and could easily guess the rest. A large estate in this country is only an imaginary fortune. You are not so much of a farmer, Joseph, that it will cut you to the heart and make you dream of ruin to part with a few fields; if you were, I should say get that weakness out of you at once! A man should *possess* his property, not be possessed by it."

"You are right," Joseph answered; "I have been fighting against an inherited feeling."

"The only question is, will the sale of those fifty acres relieve you of all present embarrassments?"

"So far, Philip, that a new mortgage of about half the amount will cover what remains."

"Bravo!" cried Philip. "This is better than I thought. Mr. Hopeton is looking for sure, steady investments, and will furnish whatever you need. So there is no danger of foreclosure."

"Things seem to shape themselves almost too easily now," Joseph answered. "I see the old, mechanical routine of my life coming back: it should be enough for me, but it is not; can you tell me why, Philip?"

"Yes: it never was enough. The most of our neighbors are cases of arrested development. Their intellectual nature only takes so many marks, like a horse's teeth; there is a point early in their lives, where its form becomes fixed. There is neither the external influence, nor the inward necessity, to drive them a step further. They find the Sphinx dangerous, and keep out of her way. Of course, as soon as they passively begin, to accept *what is*, all that was fluent or plastic in them soon hardens into the old moulds. Now, I am not very wise, but this appears to me to be truth; that life is a grand centrifugal force, forever growing from a wider circle towards one that is still wider. Your stationary men may be necessary, and even serviceable; but to me—and to you, Joseph—there is neither joy nor peace except in some kind of growth."

"If we could be always sure of the direction!" Joseph sighed.

"That's the point!" Philip eagerly continued. "If we stop to consider danger in advance, we should never venture a step. A movement is always clear after it has been made, not often before. It is enough to test one's intention; unless we are tolerably bad, something guides us, and adjusts the consequences of our acts. Why, we are like spiders, in the midst of a million gossamer threads, which we are all the time spinning without knowing it! Who are to measure our lives for us? Not other men with other necessities! and so we come back to the same point again, where I started. Looking back now, can you see no gain in your mistake?"

"Yes, a gain I can never lose. I begin to think that haste and weakness also are vices, and deserve to be punished. It was a dainty, effeminate soul you found, Philip,—a moral and spiritual Sybarite, I should say now. I must have expected to lie on rose-leaves, and it was right that I should find thorns."

"I think," said Philip, "the world needs a new code of ethics. We must cure the unfortunate tendencies of some qualities that seem good, and extract the good from others that seem evil. But it would need more than a Luther for such a Reformation. I confess I am puzzled, when I attempt to study moral causes and consequences in men's lives. It is nothing but a tangle, when I take them collectively. What if each of us were, as I half suspect, as independent as a planet, yet all held together in one immense system? Then the central force must be our close dependence on God, as I have learned to feel it through you."

"Through me!" Joseph exclaimed.

"Do you suppose we can be so near each other without giving and taking? Let us not try to get upon a common ground of faith or action: it is a thousand times more delightful to discover that we now and then reach the same point by different paths. This reminds me, Joseph, that our paths ought to separate now, for a while. It is you who should leave,—but only to come back again, 'in the fulness of time.' Heaven knows, I am merciless to myself in recommending it."

"You are right to try me. It is time that I should know something of the world. But to leave, now—so immediately—"

"It will make no difference," said Philip. "Whether you go or stay, there will be stories afloat. The bolder plan is the better."

The subject was renewed the next morning at breakfast. Madeline heartily seconded Philip's counsel, and took a lively part in the discussion.

"We were in Europe as children," she said to Joseph, "and I have very clear and delightful memories of the travel."

"I was not thinking especially of Europe," he answered. "I am hardly prepared for such a journey. What I should wish is, not to look idly at sights and shows, but to have some active interest or employment, which would bring me into contact with men. Philip knows my purpose."

"Then," said Madeline, "why not hunt on Philip's trail? I have no doubt you can track him from Texas to the Pacific by the traditions of his wild pranks and adventures! How I should enjoy getting hold of a few chapters of his history!"

"Madeline, you are a genius!" Philip cried. "How could I have forgotten Wilder's letter, a fortnight ago, you remember? One need not be a practical geologist to make the business report he wants; but Joseph has read enough to take hold, with the aid of the books I can give him! If it is not too late!"

"I was not thinking of that, Philip," Madeline answered. "Did you not say that the place was—"

She hesitated. "Dangerous?" said Philip. "Yes. But if Joseph goes there, he will come back to us again."

"O, don't invoke misfortune in that way!"

"Neither do I," he gravely replied; "but I can see the shadow of Joseph's life thrown ahead, as I can see my own."

"I think I should like to be *sent* into danger," said Joseph.

Philip smiled: "As if you had not just escaped the greatest! Well,—it was Madeline's guess which most helped to avert it, and now it is her chance word which will probably send you into another one."

Joseph looked up in astonishment. "I don't understand you, Philip," he said.

"O Philip!" cried Madeline.

"I had really forgotten," he answered, "that you knew nothing of the course by which we reached your defence. Madeline first suggested to me that the poison was sometimes used as a cosmetic, and on this hint, with Mr. Blessing's help, the truth was discovered."

"And I did not know how much I owe to you!" Joseph, exclaimed, turning towards her.

"Do not thank me," she said, "for Philip thinks the fortunate guess may be balanced by an evil one."

"No, no!" Joseph protested, noticing the slight tremble in her voice; "I will take it as a good omen. Now I know that danger will pass me by, if it comes!"

"If your experience should be anything like mine," said Philip, "you will only recognize the danger when you can turn and look back at it. But, come! Madeline has less superstition in her nature than she would have us believe. Wilder's offer is just the thing; I have his letter on file, and will write to him at once. Let us go down to my office at the Forge!"

The letter was from a capitalist who had an interest in several mines in Arizona and Nevada. He was not satisfied with the returns, and wished to send a private, confidential agent to those regions, to examine the prospects and operations of the companies and report thereupon. With the aid of a map the probable course of travel was marked out, and Joseph rejoiced at the broad field of activity and adventure which it opened to him.

He stayed with Philip a day or two longer, and every evening the fire made a cheery accompaniment to the deepest and sweetest confidences of their hearts, now pausing as if to listen, now rapidly murmuring some happy, inarticulate secret of its own. As each gradually acquired full possession of the other's past, the circles of their lives, as Philip said, were reciprocally widened; but as the horizon spread, it seemed to meet a clearer sky. Their eyes were no longer fixed on the single point of time wherein they breathed. Whatever pain remained, melted before them and behind them into atmospheres of resignation and wiser patience. One gave his courage and experience, the other his pure instinct, his faith and aspiration; and a new harmony came from the closer interfusion of sweetness and strength.

When Joseph returned home, he at once set about putting his affairs in order, and making arrangements for an absence of a year or more. It was necessary that he should come in contact with most of his neighbors, and he was made aware of their good will without knowing that it was, in many cases, a reaction from suspicion and slanderous gossip. Mr. Chaffinch had even preached a sermon, in which no name was mentioned, but everybody understood the allusion. This was considered to be perfectly right, so long as the prejudices of the people were with him, and Julia was supposed to be the pious and innocent victim of a crime. When, however, the truth had been established, many who had kept silent now denounced the sermon, and another on the deceitfulness of appearances, which Mr. Chaffinch gave on the following Sabbath, was accepted as the nearest approach to an apology consistent with his clerical dignity.

Joseph was really ignorant of these proceedings, and the quiet, self-possessed, neighborly way in which he met the people gave them a new impression of his character. Moreover, he spoke of his circumstances, when it was necessary, with a frankness unusual among them; and the natural result was that his credit was soon established on as sound a basis as ever. When, through Philip's persistence, the mission to the Pacific coast was secured, but little further time was needed to complete the arrangements. By the sacrifice of one-fourth of his land, the rest was saved, and intrusted to good hands during his absence. Philip, in the mean time, had fortified him with as many hints and instructions as possible, and he was ready, with a light heart and a full head, to set out upon the long and uncertain journey.

CHAPTER XXXII
LETTERS

I. Joseph to Philip.

Camp — —, Arizona, October 19, 1868.

Since I wrote to you from Prescott, dear Philip, three months have passed, and I have had no certain means of sending you another letter. There was, first, Mr. Wilder's interest at — —, the place hard to reach, and the business difficult to investigate. It was not so easy, even with the help of your notes, to connect the geology of books with the geology of nature; these rough hills don't at all resemble the clean drawings of strata. However, I have learned all the more rapidly by not assuming to know much, and the report I sent contained a great deal more than my own personal experience. The duty was irksome enough, at times; I have been tempted by the evil spirits of ignorance, indolence, and weariness, and I verily believe that the fear of failing to make good your guaranty for my capacity was the spur which kept me from giving way. Now, habit is beginning to help me, and, moreover, my own ambition has something to stand on.

I had scarcely finished and forwarded my first superficial account of the business as it appeared to me, when a chance suddenly offered of joining a party of prospectors, some of whom I had already met: as you know, we get acquainted in little time, and with no introductions in these parts. They were bound, first, for some little-known regions in Eastern Nevada, and then, passing a point which Mr. Wilder wished me to visit (and which I could not have reached so directly from any other quarter), they meant to finish the journey at Austin. It was an opportunity I could not let go, though I will admit to you, Philip, that I also hoped to overtake the adventures, which had seemed to recede from me, rainbow-fashion, as I went on.

Some of the party were old Rocky Mountain men, as wary as courageous; yet we passed through one or two straits which tested all their endurance and invention. I won't say how I stood the test; perhaps I ought to be satisfied that I came through to the end, and am now alive and cheerful. To be sure, there are many other ways of measuring our strength. This experience wouldn't help me the least in a discussion of principles, or in organizing any of the machinery of society. It is rather like going back to the first ages of mankind, and being tried in the struggle for existence. To me, that is a great deal. I feel as if I had been taken out of civilization and set back towards the beginning, in order to work my way up again.

But what is the practical result of this journey? you will ask. I can hardly tell, at present: if I were to state that I have been acting on your system of life rather than my own,—that is, making ventures without any certainty of the consequences,—I think you would shake your head. Nevertheless, in these ten months of absence I have come out of my old skin and am a livelier snake than you ever knew me to be. No, I am wrong; it is hardly a venture after all, and my self-glorification is out of place. I have the prospect of winning a great deal where a very little has been staked, and the most timid man in the world might readily go that far. Again you will shake your head; you remember "The Amaranth." How I should like to hear what has become of that fearful and wonderful speculation!

Pray give me news of Mr. Blessing. All those matters seem to lie so far behind me, that they look differently to my eyes. Somehow, I can't keep the old impressions; I even begin to forget them. You said, Philip, that he was not intentionally dishonest, and something tells me you are right. We learn men's characters rapidly in this rough school, because we cannot get away from the close, rough, naked contact. What surprises me is that the knowledge is not only good for present and future use, but that I can take it with me into my past life. One weakness is left, and you will understand it. I blush to myself,—I am ashamed of my early innocence and ignorance. This is wrong; yet, Philip, I seem to have been so unmanly,—at least so unmasculine! I looked for love, and fidelity, and all the virtues, on the surface of life; believed that a gentle tongue was the sign of a tender heart; felt a wound when some strong and positive, yet differently moulded being approached me! Now, here are fellows prickly as a cactus, with something at the core as true and tender as you will find in a woman's heart. They would stake their lives for me sooner than some persons (whom we know) would lend me a hundred dollars, without security! Even your speculator, whom I have met in every form, is by no means the purely mercenary and dangerous man I had supposed.

In short, Philip, I am on very good terms with human nature; the other nature does not suit me so well. It is a grand thing to look down into the cañon of the Colorado, or to see a range of perfectly clear and shining snow-peaks across the dry sage-plains; but oh, for one acre of our green meadows! I dreamed of them, and the clover-fields, and the woods and running streams, through the terrific heat of the Nevada deserts, until the tears came. It is nearly a year since I left home: I should think it fifty years!

With this mail goes another report to Mr. Wilder. In three or four months my task will be at an end, and I shall then be free to return. Will you welcome the brown-faced, full bearded man, broad in cheeks and shoulders, as you would the—but how did I use to look, Philip? It was a younger brother you know; but he has bequeathed all of his love, and more, to the older.

II. Philip To Joseph

Coventry Forge; Christmas Day.

When Madeline hung a wreath of holly around your photograph this morning, I said to it as I say now: "A merry Christmas, Joseph, wherever you are!" It is a calm sunny day, and my view, as you know, reaches much further through the leafless trees; but only the meadow on the right is green. You, on the contrary, are enjoying something as near to Paradise in color, and atmosphere, and temperature (if you are, as I guess, in Southern California), as you will ever be likely to see.

Yes, I will welcome the new man, although I shall see more of the old one in him than you perhaps think,—nor would I have it otherwise. We don't change the bases of our lives, after all: the forces are differently combined, otherwise developed, but they hang, I fancy, to the same roots. Nay, I'll leave preaching until I have you again at the old fireside. You want news from home, and no miserable little particular is unimportant. I've been there, and know what kind of letters are welcome.

The neighborhood (I like to hover around a while, before alighting) is still a land where all things always seem the same. The trains run up and down our valley, carrying a little of the world boxed up in shabby cars, but leaving no mark behind. In another year the people will begin to visit the city more frequently; in still another, the city people will find their way to us; in five years, population will increase and property will rise in value. This is my estimate, based on a plentiful experience.

Last week, Madeline and I attended the wedding of Elwood Withers. It was at the Hopeton's, and had been postponed a week or two, on account of the birth of a son to our good old business-friend. There are two events for you! Elwood, who has developed, as I knew he would, into an excellent director of men and material undertakings, has an important contract on the new road to the coal regions. He showed me the plans and figures the other day, and I see the beginning of wealth in them. Lucy, who is a born lady, will save him socially and intellectually. I have never seen a more justifiable marriage. He was pale and happy, she sweetly serene and confident; and the few words he said at the breakfast, in answer to the health which Hopeton gave in his choice Vin d'Aï, made the unmarried ladies envy the bride. Really and sincerely, I came away from the house more of a Christian than I went.

You know all, dearest friend: was it not a test of my heart to see that *she* was intimately, fondly happy? It was hardly any more the face I once knew. I felt the change in the touch of her hand. I heard it in the first word she spoke. I did not dare to look into my heart to see if something there were really dead, for the look would have called the dead to life. I made one heroic effort, heaved a stone over the place, and sealed it down forever. Then I felt your arm on my shoulder, your hand on my breast. I was strong and joyous; Lucy, I imagined, looked at me from time to time, but with a bright face, as if she divined what I had done. Can she have ever suspected the truth?

Time is a specific administered to us for all spiritual shocks; but change of habit is better. Why may I not change in quiet as you in action? It seams to me, sometimes, as I sit alone before the fire, with the pipe-stem between my teeth, that each of us is going backward through the other's experience. You will thus prove my results as I prove yours. Then, parted as we are, I see our souls lie open to each other in equal light and warmth, and feel that the way to God lies through the love of man.

Two years ago, how all our lives were tangled! Now, with so little agency of our own, how they are flowing into smoothness and grace! Yours and mine are not yet complete, but they are no longer distorted. One disturbing, yet most pitiable, nature has been removed; Elwood, Lucy, the Hopetons, are happy; you and I are healed of our impatience. Yes, there is something outside of our own wills that works for or against us, as we may decide. If I once forgot this, it is all the clearer now.

I have forgotten one other,—Mr. Blessing. The other day I visited him in the city. I found him five blocks nearer the fashionable quarter, in a larger house. He was elegantly dressed, and wore a diamond on his bosom. He came to meet me with an open letter in his hand.

"From Mrs. Spelter, my daughter," he said, waving it with a grand air,—"an account of her presentation to the Emperor Napoleon. The dress was—let me see—blue moiré and Chantilly lace; Eugénie was quite struck with her figure and complexion."

"The world seems to treat you well," I suggested.

"Another turn of the wheel. However, it showed me what I am capable of achieving, when a strong spur is applied. In this case the spur was, as you probably guess, Mr. Held,—honor. Sir, I prevented a cataclysm! You of course know the present quotations of the Amaranth stock, but you can hardly be aware of my agency in the matter. When I went to the Oil Region with the available remnant of funds, Kanuck had fled. Although the merest tyro in geology, I selected a spot back of the river-bluffs, in a hollow of the undulating table-land, sunk a shaft, and—succeeded! It was what somebody calls an inspired guess. I telegraphed instantly to a friend, and succeeded in purchasing a moderate portion of the stock—not so much as I desired—before its value was known. As for the result, *si monumentum quaris, circumspice!*"

I wish I could give you an idea of the air with which he said this, standing before me with his feet in position, and his arms thrown out in the attitude of Ajax defying the lightning.

I ventured to inquire after your interest. "The shares are here, sir, and safe," he said, "worth not a cent less than twenty-five thousand dollars."

I urged him to sell them and deposit the money to your credit, but this he refused to do without your authority. There was no possibility of depreciation, he said: very well, if so, this is your time to sell. Now, as I write, it occurs to me that the telegraph may reach you. I close this, therefore, at once, and post over to the office at Oakland.

Madeline says: "A merry Christmas from me!" It is fixed in her head that you are still exposed to some mysterious danger. Come back, shame her superstition, and make happy your

Philip.

III. Joseph to Philip

San Francisco, June 3, 1869.

Philip, Philip, I have found your valley!

After my trip to Oregon, in March, I went southward, along the western base of the Sierra Nevada, intending at first to cross the range; but falling in with an old friend of yours, a man of the mountains and the sea, of books and men, I kept company with him, on and on, until the great wedges of snow lay behind us, and only a long, low, winding pass divided us from the sands of the Colorado Desert. From the mouth of this pass I looked on a hundred miles of mountains; there were lakes glimmering below; there were groves of ilex on the hillsides, an orchard of oranges, olives, and vines in the hollow, millions of flowers hiding the earth, pure winds, fresh waters, and remoteness from all conventional society. I have never seen a landscape so broad, so bright, so beautiful!

Yes, but we will only go there on one of these idle epicurean journeys of which we dream, and then to enjoy the wit and wisdom of our generous friend, not to seek a refuge from the perversions of the world! For I have learned another thing, Philip: the freedom we craved is not a thing to be found in this or that place. Unless we bring it with us, we shall not find it.

The news of the decline of the Amaranth stock, in your last, does not surprise me. How fortunate that my telegraphic order arrived in season! It was in Mr. Blessing's nature to hold on; but he will surely have something left. I mean to invest half of the sum in his wife's name, in any case; for the "prospecting" of which I wrote you, last fall, was a piece of more than, ordinary luck. You must have heard of White Pine, by this time. We were the discoverers, and reaped a portion of the first harvest, which is never equal to the second; but this way of getting wealth is so incredible to me, even after I have it, that I almost fear the gold will turn into leaves or pebbles, as in the fairy tales. I shall not tell you what my share is: let me keep one secret,—nay, two,—to carry home!

More incredible than anything else is now the circumstance that we are within a week of each other. This letter, I hope, will only precede me by a fortnight. I have one or two last arrangements to make, and then the locomotive will cross the continent too slowly for my eager haste. Why should I deny it? I am homesick, body and soul. Verily, if I were to meet Mr. Chaffinch in Montgomery Street, I should fling myself upon his neck, before coming to my sober senses. Even he is no longer an antipathy: I was absurd to make one of him. I have but one left; and Eugénie's admiration of her figure and complexion does not soften it in the least.

How happy Madeline's letter made me! After I wrote to her, I would have recalled mine, at any price; for I had obeyed an impulse, and I feared foolishly. What you said of her "superstition" might have been just, I thought. But I believe that a true-hearted woman always values impulses, because she is never at a loss to understand them. So now I obey another, in sending the enclosed. Do you know that her face is as clear in my memory as yours? and as—but why should I write, when I shall so soon be with you?

CHAPTER XXXIII
ALL ARE HAPPY

Three weeks after the date of Joseph's last letter Philip met him at the railroad station in the city. Brown, bearded, fresh, and full of joyous life after his seven days' journey across the continent, he sprang down from the platform to be caught in his friend's arms.

The next morning they went together to Mr. Blessing's residence. That gentleman still wore a crimson velvet dressing-gown, and the odor of the cigar, which he puffed in a rear room, called the library (the books were mostly Patent Office and Agricultural Reports, with Faublas and the Decamerone), breathed plainly of the Vuelte Abajo.

"My dear boy!" he cried, jumping up and extending his arms, "Asten of Asten Hall! After all your moving accidents by flood and field; back again! This is—is—what shall I say? compensation for many a blow of fate! And my brave Knight with the Iron Hand, sit down, though it be in Carthage, and let me refresh my eyes with your faces!"

"Not Carthage yet, I hope," said Joseph.

"Not quite, if I adhere strictly to facts," Mr. Blessing replied; "although it threatens to be my Third Punic War.

"There is even a slight upward tendency in the Amaranth shares, and if the company were in my hands, we should soon float upon the topmost wave. But what can I do? The Honorable Whaley and the Reverend Dr. Lellifant were retained on account of their names; Whaley made president, and I—being absent at the time developing the enterprise, not only *pars magna* but *totus teres atque rotundus*, ha! ha!—I was put off with a director's place. Now I must stand by, and see the work of my hands overthrown. But 'tis ever thus!"

He heaved a deep sigh. Philip, most heroically repressing a tendency to shriek with laughter, drew him on to state the particulars, and soon discovered, as he had already suspected, that Mr. Blessing's sanguine temperament was the real difficulty; it was still possible for him to withdraw, and secure a moderate success.

When this had been made clear, Joseph interposed.

"Mr. Blessing," said he, "I cannot forget how recklessly, in my disappointment, I charged you with dishonesty. I know also that you have not forgotten it. Will you give me an opportunity of atoning for my injustice?—not that *you* require it, but that I may, henceforth, have less cause for self-reproach."

"Your words are enough!" Mr. Blessing exclaimed. "I excused you long ago. You, in your pastoral seclusion—"

"But I have not been secluded for eighteen months past," said Joseph, smiling. "It is the better knowledge of men which has opened my eyes. Besides, you have no right to refuse me; it is Mrs. Blessing whom I shall have to consult."

He laid the papers on the table, explaining that half the amount realized from his shares of the Amaranth had been invested, on trust, for the benefit of Mrs. Eliza Blessing.

"You have conquered—*vincisti!*" cried Mr. Blessing, shedding tears. "What can I do? Generosity is so rare a virtue in the world, that it would be a crime to suppress it!"

Philip took advantage of the milder mood, and plied his arguments so skilfully that at last the exuberant pride of the De Belsain blood gave way.

"What shall I do, without an object,—a hope, a faith in possibilities?" Mr. Blessing cried. "The amount you have estimated, with Joseph's princely provision, is a competence for my old days; but how shall I fill out those days? The sword that is never drawn from the scabbard rusts."

"But," said Philip, gravely, "you forget the field for which you were destined by nature. These operations in stocks require only a low order of intellect; you were meant to lead and control multitudes of men. With your fluency of speech, your happy faculty of illustration, your power of presenting facts and probabilities, you should confine yourself exclusively to the higher arena of politics. Begin as an Alderman; then, a Member of the Assembly; then, the State Senate; then—"

"Member of Congress!" cried Mr. Blessing, rising, with flushed face and flashing eyes. "You are right! I have allowed the necessity of the moment to pull me down from my proper destiny! You are doubly right! My creature comforts once secured, I can give my time, my abilities, my power of swaying the minds of men,—come, let us withdraw, realize, consolidate, invest, at once!"

They took him at his word, and before night a future, free from want, was secured to him. While Philip and Joseph were on their way to the country by a late train, Mr. Blessing was making a speech of an hour and a half at one of the primary political meetings.

There was welcome through the valley when Joseph's arrival was known. For two or three days the neighbors flocked to the farm to see the man whose adventures, in a very marvellous form, had been circulating among them for a year past. Even Mr. Chaffinch called, and was so conciliated by his friendly reception, that he, thenceforth, placed Joseph in the ranks of those "impracticable" men, who *might* be nearer the truth than they seemed: it was not for us to judge.

Every evening, however, Joseph took his saddle-horse and rode up the valley to Philip's Forge. It was not only the inexpressible charm of the verdure to which he had so long been a stranger,—not only the richness of the sunset on the hills, the exquisite fragrance of the meadow-grasses in the cool air,—nay, not entirely the dear companionship of Philip which drew him thither. A sentiment so deep and powerful that it was yet unrecognized,—a hope so faint that it had not yet taken form,—was already in his heart. Philip saw, and was silent.

But, one night, when the moon hung over the landscape, edging with sparkling silver the summits of the trees below them, when the air was still and sweet and warm, and filled with the diffused murmurs of the stream, and Joseph and Madeline stood side by side, on the curving shoulder of the knoll, Philip, watching them from the open window, said to himself: "They are swiftly coming to the knowledge of each other; will it take Joseph further from my heart, or bring him nearer? It ought to fill me with perfect joy, yet there is a little sting of pain somewhere. My life had settled down so peacefully into what seemed a permanent form; with Madeline to make a home and brighten it for me, and Joseph to give me the precious intimacy of a man's love, so different from woman's, yet so pure and perfect! They have destroyed my life, although they do not guess it. Well, I must be vicariously happy, warmed in my lonely sphere by the far radiation of their nuptial bliss, seeing a faint reflection of some parts of myself in their children, nay, claiming and making them *mine* as well, if it is meant that my own blood should not beat in other hearts. But will this be sufficient? No! either sex is incomplete alone, and a man's full life shall be mine! Ah, you unconscious lovers, you simple-souled children, that know not what you are doing, I shall be even with you in the end! The world is a failure, God's wonderful system is imperfect, if there is not now living a noble woman to bless me with her love, strengthen me with her self-sacrifice, purify me with her sweeter and clearer faith! I will wait: but I shall find her!"